AN HEIR OF DARKNESS AND RUIN

DAUGHTERS OF CHAOS SERIES
BOOK 2

MINA B. CASTILLO

DELPHINUS STAR PUBLISHING LLC

To the readers who want a villain:
Be careful what you wish for.

"Only a villain can show us the full extent of our humanity." — Mina B. Castillo

AN HEIR OF DARKNESS AND RUIN

DAUGHTERS OF CHAOS SERIES BOOK 2

By Mina B. Castillo

1

RENNA

My body burned.

Stepping through the mirror was like being consumed by flames until there was nothing but ash left of me.

I tried to look behind me, but the pain was crushing.

Loud swooshing noises attacked my ears, and rapidly moving black and emerald and silver lights sped past me, making me nauseous.

I vomited as my body was violently tossed until my skin felt like it was being ripped from my body. When I looked down and saw my skin charring from the intense heat suffocating me, I vomited again.

This was different from teleporting. I had never gone through a portal like this.

Unlike teleportation, where I could feel my body molded and reconfigured as I traveled through wormholes, this transport kept my body whole, and it felt as if I was tethered to a pole, rendered immobile, while flames licked my feet and began to consume my body.

The pain here would not end.

I could not scream or move but simply felt the magic carry me to whichever end. To Sethos. I hoped.

When the pain became too much and I felt my body begin to lose consciousness, a tunnel of white light appeared, as though waiting for me at the end.

The white light enveloped me in its embrace until I was blinded and closed my eyes.

Make this pain stop, I whispered in my mind to Source or whoever the creator was.

Anyone.

Please make this pain stop.

And then suddenly, I was suspended.

The pain was *gone.*

I felt weightless, and I opened my eyes.

I was floating in deep space.

In the distance, brilliant supernovae of pink, orange, and magenta adorned the nothingness of space, its stardust shining like glittering diamonds in the void. I looked down at my body, and my skin was intact and speckled with silver dots like freckles, as I myself was a star.

Had I died?

I frowned and floated around to look behind me.

A voice spoke.

You are not dead.

You will live.

"Who are you?" I moved my body in slow motion, forward and backward, testing the area I was in.

I am the Astral. You are in the astral plane. I heard your cries of pain and rushed to you.

"What are you?"

I am the embodiment of the astral night.

I shook my head. I had traveled through the astral plane with Sethos during dreamtime. None of it made sense.

And who are you?

"Renna Strongborn," I answered.

Renna . . .

Sound waves with different pitches whispered my name, floating and echoing around me, creating a beautiful cacophony.

I shivered. "How can a place speak?"

There are truths incomprehensible to mortals.

"I was in a portal," I said, touching my arms to test if anything hurt. "My body was burning. How am I alive?"

There is no pain in the astral plane.

Where did you come from?

I hugged my arms around my midsection. "It doesn't matter. I had to leave."

I could feel its presence still, and it was as if space itself froze.

"I traveled through a mirror . . ." I shared. "I did not know there was a portal until moments ago."

Portals to any dimension can be created with intention.

My brows gathered as I tried to understand what he was saying.

"I did not purposely create a portal . . ." I replied.

You must have used magic at some point and subconsciously tried to leave the place you were in, resulting in a portal.

Had I truly created the portal?

I'd spent days locked inside Khellios's home after Am-Re attacked the old ruins outside Taria. I felt alone and lost without word from Sethos, and my relationship with Khellios had been strained as he helped me train and convinced me to never use magic again.

I wanted to leave Taria. I hated being confined.

In my frustration, I'd tried to destroy a beautiful mirror that had been in my room. I recalled my magic trying to crumble the mirror to pieces, only for it to piece itself back together. On and on I tried until the mirror became obsidian.

That was the mirror I had traveled through.

A portal.

Sethos's voice and magic through the mirror propelled me to enter the portal to join him. He promised I would be safe.

And Sethos was my safe haven.

My soul guardian.

I trusted his voice when he told me to cross the portal to him.

I had to.

I closed my eyes as I recalled the pain I had experienced just moments ago.

"Will my body survive?" I asked the Astral.

Yes. I suspect you will need extensive healing.

Where were you headed?

I opened my eyes and stared at the blackness of space. "To a friend . . ." I began. "He spoke with me through the mirror to cross."

The Astral was silent.

Are you sure it was your friend?

I paused. It had been Sethos's voice directing me. His voice had been gentle, loving even, as he begged me not to take the magic suppression tincture Khellios had given me.

Sethos urged me to come *home*. Livina had also told me I would be going home, and that single word uttered by Sethos made up my mind to join him. The Goddess of Fate did not lie.

It made sense for me to follow Sethos.

Home.

To *him*.

I wanted to be by his side.

Warmth spread through me.

I would follow Sethos to the ends of the universe if he let me.

"I know where I'm headed," I replied to the Astral with more confidence. A thought occurred to me. "How were you able to hear me?" I wrung my hands together. "I called out for help."

I'm uncertain. Speaking to those traveling into the astral plane is unusual for me.

Oh.

However, given this unique situation, should you find yourself in trouble, the Astral spoke, slightly hesitating, *and you need help, access the astral plane and call for me. I have a feeling I will hear you again.*

I nodded, sensing the Astral could see me.

"The astral plane never looked like this . . ." I said, spinning around. "I have only ever been to different physical places, never space." I paused. "I thought I could only astral travel in dreamtime."

The astral plane can be accessed through dreamtime, meditation, and other moments when the brain is in an altered state.

The astral plane is not accessed every time. For example, sometimes people simply sleep—their bodies and souls remaining together. Other times, the soul leaves through astral projection and goes into the astral plane.

"Why would the soul leave the body?"

To heal. To gain introspection in the subconscious mind.

However, the conscious mind usually does not remember astral projection.

I wondered if I had astral traveled before I met Sethos and had not remembered those previous instances.

"Why do I remember?"

Once you remember one journey to the astral plane, you always remember.

Once more, silence settled between us.

I will ensure the magic in the astral plane keeps your soul here for a little while until your body gets ready to leave the portal.

My breathing hitched as I anticipated the pain that awaited me. I wrapped my arms around myself once more. "Thank you."

I must leave you. I suspect this will not be the last time we speak.

With those words, I felt a shift in the atmosphere, and it was suddenly bereft of the energy around me. It felt empty. Hollow.

I knew the Astral was gone.

I closed my eyes and let the silence envelop me as I waited to be pulled back to the portal when I reached the other side.

I wasn't sure if the anticipation of pain was worse than actually feeling it.

2

SETHOS

My blood boiled with rage.

"Ahhh!" I screamed as pain radiated from my ribs where Khellios had stabbed me.

Overwhelming nausea and adrenaline pumped through my me as I lost blood, my body thrashing and pulsating with the chaotic black magic of Am-Re—*magic I was never meant to have—*seeking revenge for the injury inflicted on me.

My footsteps echoed against the stone walls of the fortress that was my shelter when I visited Daya. I stumbled nude into a pool of magical healing waters, the water opaque black. The power of the stars swirled within its depths, giving it a sparkling black majestic color.

I looked down, and blood and black magic dripped down my side.

Wincing, I bit my knuckles when the water sloshed against my wound as I waded into the pool.

"Sethos!" A voice rang out, but I didn't bother looking in the direction it came from.

Machinery crashed to my right, and I whipped my head to the

large open archway that faced the pool. Etara's hovertor, a flying single rider vehicle, was on its side on the ground.

Etara yanked her helmet off and threw it on the ground, rushing to me.

Etara and I had been friends for a few years, having met in Daya while hunting in the Dayan forest. She was in Daya seeking shelter, running from a bounty placed on her by the King of Nightmares in the Sirius galaxy after she killed his wife.

Etara had been the chief witch in the Kingdom of Nightmares and was now a fugitive.

"What the hell did you do?" she screamed as she waded into the waters.

I moved out of her grasp, anger coursing through me. I hit the water with my fists as chaotic magic rushed from me to the surface of my skin.

"Sethos, calm down—"

"Don't pretend like you truly give a fuck, Etara. I've had enough of your criticisms."

"Tell me you did not attack Taria. Tell me you were not as stupid as to go there by yourself! That was not part of the plan—"

"I went, alright?" I submerged my body into the water and came back up, my body throbbing with pain everywhere. "You can see how stupendously well that plan went."

I sighed and closed my eyes, thinking of Renna. I had felt Renna's chaotic magic so clearly through the magical tie I shared with her because of the magic I had.

"I couldn't think straight. I had to get to her."

Etara covered her face. "Oh, Sethos . . ." She dropped her hands and looked me over. "And now you're injured. I'm sure the gods did that?"

Rage boiled inside me.

"Not gods. *Khellios.*"

"Do you have a death wish?" She scowled when she saw my torso. "You won't be so lucky next time, Sethos."

I looked down at my wound and saw how it struggled to close. Etara was right. I should have never attacked, but feeling Renna's distress ripped me to shreds.

"I will have my army next time," I said, wiping water from my forehead.

"And you'll have Renna fighting alongside you," Etara deadpanned. She crossed her arms. "*Right?*"

I lifted my chin in challenge. Renna standing in battle next to me had never been my plan, but it could be an advantage.

"And what's wrong with that?" I snapped.

Etara laughed. "You are delusional if you think she will attack her friends."

I narrowed my eyes. "She trusts me. She will hear what they have done to me and—"

"And what?" Etara lifted her eyebrows. "She will *what*? Do you honestly think that after lying, manipulating, and using her, it will make her side with you?" She grimaced.

I clenched my jaw and turned from her. I knew what I had done to Renna.

Finding Renna divided my soul and heart in two: I had found the woman I was falling for, and I had used her to lure the gods.

I did not want to use Renna at first. When I found her almost eight years ago under the tutelage of Am-Re, who was masquerading as her mentor, I saw how miserable she was and detested anything to do with magic.

After I killed Am-Re, I used his magic to keep her in a bubble, isolated from magic on her darkversity campus, making sure she had no contact with others with similar gifts. I wanted to give her a normal life.

With Am-Re dead and Renna safely at university, I searched relentlessly for the gods, to no avail. And ultimately, I knew the gods would rush to her side if they knew she was alive. They had searched for her for years—especially Khellios.

And so, with Etara's help, I staged attacks at her university with the goal to lure the gods and find their location.

My plan worked, and I was unapologetic about it.

For the Celestial Gods had wronged me twice.

The gods killed my mother and my brethren when they attacked my home planet of Isyos in an operation to extinguish Am-Re, who had resided there.

And then they took Renna from me in her first lifetime.

My Renna.

Mine.

So I would never apologize for my revenge against them.

Never.

Renna would need to understand and see things my way.

"Will you tell Renna you aren't her soul guardian?" Etara asked.

My body tensed.

"I had to do what needed to be done." I clenched my fists. "Finding the gods was the only thing that mattered."

"Sethos—"

"How else was she to trust me?" I yelled. "She hated everything to do with magic, Etara! Everything. I had to make her trust me."

"By selling her a fake story about soul guardians?" she roared. "There is no such thing."

"Are you on my side or not?" I growled.

Etara moved to the edge of the pool and climbed out.

"Sethos . . ." She shook her head. "I know you are in pain from loss. But I've been thinking." She paused and rubbed her face with her palms. "Is this what you truly want?"

"What the fuck does that mean?"

"You have Renna now . . ." Etara said carefully. "Speak to her.

Tell her what you have done. Apologize. Start a new life with her."

A fresh wave of rage coursed through me, and a viscous bout of magic began to swirl within me. My eyes blurred as Am-Re's magic pushed mine aside and began to overtake my body.

The healing waters around me began to boil, but the magic created a defensive shield around me, protecting me.

I walked to the pool's ledge and pushed myself up.

Etara's eyes grew wide, and she began to backtrack when I stood outside the pool.

I snapped my fingers, and a robe appeared on my body.

Etara hugged her arms around herself and looked away.

"I'm sorry—" she whispered. "I didn't mean to criticize."

"You overstep, witch." I seethed, my voice taking on a darker quality that was not mine.

I had a right to justice.

I had a right to revenge.

And sometimes bad things needed to happen in order to bring about goodness and salvation.

Etara's breath was shaky as I approached.

"I saw an opportunity and seized it. I will *never* apologize for this."

"You have an option to choose differently!" She clasped her shaking hands. "Please. You are like a son to me. I have gone along with this, but I now need to say something. This will end in tragedy, Sethos."

"Then I will die avenging my mother's death," I gritted out. "There is no greater honor than that."

Sharp pain shot through my body, and I bent over with a scream.

Am-Re's magic always took a toll.

Etara's hand shot to my shoulder, but I pushed it off. "I hate when his magic does this to you. I'll go to the potion room and bring you two tinctures," Etara said hurriedly. "We're running out of them, Sethos."

I grunted in response.

"You know the potions only do so much, right?" she called from a distance.

I closed my eyes as fear rumbled through me. It felt like I was standing on the edge of a cliff with nowhere to go.

The witch who had been supplying us with the potions that slowed down the damage Am-Re's magic was causing to my body had been murdered days ago. The timing was odd, and I was running out of time.

What would I do once the potions ran out?

When Etara came back, she handed me a vial.

My sweet salvation.

I snatched the vial from her hands and uncapped it, tossing the liquid back.

I squeezed my eyes shut as the vile liquid burned my throat and focused on Renna. I shoved the vial into her hands and bent over with my hands on my knees as the antidote flowed through me, cooling the chaotic magic inside me.

"Sethos, your father's magic is destroying you."

Father. The title of being his son was beneficial as I moved in his circles and then when I took his throne. Our kingdom needed stability, and assuring our allies that his son, even an adopted one, was on the throne was beneficial.

"Sethos," Etara spoke.

I looked to her.

"Show me how bad it is." She gestured to my arms.

"Etara." I looked up to the ceiling. "Don't."

"How much has Am-Re's magic spread, Sethos?" she said insistently. "Call off the glamour magic on your skin."

"It doesn't matter, Etara. The damage is done."

"Show me. You know I will not let this go."

Motherly indeed.

I groaned and arranged the robe so my shins and arms were exposed.

I whispered a spell calling off the glamour, revealing black shadows covering my fingers, forearms, feet, and calves. It looked like a black translucent veil covered my skin. The shadows moved like living tattoos.

Etara gasped.

"Am-Re's magic . . ." She shook her head, looking at my body. "It's creeping up your biceps and thighs . . . The tinctures will not reverse *this*."

I rearranged my robe, letting it fall around my body, and took the second vial from her hands. I uncapped the vial and swallowed the contents. I clenched my teeth as the foul flavor clung to my mouth.

"The more you use Am-Re's magic, the more it will overtake your soul until there's little of you left." Etara warily eyed my body.

I would never allow that to happen.

"Will you go to Vasarys tonight?" she asked, referring to Am-Re's realm—a volcanic land shrouded inside a black hole.

"I have to," I muttered and handed her the empty tincture vial. "The people are losing confidence in me avenging the Fallen." I rubbed my face with my palms. "The two assassination attempts against me have emboldened people."

"Would they truly kill you?" Etara asked.

An ominous feeling moved though my body in waves.

Yes.

Yes, they would kill me.

The question was: would a third attempt at my life be successful?

3

SETHOS

A flash of green light flooded the room.

"What's happening?" Etara shrieked and backed up, losing her balance and almost falling into the pool.

She pointed to a mirror in the corner of the room, and my heart began to race. It wasn't just any mirror—it was my mother's. The last connection I had to her.

"What is happening?" she asked.

Furrowing my brow, I bent down to grab a nearby dagger and cautiously approached the mirror.

The glass surface suddenly emitted bright light, almost like an explosion of colors that moved rapidly within its surface.

It had never done that.

Etara screamed and covered her face. "This magic is odd, Sethos. I don't like this. It feels older than anything I have ever encountered."

"It's not sea fae magic," I muttered.

As I got closer, the colors began to violently swirl until black overtook the surface. Green suddenly flashed once more, and black and emerald began to move in a counterclockwise motion.

"It's a portal . . ." Etara gasped, and she rushed next to me, pulling me back. "Don't get too close! Its sucking light into its center."

I stepped back as my heart thundered in my ears.

Who would want to portal *here*?

I lifted my hand, ready to strike in case something came through.

The mirror flared with bright white light, and I began to feel pain.

Excruciating pain.

I touched my body, confused because the waters had healed me, and I realized the pain I felt was not my own but coming from the mirror, or whatever was beyond the portal.

I waved my palm over the portal, silently sending a spell of clarity to force the portal to reveal what lay behind.

Slowly, a scene came into focus.

A darkened bedroom with scant light coming from the bottom of a door.

Soft voices could be heard behind the door.

Why was I being shown this? I stepped closer to the portal.

And then I saw her.

Renna.

She was doubled over on a bed made of quartz, groaning in pain.

My heart plummeted, and I called her name.

I narrowed my eyes when I noticed something covering her body . . .

"She's covered in black magic." Etara stood next to me, her hand covering her mouth.

"Not any black magic. It's Am-Re's magic."

"Her magic . . ." Etara turned to me. "It's integrating. She will not survive it if she does this alone. You know this."

Renna groaned, and tears streamed down her face.

I screamed and ran my hands through my hair.

Using Renna to find the gods to avenge the Fallen did not change the way I felt about her: I desired her, and her pain was cleaving my chest.

I reached out to the portal.

"Sethos, don't!" Etara screamed.

Deadly magic shocked my hand, burning my skin on contact. I pulled my hand back and cradled it to my chest.

"The portal is unstable. She must have opened the portal without knowing. It has to be the desire to join you that is the intention."

As she writhed in pain, it felt like I was being stabbed all over again, and rage consumed me as helplessness overcame me.

I recalled the pain she felt all too well.

Magic fully integrating, or activating, into the body felt like your body was burning from the inside, every cell exploding.

Am-Re's brand of magic, the one running through my veins from having taken it from him, felt worse when integrating. I had wanted to die from it.

My heart broke when I saw Renna sit up on the bed and bite into her fist to muffle a scream.

I clenched my fists and willed my body to freeze, betraying the innate instinct to run to her side to protect her.

The plan was for her to remain in Taria.

Suddenly, Renna whipped her head to her left side as if something caught her attention.

I couldn't see what she was looking at, and I cursed. I waved my hands and silently murmured another spell to bring closer focus.

On her nightstand was a black and gold vial.

I furrowed my brows, trying to determine what the vial could be.

It looked to contain a liquid spell of some sort, and an

ominous feeling spread through me. My intuition screamed that whatever the vial contained was not good.

"What do you think is in that?" I asked Etara.

She shook her head. "It's a tincture. I don't have a good feeling about it."

My chest tightened.

If I spoke to Renna, would the portal carry my voice to her?

I had to try.

"Renna," I spoke, and my voice echoed like a whisper through the portal.

Renna stilled and looked around the room.

"What are you doing?" Etara argued. "You cannot bring her here."

"And where else can she go? She opened a portal, Etara. Her subconscious is calling out for me."

"You have no plan!" She gestured around us. "Do you really want her in a run-down fortress in Daya?"

"What is the better alternative? That she stays in Taria with fully integrated chaotic magic? Whether they want to acknowledge it or not, Renna will always be an enemy of the gods, Etara. More so now."

Renna moved her gaze back to the vial. She stretched her arm toward it, her mouth contorting in pain, and took it in her palms. She weighed the vial in her hands.

"Renna," I called out again.

Renna stilled once more and looked around the room until her eyes landed on the mirror.

Yes!

Another agonizing pang shot through my body. My eyes widened when I realized why I could feel her pain.

"My sweet Renna."

Recognition flashed across her expression, and her eyes became glassy.

She pushed to stand and doubled over in pain.

I had to get her out *now*.

I closed my eyes and began to call upon my magic until it formed a fiery black sphere before me. Opening my eyes, I sent the sphere to the mirror, and the magic seeped through the portal. The Black Fire sphere entered her room in the form of black mist, quickly seeking Renna and enveloping her feet and legs.

"Sethos," she whispered, looking down at her feet and back up at the mirror.

Through the magic, I could feel Renna's body throbbing with pain. I wanted to run to her, but I couldn't. After I'd attacked Taria in my serpent beast form, the wards were restrengthened and impenetrable.

Renna would have to leave on her own.

"Wh-what's happening?" she asked, her body trembling.

"Your magic."

"I didn't mean to," she cried. "It happened so fast, and I didn't know I could—"

"Shhhh . . ."

"I'm afraid. What will happen to me? And how are you here?"

How could I explain what was happening when someone could walk in at any moment? If someone saw this, they would close her portal.

They would not know how to help her.

I was the only one who could help her understand this magic.

"Are you afraid, mejtah?"

"Not of you," she said quickly.

I needed her to come through the portal, but first, I had to get rid of whatever the vial contained.

"Put the vial down, Renna," I whispered.

She looked at her palms.

"Don't do it, mejtah."

"This is a painful existence, Sethos."

I sucked in a sharp breath. Did the vial contain poison? Was she about to take her life?

I wanted to scream, but I needed to remain calm.

"Let me help you, but don't extinguish that which makes you, you—"

"I'm afraid of what I am. What will become of me?"

I almost had everything I wanted in the palm of my hand.

I would make her see my way. She would hate me for a time, but we had the opportunity to make the universe right if we stood side by side.

"Come to me."

I pushed more of my magic into the room to comfort her, wishing I could hold her. I needed her to come willingly. If she panicked, transport across the portal would be more painful.

Suddenly, the low voices outside her room stopped. Renna noticed too, and I could feel her heartbeat speed up.

"Renna. We don't have much time. Come!"

"What will happen to me?" She began to cry.

"It's time to come home."

Home.

To me.

To *us.*

Her bedroom door handle began to move.

Someone was coming.

Renna looked to the mirror, her face hardening with resolve.

Had she made up her mind?

The answer came when she took a deep breath and nodded to the mirror.

Yes!

My magic gripped her and helped carry her closer to the mirror.

"Come to me, Renna, my mejtah."

Renna reached out to the mirror's surface, and behind her, Nera entered the room.

Her face paled when she realized what was happening.

She ran toward Renna.

"Renna!" Nera screamed. "Don't!"

In a split second, Renna looked over her shoulder toward Nera, and my heart faltered.

The vial slipped through her fingers, and she turned to the mirror and then stepped through.

4

SETHOS

The portal violently ejected Renna, and I braced my body to catch her. I fell back with her in my arms and sat up, positioning her in a cradle position in my arms. She was unconscious and badly burned.

She felt heavy in my arms, and her breathing was labored. Her eyes moved rapidly behind her lids.

"Renna?"

Her head rolled to the side.

"Fuck," I murmured and stood with her in my arms.

"You cannot do that, Sethos. Your wound!"

I clenched my jaw to keep from screaming in pain as I began walking toward the healing pool.

"This is not good." Etara paced. "What if she's followed?"

Fuck.

Fuck.

Fuck.

"We need to destroy the mirror, Sethos."

Blood drained from my body, leaving me cold.

The mirror was the only reminder I had of my mother.

Rage thrashed inside me as I blamed the gods for what I knew had to be done.

I looked at the mirror, its obsidian border encrusted with rubies.

Renna's face twitched with pain, her eyelids moving rapidly as if seeing something in a dream. I stroked my fingers through her hair as fury shot through me for not being able to protect her.

I looked at the mirror once more.

I would never forgive the gods.

"Take it from here," I said, and my voice sounded foreign, as if my mind had decided to step back and watch from afar.

"We need to destroy it—"

"Not here," I gritted out. "Take it from my fucking sight and do it elsewhere. I don't want to see you do it."

Guilt rocked me as I entered the pool with Renna in my arms. I held her body against my chest and let the water cover her up to her chin as I walked deeper into the pool.

"Understood," Etara said after a few moments.

From the corner of my eye, I watched Etara raise her palms in the air and close her eyes. Purple energy glowed from her palms, and the mirror levitated as she walked from the room with it in tow.

Alone with Renna, I gently cupped water onto her forehead. She was still bleeding black magic, and it mixed with the black healing waters as if they were one.

"I'm sorry," I whispered against Renna's skin, looking at the fortress in ruins around me.

The walls were decayed with tree rot, while tree roots created large cracks in the walls in other places. The ground was a mixture of stone and moss, with yellow weeds poking through. If you squinted hard enough, you could almost imagine flowers.

I looked up to where the roof was gone in some spots, ancient tree canopies creating shelter over the fallen stronghold.

From the corner of my eye, I saw Etara reenter the room empty handed, and an emptiness filled me.

"Can I ask you something, Sethos?"

I looked to Etara.

"Renna is here now. You have the opportunity to build a life with her. Will you choose revenge over love?"

My body tensed. "I loved my mother and my friends. I loved my life. And all that was ripped from me." I clenched my jaw.

Etara was silent for a moment before speaking again. "And what if Renna falls in love with you?"

I wanted to tell Etara that I could already feel myself falling for Renna, but it was not a privilege I could truly allow myself to indulge in.

My plan to avenge my people had been my sole goal for so long that romantic love seemed like a distraction.

I could not allow it.

"Love is not something I think about, Etara."

"I feel pity for you, Sethos. That you chose to turn your back on *love* is very telling as to how this story will go," Etara murmured.

I glared at her.

"It's a good thing she's not your mate, then," Etara said. "She deserves to be loved."

I paused, my eyes focused on the water. Chaotic magic swirled inside me, surging toward the surface. Holding onto Renna was the only thing that anchored me.

I breathed deeply before answering. "What do you want from me, Etara?" I snapped. "I am trying to do the best I can."

She groaned. "I want you to realize how precious it is to have Renna. If she feels the same for you and she never finds her mate, you will be the most important friend and lover she will ever have." She pointed to me. "Don't ruin this."

Anger flashed through me like fire, and my body began to

hurt all over again from where Khellios had wounded me and from Am-Re's magic that wrestled inside me for dominance.

I needed another tincture, but I could not afford to run out. Not until we found another way to counteract Am-Re's magic.

"So what will you do now that Renna is here? I know this was not planned. Will you take her to Vasarys?" Etara asked.

"Out of the question," I replied icily. "No one in Vasarys knows she was reincarnated. Vasarys may be safer now than when I came to power, but it's still dangerous."

"And her sisters?" Etara demanded, and I looked up.

I pinched the bridge of my nose, feeling a headache coming on. "*Half* sisters."

"They are her family, nonetheless. She should know them."

I laughed. "I don't trust them. Did you forget they attempted to assassinate me twice?"

"You knew taking Am-Re's throne would not be easy—"

"Yes," I snapped. "Thank you for the obvious reminder."

Etara grew quiet.

Renna's black magic trickled from her closed eyes down her temples. I gently wiped her skin and cupped more water onto her. Her magic pouring from her like this set off alarm bells in my mind that I was trying desperately to quiet and avoid.

"I don't remember the last time I saw someone bleed black magic . . ." she whispered. "Magic and blood bleed red for supernaturals," Etara said, her eyes on Renna's body.

My brows gathered as I thought on the significance of bleeding black magic.

"The gods," she whispered. "Their blood and magic bleeds gold."

Dread gripped my body with deathly claws until it was hard to breathe.

My voice cracked. "Am-Re bleeds black."

I looked up at her.

Etara opened and closed her mouth like she was trying to form the words. After a moment, she spoke carefully. "How much of her father's powers does Renna have . . .?"

How I dreaded this question.

"It's difficult to say—"

"That's not an answer," Etara snapped. "You know *exactly* what I am asking. You must know or suspect."

"I know—"

"There can only be one explanation, and you know it. Does she or does she not have the power of Darkness?" Etara almost yelled.

I looked down at Renna, who moved in my arms slightly as if she was flinching in pain.

"*Sethos!*" Etara bellowed.

I snapped my eyes back up to Etara. Her knuckles were paled as she gripped the ledge of the pool.

"She does, doesn't she?" Etara whispered, her eyes wide. She stood and began to back away slowly as if Renna was suddenly hazardous.

I returned my gaze to Renna, marveling at the idea of her harboring the power of Darkness. The ability would be . . . vital when fighting against the gods.

If I could convince Renna to join me and fight alongside me . . .

Etara cursed.

"How convenient for you that she has this one power!" Etara threw her hands up. "You are planning carnage! And innocents will die."

I narrowed my eyes. "That is not the reason I sought her out in the first place, and you know it!"

"You will turn her just like you. Like her father. What have I done?" she whispered while looking at the ground.

Renna stirred in my arms, and I called on healing magic to

transfer to her and speed up the process. The magic inside me felt like a small ember that refused to light. My injuries were not allowing me to generate energy for another.

A dark voice spoke in my mind.

The powers you stole are to destroy.

Not nurture.

Not heal.

I clenched my jaw and shook my head to push out the voice.

"You can't expect me to live here and lie to her like you told me they did in Taria." Etara shook her head. "I can't undo the harm I've done. But I won't continue to be in this. I should have *never* agreed to help you."

"Then leave," I snapped.

Etara turned to look at me, her intense gaze unsettling me.

"I'm going back to my camp for the time being. I cannot sway your path. You know what vengeance will result in, and you believe this lie that you will somehow be able to control the dark magic inside you."

Rage flickered through me.

"And as much as it pains me, I cannot stand by your side and watch you destroy your life."

I lifted Renna to lay her on the pool's ledge so I could get out. But once out of the water, as I placed her on the ground, her magic began hemorrhaging again.

"Fuck," I murmured and picked her up once more, covering her body with water.

"Take care of her, Sethos," Etara said. "If you ever change your ways, come and find me." She shook her head, looking down at her hands. "I want to believe that despite the hurt and dark inside you, your soul will find a way to the light."

I gritted my teeth to keep my jaw from trembling.

Everyone eventually left.

Connections were short lived.

Even my time with Renna . . . It was not permanent.

As soon as Am-Re's magic overtook my body fully, I didn't know what would become of me.

Etara met my eyes. "Renna will be your salvation, Sethos, if you let her. Don't throw away this opportunity to start anew."

Etara's betrayal, turning her back on me, sent fury surging from my center to the rest of my body, like a fire ready to escape and burn.

"I don't need to be saved," I sneered. "And I certainly don't need advice from you, *witch*. I should turn you in to the Kingdom of Nightmares."

Etara flinched as if I had struck her.

"If I see you here again," I said through clenched teeth, "don't expect me to be friendly. Do not come near Renna. I don't take threats and betrayal lightly."

"Then you should get used to that feeling, Sethos." Etara narrowed her eyes before she opened a portal to leave. "The path you are setting on only leaves room for betrayal and ruin."

5

RENNA

I was in a never-ending nightmare, running from that which haunts me.

I dreamed of the quad, the black and emerald magic exploding from the lampposts.

The chilling voice calling my name in the dark.

I relived the horrors I endured with my mentor as he forced me to imitate his magic, the black and emerald energy glowing from his palms.

Of the torment of being locked in a closet and the sickening voice coming from the other side of the door, reminding me I was nothing.

The ominous melodic whistle of my mentor whenever he entered my foster home and whenever he would leave.

Somehow, in my dreams, I escaped every time, only to run through an endless maze. Gravel covered the ground under my bare feet, making my trek painful and bloody while a feeling of doom settled in the pit of my stomach. Each wrong turn would result in me coming face to face with my mentor or a shadowy figure I attributed to Am-Re.

The nightmares ended in both men morphing into one monstrous golden serpent and catching me, the combined magic from my mentor and Am-Re attacking me and leaving me weak on the ground.

As the serpent got closer, it began to pull my life force and magic from me.

I could feel my soul being ripped from its shell as the monster absorbed my essence.

"All you have to do," the monster whispered, "is stop fighting me."

I would thrash in the dream, struggling to stand up.

"I can offer you a painless death . . ." it spoke.

More struggle.

"I can offer you anything your heart desires . . . Give me your power . . ."

"Leave me alone!"

"*Your magic is mine!*" He would rage. "You are nothing without me! I own you! You will never be anything and will never amount to anything without me! I made you. And I can unmake you."

The dream would always end the same: an eruption of golden, red, and purple lights emerging from the ground a few feet in front of us and white lights appearing in the sky to illuminate the darkness.

I could never make out the exact shapes of the lights.

When fighting the serpent grew to be too much, my body would then collapse, and the red light would catch me as if I was falling into arms. I would close my eyes from exhaustion and would feel my body slump on the ground.

The red light around me was a cocoon of safety.

I felt like nothing bad could ever happen to me while I was wrapped in the red glow.

The monster would then screech and retreat.

And on and on the dreams repeated, until the dream changed, and my mentor and Am-Re blended into one being.

And then everything clicked.

The magic of my mentor and Am-Re was the same.

Their magic was triggered by anger.

Hate.

And selfishness.

Their magic had the same black and emerald qualities.

My mentor and Am-Re were one.

My mentor was my father.

My abuser.

I felt stupid for never making the connection before. Had my brain truly blocked that much trauma from my childhood to prevent me from connecting the two?

A shrill scream broke me from my dreamtime haze, and I awoke in darkness, drowning.

The shock of finding myself underwater was terrifying, and I flailed as I tried to open my eyes and grab onto something to help me stand. Two strong hands gripped my arms and pulled me up out of the water. As soon as I broke the surface, I began to violently hack while trying to scream.

My lungs burned as I tried to breathe, but my throat, nose, and brain felt like they were on fire as water prevented me from taking a deep breath.

I was in a pool of some sort. The water was black and came up to my waist.

I bent over and vomited, gagging until I had nothing left inside.

A hand landed on my back, and I jumped.

"Don't touch me!" I thrashed and launched myself across the water to get away. "Don't!"

"Who?"

It was Sethos's voice.

I gasped and turned.

Sethos stared at me with ice-blue eyes.

My jaw dropped when I saw him standing in front of me.

My vision blurred as I tried to focus on him.

I blinked several times, and my surroundings came into sharp focus. Unlike in dreamtime, when everything had a bit of a hazy sheen, this looked too real.

Was I in dreamtime? Had I not left Taria?

"Who are you talking about, mejtah?" Sethos moved closer and cupped my face.

I swallowed and tried to slow my breathing as my thoughts spiraled. Had I imagined my transport through the mirror?

"My father," I whimpered. "My dreams . . . They revealed my mentor and Am-Re are the same. And I—" My voice broke. "My heart hurts so much—"

Sethos lowered his chin. "Renna." He darted his eyes back and forth, looking into mine. "I need you to breathe."

"Am-Re is my mentor, isn't he?" I demanded the truth as I tried to breathe.

Sethos gave me a grim nod.

Tears spilled from my eyes. "Don't let him kill me," I whispered.

Sethos crushed me to his chest. "He will never touch you. Just breathe, Renna, breathe. Please."

"Don't let him."

Sethos nodded against me. "As long as I live, you will always be safe." He kissed my forehead.

I sagged in his arms as emotions overwhelmed me, and I moved my hands to hold him, but my magic surged from me like an electrical current, shocking him. I screamed and almost fell back into the water.

Sethos swept me up, holding me against his chest, and carried me out of the pool, up the steps. He set me on my feet on the pool's ledge, which was covered in moss.

He stepped back from me, his palms up cautiously, staring at my body.

My brows gathered, and I followed his gaze.

To my horror, small rivulets of black magic poured from my feet and the rest of my body. Similar to when I was in Taria but much less than before, magic dripped from my collarbone and ears. The magic extended from me like streams of a river pooling on the ground beneath me. I moved my hands and felt the magic, thick and viscous, like petroleum, slippery and cold to the touch.

"Why is this happening to me?" I stared at my body in fear and felt the magic drain from me like it was blood.

I recalled the vial Khellios offered me to quell my magic. Had he known this would be the result of my magic emerging?

"Your magic is integrating violently and rushing to the surface after years of subduing inside you."

Tears poured down my face, and I lifted a hand to wipe them away. To my horror, black tears stained my hands.

"What does that mean?" I demanded.

"Imagine your blood and your magic were two pieces of long rope. Your magic is binding to your blood, your soul, your essence to be one."

My stomach coiled, and I doubled over, dry heaving.

Sethos knelt beside side me and rubbed my back as my body shook.

"I know you don't feel well and are in shock, but I need you to tell me if you are in actual pain."

I took a deep breath and assessed my body.

Despite the magic rolling inside me that felt like a rocket bouncing off my insides and the obvious magic pouring from me, I didn't actually feel pain.

I shook my head.

"Good. The Waters of the Rhya have healing properties and block pain receptors."

My eyes welled with tears once more, and when I took in the pool of black beneath me, I began to claw at my skin.

"Make this stop!"

"Renna—"

I screamed, trying to scrub my skin. My throat began to close, and my heart pounded to be let out of my chest. I trembled with cold until my body began to shake uncontrollably.

"Renna, the magic should almost be done integrating. I know you're in shock. You're likely having a panic attack. Sit down slowly so we can breathe through this."

He grasped my biceps, and I struggled, attempting to push against him. "Don't touch me!"

"Please, let me help you. You're having a panic attack. I have to make sure you can sit down to help you breathe through this."

I yanked an arm free.

"All I want to do is help you." He pleaded with me. "Please, let me."

Sethos let me go and held out a hand. "I'm sorry things have played out this way," he said quietly. "I care about you very much. I don't want to see you struggle like this."

I blinked away tears as my chest heaved, and I reached out for his hands.

Slowly we lowered to the ground.

"You are bleeding magic," Sethos began. "When magic integrates into someone's body, it becomes like blood. Your blood and the magic inside you are fusing. There is not one without the other. We need to stabilize you so that your blood pressure doesn't drop and make you sicker.

"As you can see"—he gestured to my hands and feet—"the bleeding has slowed. When you arrived here, you were hemorrhaging. I kept you in the healing waters for a week, and it has helped your body process the magic. The minerals and magic in the waters have sustained your physical strength."

My eyes widened. "I have been here a *week*?" Spine stiffened.

I darted my eyes side to side, taking in our surroundings, while my body seemed to only take in small, shallow breaths that were hard to exhale as I shivered.

It was nighttime, and we were in some sort of ruins. Tall gray stone walls surrounded us while moss and flowers covered uneven stone ground.

"Where are we?"

"We are in Daya. I brought you here before in dreamtime."

I nodded, recalling seeing a bit of the forest and the glowing golden butterflies.

"We're inside my home when I'm in Daya."

I went to wrap my arms around myself, but the sight of my magic escaping from my body made my stomach churn, and I bent over as nausea filled me again.

"The magic seeping from you now will only stop if you relax your body and control your magic."

I shook my head back and forth.

No.

No.

This wasn't happening.

"*Renna*—" Sethos reached out and held me. "It's okay." He patted my back as I dry heaved. "You'll be okay."

I sobbed as my stomach convulsed again and Sethos began to rub my back.

"When will I wake up?" I cried.

"*Wake up?*"

"I'm in dreamtime." I looked to him. "Aren't I?"

Sethos's face froze, and he regarded me cautiously.

"Renna," he whispered. "You crossed a portal from Taria to me."

My heart dropped into my stomach, and tears escaped from my eyes. "You don't only exist in dreamtime?"

His movements stopped. "I'm as real as you are. You are not in dreamtime. Dreamtime has been the safest mode of communication, but now that you're with me in Daya, you are safe."

I thought back on my interactions with Sethos. He had never said he only existed in dreamtime, only that we could *only* communicate through it . . .

Sethos shifted so his face was level with mine. "Now that we are together, nothing will keep me from you. I will guard and keep you safe. You will never feel alone again."

My lips trembled. "I'm scared . . ." I whimpered. "Look at me . . ." I gestured to my body as my teeth chattered. "I don't want to be like my father." I shook my head.

Sethos wiped my tears. "You will never be like him, Renna. You have the awareness to not be like him."

"Why is being his child so painful?" I cried as another shiver racked my body. "All he's brought into my life is pain. I'm tired of hurting."

Sethos shook his head and brought his forehead to mine. "If I could take all your pain away, I would. But you don't have to bear this alone, mejtah." His eyes became glassy. "You will never be alone after today."

I moved my head to his chest. "I don't recognize my body."

Another rush of cold seeped through me, and my teeth chattered.

Sethos snapped his fingers, and a heavy woolen cloak enveloped my body.

"Renna." He pulled away gently and met my gaze, gripping my arms softly. "Listen to me: you are safe. I know this is a lot, but we need to get this magic under control, okay?" He said each word slowly and calmly.

I managed to nod and laid my head against his chest once more.

"I need you to try to breathe. I know it's hard. I've gone through this before as well. Magic integration is not easy, but luckily, the healing waters have helped you this past week. All that is left to do on your part is minimal."

I closed my eyes and inhaled. The magic pouring from me seemed to slow slightly.

"Can I die from this?" I asked. "If my magic drains out?"

Sethos body tensed. "A person can be drained of their magic and die . . . *yes.*" His voice seemed distant and suddenly took on a lower, darker quality that made me open my eyes and move to look at him.

"Sethos?" I whispered, studying his face.

His eyes looked dazed for a fraction of a moment, but with a blink, whatever had overcome him was gone.

He released a heavy exhale and spoke. This time, his voice was lighter and more like himself. "You will not die. This is how magic integrates," Sethos stated.

I nodded through still-chattering teeth as my body experienced aftershocks of emotions.

I felt like a monster.

"This must be another reason why the Planetary Council banned magic," I whispered. "This is awful."

"You'd be surprised how many of the council members practice magic in secret . . ."

Before I could ask him to explain further, Sethos grabbed my biceps again and faced me.

All gentleness was gone, and his face was harder.

"You need to be fully aware of the implications of your magic integrating. There is no backing away from your magic after it's done integrating. Do you understand? It will live in you and be a part of you until the day you cease to live."

"I feel like I don't have a choice," I said. "I cannot stop this process. Yet I—"

"Choosing to help your body integrate through this is a form of control. You can choose to be miserable or fight through this and be better off. Now, breathe with me."

I nodded.

"Don't look down at your body and the magic there. Just look at my eyes. Focus on me."

"Yes," I muttered.

As I breathed, thoughts flooded me.

Control.

I had been under the control of my father for years.

I had shrunk into a defenseless victim after the attacks on my campus and the tattoo parlor.

I was ushered to Taria because I could not magically protect myself.

I would never let the man who attacked me make me cower again.

Anger continued to rise within me.

"I don't want to feel weak anymore," I whispered.

Never again.

"You are not weak," Sethos gritted out. "You are the strongest woman I know."

"For years," I began, "I thought that if I kept my head down and muted the magic inside me, I would stay safe. That it would be enough—as if it was that simple."

Sethos placed a hand on my shoulder and squeezed.

I shook my head. I was living a lie, and now I could no longer afford to deny who I was.

Sethos tilted his head. "And what good has staying in the shadows done you?"

I blinked. "It's brought me pain."

Sethos raised his chin. "And what will you do about it?"

I looked back and forth between his eyes and cupped his cheek. "Help me, Sethos. Help me through this."

A slow smile spread across his face. "That's my girl." He crushed me to him. "Don't ever back down from a challenge, do you understand me?"

I nodded.

I took another deep breath.

Exhaled.

We sat in silence for a few moments while my heart steadied and my breathing calmed.

Sethos eventually moved from me slightly and looked down between us.

"Look." The corners of his eyes crinkled with a smile. "It's almost stopped." He raised my right hand in his and intertwined our fingers.

Small drops of black slid from my hand down to my elbow and onto the floor.

Sethos brought our hands to his lips and kissed my skin.

"Now that your breathing is calm, let's try another exercise to help you visualize how to control this magic. Close your eyes."

I hesitated, but I trusted Sethos.

A shaky sigh left me, and I nodded, closing my eyes.

Never again would I feel weak.

I felt Sethos come closer to me until he was next to my ear.

"Now," Sethos whispered. "Imagine you are in a room with books, potions, and other magical items. This is your mind. Your safe space. Where you store your memories and your knowledge. In the middle of the room, imagine a large clear glass vessel. It's swirling with black and emerald magic."

I imagined it, and I found myself in that room.

I nodded.

"Are you in that room, Renna?"

I nodded again.

"Walk to your magic. Do you see how it is part of the room, just like everything else? It's not the whole room, but it's in the room. It belongs in the room."

I walked to the black and emerald glass container.

"Imagine a bronze valve attached to the vessel. Magic seeping from the container. You have the power and ability to turn the valve on and off."

In my mind, I reached for the valve.

"You don't have to make peace with the magic right now. But accept that it's there. Turn it off with the knowledge that it's there to access when needed."

I gripped the valve.

"You can access as little of your magic or as much of it as you want."

I began to panic. "I don't want to access it right this second."

"You are in control of your magic. At all times. You don't want to use it right this second? Turn it off."

In my mind, I turned the valve clockwise. And the magic slowly shut off.

Sethos moved to my ear. "Good girl. Open your eyes."

I slowly opened my eyes, and Sethos moved from me to sit back, his eyes on mine. He smiled. "Look down." He gestured to my body. "You did it."

I looked down, and the black magic around me was completely gone. I moved my hands up, and they were bare. I looked down to my collarbone and felt around my ears. Nothing. I bent my knees, and my feet had no magic pouring from them.

"I have never been able to control magic in a calm state. I always thought my magic only responded to anger. There was never any actual method to training. I would just be forced to think terrible, awful things and then direct my anger to something or someone, willing and wishing for misfortune to occur."

I would be hit, kicked, spit on, yelled at, and pushed until I became an angry thing to behold and lash out, spewing hatred through magic. I curled my hands into a fist, thinking of how my father exploited me.

"Magic is tied to all emotions. *You* were conditioned and trained to only use it in anger." Sethos ran a hand through my hair. "There was no point in him teaching you to control magic," he said. "He just wanted you to destroy blindly like a machine."

I leaned into his hand, and he moved his fingers to the base of my neck.

"If he would have taught you how to control it, you would have eventually figured out how to outsmart him. He wanted you to be rabid, with an almost bloodlust of magic, uncontrolled and feral."

A pang of grief buried its way into my chest.

"And now." He trailed his fingers down to my lips and raked his eyes across my face. "You can learn how to truly be the master of your magic. You will be a wonder to behold, Renna."

I kissed his fingers softly. "It can't be *that* easy to control?"

He smiled and dropped his hand. "You're right. Our brand of magic is not easy to wield. You will have to reframe a lot of internal thought patterns to train your body to call it with other emotions. It will take practice and time, but it's not impossible. I believe in you."

I looked down at my hands. "I lost control in Taria. Before I left. My magic . . . I've never used that much."

"Did they hurt you?" His voice was hard with an edge to it that made me shiver unexpectedly. "Why did you use that much magic?"

"A fight broke out . . ." I said quickly. "My magic spiraled out of me."

Sethos frowned and remained silent as if he wanted to say more but held back.

I looked down at my hands. "Cylas forced Khellios to tell me who I am." I frowned. "Or *was*." I looked up to Sethos. "This is not my first lifetime."

Sethos looked at me silently, his expression blank. "It is not," he finally said.

Anger awoke within me and rumbled under my skin. "When were you going to tell me?"

Sethos looked down at my hands and gave me a knowing look. "I can feel your magic stirring, mejtah. It electrifies the air."

I curled my hands into fists and crossed my arms. "Well?" I gritted out. "When were you going to tell me?"

Sethos looked up and lifted an eyebrow. "It was not my story to tell."

I paused.

"The life you lived with Khellios," Sethos began, "was his to share. You were going to marry him once."

"But I trusted you."

"*Trusted?*" Sethos's brows gathered, and he pushed off the floor and stood.

I followed him and also stood.

"Do you realize what position you're putting me in?" Sethos growled. "You're demanding I take on Khellios's responsibility."

"Sethos—"

My heart began to beat faster as Sethos paced.

"I have guided and protected you for *seven years*. I have offered to train you countless times so you don't feel *powerless*! I am not your enemy."

I froze as Sethos walked from me to an arched window overlooking the forest.

I rubbed my face, trying to figure out what to say. "I appreciate everything you have done for me—"

Sethos laughed bitterly.

"And I don't want to be at odds with you . . ." I stated, dropping my hands to look at him.

"Nor I you," he replied without turning around.

"Can't you at least agree that you could have warned me about Khellios?" I asked, crossing my arms.

Sethos did not answer, and my frustration began to mount.

Sethos had also not told me about my father.

"And what about Am-Re?" I demanded.

Sethos turned. "What about Am-Re?"

I uncrossed my arms and lifted my palms. "He and my mentor are one and the same."

"Yes."

"You didn't tell me." I pointed to him. "And *you knew*." I shook my head.

"Knowing who he was would have changed nothing. You have been in a state of fear for months in Taria. What good would adding another layer of trauma have done? You thinking your mentor was dead when you went to university helped you move forward with your life. Yes, your magic was hard to control each day on campus, but the looming threat from him was gone. Why would I bring him up again and traumatize you more? Can't you see that all I want is to help you? I'm protecting you."

I closed my eyes and inhaled, then slowly released my breath.

"I'm sorry," he said quietly.

I opened my eyes, his tone unsettling me with whiplash.

His eyes were a haunting mixture of sadness and anger.

Sethos rubbed the back of his neck. "I'm sorry I kept the identity of your father from you."

I glared at him as I spoke. "You should have told me about Khellios, my father, and my past in more detail."

"I should have. But no matter what the facts are, none of that matters now. The only thing we can do is move forward."

I covered my face to think.

Sethos was at my side then and gently pried my fingers off my face. "Renna, I will always want your safety. Your happiness. Don't let the past create a division between us. Don't allow that."

I frowned at his words and looked down to see him lacing his fingers with mine.

"Renna, we have a chance to begin again."

I met his eyes.

"Don't push me away from you," he said gently. "I have apologized. And will continue to do so. From now on, ask me anything about your past—I will tell you whatever you want to know. You are in control."

I pulled my hands from his and took a step back, putting space between us. Tilting my head back, I looked up at the roof, or lack thereof, and watched as the golden glowing butterflies native to Daya began to settle along the canopy of the trees, casting a beautiful glow on the ground.

How beautiful to be above the rest of the ground, detached from its cruelty.

"If this one action from me," Sethos began, bringing my attention back to him, "one done to protect you, is what makes you walk from me, I will understand and respect that. But is that what you really want?"

I opened my mouth, but I was at a loss for words. My hands twitched at my sides. They felt empty.

I was so conflicted.

"I don't want to be parted from you, Renna. Don't let it happen."

I didn't want to be parted from him either. He was all I had in that moment. Without him, I would be emotionally and physically alone.

Could I move past this?

My brows furrowed.

Sethos cupped my jaw and brought my forehead against his.

"Let me remain with you," he whispered, closing his eyes. "Renna, you are everything I have."

I covered his hands with mine as my heart began to thunder faster from the sheer bliss of knowing I was really with him in person. I closed my eyes, relishing in the closeness.

I memorized how his skin felt against mine, the slight coarseness of his palm, the short hairs covering his skin, and the beat of his heart pulsing on his wrist.

I opened my eyes to look at his eyelashes and nose. My eyes began to water all over again for an entirely different reason as I took him in.

Everything about him in real life was brighter, sharper, more vibrant.

He opened his eyes then, and we silently gazed at each other.

Up close, I could see his eyes were an incredible ice and cerulean blue with dark rings around his pupils.

I ran a finger up the side of his face and traced his eyebrows, feeling the blond hair there before bringing my fingers down the bridge of his nose and down to his lips.

Sethos was beautiful.

And I was here . . . with him.

Renna, we have a chance to begin again, his words echoed in my ears.

But I had been burned too many times. And if I promised not to be weak with my magic, I would not be weak when it came to my heart.

"I'm glad I'm here with you," I said and dropped my hand, straightening.

He furrowed his brow. "But?"

Sethos lying didn't sit well with me. I wasn't a young girl who could be easily convinced to overlook issues. The fact was that Sethos lied to me for months. Full stop.

"I know you apologized . . ."

Sethos groaned and rubbed his face, letting out a sigh.

"I'm not pushing you away, Sethos." I gestured between us. "But trust is earned."

Sethos grabbed my hands. "And I told you I will continue to apologize. I will fix this. Can you agree I have done everything in your best interest?"

I looked down at our hands.

What more could I ask of him? He was saying all the right things . . .

I had the self-awareness to know the hypocrisy in forgiving Sethos when I had felt so betrayed by Khellios.

I was a fucking farce.

But again, I was alone.

Where else could I go?

Not back to Andora.

Not Taria.

"Can you agree that all I have ever wanted is your happiness?" he asked and put a finger under my chin to make me look at him. "Tell me you agree. I know you do."

Sethos was my soul guardian. He was supposed to keep me safe.

And I had remained safe . . .

A small smile tugged at my lips.

Sethos rubbed his thumb at the corner where my lips curled.

"There she is," he whispered.

Why not try to have peace?

Yet, I hated feeling like I was betraying myself after my anger at Khellios.

My voice was dry when I spoke. "Don't lie to me again."

Sethos stepped into me, our bodies flush together, and he cupped my jaw with both hands, kissed my forehead, and then rested his head against mine.

"Being by your side means everything to me, mejtah."

The stare of his ice-blue eyes suddenly became too intense, and I closed my eyes.

"There won't be a second chance, Sethos." I shook my head against his. "There won't."

Sethos kissed my forehead again and crushed me to him. "I will do everything I can to make this up to you. I swear it."

6

RENNA

After my conversation with Sethos, my body began to shut down; my voice began to slur, and I could barely keep my eyes open.

Sethos called it trauma fatigue. I was no doctor, but I felt that I was finally safe—with Sethos—and it was as if my body sighed in relief for the first time in a long time.

I was with the man who had kept me safe for seven years while at university. The one who visited my dreams to keep me company. He vowed to regain my trust, and I believed him.

Daya was also a place my father could not access because it was a dimension only for fae.

Everything would be okay at Sethos's side.

I had to believe it would be.

I didn't remember the walk from the healing pool to the bedroom, where Sethos took me to rest, because my mind was solely focused on sleep.

And sleep I did. I had no concept of what day it was.

When I awoke, it was dark, with dawn just coming up on the horizon. I faced tall floor-to-ceiling arched stone windows that overlooked a dark forest. The windows were glass, but it did nothing to drown out the eerie sounds that came from the black foliage . . .

Echoes, low moans that were drowned out by the wind, slow creaks as if wood was being bent and broken, and whispers drifted in and out of my room.

A chill ran down my spine, and I swallowed hard. Sethos would never put me in a dangerous position—he trusted Daya to keep me and him safe.

Still, the noises rattled me, and I longed to leave my room. I looked around, and when I moved my body, I felt lethargic, sleep still clinging to me like a web.

I blinked to bring the bedroom I was in into focus. Gray stone spanned from the ceiling to the floor, with a tall, arched ceiling that mimicked the windows. In the center of the arched ceiling was the remnant of a metal chandelier with holes where candles should be.

The room was sparsely decorated, with only bronze wall sconces holding lit candles. A brown wooden armoire stood in the corner next to a red-screened wall where a toilet and claw-foot tub were.

I looked down at the bedsheets and realized how cold I was. This place felt far from being a home. I almost wished for the warmth and sun of Taria.

I needed to leave the room and hoped that walking to get my muscles moving would warm me . . . And a sweater. I had changed into pajamas—a short-sleeve shirt and pants—that Sethos had provided me, but I needed more clothing.

I swung my legs over the side of the bed and pushed to stand. The cold stone beneath my feet sent me scurrying across the room to the armoire to see if there were extra clothes.

Luckily, the armoire held various pants, sweaters, and boots. My eyes widened when I saw underwear and thick wool-like socks. I knew Sethos would have had to conjure them from magic, and I would eternally thank him. I happily grabbed a few items of clothing and went to the back of the screened wall to change and use the bathroom.

Minutes later, I was in pants, socks, boots, a long-sleeve shirt, and a sweater. The clothing was slightly big on me, but I was thankful for the warmth. After taking a wall sconce with me, I almost ran from the room. I needed to ask Sethos about the noises outside.

I vaguely remembered the path back to the hall with the healing pool, and my body moved automatically in that direction. Perhaps dipping my feet in the healing waters would help settle me.

As I made my way down the lengthy hallway, a voice suddenly spoke in the dark. "Good morning."

I jumped and spun around to see Sethos walking toward me. My hand was on my chest, my heart speeding beneath it.

"Sorry to have startled you," he said.

I took a deep breath. "It's okay," I breathed. "Not your fault."

"I was hoping you'd rise today. I just didn't know I would find you awake so early," he said.

"How long have I been asleep?"

"Two days."

My eyes widened. "You should have woken me," I said as my face flushed from embarrassment.

"You have been in fight or flight for months, Renna. Years even," Sethos pointed out. "Exhaustion was going to catch up to you eventually. You'll probably feel tired for a few more days as your body settles."

I nodded, my body still yearning for more rest.

"Did you sleep well?" he asked.

"The forest is . . . unsettling . . ."

Sethos shrugged. "You will get used to it. The trees glow as well with bioluminescence around midnight. You may see some fog rising."

I nodded and made a mental note to remember that.

"Did you see any star crafts?" he asked.

I shook my head.

"Sometimes fae that cannot portal arrive to Daya by star craft. You may see that from time to time."

"Good to know."

As we moved through the hallway, I could see the healing waters in the next room.

"Did you hear the echoes of the forest at night as well?" Sethos asked, drawing my attention back to him.

"Yes . . . At first I couldn't comprehend what the noises were." Goose bumps broke out along the surface of my skin. "It was as if the trees were whispering in a language I couldn't decipher or something."

"The trees have spirits," he replied. "Another thing to get used to."

We walked in stilted silence until we arrived at the hall with the healing waters.

I didn't know what to talk about now that I had Sethos all to myself. There was so much to say. I felt so awkward having him next to me in real life.

We approached the healing pool and sat down along the mossy ledge.

"Is the water cold?" I asked, not remembering what it felt like since my arrival in Daya had been so chaotic.

"Initially, yes," Sethos said. "The water is full of magic, so once your body is submerged, it will cling to your skin and acclimate to your body temperature. It should feel warm after a few moments."

I nodded while peeling off my boots and socks, and rolled up my pants.

"Are you feeling ill?" he asked, concern in his voice.

"I feel frazzled. Anxious." I confessed to him. "Coming here . . . leaving Taria so suddenly. It's a lot to process. I'm hoping whatever is in this water will help calm me a bit. I'm also cold."

Sethos snapped a finger, and a thick beige blanket appeared in his hands. He draped it over my shoulders, and I thanked him.

The water was initially cold when I dipped my legs in, but soon I could feel the water molecules hugging my legs, slowly making my skin tingle. It wasn't uncomfortable but different, and soon, the water felt warm, and my muscles began to unclench, as if tension was leaving my body.

I sat with my arms and hands behind me, supporting my weight, while Sethos sat with one knee bent.

I looked up at him, and his eyes were trained on something in the distance.

He was so breathtakingly beautiful, his silver hair glowing in the dark like stars. His ice-blue eyes were like the clearest water with streaks of bright blue, fluorescent magic.

I wondered about all the time we spent together before and our nighttime travels.

"Can you tell me something . . ." I asked.

Sethos looked to me and smiled. "Sure."

"How were you able to travel with me through the astral plane . . . ? Is it something that everyone can do?"

I knew this wasn't the case because the Astral had told me so when I traveled through the portal. Still, I wanted to hear Sethos tell me.

He shook his head. "Not everyone has that skill. For me?" He shrugged. "It's just an ability I have."

I pursed my lips. "Is it something sea fae can do?"

"No." He shook his head. "My mother told me my father was able to travel through the astral. The power comes from him."

Interesting.

In the past, Sethos had mentioned his father was someone his mother had known briefly. He shared that the man left her once she became pregnant.

"Were you ever told who your father was?"

He shook his head. "Only that he was cruel. And she was glad I inherited her silver hair color and not his black hair."

I realized how little I knew of Sethos, even though being with him felt so right.

My eyes dropped to the sheathed sword on his waist. He looked like a soldier . . .

I frowned as I realized I didn't know what he did. I had asked him before, and he avoided the question.

I narrowed my eyes and suddenly asked, "What is it you do?"

Sethos looked at me from the corner of his eye, and a slow smile spread across his lips, making my skin tingle for an entirely different reason.

"I can tell you *who* I'd like to do in this moment."

Heat spread through me as his ice-blue eyes danced with mischief, but I cleared my throat.

I lowered my chin. "Be serious."

Sethos laughed. "Who's to say I'm not? I'm absolutely serious."

I shook my head. "You know exactly what I'm talking about."

Sethos sighed and looked from me back to the pool.

"I oversee a large population," he said.

I crossed my arms. "You oversee people? In what capacity?"

He became silent and looked at the water. "I rule over your father's kingdom."

My heart plummeted to the floor. "What . . . ?"

"I overthrew your father and took his power."

I scrambled to stand and immediately backed away from him.

I shook my head. "I don't understand."

Sethos shot up and put his palms up. "I don't mean you harm."

"You don't mean me any harm?" I yelled. "You have my father's powers," I gritted out. "He's the worst of people. You know what he did to me."

"Yes—"

"Why would anyone choose to have them?"

Sethos stared at me for a long moment before looking toward the rest of the room. "Your father adopted me long ago when I was a child of fourteen." He crossed his arms. "I grew up and overthrew him."

My breath caught in my throat, and I waited for him to continue. There was something he wasn't saying.

When he didn't expound, I growled, "That can't be the entire story. There's more to it . . ."

His eyes slid back to the water. "There is," he responded.

"To overthrow someone is not an insignificant action."

"Your father ruled over a dimension called Vasarys. I orchestrated a coup and took his throne."

"Why did you overthrow him?"

"He failed his people. He oppressed them viciously and did not deserve the post entrusted to him. He enslaved his own people. I freed them."

I knew there was more to his time with my father than he shared. His posture, his tone, and his eyes, filled with detached pain and very present rage, spoke volumes about how he might have been treated. I would know.

Am-Re was a destroyer of lives.

No one escaped him unscathed.

He was a plague.

"Tell me about the time he raised you. Tell me about your childhood."

Sethos was quiet until I looked to him and found him staring at the tree canopy above.

"Sometimes I forget that part of my life," he said, not looking at me. "And then it comes rushing back to me without warning."

His tone and his demeanor made me uneasy.

"As you know, my mother was single. She raised me on her own, away from her family, on a planet called Isyos."

I nodded. "Were you happy with her?" I held my breath, waiting for his response. I always wondered what a mother's love could be like.

Sethos looked at me. "Yes. Isyos was no place to raise a family, but it was what she could afford."

"And she loved you?" I asked gently.

Sethos's eyes turned hard as he looked down at his hands, which were now clasped. He nodded.

"Tell me how you came to be under Am-Re's care."

"Isyos was attacked."

Tension coiled tight in my chest.

"Its lands were destroyed," he said with a strained voice. "One morning, the day was normal, and the next, we watched as fireballs rained down on us. I see the fire in my dreams. The fire traps me. The buildings destroyed . . . I cannot escape them." Sethos's voice suddenly took a darker tone. "I dream of missiles almost nightly. I try new ways to escape them. To hide. In the end, my body burns every time."

My chest heaved and my hands twitched as I warred with whether to reach for him in comfort or to give him space.

"The day of the attack, I was away from home during the day as I often had to be," he said and ran his hands through his hair. "My mother had her . . . clients come to our house, and I would leave to play with the children in the district. That day, we were playing in the playground . . ." He looked to the windows along the fortress walls. "I remember chasing some of the children up the play gym . . ." His brows gathered. "It was red equipment. The children began to scream, and when I looked up, I saw a fireball rushing down toward Isyos."

I couldn't hold back. I reached and grabbed his hand, squeezing.

Sethos looked down at our joined hands. "The impact of the fireball knocked me off the play gym, and I fell on my back." He moved our hands as if he was marveling at how our hands fit together. "We all scrambled home. We hid and ducked into buildings and under bridges. By the time we made it to our street, it was all gone."

My lips parted and my pulse thrummed with force inside me.

"My home . . ." He looked away. "It had caved in."

I shook my head and grabbed his other hand.

He squeezed.

"I dug. I dug for her. I—" Sethos's voice was barely a whisper. "When I got to her, my fingernails were bleeding. I couldn't uncover her fully."

Tears pooled in my eyes. "Sethos . . ."

He looked at me, and the ice blue in his eyes looked like two sad oceans.

"I couldn't pull her out." He clenched his jaw. "I could hear her cry on the other side of the stone walls . . . I—"

I freed one of my hands and cupped his face. "It's not your fault."

"I heard her die."

My tears and cries were locked in my body, and I felt like bursting from the pressure in my chest.

Crying was for the weak.

I breathed in and swallowed my tears.

I needed to be strong.

Sethos needed me to be strong.

"She died holding my hand. I slept beside her that night against that stone wall. The following morning, Am-Re walked the districts with his council and other survivors. I don't know what it was about me that made him stop that day. He saw me and knelt next to me."

Anger surged through me, knowing the vulnerability of Sethos and the cruelty of my father.

"He coaxed me to let go of her hand. And I left her." A strangled cry ripped through Sethos's body, and a shattering sob escaped his lips. "I left her, Renna."

I let go of his other hand and cupped the other side of his face.

"You didn't do anything wrong," I said quickly, my voice cracking at seeing the strong man before me break. "You were a child."

"I never knew where they buried her. He never allowed me to visit her body. I later learned that Am-Re intended to make me a symbol of the attack. A fucking mascot for people to rally around. He paraded me to garner support."

"He exploited you," I gritted out. "You had no other family."

"Am-Re had a seven-year-old daughter." His eyes searched mine, but they were vacant as if he was recalling a memory.

I dropped my hands from him.

"She became the only true friend I had. That girl was you."

My pulse hammered in my temples. That was the lifetime Khellios alluded to me living. I had meant so much to both men, and I couldn't remember anything.

"Why can't I remember?" My heart was shattering for him. For me. For everyone my father had affected.

He shook his head. "Am-Re's magic must have altered your memories. People who reincarnate remember their lifetimes through dreams or flashbacks."

Tears laced with fury escaped me as I thought of all my father had taken from me.

"What happened next?"

"Am-Re took me to his palace so he could raise the 'survivor child' of The Night of a Thousand Tears, as the attack later became called. Many thought I was lucky." He looked off into the distance and gritted out his next words. "But each day in his home, I wished I was dead."

I bit my lips together.

"Am-Re." Sethos paused. He clenched his jaw and curled his hands into tight fists. "Am-Re liked to see suffering. He preyed on the weak. It excited him." Sethos bowed his head, his forehead mere inches from mine.

"Sethos," I said carefully, moving my right hand to his chest. "What did he do to you?"

Sethos shook his head. "At first I couldn't understand why he resorted to violence the way he did. In public, I was forced to be polished and unflinching. I had to exude strength. He said I represented him in the public eye. He dressed me like royalty. I was forced to call him Father. Over time, calling him my father became second nature to me. To all he told I was the son he longed for."

I waited for Sethos to continue, but he remained silent. My chest tightened with what he would say next. I knew how difficult it was to recall trauma.

After a while, he spoke up. His fists were white with tension. "He had a man whip me."

My eyes began to water as Sethos closed his eyes and gritted his teeth.

"Every time he had a bad day or something went wrong in Vasarys—where we settled after Isyos—he would force me to strip naked. And I would be whipped. He never did it himself."

I covered my mouth and stifled a sob.

"As a child of fourteen, I could not understand why he wanted to punish me the way he did. For any slight offense. He relished in humiliating me."

With a trembling hand, I dared to touch his face, and he flinched slightly.

"Eventually, I realized he pleasured himself while seeing me whipped."

He opened his eyes and looked up at me. An ocean of pain and anger flooded his gaze with unshed tears.

I reached for him, and his eyes immediately softened. He pulled me to him, crushing my body against his as we held one another.

"I'm so sorry," I whispered, clinging to him with all the energy I had. "I'm so sorry."

He nodded against my neck. "You were the light. You were all I had. We grew up as friends. I devised a way for us to have a different life when we were older and organized an escape. You were able to get away, but somehow, you ended up in Old Xhor in transit." His body tensed. "I later learned you became involved with Khellios."

I pulled away, my eyes roaming Sethos's face. "Were you and I ever . . . ?"

Sethos shook his head. "We were never romantic," he whispered. "Although I knew you fancied me. I was quite young and good looking back then."

I blushed because he was good looking to me now.

"But I never acted on anything between us." Sethos brought his forehead to mine. "Then you turned 18 and our interactions changed. You confessed to me during a festival you liked me as more than a friend. I knew then if I ever wanted to pursue something else with you beyond friendship, it would have to be away from Am-Re. We needed to be free of him so you could make that choice freely without his shadow looming over us. I didn't want you to feel like entering a romantic relationship with someone was your only means to escape an abusive home."

I cupped his face. Our lips were so close.

"I wish I could remember how I felt about you then . . ."

"And then he took you from me." His voice broke, and he buried his face in my neck.

"I can't remember, and I'm sorry," I cried and wrapped my arms around him.

Sethos pulled away and held me by the forearms. "You're here now."

He looked down at my lips, and my breath came faster.

The energy between us began to grow, and I knew he wanted to kiss me. But this didn't feel like the right moment.

I broke our stare and looked down. "And the ones who attacked Isyos," I began and looked up again at him. "Were they brought to justice?"

Sethos's expression hardened, and he looked away. "They will pay."

A dark, ominous shiver spread through my body.

I placed my hands on his chest. "You have every right to hate them—"

"Hate is a word that will never cover what I feel," he gritted out.

"They destroyed your life."

Sethos clenched his fist. "I swear on my life I will kill them. I won't rest until the deaths of my mother and the Fallen from Isyos are avenged."

I paused and frowned.

"Sethos," I said gently, searching his eyes. "Your mother loved you. Would she have wanted you to avenge her?"

"She is dead," he snapped, his body tensing. "The dead don't speak."

I stayed silent, and he looked to the distance.

His eyes suddenly lost their brilliant icy-blue color, and a muted dark blue, almost black, moved like shadows over his irises.

My eyes flickered between his face and body several times, unease filling me.

I had never seen his eyes do that.

Then, a darker, almost foreign voice took over. "Avenging their deaths is the only thing that matters."

"Sethos..." I moved back slightly, but he still held onto me.

"I will have my revenge, Renna," Sethos said. "Do you see what I have gone through? Do you condemn me?" he spat.

I shook my head quickly. "No—"

"You never want to feel vulnerable again? Well, neither do I."

I couldn't form the words to reply.

Sethos swung his face back to mine, and in the blink of an eye, his eyes were normal again.

I froze in place, not knowing whether to pull away. Something was not right.

I looked to him and whispered, "Tell me how to help you. What do you need from me? Say it, and it's yours."

We stared at each other for a few moments.

When he spoke, his voice was back to normal. "Don't try to sway me from seeking justice."

I swallowed the saliva that had pooled in my mouth as uneasiness settled over me.

"It's my right."

I reached for his hands and squeezed.

"If someone threatened those you loved, would you not want to seek justice?" Sethos asked.

"Let me stand by your side," I said.

Sethos's eyes searched my face, and he shook his head. "You don't know what you are saying, Renna."

"Yes, I do—"

"If someone threatened you," Sethos said, his voice deadly, "I would tear the universe apart. My mother deserves nothing less."

I realized in that moment that no one had ever stood up for Sethos. Fought for him. Even as a child, he was forced to leave his mother, not even knowing where she was buried.

Rage simmered under my skin and settled in my core. "I would tear the universe apart for *you*, Sethos," I said. "I will do it."

He squeezed my hands. "Renna—"

"I'm not asking you for permission," I said and pushed myself to stand. "I am telling you."

He blinked several times and stood. "Why?" he asked, and reached for me again. He wrapped an arm around my waist and began to caress my face with his other hand.

"Because . . ." I began, as my skin pebbled under his touch.

His eyes moved to my mouth, and he pulled me closer.

"I want to be there for you like you were there for me," I breathed, our lips now close.

"You mean that now," he said, his fingertips trailing down to my lips. "But I wonder if you will feel the same when the time comes."

My brows furrowed, and I was about to ask him what he meant when he spoke.

"I cannot ask you to fight my battles, Renna."

I pulled him closer. "You aren't asking me. Stop being so stubborn!"

Sethos wrapped his arms around me and rested his chin on top of my head.

"I've missed you," he said.

I sighed contentedly. "And I've missed you."

He chuckled.

"Don't ever disappear on me again, alright?" I said, squeezing him.

"Are you asking me or telling me?"

I grinned. "Telling you. Or I'll go all blood-lusty rage magic on you."

Sethos pulled away slightly from me and raised an eyebrow, a smirk forming on his lips. "I only heard the word lusty," he said.

I attempted to pull my arm from around him to playfully punch him, but he locked my arms in place.

"Sethos!" I laughed, my skin tingling with heat.

"I'm never letting you go, Renna Strongborn," he said with a smile.

I narrowed my eyes. "Sounds flattering, but you knew I was going to hit you. You're keeping my arms in place."

He laughed. "Why can't it be both?"

I rolled my eyes.

"Can I have your word on you going all blood-lusty on me?" he teased.

A smirk formed on my lips, and a delicious, warm feeling began to build in my core.

"It depends." I shrugged, feigning seriousness.

"On what?" He tilted his head, his eyes intense.

"If you're on your best behavior, you won't meet any of my rage. No bloodlust, scary magic."

"Well then," he said, pushing my hair from my shoulders. "I guess I need to be on my worst behavior."

I bit my lip and blushed.

"I'm going to kiss you," he said.

I wanted to kiss him, but the conversation about his mother came back to me, and with my mood change, he hesitated.

"Sethos?" I asked and looked at him. "I meant it when I said I wanted to help you."

He sighed and nodded and stepped away from me. "I know."

"Teach me. Help me understand my magic, and I will stand by your side, Sethos."

He was still for a few moments and then slowly nodded. "Very well."

I reached for his hand and wove my fingers in his.

"But the first thing you need to do," Sethos said, "is go back to bed and sleep. Magic always has a price, Renna. It takes a tax. A toll every time you use it. You need to be well rested."

I nodded.

"Go back to your room and settle in. I'll bring you food. You must be starving. The healing waters provide nutrients, but you haven't eaten a full meal. You need solids."

My stomach gurgled in agreement, and we parted. When I got to my room, the gloominess of my surroundings didn't bother me as much. All I could think about was Sethos and how, with him, I felt like any place could become a home.

7

SETHOS

y eyes snapped open.

Renna's screams filled the night and echoed through the fortress.

I jumped from bed and raced to her room, expecting the worst, despite having enchanted the fortress to lock everything and everyone out.

I burst into her room to find Renna thrashing on her bed, her eyes squeezed shut, her arms reaching above her as if blocking and fighting an attacker.

She was dreaming. I knew from personal experience that after traumatic events, the mind was plagued by nightmares as the body sought to regulate itself.

"Renna?" I rushed to her side and sat on the bed. "Wake up. You're having a nightmare."

"Stop!" she screamed with her eyes closed. "Don't come any closer!"

I stilled.

"Don't hurt me, please," she sobbed, a wail wrecking her body.

I shook her gently once more. "Renna."

"I will never give in," she yelled. "Never."

She had to be dreaming of Am-Re.

"Renna!" I shouted and shook her more insistently.

She awoke with a gasp and sat up, reaching for something to grab. Tears fell from her face.

"Renna," I said again. "You were dreaming."

She wiped the tears from her face and dropped her head into her palms.

"What did you dream of?" I asked gently, my eyes tracking her every movement.

"When I was healing after the portal, submerged in the Waters of the Rhya, I had a recurring dream."

I lowered my chin. "Go on . . ."

"I am chased by Am-Re into a labyrinth. He hunts me with his dretani. It's a golden serpent."

My heart began to beat loudly in my ears, and I did my best to appear calm.

She couldn't possibly know about his dretani—especially not his color. I doubted the gods told her specific details about her father. They were cowards who would not even utter his name.

"He taunts me," Renna whispers. "He asks me to let him into my mind. To stop struggling and fighting him."

Renna still thought Am-Re was alive, and it was eating me inside.

I could not watch her go through this every night.

"I will always keep you safe, Renna—"

"You sound so sure." She shook her head.

"I am."

She frowned and wiped the last of her tears.

"Sethos, the gods in Arios's enclave fear my father. They refuse to say his name due to the terror it evokes. You can try and protect me as much as you can from Am-Re, but he's coming for me—"

"He will never hurt you again."

"He mentioned you in my dreams this time."

An ominous feeling spread over my body. I froze and pulled away from her. My vision tunneled.

My mouth was dry, and I swallowed. I was too shaken to speak.

Renna slid her arms around my torso.

I swallowed again and let her hold onto me. "What did he say?"

"He told me to tell you, *To kill a god, one must kill its soul.*"

My blood ran cold.

Renna lifted her head and looked up.

I willed myself to return her gaze.

"Sethos?" she asked, searching my eyes.

I forced a smile and hugged her to me, hoping she would not feel my racing heart.

"It's just a dream," I spoke against her hair. "Just a dream."

She nodded and settled against my chest.

"Thank you for telling me," I said against her hair.

After a few moments, I helped settle Renna back into bed and, at her request, conjured a romance novel and night lamp for her to read. I left her alone in her room with a promise to return and lie next to her once she was asleep.

Once I stood in the hallway outside her room, waves of panic gripped my heart and paralyzed me.

What if Renna was right and her dreams were . . . *more?*

To kill a god, one must kill its soul.

I could feel my sanity drain from my body like water, and my mind began to race.

There was one person who would know what to do about Renna's dreams.

In particular nightmares.

And that person would not be pleased to see me.

But I was desperate.

I portaled to the forest beyond the protective borders of the fortress to find Etara.

8

SETHOS

I stood outside Etara's camp deep in the forests of Daya, nestled at the base of a mountain. A gentle moving, glowing white stream that resembled clusters of white stars ran alongside the front of a beat-up golden star craft. Fire from a barrel with a grill on top lit the night, casting ghostly shadows along the trunks of the thick trees that stretched several hundred feet above the ground. The night was quiet save for the sound of the bubbling stream and a few star craft zipping by as people came back to their camps for the evening.

Above me, a thin layer of violet surrounded Etara's camp—a force shield to prevent unwanted visitors. Luckily, her magic allowed me passage—for now. A buzz filled the air, and I looked to my left to see Etara coming through the shield, her eyes stormy with rage.

"Why are you here?" she demanded. She held two dead rabbits in each hand.

"I need your help," I said, crossing my arms.

She paused about twenty feet from me, threw the rabbits on the ground, and placed her hands on her hips.

"You were very clear about what would happen the next time

you saw me," she said. "You say hurtful things, Sethos, to push people away. After a while, I have to wonder whether your insults and threats are all bravado."

Remorse swirled inside me, and my chest grew heavy.

"I know what I said," I began. "I'm sorry. I'm not here to hurt you."

She crossed her arms. "It's been a few days since Renna arrived," Etara began. "Have you made things right with her?"

"I'm not here to talk about that. You know where I stand."

Etara cursed under her breath and pointed at me. "Do not ask me to hurt that young woman anymore. I won't do it. No matter how much I care for you."

"I'm here because something is the matter with Renna."

She narrowed her eyes. "Something is the matter with her, alright." She spat on the ground. "She is with you! You are an embarrassment."

Anger reared its ugly head inside me, and my body vibrated with the familiar pull of Am-Re's magic. The urge inside me was to extend my magic and hurt her. Squeeze at her neck until her pulse thrashed under my hands so she would be helpless and pliant to my demands that she help Renna.

I had hurt her before, and I wasn't proud of it.

That was before we found the witch who prepared the potions.

My heartbeat echoed in my ears as I fought Am-Re's magic, and with shaky hands, I reached inside my vest pocket for a tincture vial.

As my vision blurred, I opened the vial and drank the contents.

I threw the vial on the pebbled ground below me and watched it shatter.

"Please," I said, wiping my mouth with my sleeve. "Being with her is everything to me."

Etara stared at me for a long time and shook her head, muttering curses as she picked up the rabbits and walked to the stream.

"What's wrong with Renna?" she asked as she set the rabbits down at the edge of the water and began to wash and skin them.

I stepped toward her. "She's having troubling dreams."

Etara paused, lowered her chin, and crossed her arms while holding the rabbits.

"Dreams?" She rolled her eyes. "You came to disturb my peace for dreams?"

"Yes."

"Leave me be, Sethos," she muttered. "I don't want to be a part of this mess any longer."

"I know I said hurtful things," I began. "I'm sorry."

Silence settled between us as she skinned her dinner.

"Please help me."

Ignoring me, Etara picked up her rabbits and walked to the fire and hung the rabbits above the grate and walked back to the stream to rinse her hands.

When she was done, she remained kneeling and looked out at the water. "I may not look much older than you, Sethos," Etara said, "but you remind me of the son I lost. I wish I could have saved him . . ." She turned to me. "Please, there is time to stop this madness."

"Etara." I was now next to her. "We both know my time is running out," I began. "I don't know what will happen to me once Am-Re's magic reaches my heart."

Etara's lips trembled, and she stood.

"I want to ensure the world around me is better once I . . ." I swallowed hard.

"Killing is not the answer." She grabbed my arms. "Look what my life has become after the mistake I made in the Kingdom of Nightmares. I got mixed up with the wrong people and killed the king's wife. I can never return home, and I live here"—she gestured around—"alone in a land that is cruel. Always hypervigilant, not knowing if I will ever be found out. I don't sleep. I have to force myself to eat—"

"Etara—"

"I don't want a life of exile for you." She closed her eyes and covered her face with her hands.

"I think Am-Re is back."

Etara slowly dropped her hands, her eyes wide.

"What did you say . . .?"

"I believe he may be trying to contact Renna through dreams. You are a witch of nightmares. Perhaps you can shed some light on what is happening."

Etara's eyes flashed side to side, and she grabbed my arm.

"Let's discuss this inside," she said, walking toward her craft. "Despite my force shield, it doesn't keep sound in. And I don't trust the trees."

The inside of the craft looked nothing like the beat-up exterior. The craft, which appeared to be a personal ship with two rooms, looked brand new with soft lighting and leather interiors. To the right was Etara's library, and to the left was a small white kitchenette.

Etara walked to the kitchenette and conjured hot tea in a white mug. She grabbed the mug and turned to face me. "Tell me about her dreams."

"I believe they're nightmares, but they don't seem like typical nightmares."

Etara frowned. "What is she dreaming?"

"Am-Re. He terrorizes her. She says Am-Re comes to her asking her to surrender to him. To let go."

"That sounds like trauma. A terrifying nightmare, *but* nothing out of the ordinary."

"No." I rubbed the back of my neck. "I think it's something

else. She's either having visions or is being visited by something while dreaming."

"Describe what she saw."

"Renna shared Am-Re spoke to her in the most recent dream and told her of something she could not have possibly known."

Etara came and stood next to me. "What did he say?"

I looked down at Etara, whose height came up to my elbow. "He told her to let me know how to properly kill a god."

Etara's face paled, and she began to pace, her brows furrowed. I knew she would have dreamtime information to share that would shed light on the matter.

"Have you told her you killed her father?"

I shifted on my feet and crossed my arms. "I told her I over-threw him."

Etara's face turned a dark shade of red. "You lie to her still!"

Telling Renna I was behind the university attacks would alienate her from me forever. She was the last good thing in my life, and I was selfish to keep her at all costs.

"Renna already believes Am-Re died before she went to university. That belief helped her move on with her life. If he is somehow back, it won't make a difference that I killed him before. Why would I re-traumatize her?"

Etara's eyes bored into mine. "You are a coward," she gritted out. "You take her ability to choose for herself by painting your-self as a hero when in reality"—she looked me up and down—"she should stay far away from you."

I narrowed my eyes, and my vision blurred. "Oh yeah?" I seethed and brought my face closer to hers. "And who will tell her?" I spat.

Etara's eyes moved between mine, but rather than fight me back, they suddenly became filled with emotion, and she turned her face, giving me her cheek.

"I need you to leave," she said quietly.

Black shadows moved inside me, and my hands suddenly shot out. I grabbed her and picked her up by her shoulders, shoved her down on a couch, and pointed.

"I am not moving from this fucking shithole until you help me, Etara!" I screamed. "Do not make me force you to help me because, by heavens, I will!"

Etara reached to grip my hands to free herself.

"Renna is mine," I gritted out, rattling her. "And I will obliterate any threat to her life." I lowered my face to Etara. "Now, speak!"

I pushed off Etara and I whirled to the end of the room as I glared.

Etara slowly sat up, and her voice was monotone when she spoke, her eyes not meeting mine. "Nightmares are usually either the result of hidden trauma that replays in different ways in a way that is disturbing *or* are a message from the spirit world that may cause fear to the dreamer."

I rubbed my face with both hands. I wanted to scream. "Am-Re cannot be alive."

Etara sighed, and I dropped my hands to look at her. She was now looking at me.

"If a soul exists and the physical body is dead, the soul will communicate in spirit form."

"But I killed him, Etara."

"That's *not* the same as destroying a *soul*," she argued. "Even in Renna's dream, you know this."

"His soul and body were fractured into pieces when I scattered them. How can a soul put itself back together?"

"It can't," she said, shaking her head. "Someone would have to do it through magic. If you have enough of the body and soul, the rest slowly regenerates."

Blood drained from my face.

"Who helped you kill him?" she asked.

"His councilmen."

"His councilmen, who are all mortal?" She quirked a brow. "Who would not know the first thing about killing a god?"

Rage filled me, and the dark magic inside me crept through my body like a million spiders.

"I promised the people of Vasarys I would remove Am-Re. The plan was only to overthrow and kill him, scattering his remains was a fail-safe. Killing his soul wasn't part of the 'promise' I made."

I had gathered the pieces of Am-Re's body and soul and scattered them across the seven universes. When the councilmen offered to go with me to scatter and bury his remains, I refused, wanting to do the task myself as a way to bury the pain he caused me in private.

Had I been followed?

"Sethos," Etara said, wrapping her arms around herself. "Did you go with someone to bury his remains or tell anyone of the locations?"

I shook my head.

"The manner in which you killed him would make sense to anyone, but someone knows how to put a god back together. And they likely followed you on the night you buried him."

My heart sank to the pit of my stomach, and my body threatened to tilt over. I grabbed the back of the couch for support.

"You need to seek his remains tonight," Etara said urgently. "If he truly is back, you and Renna are in even greater danger."

She was right. If Am-Re's soul had returned, that meant he would hunt for me first in revenge for having killed him.

I still needed to avenge my mother and the Fallen.

I could not do that dead.

You cannot protect Renna if you are dead either.

I had no time to waste. I would go tonight.

9

SETHOS

Even though I had killed Am-Re over seven years ago, the locations of his remains were fresh in my mind.

I portaled to the star Eusera outside Daya. The star was dying from its proximity to a neighboring black hole, and volatile matter was being pulled violently toward the inky vortex.

No one came close to black holes unless you knew how to enter their wormholes. The center of black holes were stable, and the matter being sucked into wormholes provided enough energy to sustain life inside them. Black holes had no sunshine, but the energy caught by black holes was enough to generate electricity and other tools necessary to live. That was why Am-Re had chosen to relocate the survivors of Isyos to Vasarys. Only a select few knew how to enter it.

All seven universes had an infinity of black holes with new ones forming every day, which made it difficult to explore each one and find Vasarys.

As pieces of meteor came tumbling toward me, I set up my protective shield using Am-Re's strain of magic. The magic that surrounded the shield reached out toward the meteors and crushed the rock to dust. That was the one good thing about Am-

Re's magic—it allowed me to magnify magic to an incomprehensible degree.

I sprang off Eusera and headed to the first location where Am-Re's remains were located.

This was going to be a long night.

I CLAWED through the gray soil on the black dwarf star I was on.

I was now in our sister universe, Konah.

Konah was a much older universe than the one I called home, and as a result, it had a multitude of dying stars—specifically brown and black dwarf stars.

Black dwarf stars were best described as skeletons floating in the universe, silently awaiting the end of time. They could not sustain life.

And were precisely the perfect hiding spot for Am-Re's remains.

I was in good spirits thus far, having found three hiding spots for Am-Re's remains intact.

My search in Konah, however, was proving nerve-racking.

My body temperature rose as I kept digging.

I wiped sweat off my brow with my forearm and looked up to the cosmos. The space sky here was dark purple, almost black.

The white stars I could see twinkled at me, as if mocking my efforts.

I doubted Khellios could detect me. Black dwarf stars were useless and, as such, were not important to star deities like Khellios.

I cursed the day I met him.

I thought of the first time I had ever spoken to him . . .

The night before Am-Re attacked Old Xhor—on the eve of Renna's death.

I had gone to save her, fearing Am-Re would kill her.

Khellios never heeded my warning, and she died.

Rage filled my chest and exploded down my arms in black shadows as I dug faster.

My fingernails became black as I clawed my way through the soil, desecrating the burial site. The hole around me widened and became like a tomb with me in it.

My heart sank to the bottom of the pit when I realized . . .

It didn't matter how much I kept digging.

Nothing.

There was nothing.

Am-Re's remains were gone.

10

SETHOS

"What will you do now?" Etara asked as I paced inside her camp.

I ran my palms over my face. I'd failed Renna. Every single thing I had done to keep her safe over the years was now for nothing. I had used her with the excuse to avenge the Fallen. I knew I could keep her safe because I had everything under control. But now with Am-Re back . . .

"I don't know what to do," I said.

"Who do you think did it?"

"Everyone hates Am-Re." I shook my head and dropped my hands.

"Who would stand to benefit if he returned?"

"Half the council wants me gone. They support Demira. I'm sure someone wants to see her on my throne and wants Am-Re back."

"But you have always told me Demira hated her father. Why would she bring him back when he would simply reinsert himself as ruler?"

I shook my head, not understanding what was happening either.

"I need to go to Vasarys," I said quickly and opened a portal. "I haven't been there in a month. I left Iagon, my second, in charge, but . . ." I sighed. "I can't stay away any longer."

Etara's eyes widened. "What about Renna?" She crossed her arms. "You can't just leave her here."

It was still night, and Renna was likely still asleep, but it was clear I was needed now more than ever in Vasarys to uncover who could be behind Am-Re's return.

I turned to Etara. "The fortress has the shield. Renna will be safe while I'm away for a few hours."

"Sethos," Etara began. "With Am-Re back, you must cease this agenda against the gods. Your sole focus should be on locating him and killing him for good. He is weak right now."

I glared at her. "No. On the contrary. Attacking the gods *now*, while I have Am-Re's powers, is what matters most. I will go to Vasarys to ready the troops that have been gathering for months now. While I am in Vasarys, I will also conduct an investigation as to who may have collected his remains."

"This is madness."

"I will deal with Am-Re when I come back victorious from Taria. My people need to see me triumphant in order to gain confidence in me to help me defeat Am-Re."

"Sethos, you do not know how fast his body will regenerate. You will be the first person he comes after—if not the entire population of Vasarys."

"That is precisely why I need to attack Taria *now*." I massaged my temples. "It's inevitable Am-Re will seek me out. I'd rather do it with my head held high and the death of the gods in Taria behind me."

"This is insanity—"

"I do not ask for your opinion."

"Yet you are here!" Etara gestured to her home. "Not even your right hand, Iagon, is privy to what is truly happening."

"So what would you have me do?"

I was frustrated to be on the cusp of so many things—a real relationship with Renna, justice from the gods, and freedom from Am-Re. Now it seemed to be all quickly slipping away.

"Consider calling on allies."

"My army is enough."

"I do not think Am-Re will return alone. He would not risk it."

"I will kill him—"

"Not if your army is reduced by an attack on the gods first. Where will you get more soldiers? Call for back up."

"From who?" I yelled.

"Strike a deal with the gods in Taria."

I narrowed my eyes. "You suggest I ask my mother's killers for help?" I ran my hands through my hair. "I will never see them as more than my enemy."

"You have to try something!"

"I refuse to fail."

Etara shook her head. "You are choosing ambition and revenge over the possibility of love. How very sad for you, Sethos."

Her words stayed with me the rest of the night.

Could no one understand my motives?

11

KHELLIOS

I saw red.

Pain radiated from my shoulder wound as I stormed through Arios's palace.

The wound where Sethos had cut my arm off clean when he attacked Taria.

I had been forced into a coma for a week while the priests petitioned Source to reconstruct my arm.

"*Khellios!*" Ukara yelled after me, quickening her pace. "You'll reopen your sutures!"

Nothing mattered.

I wanted blood.

Upon waking, I'd found Ukara, my cousin and the Goddess of War, at my bedside, helping the priests nurse me back to health. She had informed me that Renna and Nera were gone.

Also gone was the mirror in the bedroom where Renna had been staying.

Livina had confirmed to the other gods that Renna and Nera had been swept up in a portal formed in the mirror. Following her rule to not disturb the future, Livina, Goddess of Fate, refused to say where Renna and Nera had gone.

And I needed her now, but the Goddess of Fate could not be summoned. Rather, she appeared when necessary, and she apparently didn't think her presence was needed now. She knew I would demand to know where Renna was and the conflict that would ensue.

I walked through Arios's palace, and when I arrived at his gathering hall, I pushed open the doors, letting them slam against the glimmering limestone walls.

An ominous feeling spread through me. This scene felt all too familiar.

Arios was seated on his throne, a dazed look on his face as he leaned his chin on his knuckle, the arm of the chair supporting his elbow. An assembly of twenty gods sat in circular rows of seats.

The Goddess of Nebulas, Alisane, stood in the middle of the hall with a book in hand, facing where the gods sat as if she had been in the middle of a lecture. Her glowing white robes and gold diadem made her stand out in a room of dark and jewel-tone robes. She looked at me with an eyebrow raised in annoyance.

"I take it you are not here for my talk about the unusual dying rate of nebulae?" she asked with arrogance dripping from her voice. "Or have you not noticed the decrease in star production? These are peculiar times."

I clenched my jaw. I had too many problems on my mind, but Renna took precedence.

I slid my eyes to Arios. "Call an army," I barked at him and looked to the rest of the gods seated in the hall.

The gods shifted nervously in their seats, and Alisane cursed and shut her book.

"Khellios," Arios attempted to smile, his voice shaky. "Let's not jump to rash decisions."

"Rash decisions?" I screamed. "Renna was taken! Nera is missing."

He nodded, his face flushed, and gestured to the room. "We all understand."

I looked about the room, and the gods avoided my eyes.

"What is this?" I barked. "Have you all made up your minds without me here? *Again?*"

"Khellios, two days ago we discussed what happened and—"

"And nothing!" I screamed.

I rushed toward Arios, but before I could blink, Arios extended a hand, and a hot, invisible claw held me in place at my throat.

My body shook in anger. "We are like brothers. Don't leave me alone now," I gritted out.

Arios looked away from me and put his hand down, releasing me.

I stumbled back a few steps.

"You discussed the attack on Taria without me?" I screamed.

Arios moved to sit down on his throne. "You were in a coma, Khellios."

"One forced on me!"

After Sethos struck me from the sky and I came to seconds later, I wanted to go after him. But the gods had all pinned me down until the priests arrived to sedate me.

"Assemble an army, right now," I yelled at Arios.

I looked around the room. "Will you all leave me at this time of need?"

Some gods crossed their arms. Others refused to look me in the eye.

"Renna is not one of us," someone in the crowd said.

"She's not a god," another echoed. "Her mother was a siren. Let the sea fae find her! Why is it our issue?"

"She's the daughter of a god who used to belong to this enclave," Ukara argued back. She looked to Arios. "Father, Am-

Re was your twin! Renna is your niece, whether you like it or not!"

Arios spoke. "Renna may be Am-Re's daughter, but she has not ascended in her demigod divinity. For all we know, her magic has not integrated into her system. Therefore, she is still a regular mortal. *And* she is not part of this enclave."

My breathing began to accelerate.

"And what about Nera?" I snapped. "Will you not assemble a search party for her?" I looked to Arios. "Do you not care about your daughter?"

Arios narrowed his eyes. "Keep my daughter's name out of your mouth!" he barked. "All Sethos wanted was Renna. You should have never asked Nera to guard Renna during the attack. You wrapped Nera into this mess. I have already sent out a squadron to look for her."

I narrowed my eyes, feeling my body vibrate with anger. Help for Nera, not Renna.

Breathe.

Breathe.

Arios dropped his eyes from mine at the next words. "You put me in a difficult position, Khellios. We all witnessed Sethos leaving Taria intact."

"We want no quarrel with him," someone spoke in the crowd.

"Am-Re's successor was clear." A god stood.

The room became silent.

It was Oruk, God of the Aurora, who had spoken. His opinion carried significant weight as he was our enclave representative in the Galactic Council, which was the governing body that created and enforced laws for all seven universes, made up of beings from the fourth through seventh dimensions—gods were in the fifth dimension.

He ran a hand through his lilac hair that matched the color of his luminescent skin and crossed his arms, his mouth in a tight line.

My heart faltered.

"All he wanted was Renna," Oruk began. "I'm sorry, Khellios. The Federation has been informed of this, and they do not support military action from our enclave against Sethos. We have avoided war with Am-Re for a long time. A war now would be devastating on scales not seen for eons," he said, shaking his head and looking at his feet.

Another god stood, nodding. He crossed his arms. "We want no quarrel with Sethos. Taria is located inside Andora, and a war would bring mayhem not only to the citizens of Taria but also to the mortals on Andora. The witches and mages from Taria also demand we stay out of it, as they pledged to rise up to fight during any conflict. We do not know what warfare with Sethos would look like."

"So that's it?" I yelled at the room.

Arios, perhaps emboldened by the gods speaking up, now stood.

"Khellios, we all heard Sethos ask for Renna specifically. You were injured, yes." He looked at my arm. "But we cannot risk the death of anyone in this room. It would throw off the cosmic balance. Besides, after investigation, Livina informed us that the mirror in her room—*given to you*—enabled the portal. For all we know, Renna created the portal and *left* of her own choice—"

"Father!" Ukara cut in. "You cannot say this—"

"You will stay silent!" Arios admonished her. "I will not throw our enclave into a war conflict. Especially with the offspring of our enemies. I do not care that Renna is the daughter of my brother. He ceased being my family long ago."

Ukara launched herself toward the dais, her spear in hand and pointed at Arios.

"By choosing cowardice, you condemn Khellios to death! You know he will go after her."

I looked around the room for anyone to speak up on my behalf.

Cylas was missing.

"Where is Cylas?" I demanded, my voice taking on a deadly tone.

I slid my eyes to Ukara, and she darted her eyes away from me.

The gods in the room shifted in their seats.

"Cylas!" I screamed and looked around. "Cylas!"

"Khellios," Arios said quietly. "Cylas is gone."

I looked to Ukara, who now looked at me. She mouthed a silent *sorry*.

I snapped my head toward Arios. "What do you mean *gone*?"

"While the priests cured you, Cylas left."

My heart stopped, and my body temperature dropped.

He went after Renna.

I knew it in my core being that Cylas had gone after her.

Why waste an opportunity to be the hero in her eyes?

I clenched my fists. "Who went with him? Did he give any coordinates?"

Arios shook his head. "He went alone. We have not heard from him."

I turned on my heels and began to walk from the room.

"Where are you going?" Arios called.

I spun and faced the room.

"Renna was taken." I paused. "She was ripped from Taria. I'm going to find her."

Oruk squared his shoulders. "Khellios, we cannot condone your actions. The Federation will not be happy if we follow you."

Arios pointed to me in warning. "You would be acting alone. With no enclave representation or resources. I will not have our enclave slighted—or worse, excluded—by the Federation."

Ukara walked to stand next to me. "I am going with him. My shadow army as well."

Arios began to wag his finger at her. "You will stay put—"

"You do not own me." Ukara's voice was deadly, and she took a step toward her father. "You do not command me. You do not speak to me in that manner."

Arios blinked.

"You may be my father biologically, but I do not belong to this enclave. Source made me God of War in the womb. This enclave is for Celestial Bodies. Do not forget I *choose* to call Taria home. I *choose* where my loyalty lies at the end of the day." She pointed to me. "I stand with Khellios. My cousin. My *family*. Perhaps you have forgotten the meaning of the word."

Arios crossed his arms.

Ukara continued. "Sethos is dangerous. He killed Am-Re. I will not have blood on my hands if I stand back and Renna—or Khellios—is killed."

Arios lifted his chin to me. "You poison Ukara against me—"

Ukara cut in. "Do *not* speak for me," she yelled.

Arios fumed and pointed to me. "You walk out that door, Khellios, and you rescind your home here."

I chuckled bitterly. "This place ceased to be home the moment you abandoned the woman I love."

Ukara and I turned from the room and walked away.

As we left the hall, the room erupted in yells as the gods argued.

"Where to now?" she asked as we hurried from Arios's palace. "Shall I raise my army?"

I frowned and stopped walking.

"Let's pause and strategize first. Where are we going?" I raised my palms. "As much as Am-Re was unable to locate Taria, his realm is also hidden from us, so we cannot simply go and seek Sethos out." I shook my head. "Where would we even start the search?"

Ukara looked to the ground in thought.

"After the attack on Isyos . . ." Her brows gathered. "We know Am-Re relocated his people to a black hole. We can work our way back to determine where they went—"

"Don't speak of Isyos." I cut her off and massaged my temples.

"Khellios," Ukara said, placing a hand on my shoulder. "I know you don't like talking about the destruction of Isyos, but if we have any chance of locating him, we need to search for survivors of that day and see if they know the location of Am-Re's new settlement."

I ushered her out of Arios's palace and stopped once we were outside on the main steps, descending into the hanging gardens.

"Isyos happened a few years before Xhor fell." I reminded her. "Most of the souls are dead."

"Some of the beings there were immortal."

"And what will we say to them?" I yelled.

Ukara grew silent.

"Tell me, Ukara, because with what face will we show up and demand survivors of Isyos tell us where Am-Re went?"

"Isyos fell so long ago . . ."

I shook my head. "Many have long memories."

Ukara sighed. "Khellios—"

I squeezed my eyes shut as I recalled the day our enclave destroyed Isyos, and bile rose in my throat. I covered my eyes with my palms as if that could take away the images.

"Cousin . . ." Ukara whispered and put a hand on my shoulder.

I shrugged her off. "Gods are asked by Source to protect mortal life as part of our duties!" I reminded Ukara. "We followed Arios *blindly* to Isyos—the planet where we exiled Am-Re—and attacked the planet *without question.*" I shook my head. "We were told only the lowest types of criminals resided there, aiding Am-Re, and that we had to put a stop to it."

Ukara lowered her eyes.

"Ukara, when we attacked Isyos, we killed children. Families. *Thousands of people!*"

"We didn't know—"

"That's right! We didn't know, but we should have!" I screamed. "The attack on Isyos emboldened Am-Re to attack Old Xhor!"

Ukara folded her hands in front of her. "What happened on Isyos is no different from the carnage Am-Re unleashed upon Xhor," she said quietly. "Children also died in Xhor. Families. Generations."

"I mourn the fall of Old Xhor almost daily. I live with survivor's guilt. If I have not forgotten Xhor, the survivors or descendants of Isyos will not have forgotten our attack. So I ask you," I said, seething, "with what face do we ask for their help in locating where their descendants live now?"

Ukara looked to the heavens and closed her eyes before rubbing her face.

"The only way we will succeed in locating Am-Re's realm is through mercenaries," she said and then returned her gaze to mine. "You were a mercenary once."

"And I have not been one for a very long time."

"It's a place to start."

I crossed my arms. "Who do you suggest for the job?"

"King Miletak . . . From your mercenary days . . ." she whispered. "Do you think he would be willing to help us?"

I rubbed my chin. "Perhaps."

King Miletak hailed from a race known as Arcadians on planet Tirose-B9, an advanced civilization. Tirose-B9 was split into four kingdoms, and Miletak was the ruler of one of them.

After Renna's death, I traveled to various lands to forget and deal with my grief. I stayed in King Miletak's court for three years as a mercenary. Because of my presence in his kingdom, he asked me to train mercenaries as part of his army.

"Who do you think the king would send to lead the mercenaries?" Ukara asked carefully.

I frowned. "How would I know?"

"Well . . ." Ukara cleared her throat. "He has a daughter," Ukara said, searching my eyes. "Elrie."

I narrowed my eyes. "I am aware."

"You told me about her . . . about her beauty and how she used to follow you around—"

I growled. "Ukara—"

"Perhaps after all this time, she is the one who leads her father's mercenaries. You trained her after all." Ukara paused.

I shifted on my feet. "I did. Whoever leads Miletak's mercenaries makes no difference to me."

Ukara observed me in silence, and after a while, she shook her head.

"So what now?" she finally said.

I began to descend the palace stairs with Ukara following.

"Right now, I need to find out why the shield of Taria broke when Sethos attacked." I ran a hand through my hair. "And the portal Renna was taken from . . . It should have never happened. Why didn't we plan for something like this?"

"You will need to pay Merida a visit in the Witch District . . . I can come with you?"

I nodded. "Let's go."

12

RENNA

The dream of my father had left me rattled. I wasn't able to sleep for long because of the fear that I would close my eyes and see him again. Being awake meant I was hypervigilant with the sounds coming into my room from the forest. I jumped at every little noise and shivered when I saw the fog rise up the trees. The bioluminescence from the trees looked like glowing eyes, and I trembled as the image of my father's dretani came back to me. I wanted to run from my room and find Sethos, but I didn't know where his bedroom was, and I didn't want to yell for him.

I was a grown woman, scared of the dark. I felt stupid.

When the first signs of dawn stretched across the land like a cool cloak of violet and blue, I pushed off my bed and quickly got dressed. I headed straight for the healing pool and took a seat along the ledge, dipping my toes in the water.

"Renna."

I turned to face Sethos. He walked toward me, his brows furrowed.

"Where did you go?" I asked.

When he didn't respond, my heart began to race. My intuition yelled that something was wrong.

"I wanted to come back to you sooner. I had things to attend to in Vasarys. Nothing to worry about."

His words made me pause. He clearly looked troubled, on edge even.

I shivered.

Sethos snapped his fingers, immediately producing a cloak. He bent to wrap it around me and sat down beside me.

"Daya is a bit cold," he said. The smile on his face seemed forced.

"Are you sure everything is okay?"

He looked down at his hands as he fidgeted with his vest jacket and nodded.

"You don't seem okay."

Sethos looked up. "Would it help if I told you I feel better now that I'm here with you?"

Warmth spread through me at his words.

"You bring me peace," he said.

I smiled and reached for him, and he wrapped his arms around me, settling his chin on my head.

"I wish to never be parted from you, mejtah."

His words, which he'd said before, now had an edge of desperation, and I didn't know what to make of them.

"Let's talk about something else, okay?" he asked and kissed the top of my head.

I was used to quickly pivoting to safe topics. When you grew up in a home where abuse was a daily occurrence, you became a people pleaser. There was always a sense of duty to pacify and not be a burden.

You bring me peace. His words echoed in my mind.

Time to pivot.

"Is the weather a safe enough topic?" I tried.

He laughed. "Yes."

Hearing his laugh settled my heart, and I inwardly breathed a sigh of relief.

"Well, then." I forced a chuckle to lighten the mood. "Why is Daya so chilly? My long sleeves and pants aren't cutting it."

Sethos held me tighter. "Daya is a dimension. The daylight you see here is not real. It's an illusion created by the Tatuiyah Fae, which is why it's colder here than in other places."

I paused. "Taria was also a dimension, but it was warm. How is Daya different from Taria?"

"Taria is a dimension on Andora with a magical shield to hide it from Andorian civilians. Despite the shield, Taria shares the sun that shines down on Andora, and as a result, it heats up Taria. Daya is a dimension floating in space."

"Does the lack of a celestial body, like a sun, hide Daya from the gods?"

Sethos tilted his head and furrowed his brows. "Yes. The gods have no jurisdiction here, and that's how the Tatuiyah desired it."

"Who are the Tatuiyah?" I blushed at my terrible pronunciation.

Sethos chuckled. "It's pronounced Tat-too-ee-yah." He stood and extended his arm for me to take. "Before I answer your question, would you like some food?"

My stomach grumbled at the mention. "Yes."

"We'll pass the kitchens and can stop to eat there."

I took his arm, and he guided us out of the room with the healing pool.

"Who are the Tat-too-ee-yah?" I spoke the name several times as we walked.

"They hail from the Konah universe, the sister universe to our own. They are the royal fairy family that created Daya many eons ago as a place to spend the holiday with family and their subjects. The family has since fractured and is now ruled by a reclusive king named Oberon who has shunned contact with everyone."

"Did he intend for Daya to be wild like this and difficult for habitation?"

Sethos tilted his head. "I'm not sure. I don't think he cares what happens to his lands, quite frankly."

"What happened to him?"

"Some say he lost the woman he loved. It would drive anyone to madness, you know."

"And now his lands are riddled with crime. His reaction seems extreme. Is there more to the story? Who was she?"

Sethos paused and looked ahead, his eyes avoiding mine. "His mate. He lost his mate."

I frowned, having never heard of the term on Andora. "What does that mean?" I asked. "Is it like a romantic partner?"

"It can be." Sethos and I continued walking. "A mate is rare. It is a divine connection that forces two people to come together to procreate."

Sethos's tone was acidic, as if the term was an abomination.

I grimaced at the term myself. "Why would Source force two people to come together in that manner? I couldn't imagine being forced to be with someone like that."

As a grown woman, the idea that my sexual life could be limited in that way was horrendous.

"Does everyone have a mate?" I asked.

Sethos pursed his lips. "Only fae do. But there are seven universes, Renna," Sethos said, looking at me. "The chances of finding a mate are rare." He grabbed my hand. "You must know, as a half fae . . . you have a mate . . . somewhere. But you are safe with me."

Sethos made the mate connection seem like it was akin to . . . rape. As if I needed saving from such a connection. I shuddered.

I took my hand and crossed my arms. "I hope to never find my mate."

Sethos smiled. "Good."

We entered a long hallway lined with floor-to-ceiling stone arcs that were an arm's length away from the lush, dark forest beyond.

I tensed.

Sethos looked down at me. "Are you alright? What's wrong?"

I shook my head and loosened my grip. "Andora is a desert planet. Although I've read about human forests, it didn't seem as though they looked like this. Seeing the fog last night is still a bit unsettling. And I've never seen a forest in real life so up close . . ." I whispered, my eyes darting to the tall trunks and strange luminescent colors emerging from the depths of the foliage. "The leaves are so dark green, almost black."

"This is a fae forest. It's unique. You're safe as long as you have a clear purpose for being in the forest and stick to that purpose." He tensed a bit. "Don't veer from your path, don't stop to speak to anyone, don't pause if you hear your name."

"That sounds terrifying."

Suddenly whispers began to float on the air, as if the trees were speaking in a language I couldn't decipher. The tree spirits.

"What did you mean by the trees having spirits?" I asked.

"Each living thing has a spirit. Even trees. Fae trees speak at a frequency heard by fae ears. The trees also move."

I froze in place and then laughed nervously. "Then how is the forest safe?" My heart began to beat faster.

"Have you ever heard of crows and ravens and their impossibly long memory?"

"No. I don't know much about them other than Andora has crows and ravens in captivity. They were part of the animals that came over during the Great Migration."

"Well, those birds have an incredibly long memory. They can

like a person or hold grudges. Usually, when they grow comfortable with you, they'll coexist peacefully, but there's a warming period. The same is for fae forests."

"A fae forest can hold a grudge?" I laughed.

"Yes," Sethos chuckled. "A fae forest needs to get to know you over time so you can be safe passing through it. Luckily, the forest outside the fortress knows me and accepts anyone I bring here."

"What life or energies live in a fae forest?"

"Nymphs, ghosts, shadow people, werewolves…"

Am-Re taught me about each being he listed. "Shadow people are formed by negative thoughts and hatred," I said, recalling what he'd told me.

Sethos nodded, and I shivered.

"And you also have to factor in that you can encounter other fae in the forest as well. I mentioned last night that you may encounter star crafts or other vehicles in the forest. There are camps of fae as well."

"Who do not want to be found."

"Don't worry." He squeezed my hand and gently pulled me to continue walking. "Any fae camps are very far from here. They know this fortress is inhabited, and the magic surrounding it prevents entry. That's enough of a deterrent for those who wish to be left alone."

"Are there other fortress structures?"

"Well," Sethos began, "as I've explained, the land rejects construction and structures—the land simply overtakes and destroys man-made dwellings over time."

I nodded. "Daya is wild, yes. I remember you telling me."

"The land is slowly overtaking this fortress." Sethos pointed in front of us. "For example, take this hallway we're in right now. Look up," he said, gesturing with his hand.

My eyes widened. A tree limb ran through the middle of the

ceiling, breaking the length of the ceiling in half, with little branches sprouting off toward the edges of the ceiling.

The branches were almost gray in color as if they had become one with the stone.

"The land will eventually reclaim this structure. You can see it in places where moss and flowers have broken through the stone floor," he explained, pointing to the ground as we walked. "Because of the magic in the land and its adversity to structures, I cannot fix this fortress, but I can enchant it with a magical shield to shelter from the elements and to keep people out. I suspect this structure will last at least another hundred human years."

Once we reached the end of the long hallway, we came upon a large empty room.

"This used to be a ballroom," Sethos muttered. He pointed to a corner. "You see that raised platform there?"

I nodded.

"When I discovered this fortress, rotting instruments and chairs stood there."

I looked around and noticed how beautifully the daylight filtered through the ancient tree canopies that acted as a roof over the hall.

"You're smiling," Sethos said.

I looked to him. "I am. This place is magical, despite how it's aging—its imperfections make it beautiful."

"I'm sorry this is all I can offer you at this time . . ." He shook his head. "You are the daughter of a god. You deserve better than this."

I touched his arm. "This place is beautiful, Sethos. The trees that have sprouted in the room"—I pointed to the trunks along the walls of the hall—"and the ivy clinging to the walls and flowers that fill the cracks on the ground make this place like something out of a children's tale." I paused. "As for being the daughter of a god." I shook my head. "I have learned to make do with what I have and the opportunities given to me. You forget I was living in a tiny studio apartment at university and before that in a slum district on Andora with my foster mother."

As we continued walking, I noted interesting things I observed.

"This place must have been very beautiful and busy when it was first built. I can see some of the faded wall colors in some areas." I pointed to the dulled green wall to my left with gold detailing. "Is that some sort of four-legged animal . . .?" I squinted and recalled Cylas's dretani. "That looks like a stag?"

Sethos looked to where I pointed. "The Tatuiyah unicorn. It has snakes coiled around its hooves to represent spiritual freedom. Native to these lands, not seen for centuries."

We crossed an inner courtyard with overgrown flowers and weeds that were up to my waist. I was careful as I stepped on jagged rocks and lifted concrete.

"This hallway leads to the kitchens," he said once we entered another hallway.

"This place is like a maze."

"You'll get used to it."

My heartbeat began to slow as a sudden realization hit me. I had no steady home base. My most recent home had been my university campus. I had lived there for seven years. Since Taria, my life had become transitory, and I was starting to feel the effects of not having a haven. Even small things like sleeping in a different room, a different bed, and now getting used to a new layout were slowly wearing me down.

Nothing felt like home.

"Sethos . . ." I asked and turned to look at him. "How long will I be here?"

"Let's have food first before we dive into larger discussions. There's a lot to figure out."

My stomach grumbled from hunger as if in agreement.

AFTER BREAKFAST, the fortress tour continued, and my question about the length of time I would be in Daya was forgotten.

"The fortress has five great halls," Sethos said as we walked out of the kitchens. "You have already seen two—the hall with the healing pool and the ballroom. The third great hall"—he paused as we stepped through a large stone archway—"is the one we are now in."

I looked around, quickly scanning all four walls, my eyes widening at the sight. Rows and rows of racks holding weapons were spread throughout the room. In a corner was a fighting ring.

"This room," Sethos said, walking to the middle and extending his hands out, "has any type of handheld weapon you can imagine. I use this space for target practice. We'll do some of your training here."

"I've never seen so many weapons in one place." I wrapped my arms around my midsection. "I think the most I saw was at a tomb in Taria."

Sethos lifted his eyebrows. "They don't have an armory or military in Taria?"

I shook my head.

"Interesting."

I shrugged. "The souls there are peaceful. When I trained with Ukara, she showed me a glimmer of her army. They appeared in the desert like a mirage."

Sethos chuckled.

"What?" I asked. "What's so funny?"

He shook his head. "You would think that the gods would have armies or some sort of military presence within their enclave . . ."

"Not that I saw or am aware."

"Sounds foolish."

"It's not like they expect an attack," I pointed out. "The gods are peaceful," I repeated.

Sethos flashed me a small smile and turned, making his way toward a line of swords. He picked one up with an emerald hilt and inspected it.

"I know you shared that Ukara trained you. It will be good to see if you picked up anything formidable from the Goddess of War."

I laughed.

He turned to me. "If she's not actively defending anything or anyone, I doubt she's any good."

I crossed my arms. "I think she's pretty incredible."

Sethos lifted his eyebrows and shrugged cockily. "Allegedly."

My jaw dropped, and I walked across the room to a line of swords. I picked a silver sword with golden jewels on the hilt and pointed it at him. "Try me," I said in challenge.

Sethos tilted his head and leaned on his sword.

"Careful, little serpent." He smirked. "You'll find my fangs much bigger than yours."

I narrowed my eyes and stepped forward, sword still pointed.

"Fighting for the honor of a goddess?" he asked and began to circle me. "I wonder if she would do the same for you."

I tightened my grip on the hilt and turned my body to follow him with my sword raised.

"Don't talk like that. You don't know her," I said.

"I don't need to. Gods are fickle creatures."

"I know she would stand up for me."

"Are you sure about that?" His voice was darker suddenly.

My shoulders tensed. "Why are you talking like this?"

"The gods don't deserve your affection, Renna. You'd do well to remember that."

As soon as I opened my mouth to respond, he cut in.

"They lied to you. Even your precious Ukara."

Rolling waves of anger began to rise in my chest. "And you?" I sneered.

"Put your sword down," he said.

"Fight me," I demanded. "I know I'm good."

Sethos pursed his lips.

"Don't mock me."

Sethos remained silent and continued to circle me.

My body vibrated from the anxiety of watching him close in.

"Fight me!" I said, gripping my sword tighter.

"I don't think you're ready for the type of duel that will save your life."

"Oh really?" I huffed. "Aren't you supposed to train me?"

"I am."

I clenched my jaw. "*Fight me.* I practiced for months."

He continued to close in.

A yell ripped up from inside me, and I charged at him.

Sethos stood still, and with a rapid wave of his right hand, white-hot pain suddenly filled my palm that held the sword. I screamed as my muscles hideously contorted until I dropped the sword.

I cradled my hand as ribbons of pain shot through it.

"*Why?*" I screamed and knelt on the ground.

Sethos took a step forward and stepped on my sword before kicking it.

"You're an asshole."

He folded his hands behind his back.

"*Never* fight without an energetic shield," he said in warning. His eyes were darker than his usual ice blue.

"You didn't tell me we were going to use magic."

"*Never,*" he growled, "fight without an energetic shield."

"I would have erected one if you'd told me," I gritted out.

"You challenged me," he said, lifting his chin. "You asked me to teach you defensive magic."

"I didn't know we were starting that right now."

"You know how to wield a sword?" he knelt down beside me. "Adorable. That is child's play for the type of fighting you will need."

I squeezed my eyes shut as I continued cradling my hand.

I knew his words about defensive fighting made sense, but I couldn't think.

"Did you have to hurt me?" I yelled.

"*That*"—Sethos grabbed my injured hand with surprising gentleness—"was an example so you never forget. What if that had been a real fight? You want to learn defensive magic—that's rule one. Even when you are training, you keep that shield up."

I jumped slightly as cold magic surged from his palm to mine, and within seconds, the pain began to subside.

He shook his head. "Did Ukara or Khellios not teach you about shields or magic while fighting?"

"No." I thought back on my practices with them in Khellios's home. "Khellios said I would never have to face Am-Re. That I would never be exposed to fighting."

"Keeping the woman he loves unprotected," Sethos chuckled bitterly. "What a man."

"Ukara stood up for me. She wanted me to learn how to wield a weapon."

"How magnanimous of her."

My lips trembled at the memory of training with Ukara. She was so strong.

"Don't ever forget what they did to you, Renna," Sethos stated, his voice harsh and dark. I could feel deep hatred through his words like a mantle of heavy, dragging energy.

My chest felt heavy remembering how Ukara lied to me.

At Khellios's insistence.

Sethos stood and held out his hand to me.

Suddenly, I didn't feel like training. I wanted to sit in silence for a little while as the months I'd lived in Taria caught up to me.

I loved every single friend I'd made there.

"How's your hand?" Sethos asked and lowered his hand.

I blinked down at my hand and moved it. "It feels sore."

"And you call what the gods taught you *training*," Sethos snapped, his eyes becoming a bit darker in color, as if the ice blue had darkened several shades.

I don't know why a lack of apology and attitude made me suddenly feel emotional.

"Why are you so angry?" I fired back.

Sethos brought his face down to mine.

"Do you want to die in a real fight?" he growled.

I blinked. "No—"

"I'm angry because you are ill-equipped to handle an actual, real opponent. I'm angry that Khellios did not encourage your magic. You're not a fucking damsel, Renna. I need you to be strong."

"I am strong—"

"Then you will train. *Harder.*"

I bit my cheek, took a deep breath, and stood.

His actions and words were cruel, and I felt like my emotions would erupt from me in tears.

"I . . ." I stepped back from him. "I need to walk away right now. *I will train.*" I assured him. "I just need to be alone right now."

Sethos stared at me for a few seconds. "Renna," he began and ran his hands over his hair. "I want you to be prepared for what's coming. I know I hurt you."

I clenched my jaw and waited for an apology.

"But surviving a fight . . ." He shifted on his feet and crossed his arms. "I will be doing you a great disservice if I treat you gently." His eyes moved back and forth between mine. "You're an incredibly smart woman. You get that, don't you?"

I did. I understood he was trying to harden me for real conflict . . .

It just felt cruel.

"I'll . . ." I began and crossed my arms, not knowing what to say. "I'll walk back to my room and I'll look for you later?"

He pursed his lips. "As you wish."

I stood there stupefied for a few moments, trying to process his actions and reason with my own feelings.

I felt a little bit guilty for thinking he was treating me maliciously.

I knew the trauma of being in war had hardened Sethos in ways I would never understand.

He tried to dig his mom from the wreckage . . .

Right as I turned to walk from him, Sethos reached out for my uninjured hand, and I froze.

As if by a trick of the light, his irises turned black, but I knew I must have been mistaken because when I blinked again, his eyes were back to ice blue.

"I want there to be a future where you and I both exist, Renna," he said more gently, the darker tones in his voice gone. "Please understand how much you mean to me."

The whiplash of his sudden shift in mood made my head hurt.

I forced a smile and squeezed his hand once, then pulled it from his grip and walked from the room, my mind a jumbled mess.

13

SETHOS

I held my breath as Renna walked from the armory.

My eyes blurred, and a thick, viscous energy I knew all too well began to slither over my body.

You're getting too emotionally involved, a familiar voice hissed in my mind.

It was the voice of Am-Re's magic.

I shook my head and squeezed my eyes shut.

You have one job . . .

Does your mother mean so little to you?

Keeping my eyes closed, I reached into the pocket of my pants and took out a tincture.

I uncapped it and drank it in one go, coughing as the liquid burned my throat.

After replacing the stopper, I shoved it back into my pants and massaged my temples.

After a few heartbeats, my body began to feel normal again, as if light had found its way back into a space in my soul. My chest felt lighter, and the voice that jabbed and mocked me subsided.

And then the guilt of having hurt Renna flooded me like a tidal wave.

I had treated her horribly in those moments when the rage built inside me after talking about mates, and added to that was the reminder that Renna had been under another man's care for months in Taria.

The gods, Am-Re's magic, and Source were at fault for my outburst.

Etara was wrong to say I had to choose between love and my destiny.

I could have the woman I wanted and have vengeance.

Source owed me for the happiness and life it had stolen from me.

I was no longer that weak fourteen-year-old boy who waited for someone to save him.

I would have my happiness no matter what.

14

RENNA

Fallen leaves crunched under my boots as I walked side by side with Sethos through the forest outside the fortress.

The cool temperature of Daya was more pronounced deep in the forest, and I crossed my arms, gripping my biceps, as we walked through it.

"Are you feeling better?" he asked.

I had remained in my room for the better part of the morning as sadness gripped my body with claws threatening to pull me under.

My arrival in Daya and all the revelations since, in under two days of consciousness, left little room for debriefing how I felt.

Sethos had been incredibly mean to me, but from his background, I understood his motives in training me. Not everyone could be like Ukara, and even though she had lied to me, I missed her. I mourned her absence in my life. Would I ever see her again?

For Nera . . .

She had been there when I stepped through the portal . . . Did Khellios resent her? Where was Nera now?

I also missed Cylas. His smile. His protective arms that brought me peace.

Even Khellios and how my heart had begun to fall for him.

My brain was having a hard time completely running all them out of my heart despite the lies.

It was not so easy to immediately shut the door on people you loved, even if they hurt you. The heart did not process change so quickly.

I also grieved for my life on Andora and my friend Helena.

Would I ever see her again?

I pondered whether Helena would hate me for lying to her about my magic.

I had hidden my identity to protect her from the Planetary Council should she ever be interrogated.

In many ways, like Sethos and Khellios had done to me, I had omitted my identity to Helena because I cared for her.

"Renna?" Sethos asked. "Are you alright?"

I jumped slightly as I snapped out of my thoughts.

Sethos cared for me.

He had protected me for years.

He never stopped looking for me . . .

"I'm feeling better." I put on a smile that I didn't quite feel. I wasn't ungrateful. My body was just processing everything that had transpired.

Sethos reached for my hand and laced his fingers through mine. "I'm glad."

"Where are we headed now?"

"We're going to a clearing in the forest where we will begin your training."

I nodded. "Not inside the fortress?"

"No," Sethos responded. "And you will see why in a few moments." He pointed ahead. "Let's keep moving."

Looking between the tree trunks, I caught glimpses of a well-lit clearing ahead.

As we continued to walk, I couldn't help but hold onto Sethos's hand tighter, and he instinctively pulled me closer against his arm.

I had the power to push him away . . . But I didn't want to.

I liked being by his side.

Could I stay by his side forever?

Sethos brought our hands to his mouth and kissed my fingers.

My stomach did a somersault.

"After practice, I have a surprise for you."

I looked to him, and a lazy smile greeted me.

"There's a pond nearby where you can cool off. The water will come up to your shoulders, so you don't need to worry about swimming." He looked sideways at me. "Or drowning if you fling yourself in."

I remembered the moonlit walk in dreamtime when I almost drowned.

"I almost drowned *one time*, and you don't let me forget it," I said jokingly.

He chuckled. "One time is enough, little serpent."

I stifled a laugh.

As we continued walking, Sethos began pointing out things in the forest to look out for. Such as poisonous tree barks, ghost birds hiding in branches that had venomous claws, and snakes.

"My mind is still trying to process the bioluminescence on the trees and vegetation. Everything glows in a neon color," I whispered as we walked. "I don't like the fog. I don't know where I'm stepping."

Sethos looked down at the fog now covering our feet.

"The fog is the least of your concerns in Daya. You must know there is a magical shield around the forest surrounding the fortress. Due to its distance it is nearly invisible from down here, but up close it is purple in color. Do *not* cross it the shield perimeter without me. I don't trust the lowlifes on the other side."

I nodded and shivered at the thought of so much needed security. The fortress had a shield . . . the forest had a shield.

"Will . . . we ever go to the other side of the shield?"

Sethos was silent for a few seconds before answering. "Yes. Eventually. For real-life target practice."

My heart stopped. "What do you mean by that?"

"It doesn't matter for right now. We're here."

I covered my eyes with my sleeve as the daylight in the clearing was a stark contrast to the darkness of the forest.

"As I said, initially, we'll practice your defensive magic here," Sethos said, walking ahead of me to the middle of the field.

Behind him were three different-sized boulders.

"The first lesson of defensive magic"—Sethos clapped his hands once—"you already learned." He lifted his eyebrows conspicuously.

I frowned. "Keep my shield up."

"Correct."

I wanted to roll my eyes but opted to cross my arms. "And these rocks?"

"Boulders," he corrected.

"Still rocks."

"These *boulders*," he continued, "are so you can train your magic to lift objects."

"How is learning that *defensive magic*?"

Sethos crossed his arms and lowered his chin. "Are you going to be snippy all afternoon?"

Heat crept up my chest and neck. "I wasn't being *snippy*."

Sethos approached, his eyes on my neck. "There are two times when your body becomes flushed . . ."

I gulped, and my heart began to accelerate. "Oh yeah?"

Sethos's eyes slid to mine. "When you climax and when you're being difficult."

My jaw dropped open.

Sethos reached out and pushed my jaw closed with his pointer finger.

I narrowed my eyes and pursed my lips.

"I'm teaching you how to lift *boulders* because sometimes you have to improvise with available resources in a fight. For that reason, being able to summon objects with your magic is vital."

He had a point, but I maintained my upset expression out of embarrassment.

"I know you know how to use a sword." He crossed his arms and tilted his head. "But what if that sword is knocked from you?"

My stomach knotted as I imagined a scenario like that.

"What if your attacker is on top of you? Wouldn't you like to summon your sword—or any object—to help you?"

I nodded.

"I'm sorry, what was that?" He cupped his ear mockingly.

"Yes," I grumbled.

"Say that again?"

"Yes!" I yelled. "Now teach me!"

Sethos lifted an eyebrow. "If you acted this way around the gods, I have doubts they would launch a recovery mission for you. I'd stay away."

I rolled my eyes. "Ha, ha."

A lazy smile spread over his face, and his gaze slowly moved down my body.

"What?" I breathed, my throat suddenly dry.

Sethos lifted his chin. "I like your fire, little serpent. I like it when you fight me."

My stomach flipped, and like a switch, heat began to spread low in my belly.

I mirrored his movement and lifted my chin. "I thought you said I was snippy. *Difficult.*"

"And for the life of me, I don't know why that's attractive to me."

I was paralyzed with what to say.

I licked my lips, and his eyes followed the movement.

I swallowed and pressed my thighs together. "We should practice," I whispered.

Sethos smiled softly. "As you wish."

He spun away from me, and I wanted to sag to the ground from the break in the tension.

As he walked to the boulders, I shook my body out and took a deep breath.

I needed to focus.

"Talk to me about the kinds of magic the fae have," I asked. "Are all fae able to lift and conjure objects? You snap your fingers and can make objects appear."

"As a general rule, all fae are able to conjure small objects like clothing and food. When you learn magic you can decide if you want to snap or clap or do any action that will bring the magic forth. There are more complex categories of magic available to some fae but we won't get into that today. Levitation is a skill available to supernaturals at large."

I nodded and titled my head.

"My magic has electrical qualities to it. And its green and black in color. Is that normal for fae?"

Sethos shook his head. "The electrical quality and color comes from your god lineage. For the most part, fae magical forces are invisible. You also feel fae magic."

I thought about when I was at university and felt magic in Aramis's office. I had not physically seen the magic used by the woman Galene in his office but I had felt it. Galene must have been fae.

My magic was also at times invisible. My magic had been invisible that day and exploded the lights in Aramis's office.

"What about the gods? How does god magic differ from fae magic? Do gods have the power to do anything?"

"No. God powers are limited to a god's specific purpose. I believe this ensures no one god is more powerful than Source itself."

"So . . ." I began, "for example let's say I am the Goddess of . . ." I looked to the tree line before continuing, "*trees* . . . what would my powers look like?"

I looked back to Sethos. His lips were pursed as if he was thinking.

"If Source created you as the Goddess of Trees your powers and magic would likely be limited to vegetation and trees."

"What if my trees needed sunlight or rain?"

Sethos eyes slid to me and he crossed his arms.

"The God of Rain or the God of the Sun would need to provide that to your trees."

"And what if my trees were on fire?" I asked. "How would I be able to stop the fires?"

"The God of Fire would put out the fire."

I lifted my eyebrows. "That is *extremely* limiting."

"Source created balance for everything- even in Gods. Wouldn't you agree that one god should not have the power to do everything? What did you think gods would be able to do?"

I shrugged.

"Too many questions and very little time. Let's practice, little serpent," he said while smiling.

～

"You need to summon equal energy in both arms," Sethos called out a while later. "I've said this a hundred times at least! *You're not listening.*"

I narrowed my eyes at the boulder several feet in front of me.

"I'm trying!" I yelled. My arm muscles burned from the strain of magic coursing through me.

Sethos laughed.

"You think this is suddenly easy?" I snapped. "You must have forgotten what it was like for you to do this magic when you started."

"I'm merely saying, for you to *successfully* lift the boulder without it teetering side to side and hurting your core muscles as you squeeze your abs when you summon this magic, you should have equal magic in *both* arms."

I closed my eyes and imagined green electricity coiling at my chest's center, feeding the stream of magic running down each of my arms. I imagined pulling more energy to my left arm, the one that needed more support.

"There you go!"

I opened my eyes, and the boulder rose steadily about four feet from the ground.

"It's the smallest boulder," I pointed out.

"And that's called progress." Sethos reminded me. "We've been at this for several hours, and it's your first day. Go easy on yourself."

I sighed and lowered the boulder to the ground.

"Now go again," Sethos said. "Try to lift the boulder taller than your height."

"When will I practice with the bigger boulders?"

"When you can lift this boulder as tall as a three-story building, we can try the medium-sized boulder."

I groaned.

"No," Sethos said, "don't be negative about this. This is your first day. Give yourself credit. Every time you lift a boulder, all your muscles activate as if it was your own hands carrying the boulder."

I leaned my head to the side so I could brush sweat from my brow with my bicep.

"Are you in pain?"

"A little . . ."

"Your body will get used to it."

I squared my shoulders as I focused on the boulder again.

"I can do this," I whispered to myself and called my magic.

I imagined green magic gathering at my center, and just like before, I pictured tendrils of electric currents extending to my palms.

My fingertips crackled with green electric magic, and I mentally pushed it outward toward my target. I wrapped my magic around the underside of the boulder and clenched my jaw and abdominal muscles as I imagined lifting the boulder.

"Keep going, keep going." Sethos encouraged me. "Just a little bit higher than last time. We can call it a day after that. We'll practice again tomorrow."

My body trembled with the strain of pushing the boulder higher off the ground. My feet began to sink into the soil as I forced my thighs to work with my abdomen for the strength needed.

The boulder rose steadily.

My biceps burned.

I let out a guttural cry as I kept pushing my body.

Sethos clapped. "You got this!"

"*Ahh!*" I screamed once I raised the boulder higher than my height.

I then gathered all of my magic in my center and compelled my magic to throw the boulder across the field.

Unbidden, dark shadows snaked around my hands and

almost followed the projection of the boulder. My body temperature rose, and I felt out of breath. But just as quickly as the shadows appeared, they vanished into thin air as if they had never been there.

When the boulder fell to the ground, I laughed and rubbed my chest where it had been hot minutes ago. My chest felt suddenly sore. Had the shadows caused that?

I recalled the shadows in my room in Taria when Livina had spoken to me and then again at Misha's Place.

I turned to Sethos, who was frozen on the spot, observing me cautiously.

"Too impressed that it's left you speechless?" I taunted him.

He put a finger to his lips, as if thinking, and walked casually toward me.

"Your magic was different . . ."

I nodded. "Yes, it was."

"Is that something you experience often?"

"The shadows? It's happened a few times before. *Why?*"

Sethos smiled, but it didn't reach his eyes. "No reason, just making an observation."

I panicked. "What are you not telling me?"

Sethos was silent for a few moments.

"Your magic reminded me of Am-Re's."

My heart slowed down at the realization, and everything began to move in slow motion as if my mind wanted to detach to not deal with this news.

"This isn't good," I breathed.

"Well," Sethos said, coming to stand before me. He put his hands on my shoulders. "It comes with being his flesh and blood. You cannot escape it. You must accept it."

My lips trembled, and I gave a small nod as fear slithered inside me, reminding me of the dark legacy embedded in me.

I feared becoming my father. The fear haunted me and festered inside me like an open wound.

"Are you hurt?" Sethos asked. "Did that magic feel bad?"

I thought about the heat in my chest and the soreness there.

"It felt uncomfortable. Like a dull but burning feeling in my chest. I don't know how to explain it."

Sethos's eyes studied mine, and even though there was only curiosity in his stare, I felt incredibly self-conscious. Guilty somehow.

"Does that change how you see me?" I asked, my hands wringing, as my speech rushed forth. "Do you no longer want my help? I want to stand next to you when you bring justice to your mother. It's the least I can do for what you have done for me."

"Trust yourself, Renna," he said, bringing a hand to my jaw, and massaged my cheek with his thumb. "I think you'd make a formidable warrior," he whispered and smiled. "I'm so proud of who you are."

I swallowed as soft grief spread through my body in waves, and I forced a smile.

I wondered if children who hated their parents loathed reminders of traits within themselves that were attributed to them.

Sethos's head tilted down. "I think standing next to you in battle will be one of the best decisions I ever make." He reached for a strand of my hair and pushed it behind my ear, and my body swayed toward him, seeking comfort.

"I'm glad you think so," I whispered, moving even closer to him.

"We'll be great allies, you and I." He searched my eyes. "And to show you how much I trust you, I will accept your help, Renna. *But,*" he paused, "there is much more to learn. You won't defeat my enemies with swords and moving large objects." He moved his eyes to the boulders before coming back to meet my gaze. "Like *rocks*," he teased.

A smile broke from my lips and I laughed.

Sethos leaned down and kissed my forehead, and a warm feeling spread through me.

He moved the hand that was cradling my jaw to run through my hair.

"Plus," he said, whispering into my ear, "I happen to think you look incredibly attractive wielding magic. It alters my brain and does something to me."

A tingling feeling of satisfaction moved inside me, and my body felt suddenly hot standing so close to him. My breath hitched, and I looked to the column of his neck as he was still bent low next to my ear.

Need slowly unfurled inside me, and I longed to run my tongue over his skin.

At the thought, Sethos slowly backed from me and looked at me, his eyes searching mine as if he could read my mind.

Kiss me.

His eyes dropped down to my lips as if my thoughts had some sort of power over him, and just as he was leaning in, a dark gray and blue star craft flew over the forest and we looked up to follow it.

My eyes moved to watch Sethos, who pursed his lips and sighed as he watched the craft continue its path in the sky. He shook his head as if in annoyance.

When he looked back down to me, I knew the moment we had shared was lost and deep yearning filled me.

"Let's continue with your training, mejtah," he said with a smile and grabbed my hand and kissed the back of it as if it was the most natural thing in the world.

And although it was not the kiss I wanted, I had to be content in that moment.

15

KHELLIOS

I broke out in goose bumps as soon as the everlasting shade above the Witch District of Taria touched my skin.

Ukara rubbed her arms and shivered.

I could feel my god-like powers quickly go on mute.

My heartbeat began to slow, and my body felt heavier.

The Witch District was warded with spells to disarm any non-witch supernatural that crossed its borders. The use of the magic was dark as it took away people's choice. The energy resulted in perpetual darkness bathing the district, despite the sun shining down on Taria.

Instantly, four wraiths descended on and surrounded us.

They had no skin or bones, but were merely dark matter energy in the shape of a man. Their cloaks and hoods made them look menacing.

The air began to tingle with dark electricity, and the smell of sulfur filled the air.

These creatures were the creation of a witch and the demon Leviathan many eons ago.

A wraiths hissed at Ukara and she pointed her sphere at it. "We are granted free passage always!" she yelled.

One of the spirits hovered close to me. Its hood moved, and the foul smell of sulfur grew.

Although I was a god, these creatures always unsettled me, and I hated that they were inside Taria as a new patrol presence in the Witch District.

Coincidentally, the patrol presence occurred around the time Renna arrived in Taria.

Had the witches sensed something was coming?

Had they seen Sethos arriving through their clairvoyance?

"You are not welcome here, God . . ." the figure said, sounding like a dying man in need of water. Its voice croaked and clicked, echoing in the air.

"That is not for you to decide," I said calmly. "I'm here to speak to Merida."

"She does not wish to speak with you . . . Yet she has instructed us to escort you to her home."

Ukara stood at my side and jabbed her sphere toward the spirit. The figure moved.

"We do not need an escort," she gritted out. "We granted the witches here safe haven," she said. "The least Merida can do is give us an audience without this ridiculous fanfare."

"Merida does not have a problem with you, Goddess of War . . ." The figure turned its hood to me. "It is *you*"—its cloak sleeve moved toward me, as if it was pointing—"who is not welcome. You seek to involve the district in your games of war."

"I do not come to cause a disturbance," I said. "I will leave as soon as I talk with Merida."

"Onward," the wraith said and gestured to the street before us.

I groaned inwardly, holding my frustration inside and wishing I could attack the wraiths, but under so much defensive witchcraft, I did not have the power to do so.

But I needed to maintain our alliance with the witches—especially Merida.

Ukara and I began walking alongside the wraiths through a long, winding market street.

Floating lanterns lined the streets, and suspended candles hung in the shop windows to display wares.

Despite the eerie living conditions in the Witch District, it was home to more than a quarter of a million witches who sought refuge from persecution.

As we walked, we moved aside to let an enchanted, unmanned wooden cart of dried animal skins roll by. I observed the cart's wheels, encased in purple magic, propelling it forward.

"It never ceases to amaze me how Merida and her family designed this district to look like medieval Europe," Ukara commented. "Everything looks like it belongs in Tudor England."

I lifted my eyebrows and nodded. "Considering the mass witch persecutions there, having a place that reminded them of home was crucial to Merida when we granted her this space."

We rounded a corner and saw a black fountain with a realistic gorgon statue on top as decoration.

Water poured from the gorgon's eyes into the fountain.

"That's new," Ukara whispered.

"A recent acquisition," the wraith responded. "Merida's daughter's time travel journeys bring back many trophies . . ."

I frowned at the statue and realized the gorgon decoration was likely a real gorgon made into stone.

It reminded me of the brutality of the witches here.

But could I blame them?

They were here escaping persecution.

Our arrival at Merida's four-story home brought us to the main plaza in the heart of the district. Opposite her home was the gathering hall where witches met to discuss important matters and where criminal and civil crimes were tried.

The gods in Taria allowed the witches here to run their own society according to their ways.

The wraiths hovered toward the front door of Merida's home and knocked.

I hadn't been to Merida's home in a few years and looked up at it. Its Tudor architecture was clear, but unlike the other structures in Taria, with brown and earth tones, her home was all black, casting a stark contrast against the streetscape. But her shiny red wooden door stood out significantly.

Merida's voice came from inside the home as she yelled orders to others inside. Likely to one or all of her many young apprentices. Unlike the rest of Taria, the witches here had families and reproduced.

She opened the door aggressively and narrowed her eyes at me. "No," she snapped.

"Merida," I sighed. "We need to talk to you."

"The answer is no," the red-haired witch said, closing the door.

I shoved my hand into the gap. "You don't even know what I'm here for!"

"Oh," she laughed and swung the door open furiously. "I know why you're here. I will not play a part in this."

"Oh?"

"Yes, *oh*," she said, throwing her hands in the air and then pointing at me. "The first question you will ask is not the true reason you are here. So I'd rather not see you at all." She gestured between us. "This is already too much meddling. I will not be part of this."

"Merida." Ukara tried, her voice taking on a softer tone. "May we step inside to talk?"

"Without them, preferably." I gestured to the wraiths.

Merida crossed her arms and slid her eyes to Ukara.

"Perhaps you should have come alone, Ukara," Merida stated.

I closed my eyes and pinched the bridge of my nose.

"Please." Ukara pleaded. "We are all allies here."

"*Allies?*" Merida shouted, and I opened my eyes. "The price is too high."

After a few moments, she relented.

"Fine. Come inside." She looked to the wraiths. "Stay out here."

"But I am warning you now, Khellios, God of the Moon and Stars—or *God of Moonlight and Stardust* as you will be known when this story is told—I will not meddle!" She crossed her arms. "Let the Akashic records reflect that I refuse to play a part in what you will ask me. I will not have my name besmirched when this story is told."

I put my palms up. "I don't know what you're talking about."

"No, you don't!" She narrowed her eyes and turned around to walk inside her house, continuing to shout. "At least everything is recorded in the Akashic records."

Ukara gestured for us to follow.

Once inside, the front door shut on its own, and thankfully, the wraiths remained outside.

"Of all the timelines to tell," Merida continued, "this one is the one that will be chosen. Gods."

Ukara looked at me and rolled her eyes.

Who was Merida talking to?

My brows gathered in confusion.

"I've been told she's rambling a lot as of late," Ukara whispered as we walked. "She was the same last time I visited a few months ago. She kept going on about timelines. No one ever knows what she's talking about."

At that moment, Merida spun around. "You gods don't think your actions have consequences."

Ukara and I froze.

"Your life stories will be told to teach valuable life lessons. You'll see."

I frowned. "In the future?"

Merida laughed. "In the past. Time is not real." Merida spun back around.

We came upon a large black door, and it swung open.

"Step inside," she barked and entered the room.

Ukara and I followed.

"I'll have you know I wasn't planning on showing you this room," Merida began with a smile. "But I know some will appreciate it."

Black lace draped from the center of the ceiling in the room in question to all four corners, creating a tent-like environment. Bookcases filled with books lined the walls, petrified animals perched above them. A black animal fur carpet covered the ground.

"A divination room?" I asked, gesturing to the table in the middle of the room with a crystal ball.

Merida folded her hands in front of her. "Yes. In the style of those found on Earth. Before the Great Migration."

"I don't think I've ever been in this room before," Ukara said while looking around. "These pictures are very old. The wooden frames look ancient."

Merida looked to the wall Ukara stood in front of. "Yes, those are preserved copies of Earth photos. Passed down from generations. Frames were passed down too. My family coated them with magic to preserve them."

I walked to the table in the middle. "A single tarot card?" I said, looking down at a tarot card in a glass case.

Merida nodded. "Sent to my ancestor in the mail on planet Earth, kept in the family for thousands of years. It survived the Great Migration from Earth. It's lucky it did not get confiscated."

The Great Migration transported millions of humans from

Earth to the Andromeda Galaxy. The star crafts were like small cities housing entire families. Generations lived and died aboard as they reached their final destination.

People were allowed to bring very little.

One of the rules stated that religious and spiritual objects were not allowed aboard. The Planetary Council, which was newly formed at that time, believed that spirituality would only serve to divide people. By the time the star crafts reached Andromeda and the three planets selected for human habitation, spirituality and religions were mostly a thing of the past. Technology was used to bring people together. But like any governmental body, the Planetary Council was now ruthless in its persecution of people who were either magical or practiced religion in secret.

Luckily, the Planetary Council's rule only extended to the three human planets in Andromeda. They had no jurisdiction elsewhere. Even the Galactic Federation washed their hands of the council.

The Federation had once extended their assistance to them after the evacuation of Earth, but the Planetary Council shunned any outsider help as they grappled with control. They didn't want humans knowing of nonhuman life.

The Celestial Gods had chosen to establish Taria inside a dimension on Andora because the ruins of Old Xhor were there.

Andora used to be inhabited by the gods before Am-Re waged war on it and the humans came to inhabit it. When the Planetary Council arrived, only ruins remained, and the humans disembarking from the Planetary Council star crafts were too brainwashed to ask questions.

I tilted my head. "Any special meaning in the card?" I asked, trying to play nice.

"Yes, but I would not tell *you*."

I sighed. "Merida, I am not here as your enemy."

Merida waved her hand, and three black chairs appeared around the table.

"Let's sit." Merida gestured to the chairs.

She sat, and Ukara and I followed.

"Sometimes I forget I'm a god when I come here. You know how to command a room."

Merida glared at me. "You see"—she shook her head—"your arrogance at times, not the best quality."

I froze.

"You really should pause and consider how the words coming out of your mouth sound, God."

Ukara reached out to squeeze my arm to silence me.

"Merida," Ukara began. "We are here to—"

Merida put her hand up. "He needs to ask the question. It's supposed to play out this way in the Akashic records."

The Akashic records were a library that recorded every single event for eons. It had all events listed as if they had already happened. Livina and her goddess sister Pemira resided in the Akashic records as deities of fate.

Some witches, like Merida, and other gifted individuals with the power of clairvoyancy could access the records.

"Why was the shield around Taria broken?" I asked.

Merida's eyes went white as she began speaking.

"Renna Strongborn has an exact genetic copy of Am-Re's magic. Sethos Malachi Physerion absorbed most of Am-Re's magic when he destroyed the god's body. The magic Renna and Sethos have is almost identical and aids in tracking. The night she left Taria, she expelled a significant amount of magic, and it pinpointed her exact location."

My breathing paused and my body felt like it was floating. "How could that be? Magic does not duplicate like that. Offspring get some of their parents' magic."

Merida nodded slowly, still in a trance. "During the violent act when Renna was conceived, her mother cursed Am-Re. The curse was to take from Am-Re what he valued most. His magic. Renna was born with part of his magic. It left him weak but not enough that he could detect it. As her soul evolved, the genetics of it began duplicating at record speed. I don't think Am-Re knew the full extent of Renna's magic, or he would have never killed her."

I brought my hands to my face, and Ukara placed a palm on my shoulder.

Ukara spoke. "Do you think Renna's mother somehow cast a spell on her to protect her? To shield her daughter's magic from being fully exposed?"

At Ukara's question, I looked up at Merida.

"Yes," Merida answered slowly. She blinked several times, and her eyes became normal again. "My spirit guides are showing me that Renna's mother obtained a spell from a witch during pregnancy to shield her daughter's magic."

My pulse began to speed erratically. I had known Am-Re for a long time. I knew what types of powers he had. I battled with him multiple times . . .

My throat became parched as I formed the question. "If Renna is a genetic copy of Am-Re," I began, "then that means—"

"Renna inherited Darkness." Merida nodded solemnly.

Ukara gasped and turned to me. "Sethos will use her."

I clenched my fists.

"Her magic has fully integrated into her bloodstream now. She is no longer merely mortal. Renna is a hybrid of her own category. Not a full god. Not mortal. Something else." Merida paused and looked at Ukara. "Renna, if she trains, will have the ability to fight as well as a god."

My neck muscles tensed. "I don't want her to fight at all."

Ukara groaned.

"You don't get to decide that, God of the Moon and Stars," Merida snapped. "Stop trying to control people."

"Merida." I shook my head. "Darkness is a devastating gift," I gritted out.

"And unfortunately, many will die when she wields it," Merida added. "No one will be able to stop it. Sethos will be at her side when it happens. Operating almost like a unit."

My mind raced imagining the bloodshed, and I stood. "You're wrong! Renna will never be like him."

Ukara rose. "Khel, please calm down."

Merida crossed her arms and lifted her chin. "It doesn't matter what you think. You should know that Sethos loves Renna, although he may not know it yet. He is the one who found her soul in the second incarnation. She has been his little secret for over the past seven years."

I looked to Ukara. "You cannot believe this."

"Khellios," Ukara said in warning.

I looked to Merida and she chuckled. "At least Sethos is not her mate." Merida propped her chin on a fist and smiled. "But we won't get into that today."

I narrowed my eyes, and my jaw dropped.

"Have I said something offensive, God?" she challenged. "Or just the truth?"

"Who is her mate?" I gritted out.

Merida chuckled. "Why do you assume it's a *he*?" She shrugged. "Very single-minded of you."

My body tensed as it awaited to hear more.

"Nevertheless," Merida sighed and looked at her nails. "It is a *he*. Lovely too."

Ukara placed a hand on my bicep and pulled me to sit down.

"Who is he?"

She smiled. "Someone you already know."

Fury pummeled through my body, and I pushed to stand again. "Renna is mine," I gritted out.

She laughed. "All you men keep saying the same thing. *Mine.* It can be endearing when said in a time of passion." She wagged her eyebrows. "But very unbecoming when said to establish ownership—like an object. Nobody can own anybody."

I clenched my fists. "You twist my words, witch."

Merida rolled her eyes.

"Please." Ukara cut in nervously. "Tell us where Renna is."

"Renna's location is shrouded in a haze. I'm deliberately blocked from accessing it. She is there with Sethos." Her voice drifted off, and I saw red.

"How did she get there?" I knew it was the mirror. It had to be.

"A portal was created to Sethos. He aided her in crossing to him."

"Why was a portal formed?"

Merida chuckled. "I'm not allowed to tell you."

I dropped my face into my palms.

Merida replied sweetly, "I can tell you Renna does not mind her proximity to Sethos. In fact, if given the chance, she would remain at his side—"

I threw my hands down to look at her. "I cannot allow her to remain at his side," I snarled. "I refuse to accept it!"

"Her fate is not for you to decide, God of the Moon and Stars. Renna is not the same woman you knew."

I slammed my fists on the table. "Bullshit!"

Merida raised an eyebrow. "Careful." She leaned in and narrowed her eyes. "I do not accept violence in my home. My witch ancestors put up with too much violence against them for me to allow someone to bully me."

I glared at her.

"I helped you with the dome of Taria. I continue to help you." She pointed at me, and the room began to rumble. The table and chairs began to vibrate. "But do *not* mistake my kindness for idiocy."

"Khellios . . ." Ukara warned again. "Let's go."

I pinched the bridge of my nose and turned to Ukara.

"I have some ideas of what else we can do to intervene and protect her from Sethos."

I turned back to Merida. "We will see ourselves out."

Merida waved to the door, and it opened.

"I hope your next visit is more pleasant than the one today, Khellios."

I nodded once.

Ukara turned to Merida. "Thank you."

"We have vowed to stand up beside you in war," Merida called. "But the universes are based on freewill . . ."

I frowned and opened my mouth to argue, but Ukara quickly apologized and ushered me out of Merida's home.

"This is bullshit and you know it!" I whispered angrily to Ukara as she dragged me out of the district.

"Yes, but we need all the allies we can get right now. Despite what my father says"—she lowered her voice—"I know confronting Sethos will lead to battle."

I nodded. "I agree."

"I can feel the energy of this conflict. It *will* end in bloodshed."

I crossed my arms. "And yet Arios refuses to see it."

AFTER LEAVING THE DISTRICT, we portaled to Khira's tomb.

Ukara seldom brought people to the tomb, and I stood inside of it in silence, waiting for Ukara to speak.

"I don't like what is happening with Sethos and my father's actions."

I nodded and crossed my arms. "What ideas were you referring to in Merida's home?"

"You will contact King Miletak today. If he agrees to help you, tell him to station his star crafts in the star cluster outside of Andora and to mask the crafts with invisibility hydrogen. We don't want the air patrol on Andora to detect his ships."

"I haven't spoken to Miletak for at least two centuries."

"Well . . ." Ukara lifted her eyebrows. "You gave him and his daughter, Elrie, immortality. He owes you a life debt."

I shook my head. "That's not the way I see it. I did it gladly."

"You lost your god aura because you gave them immortality," she deadpanned. "I would *hope* he answers."

"He didn't know what I was doing."

"What you did was significant . . ." Ukara shook her head. "If this comes down to a battle, which we both know it may, with no god aura, you won't be able to fight."

"You can't tell me what to do—"

"You know I'm right." Ukara cut me off. "You knew the risks when you gave them immortality."

I turned from her to stare at the wall of armor and weapons in the tomb.

"I will petition the Galactic Federation."

I whipped back around to her, and she narrowed her eyes, crossing her arms. "Don't try to stop me, Khellios."

"You want to be at war with your father, Arios?" I shook my head. "Oruk already told us that the Federation is angry that our conflicts with Am-Re and, by extension, Sethos have been reignited. If you petition the Federation yourself, Arios would blame me."

"I am his daughter, but I'm also an individual. I am not beholden to him—"

"I never said—"

"In addition." She glared at me. "Everyone seems to forget I am not part of the Celestial Enclave. Neither is Livina. Or Pemira. There are at least a dozen gods who do not belong to any enclave. We can act alone. I don't owe loyalty to Arios. I have stood by him out of respect as my parent—"

"I know—"

Ukara put her pointer finger up. "I'm not finished. Let me speak."

I nodded in apology.

"I'm tired of merely speaking out on things I don't agree. It's not enough. I need to act and make change when I see it's needed. I do not agree that we should merely sit back and let Sethos keep Renna and wait for him to attack us. I will go to the Galactic Federation and petition them to help us because it's the right thing to do."

"I don't remember the last time a god petitioned the Federation on their own."

"Then this will be the first time it's done."

"As Goddess of War, you usually join battles. You have never asked for support in starting a campaign. Obtaining their support would mean the Federation is declaring war on Sethos. The Federation is trying to avoid war."

"When Renna was here, I told her to be fearless. I told her to fight. Khira would have wanted me to also stand up and fight." Ukara looked to the sarcophagus at the end of the tomb. "She knew I was capable of more than I allowed myself to believe."

"Thank you for all that you have done for me."

Ukara turned. Her eyes were glassy. "Just promise me something, cousin."

My breath caught. "Anything."

"When all of this is done, I want you to live your life."

My lips pressed into a tight line and I shook my head.

"I applaud you for seeking Renna. I know you love her. But don't forget—you have a life to live."

I groaned. "Ukara—"

"Listen to me, Khellios." Ukara stepped closer. "You have wasted many centuries mourning past events. And a love that was. I have watched you spiral into deep chasms of sadness and anger and make decisions I do not agree with."

A heavy sigh escaped me.

"You blame yourself for the fall of Xhor and the past death and now disappearance of Renna. You want to be a hero—I applaud you. As the Goddess of War, I applaud heroic acts." Ukara smiled sadly. "But at some point, you need to *truly* live."

"What do you mean by that?"

"That you can choose to allow happiness in without it taking away from experiences lived. Your present and your past are allowed to exist simultaneously, but each in their own box."

A wave of emotion rocked me, and I clenched my jaw.

Had anyone ever spoken to me the way Ukara had? I had continuously been told to simply move on. I could not be the only being who thought the phrase "moving on" was deeply dismissive of the pain lived. Moving on had the connotation of simply forgetting the past. For some of us, the past was inescapable.

"Do you understand what I'm telling you?" Ukara asked gently.

I nodded, and Ukara smiled.

"Now," Ukara said, wiping her eyes. "Let's go stop Sethos."

16

RENNA

y days in Daya were slowly falling into a pattern of routine.

I rose in the mornings and ate with Sethos, we trained in the clearing until the afternoon, had a midday break for food, and continued training until the early evening.

Being in close proximity, I could feel myself falling for him, and it scared me to feel so much. His lingering looks and touches seared my skin every time. I felt aflame whenever he put his hands on my shoulder, grabbed my hand casually, or placed the back of his hand on my waist as if he could not get enough of touching me for any little thing.

I craved his touch.

I watched him hungrily as he moved through our trainings with confidence, his strong body taut with muscles making me wish I could be pressed against him. In those moments, my mind always reverted back to the dreamtime moment we shared when he had crawled to me as my body surrendered to him.

I was convinced Sethos knew exactly what wicked thoughts crossed my mind when our gazes met in those moments when my body was running hot for him, and I would be rewarded with a playful smile that would cause the muscles in my core to clench. He would not say anything, but his gaze that would follow, one where he would rake his eyes down my body, told me what he had been thinking.

He never acted on it, and I wondered what was holding him back as we danced around each other and these feelings we would not discuss openly.

I sat on the grass one day, with my arms reclined behind me, as I watched Sethos demonstrate levitating two objects at once.

I knew the lesson was important, but my eyes were trained in the thick sinuous shape of his thighs. Thighs that had been pressed against me once . . .

Sethos cleared his throat and my eyes snapped to his.

My skin prickled hot with embarrassment.

He lifted an eyebrow.

"Did you hear anything of what I just said?" he asked, raking his hands through his hair. Sweat dripped down his forehead and my fingers flexed against the grass, longing to wipe the sweat from his brow.

"Yes," I answered, as my skin flushed.

He narrowed his eyes and placed his hands on his hips.

"And what did I say?" he asked.

I swallowed hard.

"You want me to lift multiple objects at once?" I offered.

His lips pressed into a tight line.

"Get up," he ordered.

Guilty, I pushed to stand and laser focused on brushing off my clothes from grass and pollen once standing to avoid his gaze.

"Are you done?" he snapped.

My eyes lifted to meet his.

"Sorry."

"I'm not standing around here for your entertainment, Renna. This is serious."

I bit my cheek as my blush deepened and nodded. Pushing all my thoughts of his body and what it did to me aside, I straightened my stance and proceeded to let him lead the lesson.

Sethos explained he wanted to train me to multitask during a fight. His idea was for me to split my mind in half while I fought off an attacker and simultaneously call on objects around me. He wanted me to use the objects to hurt my attackers and gain an advantage.

It was a brilliant strategy but intimidating nonetheless.

I squinted at him. "You want me to run while I levitate a boulder?"

He nodded. "You need to learn to move while you attack. Eventually, you'll be able to levitate several items at once and throw them at a foe while you are actively fighting them with a weapon. A boulder is a good challenge."

My eyes widened and my throat became dry.

"Why do you hesitate?" he asked.

"I can maintain my shield while using my magic to levitate objects. But running . . ." I shook my head. "I feel like I can do this, but . . ."

"Staying active will save your life. You need to train your magic to be immediately accessible. I know you can do this."

I forced a smile. "So . . . I just start running?" I scratched the back of my neck.

"Yes." He nodded. "On my mark, run toward the boulder. Direct your magic to levitate it before you get to it."

I nodded and bent my knees, my arms loose, getting in a running position.

"Ready . . ." Sethos began. "Set . . . Go!"

I pushed off the ground and took off, my breath heavy in my ears and heart pounding as I erected my shield. Next, I focused on slowing my breathing to quiet my mind as I called my magic to my center.

"Call it now!" Sethos yelled. "You're taking too long!"

My breathing sped back up, and my skin burned with embarrassment.

"I have literally never done this before!" I yelled back.

"So just do it!"

Anger thrummed through me, and I stopped and spun around. "Can you just let me try?" I crossed my arms.

Sethos cocked his head and matched my posture, crossing his arms. "Well, you're not trying."

"I was calling my magic before you interrupted me—"

"Faster." He flattened his lips into a straight line. "Call it faster."

I clenched my jaw and walked back to the starting line.

"You're thinking too much to call it forth. Believe your magic is there and capable. It hasn't gone anywhere."

I glared at him as I got back into a running position.

"Ready . . ." he said. "*Go!*"

I launched my body forward and immediately pictured green energy at my center. Cold waves rolled throughout my body as electricity coiled there, and I imagined lines of power trailing down my arms. My fingers vibrated with small shocks as the magic gathered in them.

I raised my arms and—

"Your shield!" Sethos yelled.

I groaned and closed my eyes, halting my run.

"You would already be dead," Sethos said.

I rubbed my face to prevent myself from talking back. He was right, my shield was vital in keeping me safe.

"Start over."

"Okay," I sighed and walked back, this time avoiding his eyes.

"I'm just trying to—"

"Keep me alive." I finished for him. "Got it."

I placed myself at the starting point and sprinted off when he called go.

I slowed my breathing and began to go through the motions. Shield, *check*.

Green magic at the center, *check*.

Cold flashed down my arms in tandem with the electricity rushing through them.

As soon as that power filled my fingers, I lifted my arms and willed my magic to extend before me and encircle the middle-sized boulder ahead.

The boulder barely moved before I reached it.

I cursed loudly and bent over my knees to catch my breath.

"You okay?" Sethos called.

I nodded. "It's . . ." I took a deep breath. "It's a lot going on at once. My mind is splintering to do multiple things at once."

"Do you need a break?"

I had managed to move the boulder, even if it was insignificant. That counted for something. I started off not thinking I could do the exercise at all.

I really could do this.

"No," I called back and straightened. I looked to Sethos. "Let's go again."

MY HEART THUNDERED inside my chest as I lay still on the grass after practice.

Sethos tapped my leg with his foot.

"You're dramatically covering your face with your forearm like you have perished. Should I be concerned?" Sethos's voice was laced with sarcasm.

I smiled against my arm. "Maybe."

"You did good today."

I lowered my arm and blinked as my eyes brought the world into focus.

"Ah." Sethos grinned. "She lives."

I rolled my eyes. "What's next?" I covered my face again with my arm.

"You're done for today."

I shot up to sitting. "We're not practicing after dinner?"

"We missed dinner. Can't you tell how quickly it's getting dark?"

I looked around at the incoming dusk. The sky was beginning to change from light blue to purple and deep blue with tinges of orange.

"I didn't even notice," I said.

"You didn't want to stop—"

"I was actually enjoying myself."

"I'd be hard pressed to find a woman who thinks lifting rocks is an enjoyable pastime."

I narrowed my eyes and smirked. "Well, I'm not most women."

Sethos languidly trailed his eyes along my body. "I've noticed."

Red-hot awareness flushed my skin like a tidal wave, and I lowered my eyes.

"If you're going to blush for a man," he said, "Don't lower your eyes from him."

I felt my skin heat and I knew my blush had deepened, but I forced myself to look up.

A wicked smirk was on his face, making him look roguish, and my heart flipped.

"Come," he said, extending his right hand for me to take. "Let's go inside."

I smiled and took his hand and allowed him to pull me up.

Our bodies came close when we stood, and despite all the

other times we had embraced, this felt different. There was a palpable tension in the air, and my core muscles clenched. I was too aware of him and how my body's height seemed to line up perfectly to his . . .

His eyes were intense and I felt like I would combust under his gaze.

"What were you thinking about earlier?" he asked, his tone light with an almost teasing quality.

Everything.

You.

Me.

The dreamtime moment we had . . .

Your hands on my skin . . .

Your lips . . . sucking and pulling and . . .

Fingers opening and plunging.

Taking.

Giving.

I closed my eyes for a brief moment, and I took a deep breath.

"Renna?"

I opened my eyes and cleared my throat.

"Nothing," I answered, biting my lips to conceal a smile. "Nothing at all."

Sethos observed me, and his eyes followed where I bit my lip.

"And you?" I quipped. "What are you thinking about?"

He lifted an eyebrow and met my gaze.

"Same," he said, now a brilliant wide smile on his lips. "Nothing at all."

17

RENNA

"**D**on't your subjects miss you?" I asked Sethos one morning after breakfast. We were walking through the fortress to practice at the clearing. "Isn't a king supposed to be in their lands?"

"Are you tired of me already?" He smirked and looked down at me.

I blushed. I could never tire of having Sethos near me.

I craved him.

"You know what I mean . . ." I cast my eyes to the side.

Sethos captured my chin with his thumb and moved it so I was looking at him.

"For the record, I could never tire of you," he whispered while looking at my lips.

I swallowed hard as his nearness sent a nervous energy through my stomach. The intimacy he and I shared in dreamtime flashed in my mind, and I could feel my body turn several shades of red.

The moment I shared with him in dreamtime happened because being in an altered state emboldened me. Now that I was with him in real life . . .

I was nervous because I didn't know if he would want to pursue a physical relationship with me or if what we shared had been a one-time event.

He hadn't made any indication this was more than flirtation.

Flirtation was harmless.

Something more than that?

I shifted on my feet.

"Where is Vasarys located?" I asked, trying to rein in my erratic feelings so I could focus on the training ahead.

Sethos observed me silently for a moment and smiled.

Sighing, he dropped his hand from my chin and stepped back.

"Vasarys is inside a black hole."

I paused. "That's *impossible*. The Planetary Council has definitively ruled out life inside black holes. White holes, however—"

Sethos's gaze hardened.

"The Planetary Council is also averse to magic and the supernatural," Sethos spat. "They keep all three human planets in the Andromeda galaxy in the dark, exactly as human governments used to on planet Earth. There are wormholes just outside black holes, if you know where to look, that allow you to travel to the inside of black holes and bypass the chaos outside them. Life inside a black hole is stable. Life inside white holes is obsolete."

A shiver ran down my spine. "I wonder how many other truths the council has kept from humans . . ."

"Renna." He hesitated.

"Yes?"

Sethos searched my eyes, worry overtaking his features.

"What's wrong?" I asked.

"You asked me to be open with you."

I tilted my head in attention.

"And I promised to make amends."

I crossed my arms, waiting for him to continue.

"I need to share something with you, and there isn't a correct way to start this conversation." He looked to the ground. "I hope this begins to atone for my past actions. I can't erase what I have done, but I want to show you I'm trying to move forward in the best way I can."

I froze and felt like I'd been doused with a bucket of ice. He was dragging whatever he wanted to say out, and it was killing me.

"*What?*" I snapped.

"Your father had children after your death."

My breath got trapped in my lungs as I silently stared at him.

"Am-Re had two daughters hundreds of years after you died." He paused. "Two that we know of. He could have had other children we don't know of . . ."

I shook my head, trying to force words out, but I became lightheaded as my body tilted to one side.

Sethos held my arms and guided me to sit on the ground.

"I have sisters?"

Sethos nodded.

"Half sisters. Am-Re was known to . . ." Sethos's face turned hard, and he clamped his lips shut.

"He was a terrible person, Renna. After you died, he sought out women to impregnate, hoping to replicate the power you had in your veins. But his efforts failed. You are the only one who inherited his exact magic."

My body temperature dropped, and my lips began to tremble.

"What are their names?" I whispered.

"You are the oldest. The second eldest is Demira. Her mother was a female fae Mage and a descendant of the Spirit Enclave. Demira's mother, like yours, died in childbirth."

I gripped my chest as an ache akin to grief filled the cavity there.

"Demira has lived most of her life in Vasarys. Her mother's

family wanted nothing to do with her. She is bitter and cruel to those around her. Demira's gift is witchcraft. She also wields the Violet Fire, which is powerful, divine magic."

My eyes began to water as I processed the information.

I had family.

Sisters.

"And my second sister?"

"Her name is Illona. She also lives in Vasarys. Illona's gifts are unique . . . She talks to dead prophets and wields Golden Fire. Golden Fire is considered the most powerful magic. It grants life."

My eyes widened.

"Illona's mother was a half-fae demigoddess from the Elemental Enclave. She, too, died in childbirth."

An ominous feeling spread throughout my body. "Do they know I'm alive?"

He shook his head. "Your father had them with the hopes they would inherit his magic with the goal to harvest their powers for himself. Unfortunately for him, they didn't inherit any of his magic. They only possess Fire Magic, which is magic reserved for the fae."

I covered my face with my hands.

Sethos continued. "Both Demira and Illona blame you for their existence and their mothers' deaths. Vasarys is also divided right now with those who support me and those who support Demira," Sethos said. "You are the only true heir of Am-Re, as you have his powers and are growing stronger by the day. If Demira knew you were alive, I would expect her to lobby against or even kill you."

Was it possible to feel joy and immediate grief at the same time? I felt joy knowing I had family, but intense grief knowing I would likely never have the love of a family.

My magic began to stir inside me like a black fire, raging and burning me as I realized the shadow of my father would never leave me.

His absence still haunted my life.

Because of him, I had been robbed of a normal childhood.

And even now, his deeds stole any hope I had of a family.

Shadows began to form in my palms, and waves of hatred rose to the surface of my skin.

"Renna . . ." Sethos warned, holding his palms the air.

I shook my head and ran. Dashing into the forest, I followed the path through the trees toward the clearing.

"Renna!" Sethos yelled after me.

I reached the clearing, my body shaking as black shadows continued to emanate from my hands.

Sethos caught up to me and tried to put a hand on my shoulder, but I dodged him.

"Renna." He frowned and stepped in front of me.

I sidestepped him and spun away, growling, "Leave me be."

"No!" Sethos yelled and wrapped his arms around me, turning me to face him. He moved my hair that had fallen onto my face. "Talk to me."

"I hate him," I whispered.

Sethos stilled and cupped my jaw. I thought he would tell me to breathe or sit down.

Instead, he narrowed his eyes. "And what will you do about it?" he asked darkly.

My body trembled with rage, and I stepped away from him, facing the biggest boulder.

I called my shield and extended my hands, palms facing the sky.

My chest began to vibrate as swirling magic concentrated underneath my skin. I closed my eyes and imagined green electric magic surging from my chest and mixing with the dark shadows.

"I need to destroy," I said, squaring up to the boulder.

Sethos stepped next to me.

I turned to him and saw how his eyes glittered in anger.

"Do it," he urged.

His words resonated within me, and the magic inside me turned on like a switch.

I needed to numb the wrath I felt from the hopelessness that overtook me.

My sisters would never accept me, would they?

I had no power to change how they saw me.

I was at fault for killing their mothers.

I was at fault for their lives.

I opened my eyes, and the electric magic expanded out around me, flowing down to my palms.

I looked to Sethos. "My father is a plague," I gritted out. "I don't like feeling helpless."

A slow smile spread over Sethos's face, and he lifted his chin and a single eyebrow in challenge.

I clenched my muscles and looked to the biggest boulder I had yet to try and lift.

"I'm taking control," I breathed. "He will never steal another moment of my life."

I let out a roar and shot my magic out to the boulder. Gripping it in my clutch, I lifted my arms, and my muscles shook as the boulder began to move.

Sethos began to circle my shield.

"It feels good to take charge, doesn't it?" he asked. "To mete out justice."

I screamed as the boulder began to rise. "Yes!" I cried.

"I have a better idea . . ." Sethos said with a dark smile.

In my peripheral, I could see Sethos turn so his back faced me, and he extended his arms in front of him.

The ground began to tremble, and I could feel a heavy sinister, viscous, and dark energy fill the air.

I shivered.

I slid my eyes to Sethos fully, and with a wave of his arms, a form in shadows rose from the ground at the end of the clearing.

My magic weakened with my break in concentration, and I groaned with the strain as I struggled to keep hold of the boulder.

"*What are you doing?*" I asked, switching my eyes back and forth between the boulder and the end of the clearing.

"Helping you take charge."

In that moment, a male body appeared in a cloud of smoke and ash.

My eyes widened. "No . . ." I gasped.

My concentration left me, and the boulder dropped from my grip, causing the ground to tremble.

"I didn't tell you to stop," Sethos barked. "Lift the boulder, Renna."

"What are you—" I covered my mouth with my hands as I watched the body. "What is this?"

My body turned cold like ice as the figure transformed into someone I knew.

Am-Re.

He stood at the end of the clearing in the black long coats I remembered so well, his chin lowered and his beady black eyes cruelly looking straight at me.

The body tilted its head, and his lips curled.

"He's not real." Sethos crossed his arms.

Words failed me.

"Hurt him, Renna. Prove that you're ready to take charge!"

I froze and felt the blood leave my face.

Sethos turned to me, his icy-blue eyes glimmering. "Hurt him."

I shook my head.

"He would make me hurt others . . ." I shook my head.

"I'm not making you do anything you would not truly do yourself . . ."

I wrapped my arms around myself.

"You know deep inside, he deserves no mercy."

I whimpered.

"Am-Re instructed you to hurt innocents, didn't he?"

I nodded.

"Your father is a lowlife. An abuser. He manipulates those around him. His actions stole the only family you have. Those women will never love you. They are poisoned against you. Forever."

Tears streamed down my face.

"Hurt him, Renna."

"I can't!"

"What good is your magic if you can't step up when it's needed? If you ever need to protect yourself or others you love against enemies, will you sit back and do nothing? Will you also fail *me* at my time of need?"

"No!"

"This is what you will have to do once we face the ones who wronged me. Will you back down?"

I shook my head.

"Then attack him."

Pushing my shoulders back, I took a deep breath and extended my magic to the boulder. On an exhale, I lifted it.

"Good girl."

Breathe in.

Breathe out.

I am in control.

"You have a god's gift, Renna . . ." Sethos began. "And there are terrible people in this universe. Your father is one of them. The people who wronged me are also terrible."

I nodded.

"Imagine"—Sethos's lips curled, a hand on his chin—"what good your magic could do if you eliminated just *one* bad person . . . or one bad group of people."

Pain radiated from my very soul, and it felt like it was shattering into a million pieces. I screamed and threw the boulder in the figure's way.

The apparition thrust its hands out, and black and emerald electric magic sprouted from its palms, stopping the boulder from reaching it.

"It's fighting back!" I yelled. "Are you doing this?" I asked Sethos.

"Yes," Sethos answered. "You didn't think I would make this easy on you?"

I roared as my body shook from increasing my magic to push the boulder harder against the figure's magic.

Suddenly, I felt the figure grip the boulder, and in seconds, it smashed the boulder into the far end of the clearing.

The figure then advanced toward me until it broke out into a run.

"Use what is around you to fight back!" Sethos yelled.

I looked at the remaining boulders and whimpered as I began to lift another boulder with my magic.

Steeling myself, I launched the boulder into the figure, but it waved a hand, and the boulder was ripped from my magic and thrown to the side, shattering against a tree.

I turned to another boulder, but the figure was too close now.

I needed to put distance between us so I could try to throw something at it.

What could I do to distract it?

What had my power been able to do in the past?

I thought to more recently when I had used magic in Taria.

My magic erupted in Misha's Place. Magic surged from my body, covering the floor and bar in smoke and shadows . . .

Darkness.

The darkness had come as a result of overwhelming feelings and blinding anger at injustices. But I knew better now—I knew how to control my magic. I didn't need to be like my father to use the magic inside me.

I braced my feet flat on the ground and extended my hands out.

Breathing out a slow exhale, I imagined shadows emerging to protect me. Like my mental shield, I willed shadows to cover me enough to distract my foe.

Cold magic shot through my system, chilling my cells as it ripped through me, and a great black wall of smoke and shadows erupted from me, reaching several stories high and a wide distance across. The smoke rippled from my palms and feet, making me stumble backward from the mere force of it catapulting through me.

The form shrieked in rage, and I could vaguely make it out through the shadows as it thrashed its head side to side, its sharp teeth snapping ferociously at the smoke that ensnared it like the ink of an octopus.

"That's enough!" Sethos yelled, and with the snap of his finger, the figure was gone.

I sighed in relief and collapsed onto the ground, the darkness snapping back into my chest like a rubber band.

I screamed in pain and rolled to my side.

Sethos was at my side in an instant. "Where does it hurt?"

I squeezed my eyes shut. "My chest . . ." I panted, tears streaming down my chin. "I didn't expect any of what just happened."

"I know."

"What just happened?"

Sethos was quiet for a few moments before speaking again. "You called on *Darkness*."

I opened my eyes and turned to look at him, wiping tears from my face. "What?"

"You have the power of Darkness." Sethos looked back and forth between my eyes.

I shook my head and moved to sit up. The pain in my chest still throbbed, but I couldn't lie down for this conversation.

"What are you talking about?"

"You called upon it. That wall of dark smoke? How did you do it?"

I narrowed my eyes. "I'm not sure *what* I called. I was thinking of what I could do to distract the figure. I remembered the shadows that emerged from me the night I left Taria."

Sethos rubbed his face. "You simply imagined shadows? Did you say anything?"

"Yes . . . No." I paused in frustration. "In Taria, the shadows simply escaped from me—"

"Because you were angry then."

"Yes."

"And just now, you called on Darkness because you were angry."

"I don't know what I called—"

"You called on Darkness, Renna. Your father is the God of Darkness, Chaos, Ruin."

I paused. "I didn't utter any spells or anything, I just thought of shadows to protect me."

"Do you know how incredibly rare it is to have this gift?" Sethos whispered.

"But it's just shadows . . ."

He laughed and ran a hand over his face. "It's not *just* shadows."

My eyes searched his.

"Supernaturals can see through shadows, smoke," he explained. "This is different."

My heart began to slow as I tried to process what I was hearing. "I thought your figure creation was simply pretending to stall to let me practice."

"No."

"I don't understand what this means."

"I knew you had this gift when you bled black magic. It's one of the telling signs of the gift. The Darkness lives inside you. You confirmed it today. It would explain Am-Re's obsession with you —*of hunting you*. Of replicating you."

He sat closer and grabbed my shoulders.

I shook my head.

"Renna," Sethos said quickly. "I felt the magic. I was around Am-Re for two thousand years. What you called on was Darkness. You have the ability to plunge spaces around you into complete darkness. The smoke and shadows are a small portion of what you can do."

"You're saying I can *manipulate* or override the sun or—"

He shook his head. "Not quite. Your magic can shroud an entire area in impenetrable shadows. It will block out rays of light. This is an incredibly dangerous and yet remarkable gift you have."

"I—"

"Think of the power and advantage you could have in battle—"

Blood drained from my face, and I shot up to stand, dizzy from the sudden movement. The pain in my chest was ebbing into a feeling of extreme soreness.

Sethos reached out to steady me, and I moved away. "No." I shook my head and paced.

"Renna—"

"I called on it to help me. I'm not using it to go into battle. I just want to protect myself—"

"You are not comprehending the gravity of this." He pointed at me. "This puts you in danger of being pursued by vile people. Am-Re was continuously bribed to use Darkness to win wars. Darkness kills."

I shook my head as my mind spiraled.

"The reason Darkness never worked on Arios's enclave is because of their large number of gods."

"I know what you're saying—" I closed my eyes. "This is too much. My mind is spinning—"

Sethos put his palms up. "If you ever get captured," he said slowly, enunciating each word, "and someone finds out you inherited this from Am-Re, you will be made a slave to perform this magic for the purpose of horrific war crimes."

"How do I train for something like this? I simply imagined darkness shadows to protect me."

"We will add this to our daily training. We'll start out small with you bringing Darkness to a room, and eventually move on to you plunging the fortress into Darkness. When you get more advanced, you'll be able to do this outside in large fields—"

"*Fields?* With the goal of what?" I yelled, cutting in. "Why practice to that level?"

"Renna," Sethos sighed. "I know you lived half your life in a human district, and your only exposure to magic was within the walls of your foster apartment. On your university campus, you did not experience magic either—"

"Except in the end."

Sethos sighed. "You are not on Andora. This world—" Sethos gestured around. "The cosmos outside Andora and the other two human planets are ruled by supernatural beings. Beings that war with each other. *You*"—Sethos pointed to me—"are now part of this nonhuman-ruled space. Your magic and how you use it *matter.* I never want you to go into war, but I need you strong and prepared."

I wrapped my arms around my midsection.

"All I want is to empower you, Renna," Sethos said softly. "Can't you see that?"

I thought of Khellios again and how he preferred I never use magic.

Sethos's words filled me with a wave of warmth, and I sagged slightly. Sethos made me feel safe. He made me believe I could do anything—be anyone.

"You say you never want to feel vulnerable and weak again?" he asked, stepping closer and tilting my chin up with his fingers. "Then we train this gift so you are never put in a position of weakness."

Everything he said made sense, but the gravity of a weapon to kill many was overpowering.

"I don't want to hurt people, Sethos."

"You have incredible judgment, Renna. You will make the right calls . . . Never doubt that."

I looked down, and Sethos placed his hands over mine, intertwining them. The contact ceased my trembling, and I took a deep breath.

Sethos was right . . .

I had the power to protect people—especially people I loved.

People like Sethos.

I would never allow my heart to be like my father's. I could wield Darkness and not be like him . . .

My hands trembled as I looked up at Sethos. He brought our hands to his lips and gently kissed my knuckles.

I lifted my chin. "Help me wield Darkness."

The corners of his mouth curled up. "I thought you would never ask."

18

SETHOS

I t was night, and I walked the fortress alone, unable to sleep.
I ran my hands through my hair while deep in thought over the choices I was making when it came to Renna.

She had Darkness.

A power I could have never dreamed would be available to me when I took on the gods.

I could win this war.

For once, it really seemed possible.

I thought of the army I'd begun assembling back in Vasarys six months prior, anticipating my eventual clash with the gods in Taria.

Mages and warlocks, from across the universe, and defectors from the Pleiadeans and Arcturian races, who were veterans of the Galactic Wars, were at my side. I had captured Dorions, giant frilled-neck dragon monsters, to use in battle. Sedians, or tree people, who were the ancestors of redwood trees and taller than any man-made structure, would also join us in the fight. Citizens of Vasarys, who gladly agreed to fight to bring honor to the Fallen, were also drafted. In total, we had 100,000 strong warriors.

Yet none of them could wield Darkness.

Mages and warlocks could fire effective spells, Pleiadeans and Arcturians could use their star crafts and uranium weapons, and the beasts could cause damage, but Darkness, when developed correctly as I had seen Am-Re use it, could wipe out armies with a single attack.

It blinded, boiled skin to the bone, and after, crushed bone instantly to dust.

Anger rolled inside me as I questioned why Am-Re never killed the gods while he had a chance.

He focused on enriching his pockets, forever fundraising to fund armies for an eventual attack, when in reality, his powers enabled him to take on many gods at once.

He was the God of Darkness.

Am-Re failed our people because he *wanted* to.

He dragged on an eventual attack until our people lost hope.

The suspicion he planted in the hearts of our people trickled over to me now as my citizens doubted my promise to bring them justice.

I would restore their faith.

I would be happy once I killed the gods.

It would bring me peace.

A sense of accomplishment.

Pride.

And Renna?

She had pledged to help me.

And I needed her promise.

I knew it would not be easy to convince her to kill the gods, but I would have to.

Somehow . . .

Yet—

I groaned and covered my face with my palms.

I could feel the small part of me that had begun to fall for her, yearn for something *more*.

Every moment I spent with Renna gave me a glimpse of what life with her could be like if I allowed myself to dream.

I could have all her smiles, all her laughs, and her . . . *love?*

I wanted her.

I thought of the dream we shared when she bared her body to me and the way her body sang when I held her.

I longed to touch her, to worship her . . .

And I was lying to her.

I shook my head and stormed through the fortress until I got to the armory.

Looking at the lines of swords in front of me, I swiftly grabbed the closest one.

I needed to get these dangerous thoughts out of my head.

I could not afford to lose time.

At the thought of my mortality, I felt the dark magic inside me struggle to push aside my own power to assert dominance.

A voice laughed bitterly inside my mind, and my pulse began to thump rapidly in my ears.

Love, it mocked. *What a notion.*

I closed my eyes and called my magic to my center to silence the voice. Viscous, sickly waves of darkness began to overtake me, and my sea fae magic began to recoil inside me in retreat.

Love is not for you. The voice taunted me.

"Stop it!" I said out loud and reached into my vest for a tincture vial.

My vision began to blur as the dark magic continued to slither inside me, clawing at my soul and squeezing until everything I was would eventually die.

My hands shook as I pulled out the vial.

The voice in my mind laughed, echoing inside my brain. I became disoriented and dropped the vial on the ground and it shattered.

"*Fuck!*" I screamed.

I could not afford to get another one.

I had already taken three today. That would have been my fourth.

The laughter got louder, this time seemingly moving outside me, around me.

I turned this way and that to try and chase the noise.

If love had been meant for you, your mother would have survived.

I squeezed my eyes shut as anger rose inside me.

What did I want in this moment?

To fight.

To destroy.

I screamed as I pushed aside the image of Renna and the goodness she represented and called forth my Shadow, my magical doppelgänger—one of the many skills Am-Re had taught me to become a formidable fighter for him. A Shadow had the ability to think on their own and provided extra protection in battle and was useful in training.

Like a current, black magic rushed from my body and landed opposite me, slowly swirling into a figure.

Made of obsidian, he held an obsidian sword. He stood motionless, staring at me.

I envied him.

No emotions, just raw action.

No Renna.

No remorse.

Only honor.

You will never escape who you are . . . the voice whispered in my mind.

My doppelgänger menacingly smiled, baring its black teeth.

He represented the cruelty within me.

The wars I had seen.

The loss.

The beatings and torment Am-Re put me through.

I charged the figure and raised my sword with thoughts of murder on my mind.

But I could never kill this Shadow, this doppelgänger.

He was a reflection of me.

And I could never run from my past, just like I could never run from the future I had to fulfill.

19

RENNA

"Again," Sethos said.

I tightened my core muscles and closed my eyes, focusing on the dark shadows inside me, teetering right beneath the surface of my skin.

I inhaled and visualized the shadows contracting into a ball of black in the center of my chest.

I breathed out, and the magic that had gathered at my chest fired out, thick smoke barreling toward the ceiling. I bent my knees as the power throttled from me like fast-moving currents until Darkness covered the ceiling almost entirely.

"Good!" Sethos cheered.

I looked to him and smiled as he clapped.

"See how the throne room slowly darkens as you snuff out the light trickling in from the tree canopy?" He pointed to the ceiling where a roof should be, but long, lush tree branches crisscrossed the space instead.

I clenched my jaw as I tried to nod. My movements were limited as my body adjusted to the vast power coursing through me.

"This is what you will want to do when protecting someone

from an airborne attack." Sethos gestured to the Darkness. "Arrows, beasts of flight, flying craft will see the Darkness cover but will not be able to pinpoint where to attack."

I looked up to the Darkness, twisting and swirling in beautiful round patterns—like a violent wave.

"Most importantly." Sethos continued, walking toward me. "If you ever find yourself needing to defend anyone, you can create a distraction with the Darkness and trick the enemy into thinking that you're shielding people beneath it. This will give those you are protecting time to attack from a different angle."

"Ye-yes . . ." I gritted out. I could feel my face and body turn scarlet from the exertion.

"Turn it off." Sethos instructed me. "That's enough for now."

I moved my head to indicate agreement, and Sethos positioned himself behind me.

"Turn off the Darkness, and I will catch you if your body recoils. The Darkness always rushes back. The more you use it and the more ground you cover, the stronger the return will be. You will get better at this."

I wanted to remind him that it hadn't worked out so well the last three times we'd done this.

I closed my eyes with a silent prayer that this time would be better and visualized my chest open like a secret door, welcoming the Darkness back.

I felt the magic above pause, and then, like a violent stream, the magic catapulted back to my body.

I screamed and fell into Sethos's arms.

"It burns!" I screamed. "I can't do this!"

Sethos tightened his hold on me. "I got you, I got you," he whispered as my body convulsed with the Darkness returning once more.

I whimpered, my body aching as the last of the magic seeped back in.

I visualized the open door in my chest closing, and I knew it was done.

I slumped into his arms.

Sethos held me for a long time and eventually cradled me down to the ground, where he continued to hold me in his lap until I shifted from his embrace to lay flat on the ground.

I needed my spine and muscles to relax, and laying on the ground flat brought relief.

A long silence ensued. It felt like a silence for mourning.

Was I mourning my past self?

Each time I used magic, the old me died more and more.

"Are you still in pain?" he asked after a while.

I blinked my eyes open and let them adjust to the brightness of the room. It had been so dark moments ago.

Sethos gently placed a hand on my shin and squeezed. "Talk to me."

I flexed my fingers and stretched my body. "I feel sore, but less than last time." I touched my skin. "The pain is gone."

"I can feel your pain," he said, and I stopped moving.

Sethos was looking ahead, his vision soft. "That's why I came to you in Taria."

"Can you feel all my feelings?"

He shook his head. "I'm observant, so I can sense when you're feeling sad or angry. But it's only extreme bouts of emotion that get passed to me. What I feel is muted, but anguish, fear, rage are present."

I'd never felt anything like that from him.

I wondered if it only worked one way.

"What does it physically feel like?" he asked. "To have that amount of power moving through your blood and veins?"

I nodded. "I feel like my body is trapped in a ball of fire and I cannot escape it, but then within seconds it's gone. It's like the pain was never there. Although my muscles remain sore as though to remind me it happened."

"Am-Re acted like it never bothered him."

I snorted. "I'm not a god. My body was not designed to carry this."

"Yet, somehow, Source picked you. It allowed for this transfer of magic and duplication to happen."

"For better or for worse?"

Sethos looked down at me. "If I could have Darkness as a power . . ." He shook his head, not finishing his train of thought. "I feel like everything I do is not enough."

An uneasy feeling spread over me as I noted the slight shift in his tone. It was lower. Darker.

"You have me," I said, pushing off to support my weight on my elbows.

A smile spread over his face, and he looked down to where his hand rested on my shin.

"Do I?" he asked as his gaze drifted from his hand to my face, slowly, as if he was drinking me in. When his eyes met mine, they were a brilliant intense blue.

My stomach did a summersault, and my breathing became rapid.

"Renna . . ." Sethos paused as if he was trying to form the words.

"What is it?"

"Sometimes I wonder what it would be like to not have all these duties piled against me."

My eyebrows lifted in surprise to his admission.

"That I could be a man with a freedom to choose."

He looked up at the ceiling then and then to our surroundings.

"That I could be a man with the freedom to take."

His words seemed innocent, but they made my blood and skin feel hot.

Desire pooled low in my core, and I recalled my body moving against his.

Sethos slowly moved his gaze down to look at me, and my eyes slid to his lips. His lips were perfect with the lower lip plumper than the top.

I swallowed.

I wanted to kiss him.

"And what would you take?" I whispered.

"Things that I have no right to want."

When my eyes met his, I saw the desire in his hooded eyes, and I sat up, my body urging to inch closer to him.

Sethos stayed still as I approached until we were almost nose to nose.

He tilted his head, and a slow smile spread on his face.

Feeling emboldened, I asked, "And what if you do have a right to want those things?"

"*Do I?*" he asked the question again, and his eyes trailed down to my lips.

"You have but to ask . . ." I whispered.

Sethos hand, which had stayed on my shin, began to move up to my knee and then toward my thigh . . . and up higher still.

Instinctually I opened my legs slightly as my core began to throb with want.

"*Sethos . . .*" my words were like a soft plea, and to my dismay, it made him pause.

He blinked as if he was suddenly realizing what was happening and dropped his hand.

"Maybe one day . . ." he murmured and moved backwards from me and pushed to stand.

I held my breath as my heart rattled frantically in its cage, not knowing what to do with the coiling tension inside of me.

When Sethos put his hand out for me to take, I forced myself to take it and pushed to stand.

"I'm sorry," he said and looked down between us. "We can resume training later today."

I was silent, not knowing what to say out loud when inside my body urged me to grab him to me and kiss him. To run my hands over his chest . . . to run my nose down the side of his neck, drinking him in, urging him to pull me close.

But I knew whatever moment had passed between us was gone.

"Sounds good," I said, my face suddenly feeling hot from a feeling that felt a lot like rejection.

Having too much pride to watch Sethos walk away from me, I took my hand from his and spun on my heels and walked away.

20

KHELLIOS

I slammed my fist against the wall.

King Miletak had not answered my request for assistance.

My chest was heaving, and Ukara stood by the door of my study.

My study was a mess. In a flash, I had overturned my bookshelves and thrown my desk across the room, and scattered books, maps, and records, and broken bottles and glasses covered the floor.

Ukara carefully stepped forward to avoid stepping on the debris. She opened her mouth as if to say something, but one look from me silenced her, and she stepped back to where she was standing.

"Save your words," I said bitterly, biting my cheek to keep me from screaming again.

"I'm sorry," she whispered.

"For what?" I snapped. "For not being better prepared for an attack? For my inability to kill Sethos?"

Ukara remained silent.

"The days pass, and I don't know what to think. Merida said Renna was happy at Sethos's side."

"He's clearly using her. Tricking her."

I pinched the bridge of my nose. "I can't talk to you anymore. Where is Livina?"

Ukara shook her head. "Livina speaks when she deems it necessary."

"And her sister Pemira?" I demanded.

"Neither goddess belongs to the Celestial Enclave. Like me, you know we cannot be summoned."

I snagged a bottle of alcohol off an end table and swirled the meager liquid left inside. I uncapped it and took a swig.

Ukara rushed across the room and snatched the bottle from my hand, smashing it to the floor. "I'm done with this destructive behavior. You think no one notices how you drink to cope?" she yelled. "We don't need food as gods, Khel!" She pointed toward me. "We don't need drink either!"

I rolled my eyes.

"You drink to numb and forget! Alcohol has you under a spell! You reach for it when things get hard."

"What's it to you?"

"Everything!" she screamed. "I am your family—I love you. And you're poisoning your body! You don't drink to celebrate. You drink to drown out the noise. To not deal with all that is going on inside."

"Just save it." I waved her off. "I don't need you to lecture me."

"I'm not lecturing you, Khel. I'm trying to help you! Can't you see that?"

"My body is not mortal. I will not endanger any organs," I sneered. "My body is fine. I'm healthy."

"You call this healthy!?" she laughed. "Your body may not succumb to cirrhosis like mortals, but the way you deal with pain is not healthy. You are not endangering your body, but you are chipping away at the corner of your mind, creating permanent wounds that will never allow you to heal."

I closed my eyes and massaged my temples. "Just leave," I muttered.

"I will. I only came to tell you I am leaving for the Galactic Federation today to make our plea for assistance."

I dropped my hands and opened my eyes.

"I think we have a chance, Khel. I've been hearing that Sethos's attack has made the news rounds in other supernatural circles. People are afraid of unrestricted power from a power-hungry usurper." She shook her head. "It will throw off the balance of order Source created. It's not good."

Ukara waited a few moments, and when I said nothing, she asked, "Who gave you the mirror, Khel? You said it was a fae king. It must have allowed a portal to form."

I closed my eyes and thought about those days. The days I was a mercenary across galaxies, trying to forget Renna after her death. I received many gifts as a result of my services.

"I cannot remember his name." I shook my head.

"What do you remember of him? What did he look like?"

In that moment, commotion was heard outside my study. A female yelled, and I spun toward the noise.

My door swung open, and a woman in silver armor with blond hair pushed into the room, sword in tow.

My world stopped when I realized who it was.

"Khellios," she breathed as she straightened. Her blue eyes assessed me.

"Elrie," I whispered. "You came."

She set her sword down. "It's El, you know that. And of course I did. My father sent me. He was away when you sent the message for help. But I'm here now."

"And your father?" I asked.

"He will join at a later time. He sent me first, understanding how time sensitive this situation is. You granted us the gift of life once. I personally intend to return to you the life you want . . . with her."

Ukara cleared her throat, and El and I looked toward her.

"I'll leave you two to . . . get reacquainted. I know it's been some time . . ." Ukara looked to El, and her gaze softened. "El, Khellios has always spoken highly of you and the time he spent in your father's realm. Galaxies speak of how you have developed into a seasoned warrior since then. It is said you now lead your father's mercenaries?" She shifted her gaze to mine and back to El's.

El lowered her head in respect. "Yes, Goddess. It is I who should be honored that the Goddess of War herself knows of me."

Ukara smiled proudly. "You have known Khellios for quite some time. I'm glad you are here."

Ukara looked to me again with an unreadable expression. "I leave you in capable hands."

I nodded.

"I'll send word of what the Federation says," Ukara stated.

"Good luck."

Ukara nodded a goodbye and stepped from the office, closing the door behind her.

El turned back to me, and we stared at each other silently.

She was a vision in her gleaming armor. A white cape draped from her back, making her look like a queen about to command armies.

"Do friends get a hug?" she asked after a moment.

I tried to smile. It wasn't Elrie's fault my world had imploded once more. "Of course."

A beautiful grin spread over her face, and she launched herself at me, her armor pushing me slightly back.

My body warmed as I wrapped my arms around her, and I felt her almost sink against me as I held her.

"I wondered if you would remember our friendship," she whispered against my chest.

So much had happened the last time I saw Elrie . . .

"Khel," she whispered and pulled back to look at me. "Talk to me."

I stepped back from her. "She's gone, El. Again. I failed Renna again."

"You did not fail then, and you did not fail now."

"You say that and you know it's false—"

"No." She stepped up to me, crossing her arms. "It is not your fault Am-Re attacked the old city. Your relationship with his daughter then was an excuse for him to attack the enclave. Her being taken now is not your fault either."

"You don't know that."

"I do." She narrowed her eyes. "You kill yourself every day to keep everyone safe. The attack here is widely known now."

"Renna was taken through a portal in her room."

El's hand flew to her mouth. "You brought her to the safest place imaginable. How is that possible?"

"There was a mirror in her room. I became a portal and . . ." I shook my head and squeezed my eyes shut. "I should have made sure nothing dangerous was in her room—"

"How were you to know the mirror would be dangerous? You cannot keep doing this, Khel. When you came to my father and me, you were broken with guilt."

I opened my eyes to look at her. "Some days it feels like nothing has changed."

"You spent three years in our kingdom. When you left, the light had returned to your eyes . . . You laughed. You smiled. And now." She shook her head. "Now I can see deep sadness coming back."

She was right, in part. Some days or years, I felt fine, like life was normal again. Then something would trigger me—perhaps a word or sentence—and plunge me back into a darkness with no escape. I would hit bottom, and my body would become chained with memories.

Elrie gently gripped my forearms. "Khel, this cycle of pain is no way to live out your existence."

"I've lived this way for a long time. It's hard to remember a time when I was not . . . grieving."

El narrowed her eyes slightly. "And you still refuse to truly talk about your feelings beyond the surface level?"

I paused and thought about her question. "I think you're the first person I've opened up to in a long time."

El sighed and dropped her hands. "You need to make a commitment to get better."

I smiled.

El lifted her palm to my face and cupped my cheek. "That is the saddest smile I have seen. You have so much to live for, Khel."

"Are you the expert on living?"

She smiled and stepped back from me. "I guess I am. Or do you not recall my ability to throw a party?"

A laugh escaped me. "You sound like an immortal."

"It suits me." She lowered her eyes. "I just wish it didn't come at a cost to you."

I couldn't help but step closer to her and tilt her chin up. "I never regretted giving you both immortality."

"You angered Source when you did it. You knew gods are not at liberty to grant eternity to mortals."

She lifted my hand in hers and looked at my skin, lacking the silver aura gods typically have. "You gave up part of your divinity for me."

"You were dying. I would do it again."

"And in exchange, I promised you I would live my life fully."

"And have you?" I searched her face. "I have not seen you in —" I looked up, trying to count.

El turned from me and straightened a chair I had thrown. "We're not here to talk about my life, Khel. I'm here to help you. I am now commanding my father's troops. I have three crafts and a crew of one hundred stationed outside Andora as instructed. I will be the one to help you search for Renna."

I couldn't help but smile.

"What?" she demanded.

"You are no longer the damsel I rescued."

She lifted her chin. "I am not." She laughed. "Plus, I like who I am now."

I lifted my eyebrows. "I liked you then. I like you now."

"As a friend . . ."

"As family." I reminded her. "You know what you and your father mean to me."

El looked down and nodded. "Well." She straightened and stood a little taller, looking up at me. "Let's get going." She turned to walk from the room.

Something heavy and tight stirred in my chest.

I caught El's elbow, and she paused without turning.

"El," I began. "I know we haven't seen each other in a while. I . . . remember how we left things last time I saw you."

El turned and gently took back her arm. "It was so long ago." She shrugged. "I barely remember."

The tightness in my chest continued to expand, and I shifted on my feet.

"Should we get going?" she asked.

I nodded slowly, not knowing what to say.

"Good," she said quickly. "Let's go."

I followed her from the room with one question on my mind: Now who wasn't talking about their feelings?

21

RENNA

It was a beautiful golden-red evening when I came upon Sethos sharpening his sword in the hall he used as an armory. He was shirtless, and I watched as his back and arm muscles flexed as he worked.

I wanted to run my fingertips over his and—

"I know you're there." He continued to work, not bothering to look over his shoulder.

"Hi," I said, my voice coming out softer than intended.

"Will you stand there staring at me all day?"

That could certainly be an option . . .

"Might be better than what you're doing," I teased. "It looks incredibly boring."

He chuckled. "What did you think training for conflict was going to entail? Sometimes it involves mundane tasks. Do you think soldiers pass the time fucking off?"

His words made me blush, and when I did not answer, he looked over his right shoulder.

Our eyes met, and his intense gaze made my skin break out in goose bumps.

"No. You're not going to seduce me as a pastime," he said.

I choked on my spit and coughed.

"Excuse me?" I asked, hitting my chest with my fist.

"You know exactly how you were looking at me just now." He dropped his weapons and tools and stood.

I laughed nervously.

"And how was I looking at you?" I asked.

Sethos turned to face me and crossed his arms.

"Like you wanted me to fuck you."

My eyes widened, and my lips parted.

His eyes focused on my lips, and he drew in a breath before his eyes met mine.

"You're trouble, mejtah," he said while shaking his head. "Surely you know that?"

I chuckled and then pursed my lips. "You're the one talking about . . ." I paused and lifted my eyebrows, "*fucking.*"

"Such filthy words from such a pretty mouth."

His statement made my pulse quicken, and a delicious shiver rolled through my spine as I watched him approach.

"Is there a problem with what I said?" I lifted my chin as if ready for a challenge.

Sethos stopped right in front of me, and I was rewarded with a lazy smile.

"You're treading on dangerous waters, Renna."

"Am I?" I pouted.

Sethos leaned down to my cheek, and I almost jumped when his skin made contact with mine. He rubbed his skin slightly against mine and moved his lips to my ear.

"I can think of better ways to spend our time today . . ." he said.

I squeezed my thighs together.

"How?" I asked him.

Sethos straightened with a satisfied smirk.

"I'm going to teach you how to use Black Fire," he said and turned around.

I inwardly groaned as I watched him set space between us.

I crossed my arms. "More training. *How thrilling.*"

"Don't you want to stay alive?" he said, his tone more serious.

I rolled my eyes. "I would prefer to live, yes."

"I also would like for you to live."

I sighed and ground my teeth with frustration as the sexual tension evaporated from the room.

"Fine. So what is Black Fire? Is it actual fire?" I asked. "Or is it like the Fire Magic you mentioned my sisters have?"

"The latter."

"I take it Black Fire is another trait I inherited from my father?"

A slow smile spread across his face. "I believe so, we have only to try to confirm. This, too, is something you should possess."

He lifted his palms, and within seconds, two glowing black spheres emerged. The spheres swirled with black shadows, and an almost blinding white light encircled them.

"I know it's hard on the eyes at first," he said. "You'll get used to it in time. Try to relax the muscles around your eye. If you squint like you're doing now, it will only strain your eyes."

I recalled how terrible Darkness was on my body. "Does Fire Magic burn your skin?"

He shook his head. "It feels cold. But not uncomfortable. It feels much like our own brand of magic."

I took a breath and tried to relax my face. "Where does Black Fire come from?"

"Black Fire hails from Fire Magic, which I'd alluded to before. Fire Magic is the purest form of magic directly from Source. While there is magic in the universe that can be created through spells and passed down in lineages, Fire Magic is gifted straight from Source.

"There are six types of Fire Magic. Red Fire, Black Fire, Golden Fire, Violet Fire, Green Fire, and White Fire. For our immediate purposes, you only need to know about Black, Violet, and Golden Fire.

"Violet Fire was spiritual magic used by metaphysicians and prophets of old who had reached enlightenment. The spiritual magic allowed them to alchemize new realities and possibilities to benefit themselves and many more."

I crossed my arms. "That sounds a bit like witchcraft."

"Some witches do have the power of the Violet Fire." He nodded. "As I've told you, Demira wields Violet Fire. She is able to imagine physical objects and conjure them into reality."

"Such as?"

"Money." He frowned.

"Violet Fire sounds terrible in the hands of the wrong person."

His lips pressed into a hard line. "Which is precisely why I have an issue with Demira. She abuses the Fire Magic by granting the nobles and council in my court boons to draw on their support."

"To topple you."

The air suddenly electrified with rage. "She can try."

I scrambled to bring his focus back to me so that he would calm down. "And what about Black Fire?" I asked.

"Black Fire is used to wield magic for war." He waved his palms elegantly, and a black sword with a glowing white outline appeared. "I wield Black Fire. Anyone can create weapons for self-defense. Ones made from Black Fire will always be more effective and ten times more deadly."

"Black Fire is used only for war?"

"Correct. It only produces weapons. It's quite limited. It cannot produce riches. Or other material things."

"Well," I said, thinking out loud, "if you have the most effective and deadly weapon, you could conquer a land and get those riches without having to create them from magic."

Sethos nodded. "Magic is always about balance."

"How do I call it forth?"

"The first time you use any Fire Magic, you have to petition Source. The way to do it is to imagine a golden thread extending from the heavens down to your center. That thread is your divine connection to Source. Imagine Black Fire surging through there when you call your magic. Source will immediately decide if it wants to grant it."

"Has it ever rejected a Black Fire petition?"

"Source will, from time to time, decide that the ask comes with too great a cost."

Suddenly a foreboding feeling spread through my body then, and an image materialized in my mind.

One where I fought alone.

And Sethos stood on opposite lines.

A shiver rippled down my spine, and I closed my eyes. I shook my head to clear the image away.

Sethos was my friend. I wanted a future with him in it.

When I opened my eyes, Sethos had turned away from me, looking at something far off in the distance, as if he, too, was lost in his thoughts.

"What about Golden Fire?" I asked to pivot the conversation.

Sethos looked back to me. "Golden Fire grants life to beings on the verge of death," he said quietly. "Your sister, Illona, has this power. It is the most potent of all flames. This is why I mentioned she is more powerful than Demira."

His words made me pause. "The Fires seem to teach restraint in what you can and cannot do with them."

He nodded. "Source designed it that way. To make sure that magic did not go unchecked."

"Will Black Fire feel different from using regular magic?"

Sethos tilted his head and gestured at my hands. "Call it forth. There's only one way to find out. It may feel uncomfortable at first."

"Will it hurt?"

He shook his head. "Try and see."

I nodded and closed my eyes. I didn't know what Source looked like, whether it was gendered, or if it spoke, but I imagined a rounded glowing silver portal in the vastness of space. Silver rings of energy moving in a clockwise motion surrounded the portal.

I spoke to Sethos while my mind remained trained on my interpretation of Source. "Do I have to say anything specific?"

"No," Sethos responded. "Just imagine the energy flowing from it to you. Source will either grant or deny the power at that time."

I nodded and imagined a glittering, solid golden cord, almost like a ribbon, extending from my solar plexus up toward the sky, directly to the center vortex of Source.

Like Sethos instructed, I pretended that Black Fire traveled down the cord to me.

Was this it?

I flexed my fingers, waiting for the fire to materialize in my palms.

Seconds went by.

Nothing.

I couldn't feel my energy change in any way, and I peeked at my hands. They remained unchanged.

I shut my eyes again and imagined my golden connection to Source.

Why wasn't the Black Fire coming to me?

The vortex that was Source began to glow silver and white.

And suddenly, a tall figure with blue-spotted skin appeared in front of Source, floating in the cosmos. Its eyes were slanted and indigo, almost neon, and glowing in the dark. I couldn't decipher their features clearly, but I knew I couldn't possibly be imagining what I was seeing.

The figure folded its hands in front of itself, and then it spoke without moving its mouth.

Black Fire was granted to one like yourself.

For battle, it was used, but chaos ensued.

Now, its ghost cannot wield it.

My pulse began to race.

Was I supposed to answer? I recalled speaking to a voice in the darkness as I portaled to Sethos. This voice was different, but still, I wondered.

Who are you? I asked. *You are not the voice of the Astral.*

You are correct, I am not the Astral. I am from the sixth dimension. We are the guardians of Fire Magic, on behalf of Source.

I seek Black Fire.

We deem the cost too great. Why should Source grant this Fire to your lineage again?

I don't seek to destroy, I answered in my mind.

Then why do you need it?

I thought of Sethos's comment about being able to do good for others with my magic. I recalled the attacks on my campus and my inability to protect others and how useless and lost I felt in those moments.

To protect those I care about.

I also thought of Sethos's grief and my offer to help him fight his demons.

To make sure I, and those around me, never feel hopelessness or fear again.

Why?

Because to live in fear is no life at all. Why be granted life if we are terrified to live it?

The silver rings around Source stopped moving, and everything went still.

My skin turned cold, and my heart slowed down as I waited.

The figure in blue stared at me for a long time.

What is given can be taken away, Daughter of Darkness, Chaos, and Ruin.

I am not my father. And I never will be.

We shall see.

Goose bumps spread over my body at its words.

Suddenly, Black Fire emerged from Source and trickled down the golden cord toward me.

The Fire moved slowly, as if burning down the length of the cord.

I lowered my head in respect. *Thank you.*

The image before me went black, and my body felt like it was falling through space in slow motion. I felt no fear as I knew this was all in my mind.

"Renna . . ." Sethos whispered in an echo around me. "Come back . . ."

Within moments, my feet touched the ground, and I opened my eyes.

Sethos stood before me with a sly grin on his face.

"Look, little serpent," Sethos said, his eyes glowing as he looked at my hands.

I raised my hands to see black flames in my palms.

It felt like cold vapor, skimming my skin.

Sethos chuckled. "And now you wield Black Fire. How do you feel?"

I grinned as I moved my hands, admiring the Fire. "Pretty good, not going to lie," I answered.

"You should feel good. You wield Black Fire and Darkness. Not so helpless now." He moved closer and brushed my hair off my shoulder. "You are a formidable foe."

I blushed and called back my magic, turning off the Black Fire in the same way my regular magic retracted.

With the magic out of the way, Sethos closed the distance between us, cradling my head with one hand and placing his hand on the small of my back.

My skin felt hot where he touched me, and I moved more into his body, relishing to be held by him.

"*We* are formidable," I breathed as he lowered his face to mine.

"You're doing things to me, mejtah . . ."

I moved my hands up to his chest and loved feeling his heart beating as fast as mine.

"And are they bad things?" I teased.

He smiled. "Not at all, little serpent. Not at all."

22

RENNA

A woman in black stood on a turret.

Her black hair moved violently in the wind. A white streak of hair contrasted against her dark hair.

I had never seen her before.

She hugged her arms around herself as she looked toward the horizon.

I couldn't make out where we were, only that she was on a place high above the ground.

I walked to stand next to her.

Her violet eyes looked worried, and she chewed her bottom lip.

I tried to determine what she was looking at, but all I could see was a red haze. My dream didn't permit me to see where in the universe we were located.

"Who are you?" I asked, but the woman didn't move.

Did she not hear me?

I moved closer to her, placing a hand on the stone turret like she was.

The woman suddenly looked up, her eyes rapidly moving to the heavens.

I followed her gaze, but all I could see was red haze.

I looked down at her to see her frown.

"No," she whispered and closed her eyes.

She reached inside her black leather shirt and pulled out an amulet. An intricate pentacle encircled by a serpent.

She began to murmur words in a language I couldn't understand, and my eyes widened when dark purple sparks shot from her palms.

Then suddenly she became deathly still.

And that was when I felt it.

A dark, viscous energy that reminded me of a rattling closet handle and the fear of holding the door closed. Energy that brought memories of being physically assaulted and held down. A male voice screaming that I was nothing without him.

"No, no, no . . ." the woman said, her eyes remaining closed.

And whatever she was seeing behind closed lids made her physically recoil as if she had been struck.

I wanted to reach out and comfort her.

Her eyes flew open, and she stared straight at me.

"Am-Re is alive."

My heart raced, and I stumbled back a step, but the woman grabbed my hand to stop me.

Her grip turned deadly as her fingers clawed into my flesh.

Her eyes went white, and her lips moved, whispering, "He comes for the heir of darkness and ruin."

I woke up screaming, and the hands pinning me down caused my heart to go into overdrive.

My father would hold me down, too, until I produced magic.

"Don't touch me!" I fought and clawed with all my strength.

"Renna!" Sethos said quickly. "Open your eyes. It's me!"

I opened my eyes and scrambled to sit, looking wildly around the room. My brain was disoriented.

"You're safe," Sethos said, kneeling next to me. "We're in Daya. In the fortress. You're in your bedroom."

Sconces lit the room, giving it a dim glow.

"He's back," I breathed, my chest heaving.

"Who?"

I wiped sweat off my forehead. How long had I been dreaming? My clothing was soaked in sweat as if I had been in a pool.

"What did you dream of?" Sethos reached out but pulled his hand back.

I tried to slow my breathing to calm my heartbeats.

"She told me . . ." I whispered. "She told me he's alive."

"*Who?*" Sethos's voice was raised. "You're not making sense."

I dropped my head in my hands, and my lips began to recite the words the woman had said.

"What are you saying?"

"*He comes for the heir of darkness and ruin.*"

Sethos paled, and he lowered his chin. "What are you talking about?"

"In my dream, a woman spoke to me." My lungs tightened. "She—" I stumbled on my words. "She said those words and looked right at me." Tears now ran down my face, and I didn't have time to berate myself for crying in front of him.

"You're shaking," Sethos said and ran his hands down my trembling arms.

"Am-Re is coming for me."

Sethos paused and grabbed my biceps. "Renna," Sethos said. "We are safe in Daya."

"It doesn't matter!" I screamed. "I know. He's coming for me, I'm the heir of his darkness! My magic brings about ruin!"

Sethos shook his head. "You've been using the magic inherited from your father. I suspect it's triggered your emotions."

"It felt real, Sethos."

"Dreams are just dreams."

"And you?" I asked, sitting straighter. "You visited me in dreams. Those were more than just dreams."

Sethos ran a hand over his face and sighed. "Renna—"

"So you're going to dismiss my dream?"

Sethos stood and put his hands on his hips. "I believe you had a terrible nightmare, and I'm here to tell you that you're safe."

I wanted to believe him, but there was something ominous about the dream I couldn't shake. I knew what regular dreams and nightmares felt like.

This dream, however, had the qualities of the nightmares I had while in the healing waters after I portaled to Daya—they were *too real.*

Those dreams had revealed that my mentor was Am-Re. I knew deep down it was true. Their magic had the same qualities, but it was as if something inside me refused to put the pieces together before. I wondered if the healing properties of the water helped me find clarity.

Would the waters help me find clarity now?

I pushed the covers off the bed and stood.

"Renna," Sethos sighed. "Get back into bed."

I reached for the robe that was at the foot of my bed. "I'm not tired anymore."

I lifted the robe and put it on and crossed my arms.

"Yes, you are tired. You'll only hurt your body if you don't rest properly with the training you've had."

"I'm not tired. I'm going to the armory."

I walked to my armoire and pulled out my usual black cargo pants and black shirt, then moved behind the dressing screen and began to change.

"You're going to the armory to train? It's nighttime. I'm tired. Just get back in bed."

"Sethos," I said as I began to change. "If I tell you I'm not tired, *I'm not tired.* Stay here. I can go on my own."

He remained silent.

Once dressed, I walked to my bed and sat to put on the combat boots I'd left next to it.

Sethos stood in the corner of my room with his arms crossed.

"In my dream, the fear of him returning was paralyzing." I looked up at Sethos as I laced up my boots. "One of my first memories of my father was watching as he pulled my foster mother by the hair, dragging her across our apartment."

Sethos's jaw visibly clenched, and he curled his fists at his sides.

I put my forearms on my thighs and looked to the ground. "He was terrifying. I used to cower in his presence as a child. If I got too physically close when he was in one of his moods, there was always a fear he would grab me and beat me." I stood. "He used to rape my foster mother as well. I heard my father force himself on her almost every week. As a child, I didn't understand what the noises were at first. Then I became older, and I could comprehend."

Sethos closed his eyes as if he were in pain. "I'll kill him," he gritted out.

"I tried to confront him one time after he raped her. I believe I was about fifteen. I sat on the couch, waiting for him to leave her room. I demanded he confess what he had done, and he just laughed and left."

"I'm sorry you lived with a monster."

"I've never told anyone that story. I always thought no one would believe me. I fear even now, as an adult, that if I tell people what I truly lived, people will think I'm making it up."

Sethos's eyes were furious. "I will always believe you. And I want you to believe me when I tell you that I *will* kill him."

An ache spread through my chest at his words. The ache was not sadness but an empty hollow happiness at being seen and believed, but also shame that I burdened him with my experiences.

It was odd how so many feelings could exist at one time.

"So." I crossed my arms. "I train tonight to get the rage out of my system. To pretend that it's him I'm destroying and never letting him hurt anyone else while I live."

"Do you need me to come with you?"

"No." I needed to be alone.

Sethos nodded. "Alright. I must go to Vasarys for a few hours. Stay within the shield that covers the fortress and forest. I trust you'll be alright?"

"Yes. I won't venture off. And as far as the training goes, we have been training for several days. I've got it handled."

He smiled.

A thought crossed my mind, and thoughts if impending doom began to race through my mind.

"Sethos, you've told me Vasarys is not welcoming for you at present." I fidgeted with my shirt. "What if you need help while you're there? How would I be able to reach you?"

He frowned and crossed his arms. "That would never happen. I would never allow it to get to that point."

"But what if it does?"

He shook his head.

I walked up to him. "Teach me to portal."

He raised his eyebrows.

"My father forced me to portal a few times as a child. I only did it for small distances, like across the room, but I was small and blocked most of it out."

"You want to learn to portal to save me?" He chuckled.

I narrowed my eyes. "Don't laugh at me. I'm serious."

Rolling his eyes, he placed his hands on my shoulders. "And I'm serious too. Portaling to Vasarys on your own would be stupid and reckless."

Something inside urged me to press the matter, and I lifted my chin. "I still need to learn."

"Well . . . technically yes."

I tilted my head. "I'll need it in a fight, won't I?"

Sethos lowered his chin in thought. "If I teach you to portal, promise me you won't do anything stupid." He paused and studied my face. "Would you go back to Andora?"

A deep sigh settled in my chest, and I shook my head. "I would never risk the lives of innocents on Andora if Am-Re traces me back there."

Sethos was silent for a few minutes. "Are you sure you want to take this on, on top of everything else?"

I lifted my chin. "Yes. You won't be able to protect me forever, Sethos."

A look crossed his eyes that I couldn't understand, and he blinked several times.

He ran a hand through my hair, making me feel like I was the most precious thing in the world.

Looking directly in my eyes, he said, "Nothing will keep me from remaining at your side," he whispered fiercely and cupped my jaw. "Not even death."

I placed my hand on top of his. "I won't let you die, Sethos. If you go down, we'll go down together."

Sethos looked to the ground. "If I have your word that you'll use caution, then we can add portaling to your training tomorrow . . ."

A grin spread on my face, and I hugged him. "Thank you," I said against his chest.

Sethos nodded. "Now go train to clear your head." He straightened. "Go sort yourself out and get some sleep after. Portaling will be brutal tomorrow."

I kissed his cheek. "I will."

"I'll be back long after you fall asleep."

I nodded, and we walked out of my room. He portaled to Vasarys outside my door, and I headed to the armory.

23

RENNA

My body shook with the strain of controlling the Darkness that rushed from my chest and now formed a barrier of black smoke and shadows, slightly curving around me like a shield.

I didn't know how many hours had passed since I began to practice after I left Sethos's side, but my eyes were dry and my muscles ached.

Still, despite the strain, I persisted.

After spending all night training in the armory, I decided to walk around the fortress and try to use my magic while on the move.

I ended up in the hall with the healing waters.

There was very little I could do inside Daya, but at least in this, I had control. At least it was better than in Taria, being locked in Khellios's home and restricted to only using weapons he chose for me.

At the memory, I pushed my magic harder, and more surged from me. I screamed as it continued to bend around me even more, in a semicircle, arched shape now. If the goal of Darkness was to protect myself and others, I had to master how to manipulate the shadows. It wasn't enough to erect a rectangular type of barrier wall; I had to move with it.

I imagined walking with soldiers behind me and the Darkness creating a shield as we plowed toward an enemy.

I looked above me at the towering shield of Darkness and wondered whether I could bend it even more so it would form a full circle behind me.

Could I push my body just a little bit more?

I squeezed my eyes shut and bent my knees slightly, imagining myself pulling the edges of Darkness around me to enclose me within.

Sweat dripped down my brow in buckets now, soaking my shirt as my skin heated from exertion.

When the room darkened completely behind my closed eyelids, I finally opened my eyes, and my jaw dropped in wonder. I was in the middle of a black cylindrical storm with violent energy swirling in blacks, grays, and silvers throughout the Darkness.

I blinked as bolts of electricity flashed within the chaos. While the energy surrounded me, a high-pitched noise reached my ears, sounding like the whistling echo of a stormy wind. On the surface of the walls, tiny bits of silver and black misted off like stardust and wafted to my skin. Expecting the Darkness to burn me, instinctively I called forth a Black Fire shield and watched as the mist bounced off and disintegrated into nothing.

I blinked down to my Black Fire shield as the realization hit me.

I was successfully wielding Darkness and Black Fire simultaneously.

I almost expected Sethos's clap at that moment, but none came. He was likely sleeping.

I laughed in shock as I moved around, marveling at the magic encasing me. Pride swelled in my chest.

I had done this.

I was powerful.

And I could trust myself to use my powers without Sethos next to me coaching every move.

Wanting to see just how much more I could do with the current Darkness shape, I pushed the magic up to the ceiling of the fortress, to the canopy.

The trees were several hundred feet high, and I narrowed my eyes as I concentrated, funneling my magic upward.

Suddenly, yellow and white sparks flashed on two of the trees.

I covered my mouth as dread filled me.

More sparks flew, and the beautiful trees caught on fire.

I immediately called the Darkness back to stop the flames from spreading. The shadows snapped back, throwing me backward several feet.

Anticipating the impact, I called forth Black Fire and imagined a soft, protective buffer to fall on before my body hit the stone floor.

I screamed, not knowing whether it would work.

As soon as my back made contact with the barrier, the magic felt like a tight woven net that moved with my body, almost molding to it and minimizing the blow. I never hit the stone ground.

I went completely still as the barrier stabilized me. Letting out a shaky breath, I ran my hands over my body to make sure I'd made it in one piece.

When my hands brushed over my chest, the skin was sore to the touch. I had used too much magic this time. I would need to pace myself.

I groaned as I turned to the side and curled my knees. Pushing off with my hands, I sat up.

I examined the surface beneath me. A glowing neon black rectangle, the size of my body, it was elevated from the ground so that if I were standing, it would likely come up to my waist. Although I had never asked for the specific barrier that the Black Fire created, the design was brilliant. Once more, my magic had shown me that all I had to do was trust myself.

The burning canopy crackled with red embers, and I looked up, quickly jumping off the barrier.

"How the fuck am I going to put that out?" I gripped my hair at the roots as the red embers spread.

I had to use magic to somehow transport water.

Water...

Water from where?

I slowly dropped my hands as I remembered the healing waters were nearby. I looked down at my palms.

Black Fire was supposed to turn into weapons of war. The net I had just created could be a weapon to trap someone, even if it had aided me. I doubted there was something I could devise to transport water.

Darkness would not help me either as it would singe the trees even more.

Flames licked the air above me, and I ran to the healing waters.

Would my regular magic work to somehow manipulate the water to travel up?

I recalled using my magic on my campus when Am-Re had attacked my university quad.

Am-Re's magic was shattering the lightbulbs that lined the quad to encase the space in darkness.

I had compelled my magic to keep a single lamppost on as people ran to find shelter.

Could I compel water to do what I wanted?

You've learned to trust yourself today, my brain reminded me.

I squared my shoulders. Okay, I could try to do this.

As the flames spread, my chest began to close up as panic gripped me.

Trust myself.

I breathed in and out slowly.

Would the electrical quality in my magic hurt me? I had healing magic, so I had to at least try, and I'd heal myself if it came to it.

On instinct, I bent next to the pool and hovered my hands above the water.

"Okay," I breathed, looking down at the glimmering surface. "I'm talking to water, a perfectly normal thing."

Cinders began to rain down into the room, and when I looked up, the entire top branches of both trees were now in flames.

I looked back down at the water.

"Water." I pleaded. "You heal. You healed me. I don't know if you heal objects?" I asked it. "And I don't even know if you can understand me?"

A fiery branch fell onto the floor, and I jumped.

"Fuck!" I yelled and crouched next to the pool's ledge. "I need you to heal these trees. They're burning. Please work with me to heal. Help me defend the health of these trees. Work with me and on my behalf to help."

Something in the air tinged, like a single high-pitched bell.

And everything froze.

The cinders stopped moving, the fire froze, and the air stilled.

Whispers murmured by a female in a foreign tongue began to fill the room, and waves of power rolled inside me, starting at my crown and moving to my feet.

A shiver ran up my spine, and I glanced around, expecting to find someone in the room who might have caused such magic.

Suddenly, the healing waters began to vibrate, and mist rose from the surface, jumping up to meet my hands. Instead of pain, the water met my electrical power and began to fuse with the currents in my palms.

Then, the waters began to glow within as if an enormous light shone in its depths. It made the pool look like it was deep, deeper than I knew it to be, as if it went on forever. It was magic, giving the illusion of an unimaginable depth.

I fell back on my ass and scrambled to stand, immediately calling my protective mental shield and Black Fire hand shield.

Something moved within the waters, casting shadows on the light that shone from below.

And then I saw its shape.

My eyes widened, and my jaw opened as an enormous serpent emerged from the depths.

A Black Fire axe appeared in my other hand, and I took several steps back, ready to call forth Darkness.

When the deep green head of the serpent rose from the waters, it whipped its gaze to me, locking eyes with mine.

A cry escaped me as my body shook from terror.

The snake rose farther and slithered onto the stone ground outside the pool, coiling several times, showing its enormous length. It never broke eye contact with me.

"I'm not afraid of you," I whispered through clenched teeth, trying to appear brave.

The serpent almost seemed to tilt its head to the side.

I looked to the water briefly. "I asked you for help!" I screamed. "Not this!"

I snapped my eyes to the beast's again, and it rose and angled its body back, as if it was going to strike me.

This was what Sethos was training me for. The world was never safe. This was proof of that.

The serpent lunged toward me, and I screamed as I called forth Darkness, erecting a barrier to protect me.

The serpent didn't break its course as it raced toward me. But at the last second, skimming my Darkness barrier, it angled its body up and took flight, soaring to the tree canopy.

My jaw dropped once more, and the beast turned a shade of translucent ice blue and launched itself at the burning trees.

On contact, the serpent disappeared and became water, instantly putting out the fires.

Water splashed against the foliage, and then everything became animated again. The cinders rained down, although now soaked and disintegrated into gray dirt, and water from the violent clash splashed onto the ground and bounced off me, soaking me through, and little droplets of rain filled the room.

I recalled all my magic then and lowered myself to kneel on the ground, looking up at the trees that were saved. Tears streamed down my face as the terror and whiplash of emotions passed through me.

Then a voice I had never heard before spoke inside my head.

Dretani.

24

SETHOS

When I portaled into Vasarys, the throne room in Vasarys was as dark as it always was, and I straightened my clothes upon landing before heading to the banquet.

My eye began to pulse, and I pressed my fingers to my closed lids to calm the nerves there.

My vision was one of the first signs Am-Re's magic was slowly overtaking me.

I dug my hand into my pants pocket and took out a tincture. It glowed purple in the dark, and the black in the mixture looked almost ominous as the liquid swirled.

I unscrewed the cap and took a swig.

As I wiped my mouth with my sleeve, almost gagging from the taste, something moved in the room.

"The king finally arrives," a dark, mocking voice said in the darkness.

I turned.

Perched on the throne—my throne—was Demira.

Dark black hair fell down her shoulders, giving way to a deep

V dress meant to scandalize. That was always Demira's goal. To shock.

"Demira-Titania." I grimaced as I pronounced her full first name. "You look cozy." I gestured to the casual way her legs were spread as she sat on my throne. Her dress barely covered the area between her legs.

She shifted, slightly opening her legs more, and laughed. "You used my full name." She scowled. "How official."

"If only Am-Re had given you his last name." I tapped on my chin and pretended to think. "Did he marry your mother?"

Demira's eyes were hard like steel. "I would invite you to sit here, Sethos, but only one person sits on this throne. And I rather like how the room looks from up here."

"It doesn't matter where you sit." I stepped toward her and crossed my arms. "The truth will always remain that your father did not name you as his heir."

Demira smiled. "Your words don't wound me, Sethos." She leaned forward.

"They are not meant to wound. They are mere observations. You simply didn't measure up."

She paused before answering and stood. "I wonder if my father would think the same . . ." She stepped down on the dais to where I was. "If he were alive, of course."

I erased any expression from my face.

Demira pointed at me. "But you killed him."

She took one more step toward me.

"And you took his power." She continued.

One more step toward me.

"Where do you go, Sethos?" She tilted her head. "You are missed."

"I don't owe you an explanation."

She cocked her head to the other side and crossed her arms. "You see," she said with a cruel smile, "you say that. But when you leave here, without an explanation, a majority of the nobles look to me for guidance because I'm the daughter of their last king. They ask me where you go. Who you are with."

"I leave Iagon in charge."

"And yet the people choose to listen to the daughter of a king." Demira brought her pointer finger up and outlined the top of my jacket, running her finger across my collarbone. "So what do I tell your people, great king?"

I grabbed her hand and threw it off me. "You can tell them I don't owe anyone an explanation." I moved past her in the direction of the banquet.

"And what of their support for you?" she yelled after me.

I kept walking.

"You know what you did," she yelled. "You convinced them all that you would be a better ruler than my father. That you would finally bring justice to the descendants of Isyos. That you would kill the gods."

I paused.

"Where are their heads, Sethos?"

I turned slightly toward her.

"The deaths you promised in exchange for their betrayal of my father when you led a coup to kill him." Demira stepped in front of me. "Don't you think, for a second, I have forgotten."

"Don't act like you cared whether he lived or died!" I screamed.

She tilted her chin up. "It's been over seven years of promises since you took a throne that by blood should belong to *me*. The nobles grow weary of their king."

I crossed my arms. "Tell me, Demira, does it sting that the only reason you are alive is because your father sought to have offspring that would inherit his magic? But when his magic skipped you, he simply went on to have more children, trying to find something he would actually like."

Demira flattened her lips into a tight line.

I leaned into her ear. "You are an accident of birth. And your father knew that. You should have died when your mother birthed you."

Demira stilled.

"Let's be grateful your mother didn't live to see what a disappointment you grew up to be," I gritted out.

Demira blinked several times.

I straightened and walked out of the throne room.

When I didn't hear Demira follow, I called back, "Make sure to close the door behind you."

"DON'T LOOK TOO excited to be here," my right hand, Iagon, said, leaning toward me, his voice full of humor.

I looked to my right at him and rolled my eyes.

He sat back, drink in hand. "You know these dinners drag on every night. What else are these people supposed to do? Am-Re hosted nightly banquets."

"Leave. Everyone should leave."

Iagon took a sip of his drink. "Am-Re set this palace up with the purpose of having the nobles live in residence. They are never meant to leave. They have no jobs, no occupations, no worries. Banquets keep them drunk and appeased."

"A bunch of fucking freeloaders."

"Who all have ownership in the Vasaryan mines." He set his drink down and turned to me. "Mines you need to fund the army you organized to attack the gods."

The milesea mines contained a mineral that fueled star crafts and other machinery, but it was outlawed by the Galactic Federation, which set standards for the safety and speed of all star crafts. Milesea was fuel on steroids and was used by outlaws to outrun Federation monitoring crafts. We exported and traded milesea on the black market. It was what filled the coffers of Vasarys.

"I know," I growled.

He shook his head. "I think you forget that you sit on this throne because of them."

I pinched the bridge of my nose.

Iagon pointed to the nobles around the room. "All of the people here backed you as the ruler. They helped you overthrow Am-Re."

"Iagon—"

"It's my duty as your second to keep you on this throne, and I'm telling you the people here are growing impatient. You have been gone for a month with no word and left me to fill in with excuses. You have not devised a concrete plan to attack the gods."

"I'm taking care of it—"

"It's been seven years, Sethos!"

Demira's laugh cut through my conversation with Iagon, and we turned to look at her. Two nobles were draped on her shoulders, one on either side, whispering in her ears.

I groaned and grabbed the goblet in front of me.

"Drink mine," he said and handed me the cup.

I discreetly passed him my goblet.

"They refilled your cup, and we cannot trust them." Iagon's voice was low.

I took a large swig from Iagon's cup.

"What's going on?" Iagon looked at me. "I have been patient with your absence, but I'm your oldest friend. You made me your right hand. Yet I never know how to respond to the councilmembers when they ask about your whereabouts."

"I know. I'm sorry."

"So?" he asked.

"I have found a way to solve most all of our problems, Iagon. Finally."

Iagon's eyes widened. "What do you mean?" He looked to Demira and then back to me. "Surely you don't mean you're heeding your councilmen's suggestions that you marry Demira?"

Iagon had confided in me of his love for Demira.

I laughed bitterly. "Marry the woman I can almost guarantee is behind both assassination attempts?" I shook my head. "Never."

"But marrying her would fortify your position as ruler. Demira's magic and yours . . ." He shook his head. "No one would question you."

"I'm not marrying her. I detest her."

Iagon leaned to look at the rest of the people seated at the table. I followed his eyes and paused on a beautiful woman with ebony skin and silver hair.

"Illona?" Iagon whispered, looking at me. "You will marry the second daughter?"

"Why are you trying to marry me off?" I growled. "Illona is far more beautiful than Demira, but she is not made for the rough life in politics, and you know it."

"So what's this solution you have conjured?"

I looked to my sides and saw that our table was now mostly empty. The only ones left were Illona at the end of the table and an older woman who was married to a councilman.

Illona shook her head as she looked at Demira and the scene she was making on the dancefloor with the noblemen.

Am-Re's banquets were known for their debauchery.

"If Illona would let me offer her hand to a prince from a distant land, her life would be better," I said.

"You have offered, and she has refused. Her life is her sister. Demira has also turned down the prospects you have selected for her."

I glared at Demira and her display.

"You cannot win with them," Iagon said. "Am-Re's children hate you, and that loosens the confidence of the nobles."

I leaned into Iagon and spoke in a low tone. "Not all of them."

Iagon's chin lowered, and his eyes darted between mine. "What do you mean?"

"I have found the heir of darkness."

Iagon froze. "Speak plainly, Sethos."

"Renna is alive."

Iagon's jaw dropped. "You don't mean—"

I nodded. "The bastard reincarnated her. I have found her at last. And she led me straight to the gods in Taria."

Iagon shot up in his chair, but I quickly dragged him back down.

"You need to tell the council!"

"And I will," I gritted out. "Give me some time."

"Time?" Iagon exclaimed. "You don't have time."

"Renna inherited the power of Darkness."

Iagon's face paled, and he suddenly looked ill.

"Sethos . . ." he said slowly. "That—" He shook his head. "That's—"

"*That*"—I cut in—"is how we will win our battle with the gods. It will restore the noble's faith in me."

Iagon covered his mouth with his palm. "We really *can* win this . . ."

I nodded. "We have hundreds of mages, warlocks, and star crafts ready to attack. Add in Darkness . . ." I smiled. "The gods won't have a chance to flee."

I could imagine it so clearly. Trapping them in Darkness while we attacked from all sides . . . Even if Renna trapped one at a time, every kill mattered.

A smile spread over my face as I thought about how killing each god, one by one, would be time well spent. I would favor their screams for mercy. Their cries for help. Seeing their bodies ripped to shreds . . .

Suddenly, a heavy, ominous feeling swept through me, making me feel off.

I shifted in my seat and cleared my throat.

"How did you find Renna?" Iagon asked.

"I will tell you that when I return." I stood and cracked my neck and my hands, trying to shake off the feeling that had overcome me.

"Is that where you go?" Iagon stood. "To her?"

I nodded.

"When will you bring her?"

"Soon. I imagine the nobles and council will want a demonstration of her powers. I have been training her."

"She's to be your pet?" Iagon laughed. "Exhibiting her like an owner? Does she purr when petted?"

Anger rushed through me, and I grabbed Iagon by the collar, dragging him off the dais and pushing him behind the table toward a hallway that ran along the back of the banquet hall.

He stumbled, and I pulled him into the hallway. It was empty.

"Speak like that again and I will cease to see you like a brother," I growled. "Never, ever, utter words like that in your fucking life."

The music in the banquet hall stopped, and loud murmurs floated from the room.

Servants began to peep into the hallway, their curiosity piqued.

"I'm sorry," Iagon said, rubbing his neck. "It won't happen again."

I pointed to the banquet hall. "Go back in there and fix the scene you have made. Ensure no one questions our argument. I'll see you soon."

Iagon nodded and began to move to the doorway.

"One more thing," I said.

Iagon turned.

"Keep an eye on the council members loyal to Demira. We need to start paying more attention to what they do daily. If they meet with her. Who is the latest noble she grants boons to."

"As you wish." His voice was quiet.

"Good."

I turned from him and made my way to my rooms. Portaling to Daya out in the open was out of the question since portals, when opened, revealed the image of the destination.

Pausing, I closed my eyes and tried to breathe deeply to will away the uncomfortable, heavy feeling in my body. When the feeling passed, I began to walk again.

"Leaving us again?" a male said behind me.

I stopped and clenched my jaw. I had an urge to clench my fist, but I slipped on my usual mask of indifference instead.

I turned to face the person in question. "Velos." I inclined my head. "Vasarys's treasurer. Shouldn't you be enjoying the festivities?"

He smiled, sliding a hand into his pocket while holding a goblet in the other, and walked toward me. "Am-Re hosted the nightly banquets so we would enjoy his presence." He tilted his head. "You have not graced us with your image in a month . . . I wonder what is so important that you neglect the throne we placed you on?"

My eyes narrowed, and I pointed a finger at him. "You ejecting Am-Re from his position was something you had no issue doing." I reminded him.

"Am-Re was my closest friend. He granted my family and me immortality. What mortal would turn that down? Once it became clear he was causing harm to all our pockets, we had to do what had to be done. To be immortal and poor was not something I wanted for myself and my family."

"And the suffering of the common citizens in Vasarys?" I snapped. "Their plight also played a role in overthrowing Am-Re."

He chuckled. "Of course." He put a finger up in the air dramatically. "Although I don't recall we ever foresaw Iagon becoming regent."

"I have been away looking for allies to fight the gods." I knew sticking close to the truth was the best course of action.

Velos drank from his goblet before speaking. "And the one-hundred-thousand-soldier army we are funding, which is draining our coffers, is not enough?"

"I need more time," I gritted out. "I am at a potential breakthrough. I won't fail Vasarys."

Velos lifted his eyebrows. "You know you can always count on me, Sethos. That is how this relationship works."

He snapped a finger, and a servant stepped forth with a tray and my goblet from the banquet table on it.

"To show you how much I continue to value you," Velos began, "I wanted to show you something . . ." He pointed to the servant. "Drink it," he demanded, gesturing to the goblet.

The servant blinked. "Sir?" he asked, looking between Velos and me.

"I said," Velos grated and took a step toward him, "drink from the fucking cup!"

The servant reached up, hands shaking, to the goblet and slowly brought it to his lips.

Iagon's earlier warning about drinking from my cup flashed through my mind.

Did someone try to poison me?

My heart beats echoed in my ears as I expected the servant to fall to the ground from poison.

My throat became dry, and my chest began to expand with uncomfortable tightness.

A third assassination attempt.

No.

No.

No.

The servant began to drink slowly. Liquid spilled from the corners of their mouth while their wide eyes moved between Velos and me.

I wanted to scream.

I clenched my fists to prevent myself from ramming the cup farther up so he would drain the contents faster.

When he was done and had settled the cup on the tray with trembling hands, I looked to Velos. I narrowed my eyes at the servant and took a step forward.

The servant coiled back as if I would strike him, and Velos chuckled.

I grabbed the servant by the shoulders and examined his face for any potential poison effects.

Nothing.

I pushed the servant back, and the goblet fell over on the tray.

Velos smiled and patted my back. "You see," Velos said, "I continue to monitor your food and drink for poison."

I forced a smile.

Velos lifted his own goblet in the air. "To your everlasting health," he said, without breaking eye contact, and drank from his cup.

The stakes I faced could not be clearer. I had to get control of Vasarys and defeat the gods.

Renna was essential to me as a tool of destruction, and I would not fail.

25

RENNA

I had a dretani.

I had a dretani.

How?

I paced around my room and massaged my scalp, where a dull headache had bloomed.

I had not slept at all and watched the night trickle into the morning. My eyes burned from exhaustion.

Why had Sethos not mentioned the possibility of me developing a dretani?

I recalled seeing Cylas's dretani, a majestic stag made of white, almost blinding light.

Besides him, Khellios and other gods had not talked about their own dretanis.

I wondered whether a dretani was a deeply personal part of one's identity, only to be shared in private like Cylas had done, or during battle to defend and fight alongside their person.

Did I have a dretani because of who my father was, which meant my half sisters also had capabilities for a dretani, or did all half gods have one or the potential for one?

My dretani being a serpent should not have come as a great

surprise. I knew my father's dretani was a golden serpent, and my magic stemmed from his. I wondered whether his serpent also took on different qualities like mine did when it became water.

I sat on my bed and continued massaging my head as thoughts rushed through me.

My dretani had transformed into water and saved the trees, but it had brought up healing waters with it because the trees now looked intact. I knew the healing properties in the water had cured and reversed the damage I had caused. Even the cinders that had turned into black mud had evaporated into nothing.

The room where the event had taken place looked like nothing had happened.

Part of me wanted to tell Sethos what had transpired and how I had solved the problem, but I was also scared for him to hear I could have burned the fortress down. This was his home and haven—especially with how unwelcoming Vasarys was becoming.

I didn't know how I'd react if someone told me they'd burned part of my home but "fixed" it and to not worry about it moving forward.

Khellios had not wanted me to use magic.

Would Sethos go back on his support of me using magic under his roof?

His hesitation about teaching me to portal made me uneasy. He had agreed to teach me after I pressed the issue, and I was grateful, but knowing I had set something on fire?

I closed my eyes and lay down on my mattress, my feet dangling on the edge.

I would not tell Sethos about my dretani right away. I would have to explain how and why the dretani emerged. I needed to let time pass from the burning incident.

Mind made up, I breathed easier and focused on reliving the moment I saw my dretani emerge from the waters.

Its beautiful deep green scales reminded me of the emerald color quality of my magic.

I wondered if my dretani would simply materialize out of thin air next time it stepped forth, or if water was important for its presence.

You are the daughter of a siren . . . My brain nudged me.

My eyes snapped open.

I wondered about my mother then.

Perhaps that was why water played a role in the beast I'd summoned.

I needed to somehow summon my dretani again by the healing waters to understand how it worked. I slid my eyes to the windows and the morning light outside.

Sethos was likely already in the fortress, so I couldn't do it now if I intended to keep it from him. I would need to wait until he left for Vasarys again.

If I could now wield Darkness without Sethos's help, I could learn to master my dretani as well.

Letting out a heavy exhale, I rolled over and crawled into bed and under the covers, willing myself to sleep.

Today, Sethos would teach me to portal, and I would not miss that for the world.

26

RENNA

I overslept.

And Sethos was not in a good mood.

"You slept through the morning," he growled. "My need to split my time between here and Vasarys grows. I am needed there again tonight."

"I said I was sorry," I sighed as he treated me with cold indifference.

Sethos pointed a sharp finger at me. "If I'm going to train you, and you're going to take this seriously, you need to wake the fuck up and be ready as soon as daylight emerges."

The muscles in my jaw clenched, and I crossed my arms. "I am taking this seriously. It was one mistake. One time. Don't talk to me like that."

"Well, can you be ready next time?"

My eyebrows shot up. "So unless I wake up on time, you're basically going to continue to treat me like shit?"

Sethos sighed and rubbed his face with his palms. "I can't do this today, Renna."

"Do what?" I demanded. "Train me or listen to how much you're being an asshole?"

Sethos lowered his hands and looked at me, his eyes cold. "Well, are you ready?" he snapped.

I lifted my chin. "Teach me to portal."

Sethos grabbed my arm, and within the blink of an eye, we were gone.

27

RENNA

We landed in the middle of the forest right next to a pond in a swoosh of air and swirls of black magic. Echoes of my screams from transit filled the air.

I pushed off Sethos's chest when my feet touched the forest floor.

"What the fuck!" I yelled as I stumbled back and fell.

Sethos crossed his arms. "You wanted to portal."

I pointed at him. "You gave me no warning."

He tilted his head and raised his eyebrows. "You said you were ready."

I pushed off the ground.

"Are you in pain?"

"No!" I crossed my arms.

Portaling stretched the body into what I could describe as dust, pulling and rearranging the fibers on a cellular level. I was thankful the portal we had just gone through was nothing like the one from the mirror.

However, I still felt out of sorts, like my joints were moving back into their correct positions. I was not in pain, but it was uncomfortable.

"I'm sorry," Sethos said softly. "I'm fucking up today, and I'm sorry."

I glared at him. "I get startled with sudden portaling because of the training Am-Re had me do as a child."

"How many times did Am-Re force you to portal?"

I closed my eyes recalling. "A handful of times. I never traveled farther than across the room." I opened my eyes and shook my head. "My subconscious blocked most of my training with him, but the feeling of pain and fear and the insults are fresh in my mind."

Sethos ran a hand through his hair and pressed his fingers against his eyelids. "I'm sorry." He shook his head. "I'm sorry I'm adding to what he did."

I was quiet for a few moments as I processed what had transpired today.

Part of me wanted to tell him that it's okay, shit happens. That I forgave him. I didn't want to fight with him. It was easier to push it under the rug. Move on.

But Sethos's rude behavior was recurring.

"You've treated me really badly, Sethos."

His fingers came off his eyes, and he blinked.

"You've yelled at me, made me feel like the worst sort of person for oversleeping, and portaled me here in anger. The way you portaled me here is the equivalent of manhandling."

Sethos was silent.

"That can't happen again," I said. "I didn't endure years of being treated badly to now be with someone who takes out their bad days on me."

Sethos blew out a breath dand looked to the ground. "I'm not proud of how I've treated you," he began. "My mother would be ashamed." He shook his head and ran his palms over his face. "I'm a fucking idiot. I know I am," he continued. "I'm sorry."

I was quiet for a few moments.

"Thank you for your apology," I said. "I can see you're under a lot of stress right now. I think next time, if you need to take a day and just sit with whatever emotion you have, you need to do that. You're entitled to have a mental off day. You cannot be on all the time, Sethos. You rise and train me, and then you leave and are in Vasarys until dawn. It's not healthy for you—or me."

"I know."

I nodded. "Do you want to take today off or—"

"No." He shook his head. "I promised I would teach you to portal today. Let me make it up to you." He took a step toward me. "Please," he said.

I needed to learn to portal.

I could sense the escalation of Sethos's stress from his time in Vasarys, likely indicating conflict with his enemies was near. I needed all my magic at my disposal.

"Alright." I nodded. "Let's train."

Sethos smiled. "You mentioned you don't really remember a great deal from Am-Re's portaling lessons. I'll start from scratch as if you've never portaled before."

I nodded again.

"Portaling is the ability to manipulate the body to materialize into another place. It can only happen if you mentally imagine and visualize yourself in the location you would like to be in. You have to force your body to pretend to experience what standing in that new place would be like. How would the surface you are on feel against your shoes or feet? What is the temperature? Will you shiver there or sweat?

"It's also about the smells and sounds. For example, if you're portaling to your favorite outpost tavern, you may want to imagine and recall what food they serve and the smells of fresh bread and tavern food. Is the tavern noisy with many star craft travelers? Is there live music?"

Sethos turned to face the pond. "Now, we're going to portal

across the pond. If it doesn't work, then you'll fall in the water, and no harm done. The water is shoulder deep. I'll be here to pull you out if you panic."

"So," I began. "It's all about altering my mind and putting myself in that location before I am there?"

"Correct. That and also using your magic to open a portal, and then it's a matter of stepping through."

"What if you have never been someplace?"

He lowered his chin. "I don't ever recommend portaling to a place you have never been. *However* . . . if you must," he continued, "I would recommend you speak to people from that area so they can describe it for you and you can imagine yourself there."

I frowned. "Would that work for portaling to a person?"

Sethos shook his head. "Not for you or me. That would be dangerous. The ability to portal to any person would be catastrophic for the safety of many. Source limits that power to gods not affiliated with an enclave and who are essential for the safety of supernaturals and angels."

I thought of Livina and Ukara and their essential powers of fate and war. It would make sense for them to portal to people and prevent conflicts.

Angels having the ability to portal to mortals in their care made sense as they were charged with aiding them.

"So, how does my magic open a portal?"

He flicked his wrist, and emerald and black magic appeared in his palms.

I followed suit, and the same type of magic appeared in my palms.

"Our magic can do so much. Just like you have learned to lift objects, you are the one who tells your magic what to do. You are in control. Close your eyes."

I closed my eyes.

"Now imagine that by waving your hand in a clockwise

motion, you have the power to create a doorway that is wide and tall enough for you to step through."

I moved my hand in a clockwise motion and imagined an oval a little over twice my height and width.

I opened my eyes and saw nothing. The magic in my palms remained ignited.

"That's okay," Sethos said. "Try again. You have only created something with Black Fire. This is new for your regular powers. You have to really imagine that you have the ability to create the portal doorway. It's not just moving your hands. *Remember*: it's the intention that matters when you are performing magic."

I cracked my neck and shifted my body. "Okay."

Once more, I closed my eyes.

I called forth more magic, and the familiar cold swirling sensation rose inside my chest and shot up to my shoulders, then down my arms to my palms.

I imagined the doorway once more and moved my hands in a clockwise direction. I could see the green and black delineation of the portal in my mind's eye with a black vortex swirling inside it.

I opened my eyes once more.

A faint outline of an oval doorway appeared but vanished into thin air just as quickly.

My heart sank into my stomach, and I clenched my hands into fists.

"Progress is progress," Sethos said gently. "You will get better."

I groaned and closed my eyes, preparing to call my magic forth again. "Once I make the portal, do I imagine where I'd like to go?"

"Ideally, you want to have the place you are portaling to in mind when you create the portal doorway. This is just an exercise to help you form the doorway as a first step."

A heavy feeling entered my system, and I frowned, opening

my eyes and stopping what I was doing. "What happens if I create a portal doorway with no destination in mind and simply step through?"

Sethos's eyes widened. "Never ever do that."

"Why?"

"You would be stepping into an unstable portal. You would not know where you'd end up. It would be like a lottery—leaving your portal to chance."

I nodded. "I understand."

I continued to practice portaling until evening settled, and it was time for Sethos to leave for Vasarys. My attempts had not been fruitful. I'd only gotten as far as creating a portal doorway but was never able to sustain it long enough to cross through.

As I hugged Sethos goodbye for the evening, he brought his forehead against mine.

"I'm sorry for today," he whispered.

I brushed my nose against his. "I know you are."

Sethos straightened up. "Will you let me make it up to—"

I rose on my tiptoes, wrapped my arms around his neck, and without a second thought, kissed him.

I was tired of waiting for him to take the initiative, and the tension that swirled around us was making me yearn for more.

I ran the tip of my tongue along the seam of his lips, coaxing him to open and let me in.

He moaned, and when he opened and I thrust my tongue in to taste him, he met me with his own tongue and explored me as well, his tongue sweeping to establish dominance, making my toes curl.

I pulled him fully against me, and aligned our bodies so that I could feel all of him, deliciously and suddenly hard.

Sethos moved one hand from my waist to the small of my back, his large palm taking up space and warming me, and the other to the crook of my neck, and tilted my head back with his nose to deepen the kiss.

I snaked my hands down to his jaw, fully throwing myself in the kiss, never wanting it to end.

When we came up for air, Sethos said, "I wish I could stay with you." His tone was suddenly melancholy, and I frowned. I felt in my gut that his words had a deeper meaning than him just leaving for Vasarys.

I could take Sethos's anger and irritability because I knew the stress he was under, but his sadness? That was my weakness. I wanted to cover him with a shield of protection and soothe his pain.

I could soothe his sadness with my body . . .

I craved him as much as he wanted me.

Could I make him forget the duties that pulled him from me?

Part of my mind screamed that I should wait for a better time because Sethos and I had argued and that sex was not the answer. My mind warned me his behavior was not normal.

But we lived a reality that was far from normal. It was harsh and cruel and was threatening to destroy us.

A sudden urgency filled me—one where I felt like a tomorrow with Sethos was not promised.

And I needed him.

"I want you," I breathed and moved my hand down to his chest and farther down still toward his abdomen.

Sethos smirked against my lips and grabbed my face, pecking me with innocent kisses until I moved my hand to the front of his pants and began to stroke him.

He moaned into my mouth, and our kiss became frantic and rushed. It was teeth and nips and whimpers and groans as we fought for breath before returning to the kiss. I gripped his hair and began to pull open his pants.

"I need you," I whimpered.

"Oh yeah?" he teased and moved his mouth to my neck, licking and sucking me there.

Sethos pushed a knee in between mine, and when his thigh made contact with my core, I moaned into his mouth, but he didn't relent.

"You're teasing me, mejtah," he groaned against my skin when he came up for air, resting his forehead against mine. "You know I have places to be."

I moved my lips to his neck and sucked and kissed the skin there just like he had done to me.

"Maybe you should stay with me instead . . ." I suggested.

He pulled back to look at me, smirking. "And why is that?"

I cupped his face. "Because . . ." I said and brought my hands to the zipper on my shirt. When my shirt gaped open, I moved to unzip my bra in the front.

Sethos followed my movements, and he groaned when my breasts were free.

"I need to feel you," I said. "And you've been driving me crazy."

Before I could do anything else, my back was against a tree, and Sethos moved his hands on either side of me, caging me in, while his lips latched onto a nipple.

I could feel him smile against my skin.

"Should I?" he said, letting his teeth graze my skin. "Should I stay, mejtah?"

"Mhmm," I said, tilting my pelvis toward him and arching my back. "*You should.*"

Sethos pushed against me, his cock straining against his pants, and I reached down again and moved my hand inside and gripped him. He was hot and silky and hard. I could feel the veins covering him, and I squeezed.

Sethos bucked and pushed into my hand, and I gasped from the force of him pushing against me.

He next moved his mouth to my ear lobe, sucking while kneading and pulling on my breasts.

I shivered and squirmed against him, and his leather top and zipper brushed against my nipples, the rough, cool metal of the zipper making my skin tingle and feel raw. My nipples hardened, waiting for his attention.

I grinned and pushed my chest out toward him.

"Fuck it," he said wickedly, pinching my nipples and pulling them toward him. "I'd rather stay here"—Sethos knelt, his face level to my breasts—"with you and these glorious breasts."

He laughed, and I moaned when he began to rub his face against my nipples slowly, his skin branding my already sensitive nipples.

"I need you too, Renna," he whispered, his voice now more serious, as he echoed my earlier statement.

I leaned my head against the tree and looked down at him, a small smile on my face.

He looked up at me. "I'm sorry, again."

I nodded. "For being a rude asshole to me or for keeping me waiting for weeks?"

Sethos's eyes turned dark, and he opened his mouth and clamped his lips on my nipple. His ice-blue eyes were on me as he suckled.

I whimpered, and my core throbbed as sensations shot through my body. I wiggled and pressed my thighs together to create friction.

"For both," he said and began to undo the laces on the front of my pants.

"I was starting to think you didn't want me like that . . ." I confessed, my voice husky. "That when you said you wanted to remain by my side you meant it as a friend . . ."

"Hmm," he cooed as his fingers worked while he moved his lips to my other breast and latched on. "Do friends do this?"

When he opened my pants and brought his fingers to my clit, I cried from the sensation.

"*Maybe?*" I offered.

Sethos released my breast with a loud pop. "Then you have some interesting friends," he said and began to circle my clit with his pointer and middle finger.

My eyes rolled to the back of my head.

"*But I wonder,*" he said and moved to my other breast and began suckling again, hungrier. He let my breast go. "If they move their fingers like *this* . . ." He pushed those two fingers inside me and curled them up, hooking them and pulling me toward him. "Will they bring you to the edge . . ."

I moaned and began riding his fingers.

"Yes . . ." he urged me.

I opened my eyes and watched as he worked me, his eyes trained on my pussy as he pleasured me.

"I need more," I whimpered.

Sethos moved faster. "More?" he asked.

I nodded.

"What you need, Renna," he growled, "is my cock."

Gods, I needed it.

"Give it to me," I begged. "*Please.*"

Sethos straightened and, with the snap of a finger, he was nude.

My eyes widened at how hard and dark his cock was, pulsing and straining at attention.

My mouth watered thinking of kneeling before him while I pleasured myself. I had wanted to bring him pleasure during dreamtime, and he had not let me.

"You have made me stay here, Renna," he growled, grabbing his cock, "when I should be working."

I bit my bottom lip and dragged my hand to my clit, rubbing myself as he spoke.

"And now," he said, stepping toward me, "you're going to make my time worthwhile. You're going to let me fuck you so I don't remember who I am or anything else going on in the world. You are the only thing that matters to me in this moment."

Yes.

"But first," he said with a slow smile. "*Kneel.*"

I could not kneel fast enough and immediately spread my legs. One of my hands went to my clit and the other to his waist. My core pulsed and pooled around my thighs at the thought of bringing him pleasure.

I wanted to watch him lose himself in me.

"Good girl," Sethos whispered and moved forward so we were lined up with his cock by my lips.

"Open up for me, mejtah," he groaned and pushed my bottom lip down with his thumb.

I opened and poked my tongue out to touch his length. His skin was smooth like velvet and tasted salty. It jerked against my lips.

"You're going to be the death of me, Renna."

In a swift movement, Sethos grabbed his cock and pushed into my mouth, filling me until I gagged and tears sprang from the corner of my eyes.

With a hand, he grabbed my hair and pulled my head back and forth, setting a slow pace.

"Do your friends do *this*?" he growled.

I moaned as he fucked my mouth, and I began to work myself, applying pressure to my clit how I liked.

After a few thrusts, Sethos cursed and pulled out.

In an instant, Sethos grabbed me, and I was airborne until my back was against another tree with my legs straddling Sethos's waist and my arms around his neck.

And then he thrust into my core.

I screamed as he filled me completely and breathed against his shoulder through the sting of his sudden intrusion.

Sethos stilled for a moment and, keeping one hand on my bottom, he cupped my jaw with the other. "Did I hurt you, mejtah?"

The initial sting began to fade.

"I haven't had sex like this in about three years," I admitted.

"Well, then." Sethos brought the hand that was on my jaw to my bottom. "Allow me to remind your body how it sings."

Sethos began to move me slowly, and my legs matched his rhythm by pushing my body up to meet his shallow thrusts.

"Gods, you're so beautiful," he murmured as he increased the speed.

I could feel my body clench around him, creating so much pressure I feared I would squeeze him out.

"You should see how pretty your breasts bounce every time I thrust inside you." He leaned down and licked one of my nipples.

I moved my hands to my breasts and cupped and squeezed them as he moved.

"Yes," he hissed. "Look at you."

Sethos snaked one thumb to my clit and began to rub as my body throbbed and pulsed around him.

I mewled and thrashed against him as he did with my body what he wanted, and I encouraged him to use me, getting lost in the moment until we wrapped our arms tightly around each other, spent and sweating.

Afterwards I'd remember each time I climaxed and screamed his name into the darkness surrounding us. The way his thrusts had become increasingly savage. I wondered whether he forgot his worries each time he thrust harder, his fingers digging into my skin, surely leaving bruises I welcomed.

I wanted to live in him and for him to remain inside me so that there was no beginning and ending to us. I wanted to be full of him so that my skin and body smelled of him. Sore of him so that my muscles remembered Sethos had been my choice—not some ridiculous notion of a mate.

When he portaled us to my room and we lay together, our chests heaving, and my leg draped over his, there were a few blissful moments of peace. Lying in his arms was preferable to the inevitable absence that filled me when he rose from my side to portal to Vasarys.

The same ominous feeling of being separated from him spread through me when he quietly dressed to leave.

I'd wanted to demand he promise that nothing bad would happen to keep us apart . . .

That allowing my heart to truly fall for him, as it was already doing, would not put me in danger of heartbreak.

But something inside me had known that to ask such a promise would lead to an answer I didn't want to hear. Vasarys wasn't safe for Sethos, and my father hunted him and I.

I wanted to believe I would have an opportunity to build a life with Sethos. That my body would never forget the imprint of him melding to me.

Stay with me, my heart whispered as I watched him open a portal to Vasarys. *Just stay with me.*

I wanted to stop time.

I wanted so many things.

Oh, how I wanted.

28

CYLAS

"Find my purpose," I muttered angrily as I raced through galaxies.

That's what Livina had called it.

Like a biblical messenger angel, Livina came to me after Renna left Taria to announce I was to follow Renna, who was with Sethos, to "find your purpose, find life."

In typical Livina fashion, she never elaborated on what I was to find.

Was Renna my purpose?

Livina refused to answer.

Find life?

I was the God of Creation. The God of the Planets.

She was ridiculous.

After Livina appeared to me, I petitioned Arios to assemble a group of gods to go after Sethos. I had spent millennia sitting back watching mortals destroy my planets without the authority to do anything about it. Source prohibited direct intervention in mortal affairs with the godsforsaken Trojan War of eons past as a cautionary tale of what happened when gods interfered in mortal conflict.

But this was different.

A supernatural had attacked Taria and threatened Renna's life. If we were banding together to defeat Am-Re's predecessor, we had to switch gears and pursue the new foe.

Arios refused to help, not wanting to dive into a war conflict. When I pressed, he began to personally attack me for all of a sudden "giving a shit" about matters concerning the enclave. He mockingly suggested I find help elsewhere—perhaps with his rival, Istron, the Chief God of the Elemental Enclave and also the God of Air.

And that was exactly where I was going.

I would not wait for Khellios to recuperate. He had embroiled Renna in this mess.

I would get her out of it.

I knew where Vasarys was, but I had to plan. Knowing the charms around Taria, Sethos had gone through a huge undertaking to attack Taria, which meant he would keep Renna alive. For now.

I should have taken more care after speaking to Sethos when I visited Vasarys last. I should have never underestimated him. I could have never imagined the extent of a mere fae's magic—especially one who had toppled Am-Re.

As I neared Delphinus Galaxy, I propelled forward to Moringa, the planet of the Elementals.

The planet Moringa greeted me with lush jungle greens and blues as I neared. It reminded me of planet Earth from a distance, with so much life visible from space. Unlike Earth, Moringa was exclusive to gods, which meant the typical mortal structures didn't exist. Gods on Moringa had very peculiar building tastes, often relying on the elements to build their palaces.

My skin boiled for mere seconds from the heat of the atmosphere, and the air pulled back the skin on my face as I descended. Air then enveloped me in a supersonic pocket as I navigated to Istron's palace, on the edge of a cliff overlooking the ocean.

"Cylas," the air spoke to me.

I slowed down.

"Istron," I said back to the nothingness. "You miss nothing."

The wind enveloped me.

"Unlike Arios, you mean," the god replied.

I laughed. "He suggested I seek his rival in solving a problem."

"How typical of Arios to turn his back on issues. I hope I may be of assistance. Come to my palace."

I nodded, knowing even if I couldn't see Istron, he watched me from somewhere. "I'm headed there now."

I landed in Istron's hanging gardens and blinked as I looked at the peculiar scene around me.

An elegant garden with floor pillows and intricate outdoor wooden bamboo furniture was before me with a pool in the middle. Surrounding the pool and draped on the various pieces of furniture were various Elemental Gods and nymphs engaging in . . . an orgy.

My eyebrows rose, and I tilted my head as I tried to understand the particular position the Goddess of Rain was partaking in.

She was on all four with her legs open while five male nymphs—

"*Cylas!*"

I spun to find Istron headed my way.

"You greet me with outstretched arms," I chuckled and returned his embrace. "I feel much more welcome here than in Taria."

"We greet the God of Planets openly and with appreciation always." Istron nodded. "See what your creation allows . . ." Istron's brown eyes gestured to the gathering before us.

"I—" My skin heated as I looked my fill. "This is certainly one way to enjoy my creations..."

Istron chuckled. "The lovely nymphs and dancers you see before you are performers sent by Misha, the delectable Goddess of Lust."

"I didn't know Misha sent nymphs to gods." I raised my eyebrows. "You must be on her good side. You have quite the gathering of gods here," I murmured and politely smiled to the gods and goddesses lying on several floor pillows, enjoying the dancers and nymphs.

"I recently granted Misha a favor, and as a token of *alleged* appreciation, she sent her performers."

"Ah." I nodded. "Alleged. You mean alleged because Misha siphons sexual energy." I narrowed my eyes as I noticed that each performer had a necklace with a red glowing crystal.

Istron laughed. "Exactly. She sent the performers as a thank-you, and the gods and goddesses here are delighted. However, the ever industrious Misha is siphoning their sexual ... er, energy for her enterprise. If you look closely, you'll see the red crystals exacting some of their energy."

"You don't ... *say* ... the gods here don't seem to mind at all," I replied, tilting my head to examine a peculiar position another god was engaged in with two nymphs in the distance. "To each their own." I turned to Istron. "You're not partaking?"

Istron shook his head. "I'm the chief god here, Cylas. Nearly all the gods in the Elemental Enclave are here for this gathering. Unlike Arios, I do not negate my duties. If we are attacked, I need to be alert. Besides." Istron turned away and began walking into his palace, gesturing for me to follow. "Livina visited me yesterday. She told me to expect you. She explained the situation with the attack on Taria and Renna Strongborn, Am-Re's daughter. I've been anxious."

Of course Livina would know I'd come here. I wished she'd told me to come here straight away.

"Hopefully Livina told you more than me."

Istron nodded, and we began to climb the golden stairs. When we reached the landing, an airy courtyard met us with lawn chairs and tables.

Istron waved for attendants to come by with refreshments, and food and drinks were set on a white iron table. Istron gestured for me to sit, but he remained standing.

"Livina is quite the busy goddess spreading impending doom," he chuckled. "She told me you would be seeking my help. But before we begin"—he pointed to the food—"we prepared food expecting your arrival today. Eat and tell me how I can help."

I grabbed a goblet of ambrosia and sat back. "I can always feel the electricity around conflict," I began. "I'm attuned to it because I am the creator god. I can always feel when wars are coming. It means the death of something I created."

"And for that, I'm sorry. You and Livina are kindred souls. You both feel death deeply."

I frowned and looked at my cup. No one had ever acknowledged the burden it was to feel my own creations dying or being destroyed.

"Thank you."

"So." Istron crossed his arms. "You feel war coming as a result of the attack on Taria?"

I set my cup down and leaned forward. "I do. It's a palpable energy. It's almost like I can taste the blood that will be spilled on my tongue. I can hear the battle. The armor clashing in my ears. Renna being under Sethos's custody is the catalyst."

"Have you spoken to Ukara about this? She leads the Army of the Ever Dead, you know."

I scratched the back of my neck. "Ukara and I seldom speak

nowadays. Her allegiances are with Khellios. He and I are . . . at odds often."

"I see. Ukara would be valuable to have in battle."

I knew that. But I would not rely on her alone to take on Sethos. She would likely already be planning an attack with Khellios and would ignore any suggestions.

I was diplomatic in my answer. These were becoming very fragile times. "Perhaps we will join forces in time."

Istron nodded enthusiastically.

"I am headed to Vasarys to get Renna. I know of Vasarys's location, and I will give you its coordinates. I need you and the gods here to fly a star craft outside of Vasarys in case I need help."

Istron stroked his beard, and a slow smile spread across his face. "It's been far too long since I joined a good battle. I thirst for it." He put his hands on his hips. "Count me in."

"Vasarys," a male said from behind us.

When we turned, a god with bronze skin, ice-blue eyes, and white hair stood at the landing, arms crossed.

"Berion," Istron said. "Nice of you to join us. Cylas has come to visit."

Berion ignored Istron and walked right up to me, his eyes narrowed. "Livina told us you would come here. You're seeking help in defeating Sethos. Sad to hear that a mighty god like Am-Re was killed. I respected his might."

I nodded, but an uneasy feeling spread over me.

"I'm sure our chief god, Istron, has informed you, the gods of the Elemental Enclave don't like to be told what to do?"

I pursed my lips.

"Perhaps we can"—Berion smiled—"convince them to join you. Many of them respect my counsel. Wouldn't you agree, Istron?"

Istron's gaze was hard as he looked at Berion.

"The gods here live a life of leisure and pleasure." Berion

gestured outside. "As you have probably seen. Why would they leave this life for battle?"

Berion's drawn-out conversation was irking me, and I narrowed my eyes. "You want something in exchange." I crossed my arms. "What is it?"

Berion laughed, his eyes glittering. He also crossed his arms and widened his stance. "My sister."

I lifted an eyebrow. "I don't follow."

"My mother and Am-Re birthed a child, Illona-Rene. As you can probably surmise," Berion said, "my dear sister lives in Vasarys. Am-Re raised her and has kept her there. I want my sister back. You need to retrieve her when you get Renna."

There was something off about his request. He didn't seem like a desperate brother seeking his long-lost sister . . . Why did he need his sister? Something dark moved within me and settled in my gut.

"You need me in the conflict with Sethos," Berion said with a smile that didn't reach his eyes.

He was right. Having the God of Fire on my side in a battle was imperative. The fire weapons we would be able to forge would be vital.

Berion extended his hand to me. "Do we have a deal, God of the Planets?"

"And if Illona doesn't want to go with you?"

Berion laughed. "Family is family. She'll be in good hands here."

"Take the deal, Cylas," Istron said suddenly.

My heartbeat pounded in my chest as I stretched out my arm. He shook my hand firmly.

"Great!" Berion's face brightened with an eerie smile. "I'll go round up the gods and goddesses," he said and let go of my hand.

Istron's face tightened slightly.

"I'll see myself out, old man," Berion said, patting Istron on the shoulder before sauntering off.

"You need him," Istron said after a moment.

"Apparently so do you. He acts like the chief god. Why would Berion want her here?"

"Something has been off about Berion lately . . ." Istron shook his head. "Much more than usual . . . Keep an eye on Illona when you come across her. I don't trust him."

I nodded and prepared to leave Moringa.

29

KHELLIOS

I stared out the window before me.

We had just jumped out of another galaxy.

We had traveled to two different galaxies with no luck.

Renna had left no trace.

I had failed her once more.

We had not received word of Cylas's whereabouts.

Nera was still missing.

I massaged my temples as I tried to think of how to continue the search.

"We will find her." Footsteps drew closer as the speaker approached me.

Two hands gently grabbed my biceps, and I dropped my arms down by my sides.

I opened my eyes, and blue eyes met mine.

"Khellios." Elrie's eyes darted as she searched mine. "It'll be okay."

"Your soldiers won't begin to question why they've been on a fruitless mission for weeks?" I shook my head. "They don't deserve this. Neither do you."

El set her mouth into a tight line. "My soldiers will do what I tell them. They are loyal to my father. They are loyal to me." When she saw I was about to speak, she cut me off. "They are mercenaries, Khel. This is what they do. They execute missions."

"And won't your father object to three of his starships being commandeered from his kingdom?"

El tilted her head and raised her eyebrows. "He knows I'm here. We promised we would be with you whenever you needed our help."

I nodded, but guilt wrecked me. "I feel I don't deserve it." I looked at the window behind me to avoid her gaze. "Not from you."

El was quiet for a few minutes. "I was young."

I wanted to clench my teeth. "I wish I could have—"

She cut in. "It's alright."

I looked at her now. This time, it was she who avoided my gaze.

She smiled softly. "You came into my life like a rogue fire. I had never met anyone like you before."

"You were too young to die."

"And impressionable." She looked down at her feet.

"I never made you any promises."

She shook her head. "I never expected any." She chuckled suddenly and looked up at me. "Who would want to compete with a ghost? I knew you were in love with Renna."

I swallowed a large lump in my throat.

"I always wondered what she looked like." Elrie smiled. "She is lucky to be loved by you."

I didn't know what to say, and I looked to the side, remembering my time in her father's kingdom.

"Do you still think me too young?" she suddenly asked, bringing my attention back to her.

"You're twenty-three. I'm much older."

"You made me immortal." Her voice took on a tone I couldn't understand. "I've lived twenty-three for a thousand years."

I wanted to ask her if she regretted me saving her life. I didn't regret saving her.

"I understand you now," she said quietly.

"How so?"

"You likely search for her in part because you have a fear of being alone."

There were many reasons I wanted Renna. I had never considered loneliness one of them.

"Being immortal is one of the loneliest existences in the world."

My voice cracked. "I never meant to cause you harm."

El smiled as her sad eyes observed me. "I know." She shook her head. "I must take my leave. I need to meet with the general to go over the coordinates for the next stop."

I nodded and looked to the window once more.

When she didn't move, she spoke up. "Khel?"

"Hmm?" I said absentmindedly.

"I need to go."

I turned back to her, confused.

She blushed and looked down. "You're holding onto me."

I then realized that while she had been holding onto my biceps this whole time, I had gently wrapped my hands under her elbows, holding her in place.

I cleared my throat and dropped my hands. "Apologies."

"I'll see you for dinner," she said as she walked away. "The soldiers want to speak with you more than in passing, by the way. I'll keep inviting you to dinner until you show up."

"I know."

"It might be nice for them to hear about the great Khellios's mercenary days across the galaxies."

I chuckled. "Are you sure they would like that?"

She turned her head slightly but didn't meet my gaze. Her lips curved into a secret smile. "*I* would."

She met my gaze then and quickly left the room.

I stood in the same spot for a long time, trying to figure out the strange feeling her look had stirred inside my chest.

Longing.

30

RENNA

I finally managed to portal a week after practicing.

It happened one evening when I was alone while Sethos was in Vasarys.

I was throwing spheres of electrical magic across the room, practicing my aim, when I wondered what it would be like to portal to the other side of my throw and catch the sphere.

So, when the next sphere left my hand, I immediately extended my right hand and drew a circle in a clockwise motion, imagining the end of the armory where the sphere was headed.

The portal opened, and without hesitation, I ran through.

My body evaporated inside the vortex and broke into trillions of pieces that felt like effervescent bubbles. I could see and *feel* all the colors of the rainbow in the portal, and each color had a temperature to it. Reds and warmer colors had a hot feeling while the darker colors, like purple and blues, had a cold, almost subzero temperature to them.

I felt it all at once.

The portal had so much sound too. Swooshing and echoes of words I couldn't quite understand filled my eardrums. It all filled me, but at the same time, it culminated into nothing as I was nothing.

Then, just as quickly, it all vanished, and I jumped onto solid ground, my body again whole. My hair swung around me, and my skin was flushed as if I had run a short distance very quickly. My heart raced, the beats echoing within my body.

I turned and caught the magic sphere in my hands. As the power crackled against my palms, I could only stand still, my chest heaving.

And then I screamed and jumped and laughed and threw my fist in the air as I rejoiced.

I had done it.

I had portaled.

Without duress from my father.

Without fear.

I felt unstoppable.

I dismissed my magic and sat on the floor, taking it all in.

Once again, my magic reminded me that anything was possible if I simply trusted myself.

I looked around the armory and felt Sethos's absence.

I was making incredible progress with my magic . . . and he wasn't around.

My head bowed.

I knew his absence wasn't on purpose.

Still . . .

That part of me that had been emotionally abandoned as a child wished he—or really anyone—could see my progress in real time.

I walked to my room in silence, my mood suddenly deflated.

Why was it that no matter how successful people could be, those with childhood trauma craved recognition and praise? It was a toxic cycle of thinking we weren't good enough unless someone acknowledged our achievements.

31

RENNA

"I think you're ready to increase your training today," Sethos said one afternoon when I was lying on the ground, face to the tree canopy above me in the throne room, my skin damp after portaling practice.

Portaling was my favorite activity—even more than using Darkness.

The supreme control portaling allowed me over my body was unlike anything else I had ever experienced.

Sethos was so impressed with my progress that we began to incorporate Black Fire weapons-simulated combat with portaling. He would attack me, or I would attack him, and we would portal to escape.

"What do you mean increase my training?" My whole body was sore, and I groaned thinking of what else he was going to throw my way.

Sethos raised his eyebrows and put his sword away.

"You've mastered Black Fire, object levitation, portaling, and know how to use Darkness. Now we raise the stakes."

My eyes widened. "I'm not following."

"I'm going to attack you in a way Am-Re would."

I scrambled as I sat up, and uneasiness spread through me.

"Am-Re never attacks the same way twice in a fight. It's my job you are prepared for the worst of it."

My heart jittered in its cage, and my lips trembled. "What will you do?"

"You'll see. I'm going to give you ten seconds to run."

There was no playfulness in his tone.

"Ten seconds isn't a lot of time—"

"You won't have time in a true attack."

"Can I use any weapon? Can I portal?"

"You can use your weapons. But"—he paused—"you cannot portal." He crossed his arms. "Not for this. I need you to deal with the attack head-on."

Anxiety coursed through my veins.

I also wouldn't call forth my dretani. I would keep it a secret for a bit longer.

"And you'll stop the attack if I ask you?" I asked quickly.

"Yes." Sethos's voice was serious. "Tell me to stop and I will."

I bit my bottom lip and looked around the room. We were in the throne room, and on each side were large archways that led to the forest.

I could run and hide among the trees to buy time.

Sethos squeezed my hands reassuringly. "Ready?"

I looked to him and nodded.

Sethos smiled. "One . . ." he said loudly.

Adrenaline shot through me, and I ran.

"Two . . ."

I nearly tripped on gravel as I ran into the forest.

"Three . . ."

As I ran, I could no longer hear him, and the darkness of the forest made me more paranoid that he would attack from behind a trunk or bush.

My feet carried me toward the clearing I was familiar with.

The sun beat down on me as I sweated, and I felt like passing out.

I called the Black Fire and my sword. I held it in front of me, my knees bent. Looking around me, I trained my eyes on the ground. I looked briefly to the ledge behind me and felt confident.

He couldn't fly . . .

Could he?

Suddenly, a great chilling cry pierced the air.

I lifted my sword high and whipped my head back and forth, my heartbeat almost blocking out all other noise.

The sky was empty.

I swept my eyes side to side.

Back to the forest.

My breath was loud.

Something black and emerald and gold shone in the sky.

I turned around, and all I could see were clouds.

I moved closer to the ledge.

A great gust of wind pushed at my back, and I spun around.

Emerging from the bottom of the cliff was a flying serpent beast.

It had flown right past the ledge and was now shooting to the heavens.

I had never seen a beast like this, and I stood stupefied as it turned its body around and quickly zoomed back down to the ground, coming directly at me.

The beast had to be the size of a skyscraper seen on Andora.

"Run, little Renna . . ." The beast's voice reverberated around me. "Run as fast as you can."

I ran toward the forest, but before I could get there, the beast let out an unnerving roar, and I turned around just in time to see it breathing Black Fire toward me.

Fight fire with fire.

I willed my magic to transform from a sword to a dome of protection.

The beast's fire made contact with the barrier, and I watched as the fire from its belly bounced off. As the shield deflected the attack, I could feel the strain of my magic.

I didn't know how much longer I could hold the dome, and I imagined a bow and arrows in my hands.

Once the weapons materialized, I aimed at the throat of the beast, who was still hurling fire at me.

As soon as I released an arrow, the beast dodged, and I screamed in frustration.

I shot again.

It moved once more.

It circled the dome, taunting me.

My fingers were sore from releasing arrow after arrow to no avail.

I wouldn't last against this beast, or one like it, with a sword and arrows since it had the power to rapidly move ...

I needed to distract it to get far enough away so I could shoot it from a distance.

What could I do to distract it?

Darkness.

I braced my feet, hands extended out.

I breathed out and imagined shadows emerging to protect me. Like my mental shield, I willed shadows to cover me with enough to distract my foe.

Darkness surged from me in a rapid vortex, and shadows emerged forming a wall of black that shot up to where the beast was.

Sethos's beast cried in rage as it avoided the dark wall of magic, furiously thrashing its head from side to side as it tried to find a way to get to me.

As the beast struggled, I ran until my lungs and thighs

burned. My magic stopped flowing from my feet and palms, and I turned for a mere second to see if the Darkness was still active. But that second cost me when I tripped.

The beast roared, and I flipped to my back. My magic slowly began to vanish like shimmering black stardust, revealing the serpent monster. From where I lay on the ground, I called Black Fire and shot an arrow straight to its head, not wanting to shoot Sethos in the heart.

With a glittering cloud of emerald, the beast disappeared and revealed Sethos, holding the arrow I'd shot in his hand.

He was naked and glorious.

I sighed in relief and lay back down.

"I can't believe that just happened!" I yelled, my chest heaving, and closed my eyes.

I could hear Sethos walk toward me.

"Get up," he ordered.

His voice was dark, and a shiver ran down my spine. I opened my eyes and saw a clothed Sethos with a Black Fire bow. He cocked the arrow he'd caught and aimed at me.

My eyes widened, and I rolled out of the way as he released the arrow.

I scrambled to stand and called the Black Flame, producing an arm shield and sword.

"What the fuck are you doing?!" I screamed as I ducked another arrow.

"You don't give up."

Another arrow sailed toward me, and I deflected it with my shield.

"Good!" Sethos encouraged me.

"Sethos!"

Another arrow.

"You fight until the very last breath leaves your body."

I looked up from the shield, and he was gone.

I whipped my head around, but suddenly his strong arms grabbed me from behind, and we portaled a few feet away from where we were standing.

"Your energy shield!" he gritted out through his teeth as we landed and rolled to the ground.

Lying on our backs, our chests heaved. I turned my head to look at him.

"Never let anyone touch you in battle. Always have your energy shield up," he said, breathless, and turned his face to me. "If they know how to portal, they can whisk you away." He brought a hand up to his chest and continued to pant. "Shooting from your dome was smart," he said. "Your own Black Fire weapons will pass through it. If you use regular weapons made of steel or any other materials, your shield will block them."

I was speechless as he spoke. All I could think about was his beast. I recalled the chosen animals of the gods, or dretani, used in battle to fight on their behalf.

"You also need to be faster."

"You have a dretani." I blurted out.

Sethos shook his head and pushed to stand. He extended a hand to me, and I took it, allowing him to pull me up.

"A dretani is only reserved for gods," he explained. "Am-Re's dretani is a flying golden serpent. Remember that. It will save your life."

I waited for him to continue.

"Am-Re's magic allows me to shift into beast form. That was merely a shift—not his dretani."

I couldn't believe how much of my father's magic he had.

"And half gods?" I asked carefully. "Can they have dretanis?"

Sethos frowned. "A half god?" he asked like it was a ridiculous question. "Like you?"

I lifted my chin.

"It's not what usually happens."

I crossed my arms. "But has it happened before?"

"Yes. But it's not the norm."

The manner in which he brushed me off made me angry, but I couldn't show it. My intuition screamed at me to keep my dretani a secret for the time being.

"Could someone be transformed into a dretani?" I asked.

Sethos shrugged. "If it were possible, I would imagine it like a perpetual, horrific sentence of servitude."

An ominous feeling spread through me.

"Does it hurt to transform into a beast form?"

Sethos blinked several times, and he looked down at his hands. "The magic flows so rapidly that before I have time to register the flash of pain, it's gone."

"What triggers your transformation?"

Sethos looked away from me. "Extreme bouts of anger. The need to destroy." He shook his head.

I wanted to reach out to him. "What triggered your anger this time?"

"Childhood memories of living with Am-Re." He turned his face to mine. "And the risk of losing you to him again."

My chest tightened.

"The ability to transform is not something I ever wanted. It provides an advantage over people with lesser magical powers. But against a large army, it can make me an easier target and potentially at risk of being killed, unlike a god who never has to dirty their hands in a fight."

Thoughts of Sethos being fatally wounded made my nervous system plummet.

"If Am-Re attacks"—I searched his face—"will you transform into beast form and fight him?"

Sethos observed me and smiled slightly. "Are you worried?" he asked.

"I am. I don't want you to get hurt," I said, looking up at him.

"Renna, I was trained in his army. I know how he fights. I know what to expect. I know the risks. I've killed for him many, *many* times."

"I will still worry."

Sethos closed the distance between us and ran his palms through my hair before cupping my jaw. He tilted my face up toward his.

"I know." His eyes roamed my face until they settled on my lips. "This is not the reality I want for you."

"Nor the one I want for you," I whispered back.

32

SETHOS

More than two months had passed since Renna arrived in Daya, and I was now shifting almost daily to train with her. I couldn't deny the toll it was taking on my body.

Each time I shifted into a beast, I used more of Am-Re's magic, and it consumed more of my soul, the black of his magic inching its way closer to my heart.

Shifting back to human form was getting harder as Am-Re's magic clawed its way around my soul while I was in beast form.

The only thing that helped settle me was the tinctures, and now I was taking five to six potions a day.

My time was ticking.

But I needed to train Renna to survive what was coming if she was to stand next to me and use Darkness to kill the gods.

I wondered if the gods would immediately turn against her after she used Darkness on them . . .

We had to be successful.

Luckily, I continued to encourage Renna to train her Darkness every day, and even her portaling was getting better, faster, stronger.

She was magnificent.

I spent all my days with her, and every two to three days, I would spend my evenings and nights in Vasarys.

What I would give to be by her side all hours of the day . . .

Renna was getting under my skin.

Sometimes I could forget why I was with her in the first place and pretend it was just the two of us living day by day.

Back in my rooms in Vasarys, I groaned, a melancholy ache spreading through me, and gripped the pool ledge I was sitting on.

Not wanting to think about Renna, I pushed off the ledge and submerged myself in the healing waters I had placed here.

I closed my eyes and let my body drift under the surface, glad for the quiet nothingness that was the waters here.

During quiet moments like these, I wondered what it would have been like if my mother hadn't died. Would I have remained at her side, or would I have been drafted into Am-Re's army for his campaigns?

My mother was always adamant that we remain in Isyos, and it was something that always troubled me. She was never forthcoming about the topic and would simply tell me that my place was in Isyos.

Perhaps that is why my hate toward the gods was exponential—my mother had told me my place was in Isyos, and they had killed her and destroyed the place where I was supposed to be.

Isyos was my last connection to her, and that was gone.

I would destroy Taria to show the gods how it felt to lose their home and loved ones.

I would show no mercy to anyone living there—just as they had done to us in Isyos.

An eye for an eye.

A soul for a soul.

A dark feeling spread through me then, similar to what I had felt outside the banquet nights before.

Movement in the water made me open my eyes.

A black mass swirled ahead of me, and the hair on my body prickled.

I reached out . . .

"*Sethos* . . ."

My ears perked up. Someone was calling me from above the water.

"*Sethos* . . . You have to come up . . ." the voice said.

Whatever had been in the water with me was gone.

I frowned and pushed up to the surface.

A familiar face met me.

Iagon stood with his shoulders squared, legs wide, and hands at his sides, in his typical military pose.

I wiped water from my face.

"I did not want to disturb you," he said apologetically. "You have been taking the cure"—he gestured to the water—"for more than an hour."

Had I been in the pool that long?

I felt like I'd been in the water for mere seconds.

"I did not realize," I said as I moved to the edge of the pool and pushed myself out of the water.

Iagon lingered, and I could feel his anxious energy.

He handed me a towel. "I know the strain of Am-Re's power weighs on you and that you need to use the waters to regain strength, but this is urgent," Iagon said diplomatically.

"What is it?" I snatched the towel from his hands.

Iagon shifted uncomfortably and crossed his arms.

I put a palm up in the air. "What?"

"It's Demira."

I frowned and wrapped the towel around my waist. "What did Am-Re's godforsaken daughter do now?"

"Leteah Demira," he said, using her formal title, which was one given to the daughter of an Ahtar, "held another meeting last night. Velos attended this time. He did not mask his attendance to the people in the palace. It's as if he wanted people to know he was going to visit her."

I massaged my temples. "Demira is an idiot. Velos is loyal to no one but his own pockets, which is ironic since he's treasurer."

"You know Velos has power, Sethos."

"But not magic," I pointed out.

Iagon nodded. "He doesn't have magic. But he has influence. And he *was* Am-Re's friend."

I laughed bitterly. "Some friend to Am-Re he was. He was the one who handed him over to me to kill. He agreed to the coup and set him up. He wanted power in the council. I gave it to him. I've made him richer than he could have ever hoped to be."

"For that reason, Velos meeting with Demira can't be good. You know that," Iagon added.

"I thought Demira would go away once I took power. The men clamor for her, she's not terrible to look at—despite her past. They don't care she's a young widow and the mess surrounding that whole episode."

Iagon grew quiet before saying, "Perhaps she is in mourning for her husband still?"

I rolled my eyes. "You see how she acts around the men in court." I shook my head. "Those are not the actions of a young woman mourning the love of her life. She turned down the latest marriage contract I drew up for her. She could have her pick of *anyone*."

"Perhaps she dreams of more than marriage?"

A bitter laugh left my lips. "*Yes.* She wants my throne. She wants me dead."

"I have more information . . ." Iagon continued carefully.

"Well?"

Iagon placed his hands on his hips. "My source at the meeting shared that because there has been no movement made on your part with the army, she is now promising new alternatives for finding the gods to take revenge."

I laughed. "And what would those be?"

"Demira speaks of a vision she had . . . It's raising a lot of eyebrows . . . and many are listening. She's planning to amass an army of sky beasts from Konah to attack the gods."

I paused.

Konah . . . the universe where Am-Re's remains had been disturbed . . .

"What kind of sky beasts?" I asked. "There are many that reside there."

Iagon paled and shook his head. "Metidons."

Blood drained from my face. "What?" I yelled. "She's planning to command an army of Metidons—the beast equivalent to a god?"

"I couldn't believe it myself."

Demira was on a suicide mission if she thought anyone could control the winged beasts.

"She's a fool. Those beasts don't take commands from anyone —not even gods!" I argued.

What worried me more was her spewing that she had received a vision of commanding the beasts . . . Lie or not, Demira's skills with witchcraft and clairvoyancy were impressive. People would be listening to her.

I wished now more than ever I could have inherited Am-Re's dretani. It would put me on an equal playing field with the gods. I couldn't only rely on Am-Re's magic. I needed the godsforsaken army I had assembled.

I needed to assemble my generals and cabinet immediately and tell them I had found Taria. I would tell them of Renna as a surprise once I brought her to Vasarys.

"How many people met with Demira?"

Iagon cleared his throat. "Yesterday's meeting had thirty councilmen. That's ten more than her previous meeting."

"Fuck!" I covered my head with my hands.

Iagon remained silent.

I was so close to winning the complete respect of my people.

"I need you to call a cabinet meeting immediately."

Iagon nodded. "Will you call for the arrest of Demira?"

I shook my head. "*No.* Unless she explicitly calls for my removal, politically, I cannot arrest her. The nobles and councilmen would rise against me."

Iagon regarded me with a careful stare.

"Let us wait until Demira slips up. We need her comfortable and reckless enough to make a mistake."

33

RENNA

Practicing the attack with Sethos in beast form and knowing my father's dretani would waste no time attacking me, like it had in my nightmares, urged me to call forth my dretani.

If I wanted to master my magic, this was something I had to learn.

My or Sethos's life could one day depend on it.

And so, I stood next to the healing waters, my hands buzzing with energy as anticipation built.

If I was able to portal, surely I could summon my dretani again.

I hovered my hands above the water and closed my eyes. I called my magic forth, letting the electrical currents travel from my core down to my arms and concentrate on my palms.

"Water . . ." I whispered. "I'm not entirely sure if this is how it works, but I'm going off instinct . . ."

The air stilled, and like before, the sound of a high-pitched bell chime echoed around me.

There was a pause as if whatever magic was in the waters was waiting for me to bring forth a petition.

I opened my eyes.

"Show me my dretani."

The air continued to stand still, as if holding its breath.

I looked around me, expecting to see maybe magic in the air. Nothing.

I looked down to the water, expecting to see it glowing. Nothing.

I cursed and began my petition again.

Again, nothing happened, and the stillness that had filled the air moments ago began to vanish.

The voice I had heard when my dretani emerged was also nowhere.

I pulled at my hair after a few more tries and stood, my frustration threatening to spill over.

Defeated, I turned from the pool.

Familiar feelings of unworthiness began to creep over me.

Had my dretani been a one-time thing?

I began to understand why Sethos said dretani were not common for half gods, but as doubt began to seep into my bones, I shook my head to clear my mind. I had come so far with my magic these last months. I wasn't the same person I was a year ago.

I would try to summon my dretani again.

I would not allow myself to quit now.

Sadness spread over me as I thought about how I was concealing my dretani from Sethos, but I knew I was doing the right thing.

I hoped he would be proud of me when he could see me summon my beast.

34

SETHOS

I leaned forward on the long table in front of me and massaged my temples as councilmen around me yelled profanities at each other and argued. We were trying to find funds for the army.

Iagon side-eyed me from his seat to my right. His elbows were on the table, hands fisted together against his mouth to prevent him from speaking out.

I was losing control of the council meeting.

Just like I was losing control of Vasarys.

Everything was a nightmare.

A council member shot up from his seat and pointed at a member sitting across from him. "Perhaps we should ask the Ahtar what he would do so we can stop speculating for once!"

The man being pointed at shot up and leaned across the table, his face red and eyes wide with rage. "Your side bolstered his claim to the throne, and now look at where we stand!"

The first man slammed his fists on the table. "Watch your tone for you verge on treason with a faint suggestion he should not be on the throne to begin with—"

I rose. "*Enough!*"

The men turned to face me, along with the rest of the bodies present around the table.

I closed my eyes briefly and took a breath. "How many trading partners have we lost since the beginning of the year?" I asked the man seated to the left of me.

The man in question, Brakzo, folded his hands calmly. "Four partners have pulled out of deals. As your Minister of Commerce, I have to tell you it's not good." He looked at me briefly, then glanced back down at his hands.

A familiar person spoke up. "We have lost thirty-three trading partners in seven years. A pity."

I looked to the person who had spoken at the end of the table. *Velos.*

He grimaced.

Iagon growled and stood, leaning over the table. "You sound pleased, Velos."

Velos smiled back to the room, baring a row of sharp yellow teeth. He reclined back in his chair and folded his hands on his rounded stomach.

"Not pleased," Velos said to the room. "The situation in Vasarys pains me greatly. Our economy was already in decline in the last years of Am-Re's reign."

Men nodded in agreement.

"We want Sethos to succeed," Velos stated. "Many of us supported his claim to the throne. After all, Sethos was born in Isyos. He is a child of the Night of a Thousand Tears. He has vested interest in our success . . ."

A cruel smile formed on his face.

"*But.*" Velos paused and looked to the men seated before looking straight at me. "I did warn you all, deposing my old friend Am-Re would have consequences. I hoped we would not be in this position."

The room was silent.

"Am-Re was not native to Isyos, but our planet flourished under his guidance. At the time his leadership brought many insurmountable riches."

An ally of Velos spoke up. "We want to get back to a time of prosperity. The Minister of Commerce has spoken: we are in the red. Vasarys cannot function with the deficit and also successfully wage a campaign to attack Taria."

"And leaving Vasarys is not an option," Velos added. "The milesea mines harvested by Am-Re in here have existed for two millennia. We cannot simply take them with magic elsewhere and start anew."

Watching the men around me nod in agreement with Velos as he slowly controlled the room made me simmer with rage. I knew he didn't care who sat on it as long as his pockets were rich.

I leaned back on my chair, trying to appear cool and unaffected before speaking. "Velos, thank you for being so vested in the welfare of Vasarys. I know more than one council member wishes they had the wealth you have amassed over these years. I'm sure, should the kingdom need to borrow coin, you would be the first to offer us stability."

Velos narrowed his eyes. "But of course."

I nodded with a forced smile, and it took everything in me not to roll my eyes. I spoke to the room. "I know the situation isn't good. When you all supported me seven years ago to depose Am-Re, I promised justice against the gods." I stood. "I know where Taria is."

The men in the room gasped, and several shot to their feet.

Velos was the only one who sat in silence, his face revealing nothing.

His reaction was . . . *odd*.

My eyes narrowed into slits.

"Where is it?" the closest commander to me asked.

I waved toward a cartographer in the corner of the room with a map of Andora, and he rushed to me.

He set the map down and spread it over the table before me.

The cartographer offered a marker, and I began to draw out the coordinates.

"Velos," the Minister of Commerce gritted out. "How is it possible that Am-Re never found Taria? You were his right hand? Did he simply stop looking?"

Velos picked lint off his shoulder. "Am-Re had many things to take care of and attend to," he replied, entirely unbothered.

In that moment, I *knew* Velos knew where Taria was.

Am-Re perhaps had known as well.

Am-Re's and Velos's constant fundraising for a battle that I knew now they would have never pursued was pure corruption at its finest.

Rage swirled inside me as I realized I was the only one who would bring justice to my people.

I wanted to kill Velos on the spot, but I needed him and his influence.

"We need to do what we must to fund the army," I said to the room. "Someone provide a solution *right now*."

The minister to my left spoke.

"Sethos . . ." He shook his head. "We do not have the money to sustain the military camps on Vasarys for another six months. The mages and warlocks are demanding higher coin for their participation in this war, and we need them. Your magic is impressive, but we need multiple supernaturals to help defeat the gods."

The military commander who stood by the door listening nodded to me in silent agreement.

"So what are our options?" I asked the minister.

He sighed. "I know you don't want to hear it, but we *need* to increase production in the mines and reduce our prices to entice buyers. I have devised a plan where we could see a twenty percent increase in profits in just a few short months."

I clenched my jaw to stop myself from verbally objecting. "We don't have months to wait to attack!"

The minister shook his head. "It's the only option we have now."

Velos spoke up. "Sound advice, minister. Let us raise production in the mines. It's a plan I have stated for many months."

My head snapped to Velos. "You also assured the men assembled here that you would make sure our trade partnerships would remain strong."

"That I did." He nodded with an exaggerated sigh. "You also recently appointed your own minister of trade."

I leaned on the table. "I had to. The last person on that post, *your brother*, was caught embezzling funds."

Velos stood. "And what a pity he died after discovery of his misdeeds before I could clear my family name."

Iagon chuckled next to me. "It would take more than that to clear your name."

Velos seethed toward Iagon. "You have no place here."

"Velos, you forget yourself." I reminded him.

Velos chuckled. "I forget myself?" He pointed to Iagon. "You mock us by appointing a low-birth mortal as your right hand! And he dares to insult me."

Iagon bristled and put his hand on the hilt of his sword, and I put my hand on his chest to halt him.

"And you could have been up for the job as my right hand?" I snapped to Velos.

"Any of us!" he yelled. "We have supported you for years!"

"It seems you have a long list of grievances."

"Not just me, sir." Velos retorted. "I refuse to leave this room until you commit to increasing production."

I looked to the two councilmen in charge of the mine workers and mining infrastructure. "What is the risk to the workers?" I demanded. "Can our equipment handle the increase?"

One of them answered. "The risk to the workers would be minimal. We can adjust the systems in place as needed."

"That's not a ringing endorsement," I snapped. "The regular citizens of Vasarys are the ones suffering the most today. I will not have them die in those mines."

"They will suffer more if we continue in this decline." Velos interjected. "They either die of hunger slowly, or we take this chance."

I looked to the councilmen overseeing the mines and jabbed a finger in their direction. "If I agree to this, you are responsible for the well-being of the workers and their families. I need you to report to me weekly about the health and status of the workers. I want *no* children in the mines."

They nodded.

I looked to the minister next to me. "How long do we have to act?"

"We don't." He straightened in his seat. "Sethos, you need to make a decision."

When I became Ahtar, I never imagined dealing with a financial crisis. I never anticipated our trade partners pulling from us because of how closely connected they were to Am-Re. My only goal had been to avenge the night of terror unleashed on Isyos. Now I had to keep Vasarys from collapsing. The responsibility to my people was like a dead weight on my shoulders.

I wanted to scream as rage and anger rose within me at the impotence I felt. My magic stirred within me like a chaotic storm lashing to get out. My skin bristled with magic as my anger begged me to shift and transform into the beast within.

I looked to the minister and nodded. "Do it." I pushed off the table and stormed from the room.

I barely made it to my rooms before the beast inside gnawed at me with sharp fangs, crawling from me. My bones began to break in the sudden rush, and I quickly portaled to Daya.

35

RENNA

It was raining in Daya, and I marveled at the droplets gathering and rolling on my skin.

I was in one of the large inner courtyards of the fortress, and I had come outside as soon as I heard the rain to try and summon my dretani once more. I thought perhaps with rainwater it would work. But my dretani was nowhere to be found. The voice I had heard from when my dretani emerged was still silent.

I tried to be positive as the water came down on my body and closed my eyes, taking deep breaths to banish the disappointment I felt.

But then, a terrible roar split the air. The water pooled at my feet trembled as the floor beneath me shook.

Part of me wanted to run inside, but an electricity filled the air that I recognized. It felt like my magic . . .

Sethos.

I lowered my hands and searched the night sky.

The roars in the sky were different from the typical sounds his beast normally made.

He was angry.

My body trembled.

A flash of emerald and gold scales flew overhead, and my mouth dropped open when his beast dove for the courtyard.

He was terrifying. And marvelous.

The beast settled in the courtyard, its great body filling the entire space and coiling around me.

The beast lowered its head toward me, slowly advancing, emitting a low growl.

Its eyes were entirely black this time . . .

Not ice blue like Sethos.

Its throat moved, and I imagined fire building there.

He wouldn't hurt me.

The beast opened its mouth and let out a terrifying roar that shook my body.

Sethos wouldn't lose control.

Right?

I clenched my fists and kept my body still, forcing myself not to blink so I could look the beast in the eye.

"You won't hurt me," I said in barely a whisper.

The beast slithered closer, its eyes furious, and began to recoil, as if gaining momentum to strike.

I took a step back.

"Sethos?"

The beast thrashed its head side to side and roared again, the vibration of the noise rattling my bones.

I had to trust that Sethos wouldn't hurt me.

And because of my unwavering trust in him, I didn't erect my energy shield.

I didn't call any Black Fire weapon.

I didn't call Darkness.

And I didn't have time to scream when the beast's tail rapidly slithered and coiled around me and began to squeeze my body in a death grip.

I struggled against it, the breath gone from my lungs.

I wanted to scream and tell Sethos to stop. I knew Sethos's ability to turn into a beast came from my father's magic, and I wondered what had happened for him not to turn back into the Sethos I knew.

Sethos believed in my strength to fight against my darker urges that stemmed from my father's legacy.

Did he have the ability to also fight back?

Would he fight back for me?

As my lungs burned and screamed for air and my throat began to close, my mind began to float. Everything suddenly felt lighter somehow.

My muscles relaxed, and my head dropped to the side.

Let go . . . a voice whispered.

Suddenly, the thought of letting everything go silent seemed like bliss.

I looked up at Sethos's beast as my body began to convulse.

My eyes closed.

Through closed eyes, I saw light flash, and the grip around me vanished, and I fell to the ground.

My eyes cracked open, and I watched as the beast disappeared and Sethos, the man, fell naked to the ground.

As I sucked in air, my body protested with the sudden oxygen, and I coughed violently, my body spasming painfully.

I reached an arm toward Sethos. My throat was still raw, and no sound came out.

I watched in horror as the rain bounced heavily off his unconscious body and slid to the ground beneath us, where it had begun to pool.

I screamed internally in panic as I watched him.

Was he dead?

No.

No.

I needed to move!

I pushed onto my forearms and began to slide toward him, my heart beat galloping out of my chest.

"Sethos?" I whispered as much as my sore throat would allow, but the rain drowned out my voice.

Nothing.

And then, my eyes zeroed in on the smallest muscle movement of his shoulders.

I froze.

In an instant, Sethos began to push his upper body up on his palms.

"Sethos?" I asked again.

Slowly, he moved until his arms were extended and he sat up, leaning forward on his arms. His head was down, his silver hair covering most of his face as the rain pelted down.

I groaned as I also pushed my body to sit up, and my muscles shook as I worked my way to a kneeling position. As my breath struggled through my lungs, I was able to eventually push to stand, and I walked to him, each step feeling stronger.

I knelt by his side and placed my hands on his bare shoulders.

"Talk to me," I whispered.

Sethos stilled, and after a few minutes, he turned his face toward mine.

Ice-blue eyes met mine, and the look on his face of pure shock and immense grief made my breath hitch.

He shook his head and reached for my face with one hand as if he couldn't believe I was there.

"Renna . . ." His voice was shaky.

I pressed his hand to my cheek.

"I thought I . . ." His voice broke off. "I-I'm sorry."

I sat on the ground in front of him. "What happened?" I said, pushing hair from his face.

With his other hand, he cupped the other side of my face.

"It was like I was in a haze," he said and began to frantically look me over. "I lost control of the beast. It overtook me. The magic made me . . ."

I brought our foreheads together. "You would never hurt me," I murmured. "It's my father's magic."

He nodded against my forehead and closed his eyes.

"I thought I killed you," he said after a few moments. "I didn't want to move after I shifted for fear of seeing you dead."

I didn't want to tell him that I thought he would kill me too. Of how easy it felt to just give in. Of my brain tricking me with my father's voice in those moments, taunting me to end it.

"I didn't mean to . . ." he said, looking at the ground. "These last few days have been hell . . ." Sethos broke from me and pulled at his hair in frustration. "I'm sorry for letting this anger get out of control—"

I put my fingers on his lips to silence him.

Sethos looked up.

"I don't want to lose you," he said, his voice breaking, and I could see him begin to spiral into a pit of anxiety. "Everything is slipping from my grasp—"

"Sethos—"

"I don't understand my body anymore—"

"Sethos—"

"And—"

I didn't know how else to silence him, so I kissed him.

And I must have stunned him so much he finally quieted, and he threw his arms around me, gripping me to him, and began kissing me back.

I could feel the tension in his body wrapped like a tight coil, and the way he clung to me and moved my body to get better access to my mouth, my neck, and my chest as he ripped open my shirt, I knew he needed this.

And I wanted him.

The thought of losing Sethos made me frantic, and I wrapped my arms around his body, pulling him closer, and with one quick movement, he shifted me so I straddled his naked body.

When he pulled back, brought his mouth to my nipple, and began to suck, I moved my body against him to relieve the pressure building in my core.

I tugged his hair as I closed my eyes, and a kaleidoscope of colors exploded behind my closed lids as he suckled and pulled my nipples one by one into his mouth.

I reached down to his cock and wrapped my fingers around him. He was stiff and ready for me, straining between my stomach and his torso, and Sethos moaned as I moved my hand up and down his length.

"I'm going to stand up with you," he said after pulling his mouth from my flesh. "And get us out of this rain."

I nodded, and in a flash, we were inside, and I found myself against a stone wall, Sethos caging me in with both arms, his mouth pressed against the underside of my jaw as he peppered kisses on my skin.

"I never want to lose you," he said in between kisses and then looked up. "Stay with me," He searched my eyes. "Always."

"You have me," I said gently and wrapped my hands around his waist.

The look of desperation in his eyes suddenly made me fearful, as if Sethos knew something I didn't.

"Why are you so scared?" I asked him.

Sethos didn't answer me but merely pulled me against him and kissed my lips, devouring me as our tongues met and breaths mixed. Sethos pushed his cock against me and then he unlaced the front of my pants and yanked them down.

I hastily helped him pull my pants off the rest of the way, happy that I had been barefoot. Next, he ripped off my shirt the rest of the way and discarded it over his shoulder.

As I stood naked before him, my magic moved within me, and I felt it reach toward him, as if it was grasping with desperate tendrils to hold him to me.

Sethos must have felt the magic around him because he smiled sweetly for a moment, but the sweetness was quickly replaced by wildness as he hoisted me up around his waist. With one hand, he reached down to my bundle of nerves and began stroking me, making the heat inside me rise until I cried out, begging him to take me.

"Tell me to stop," he said frantically between kisses.

I knew I couldn't ask him to stop.

I didn't want to.

"Don't stop," I whispered and gripped him closer to me.

In one quick thrust, Sethos was inside me all the while his touch on my clit was painstakingly slow as if he wanted to drive me insane with want, and I pushed my body against him, urging him to move.

I felt so full of him and so hot and flustered, I needed more.

When Sethos's lips curved into a smile against my mouth, I knew he was doing it on purpose.

"Move!" I yelled as I gripped him closer with my legs.

"I believe the words you are looking for are, fuck me," he said, suddenly thrusting. "You want me to fuck you, don't you? You're so slick and wet for me."

I cried out as he increased his speed.

"Do you feel that?" he growled. "How your walls squeeze and milk me, trembling around me as your orgasm builds? As I take you against this wall?"

I felt bliss, and I never wanted it to end.

"Do you want me to come inside you, mejtah?" he asked. "Do you want me to fill you with my cum and then greedily push it back inside with my fingers you so that it never leaves? Do you want to watch as your swollen pussy tries keep my fingers inside you as I make you come again from that alone?"

"Yes!"

"You're going to be so full of me that your pussy will weep with the remnants of me for hours and days to come."

I wanted everything.

And he gave it all to me.

Later, when we lay in my bed after he portaled us there, I was draped over Sethos's bare torso. Sethos lazily moved his fingers along my back, creating shapes.

"Do you hate me for the monster your father's magic has made me?" Sethos suddenly asked.

His words broke my heart, knowing all he had done for me. I lifted my head to look at him. "I will never look at you like that."

"And what do you see when you look at me?" His eyes moved back and forth between mine as if he was hanging on every word I was saying.

I pushed my body up to move closer to his lips. His face was now mere inches from mine.

"I see someone who has been molded through pain." I cupped his jaw with one hand. "But I also see someone who loves deeply and protects those around him. There is goodness in you, Sethos. I'm glad it was you who was chosen to be my soul guardian. It brought you to me," I said against his skin, feeling my body on fire.

Sethos stilled.

"What's wrong?"

He let me go and sat up.

"Sethos?"

Ignoring me, he swung his legs over the bed. "I have a lot on my mind, Renna. The situation in Vasarys isn't good. My people are losing faith in me to bring justice to our Fallen."

I gently placed my hand on his shoulder, but he shrugged it off.

His dismissal stung.

"I have vowed to help you in battle," I said. "What can I do now to help you? Tell me and it's yours."

Sethos turned and stared at me for a long while before answering. "Yes. There is something you can do."

I lifted my eyebrows to signal him to continue, and he stood.

"I am bringing you to Vasarys in a few days' time."

Shock spread through me and my breath paused in disbelief.

"I will show my people that we have the power of Darkness on our side to defeat the murderers of our people." He lowered his chin. "Your people too."

I nodded.

"This is not just my vested interest, it's yours as well. You may not remember your first lifetime, but you were born in Isyos, and you were there when it was attacked. In many ways, you also have a duty to the Fallen."

I thought of my half sisters and how I would be received once I arrived in Vasarys.

"And what of Demira and Illona . . ." I began to fidget. "Will they accept me?"

Sethos growled and he began to pace the room. "We don't need them to accept you. We need them to fear you."

I lowered my chin and lifted an eyebrow. "*Fear me?*"

Sethos stopped pacing and faced me.

"To be a formidable soldier, Renna, you have to be feared. That is how you earn respect."

My father led me with an iron fist and a healthy dose of fear.

Was that what I wanted for my future? My father had stolen my family with his hatred. If I had the opportunity to mend the bridges with my sisters, would I take it?

"I don't know if I agree with that entirely, Sethos . . ."

I bit my fingernails.

"To lead with fear." I shook my head. "I have vowed to help you in battle because I believe in your cause, not to become tyrannical through my powers. There's a difference."

Sethos turned from me and walked toward the window.

My chest tightened. "Are you angry at me?"

Sethos ignored me and continued to stare outside.

I frowned and moved from the bed to stand. I crossed my arms. "I'm talking to you."

Sethos did not turn around when he spoke. "It's late. I'd rather not argue."

I shook my head. "No. Let's talk about this. We just had sex. We can't just avoid—"

"*I said*," Sethos snapped, now looking at me, "I don't want to argue."

I swallowed and fisted my hands. "Then get the fuck out of my room," I gritted out. "I won't stand here and have you be an asshole to me after I gave myself to you."

Sethos clenched his jaw and stormed out, slamming the door behind him.

I stood in silence, my brain not knowing what to do with the whiplash from Sethos's back and forth.

36

CYLAS

y arrival in Vasarys was as chaotic as could be imagined.

I had portaled here one other time, when I had spoken to Sethos months before and asked him to leave Renna alone, thinking I would meet with Am-Re.

Portaling here a second time was no easier than it had been the first. The wormholes outside of this particular black hole were ever changing.

I arrived in the throne room, apparently during a council meeting of sorts, as several men in black robes sat in an audience, listening to a man talk from a podium next to the throne.

I now stood with several soldiers pointing weapons in my direction, my magic creating a green barrier of fire around me to ward them off.

I waited to speak with Sethos.

The black pool of healing waters was in the middle of the room as evidence of Am-Re's weakness in how much the black magic he wielded consumed him.

"Anyone want to go in for a swim?" I asked the guards.

They merely growled at me and closed in.

"You realize, none of your jabby weapons will actually work against me?" I asked the soldiers. "This"—I gestured to the ring of fire—"is just a kindness on my part so I don't kill you and further inflame relations with your boss."

A soldier growled fiercely at me, and I rolled my eyes.

"You puny little mortal," I whispered.

"Who the fuck are you?" someone said.

I spun to face the speaker.

Angry violet-colored eyes greeted me at the end of the throne room.

A woman.

A very beautiful woman.

A lazy smile naturally formed on my lips as she approached, her fists clenched.

I raked my eyes over her body as she moved. She was about average height, lean in a muscular way, if her toned bare arms indicated anything. My eyes moved to her bosom, which was on the smaller side, but I didn't care.

My tongue would not care.

All women were beautiful to me.

Especially angry women.

"Every time I come here, there seems to be another in charge," I quipped. "I *much* prefer this latest version."

The woman almost growled, and purple fire rose from her palms.

I jumped slightly and frowned.

She wielded Violet Fire.

Interesting.

"Step back!" she yelled at the soldiers.

The soldiers immediately retreated in unison and lowered their weapons.

"That's hot," I breathed.

She lifted her chin and stepped forward, stopping at the

border of my shield,

She crossed her arms.

"You play with fire, little witch," I growled in warning. "Do you want to get burned?" I gestured to the magic surrounding me.

"Who the fuck are you?" she snapped.

I opened my mouth to answer but paused as I studied her face.

"I don't understand . . ." I muttered, leaning back.

"Speak," she demanded.

She looked like Renna, in a way. Where Renna's hair was dark and wavy, almost curly, this woman's was straight, black, and had a streak of white.

But it was the eyes, the shape of them. The curve of her nose.

The way her jaw was formed, and her neck . . .

I shook my head. "You look like her . . ." I said. "And yet." I squinted. "You are nothing alike."

"Do you make a habit of sounding like an idiot?" she snapped. "I asked you a question."

"Where is Sethos?" I gritted out. "Bring him to me."

She blinked in confusion. "Who the fuck do you think you are?" she yelled. "You come to *my* lands uninvited, breaching our borders, sending everyone in a panic, and you have the *audacity* to make demands of *me!*" She laughed as if in disbelief. "I don't answer to *you* or any other person."

I lifted an eyebrow. "Testy."

"So I ask you again," she gritted out. "Who are you?"

I recalled my magic and let my god aura glow in its full capacity. It encased me in silvery white, showing my divinity.

Soldiers shielded their eyes.

But the woman stared on, unflinching.

Only a god or a half god would be able to look straight on when a god's aura was in its full divine glow. But she wasn't a god. I would have felt it.

She clenched her jaw. "Your tricks don't scare me," she spat.

"Where is Sethos?" I demanded.

She folded her hands in front of her. "He's not here."

"Your name?" I demanded.

She crossed her arms. "I asked you first."

I crossed my arms too. "Cylas."

Her eyes widened, and her jaw dropped.

"And yours?" I demanded.

"Demira-Titania, Leteah of Vasarys. Daughter of the Most High Am-Re, first king of Isyos, former Ahtar of Vasarys, God of Darkness, Chaos, and Ruin, formed by Source at the beginning of time."

It was my turn for my jaw to drop.

She was Renna's sister.

She smiled, but there was nothing sweet about it. It sent a chill down my spine, and I was a god. I feared nothing.

"Cylas," she said out loud to the room, which now had about a hundred people present. "Cylas is the *only* god from the Celestial Enclave who decided not to attack our people in Isyos."

My body tensed, and I clenched my jaw and fists.

"Were you busy that day?" she asked, a bitter edge to her voice. "Inaction is often times action, great God."

I shook my head. "I don't attack my creations," I said. "Isyos, despite its unruly and criminal history, for better or worse, was a planet *I* created."

She nodded.

I hated the reminder of my complicity in letting my enclave attack Isyos.

I shook the thought aside and focused on the present. "Where is Sethos?"

"I really don't think you're in a position to be asking questions, God."

Suddenly, hurried footsteps sounded, and we all turned.

My eyes widened as I beheld the most beautiful woman I had ever seen approach.

She had curly silver-blond hair and ebony skin. Her eyes were like ice, and when they met mine, I felt like her icy stare encased the chamber housing my heart and held it hostage.

I struggled to breathe as she continued to approach.

What the fuck was happening to me?

Demira looked back and forth between the silver-haired woman and me.

When the woman finally stood a mere arm's length away from me, she bowed her head in respect.

I became deathly still and then looked at Demira.

"What is this?" I asked, putting my palms up. "You are all wasting my fucking time. Bring me Sethos."

"I know why you are here," the woman with silver hair said.

"Oh, yeah?" I tilted my head. "And yet Sethos has not been brought to me."

"You were sent here." She was slow as she spoke. "To find your purpose."

I froze.

Livina's words.

"And how do you know that?" I snapped.

She stepped closer to me, her eyes suddenly growing softer. "I know a lot of things," she whispered. "The dead sometimes speak too much."

Words stumbled out. "You're a necromancer?" I asked.

She looked down at her hands, which were folded at her middle. "My name is Illona. I am Am-Re's third child." She gestured to Demira. "Demira is my older sister."

Berion's sister. I needed to leave here with her.

"My sister and I have lived under the tyranny of my father. And now Sethos," Illona explained.

Illona reached out and touched my arm, as if we were familiar with one another. A natural reaction would have been for me to step back as she was a stranger. But my heart wouldn't let me move.

"You will help us," Illona said, and she nodded. "I know you will."

Words left me almost automatically. "*Yes,*" I said quickly.

In that moment, my body was stunned with magic, and blinding pain shot through my arms.

I screamed and looked down to see death in physical form.

Alaric Chains.

The chains were actually handcuffs, used to slowly drain a supernatural of its life force and magic.

It was a death sentence.

Not even a god could escape them.

"Demira, *no!*" Illona screamed. "We need him!"

I watched in horror as the cuffs branded themselves to my flesh and began to siphon my magic from me.

"What have you done?" I roared, battling to escape them. It was futile, yet I had to try.

"Why are you doing this?" Illona cried, tears streaming down her face. She launched herself against her sister. "Please don't hurt him! Not him."

Demira laughed, her eyes locked to mine. "Because this *little witch* can."

"Help me!" I screamed.

Illona shook her sister. "Demira, this is not the way it's supposed to play out. *Let him go!*"

When Demira shrugged her off, Illona knelt at my feet to help me.

I shifted my body to shield her from touching the cuffs. Her skin would burn if she made contact.

"No!" I screamed at her. "Get off!" I had to protect her, but Illona wrestled with me, determined to help.

"Cylas," she cried as tears streamed down her face. "I'm sorry," she repeated on and on. "I failed. I failed."

As pain thrashed inside me, I tried to comprehend her words, but nothing made sense.

"*Guards,*" Demira yelled. "Escort Illona to her rooms."

Illona paused and looked to Demira through tears. "Demira, please, don't do this! We have to help him."

Who was this magnificent brave woman who was risking everything for me?

I swallowed the lump in my throat and clenched my jaw as the guards approached her.

Something about the soldiers putting their hands on her made my blood boil. I wanted to kill them all.

"Your heart is soft, sister. We cannot be nice to prisoners," Demira gritted out. "I am in charge. You will listen to me."

As the soldiers closed in, I saw red.

"Don't fucking touch her!" I yelled, and the soldiers paused.

Illona whipped her head to mine, and something passed between us in that moment that I knew I'd never felt for another being in my entire life.

Admiration?

"He can't hurt you," Demira said, bored. "He grows weaker with every moment that ticks by."

The soldiers nodded and removed Illona from my body.

She kicked and screamed and clawed and spit as she fought them, but they overpowered her.

She screamed for her sister.

And she screamed for me.

And I could do nothing but watch as they dragged her from me.

The magic of the Alaric Chains overpowered me then, and the last image I saw was a pair of hauntingly beautiful ice-blue eyes boring into my soul.

37

KHELLIOS

"We made progress today," Elrie said as we boarded her craft.

Her crew walked behind us, rolling crates of supplies and chatting quietly among themselves. El had us stop at an outpost to load fuel and food, and it had brought a welcome break to the almost two-week confinement in the craft.

"I feel I'm no closer to finding her than when I started."

El put her hand on my shoulder. "That's not true. We know several of Am-Re's and Sethos's trading partners stop here on their way to and from Vasarys. Also, the Galactic Federation is hosting a gathering in the next few days, and this outpost is the closest to the meeting. This place has to be full of people with information. I refuse to believe otherwise."

I shook my head. "El, I doubt anyone here will tell us anything. We know nothing of what the Federation's meeting is about. There are billions of black holes where Vasarys may be located. I won't risk the crew and you with entering just any black hole."

"I know the risks," she said defiantly, taking her hand from me and continuing up the craft's ramp.

I stopped her and turned her to face me. The way the setting sun star settled on her face made her skin glow and her hair look like spun gold. Her dark brows, which were a prominent feature on her face, furrowed over her crystalline-blue eyes.

I cleared my throat. "I won't risk you, El."

She lifted her eyebrow. "That's not a decision you get to make."

"This isn't a payback situation for me—you know that. I don't need you to pay me back for saving your life."

"Why must you be so stubborn?" She frowned. "I want to help you. I have been helping you. Accept my help, godsdamn it!"

"It's not about being stubborn," I growled. "A star craft can only take so many passages through a black hole before the equipment stops working. I don't want to leave us stranded. My particular magic is lessened in black holes. I draw energy from moons and stars, none of which exist inside black holes."

El crossed her arms. "We have one of the best star fleets in several galaxies. I didn't convince my father to invest his money in just any equipment, and it bothers me that you have such little faith in my leadership as to think I would blindly risk my crew."

I recalled how weak El had been all those years ago. An illness was killing her, and her father had asked me to save her.

"You still see me as someone who is weak." Her voice was low but enraged.

"I promised your father I would always look after you if I was ever near."

"And where have you been all this time?" she snapped. "You seldom ever came back. I have managed fine on my own, thanks." El turned from me.

Something akin to hopelessness stirred within me as she walked away, and anger washed over me. I stalked after her and turned her around.

"I'm leaving you out of this search."

El growled and shrugged her arm out of my hold. "You have a problem!"

I laughed and pointed to my chest. "*I* have a problem?"

"Yes! You do!"

"Oh yeah?" I stepped closer. "And what is that?"

She brought us toe to toe, her eyes narrowed. "You're a control freak."

I blinked.

"You have an issue with wanting to control and lord over everything! I'm sick of it!" she yelled.

"You're sick of me?" I yelled back.

"*Yes!*"

"*Fine!*" I spun around and walked back down the ramp.

"Where are you going?" she yelled after me, and her heavy boots thudded on the ramp.

"Removing myself from your vicinity. Getting rid of your problem," I called back.

I stepped on the gravel of the desert planet and began to walk back to the town we had just left.

"Coward!"

I paused.

"That's right!" she said louder now. "Coward."

El stepped in front of me, her skin flushed and chest heaving. I had never seen her this angry.

"You don't want to accept help because that would mean you don't know what to do." She stepped closer. "You're afraid."

"Afraid?" I crossed my arms. "You think I don't know that?"

"I'm not talking about the regular fear of what if you don't find her, Khellios."

"You don't know anything."

"You're afraid of what your life will look like if she decides she no longer wants you. You want to find her in time—as if that will make her want of you materialize."

"You don't know anything."

She lifted an eyebrow. "You're afraid of what your life will look like after grief."

I blinked at her words. Was fear truly keeping me back?

"Terek," Elrie called to her second general, who conveniently was just beyond the ramp entrance.

The man walked down the ramp, his polished navy blue armor gleaming. He held his helmet in his hand.

"Yes?" he said, eyeing me with suspicion.

"Tell the crew I've decided to stay overnight. This outpost city is busy, and there are many taverns and places to stop for food. The tab is on me. The crew has earned it."

He nodded. "Certainly, Princess El."

He bowed, swiftly turned on his heels, and walked up the ramp.

El turned her eyes to me and lifted her eyebrows. "I'm going into town to get a drink." She paused. "You are free to join me."

I frowned and watched as El strode back into town alone, her white cape swishing as she walked, making her look like a majestic knight on a mission of salvation.

Did she know I was a lost cause?

This outpost was filled with an unusually large number of people. I knew El could defend herself—she was commanding three spacecrafts—but something inside me craved to protect her.

I shook my head and followed her.

I GRUNTED over the cup I held under my nose.

I slid my eyes back to Elrie, who talked animatedly with a group of several men. They all looked enthralled as she spoke, her hands flying through the air as she explained something funny.

When the group of men broke out in laughter and she blushed, I groaned and took another sip of my drink.

Why did I care who she spoke to?

Had I not made it clear to her to steer clear from me?

Still, a feeling of discomfort gnawed its way inside my chest.

The bartender in front of me leaned in across the bar. "She's magnificent, isn't she?" he asked, his eyes glittering.

She was one of a handful of women in the tavern.

"She's something, alright," I growled.

She *was* magnificent.

She was regal.

She was fearless.

She was beautiful.

All things I knew from the moment I met her.

"How long have you two been together?" the bartender asked.

I looked up and chuckled while shaking my head. "She's not mine."

The bartender lifted his eyebrows and wiped down the counter in front of him. "You don't say . . ." He frowned. "Well, you're scowling every time a man says something to her that makes her blush. *Could have fooled me.*"

I grunted.

"But you're right." he said, side-eyeing me.

"What does that mean?" I set my drink down.

The bartender whistled. "A woman like that." He shook his head and grinned. "She's no match for any man."

"Well, I'm no *man*." I frowned.

I didn't have my god aura to show others who I was.

I had given that up to save Elrie.

"Yeah, yeah," the bartender said. "I know you're some type of supernatural. Most of the people who pass through here are one way or another. Mortals are rare."

"So what's your point?" I snapped.

He gestured to the crowd around her. "She attracted the attention of three different royal fae courts. All those blokes you see around her are from three different kingdoms."

Alert bells began to ring in my mind.

The fae were known to stay in their lands.

"And?" I asked, hoping he would offer more information.

"Well, if you know anything about the fae, it's that they're snooty as fuck. They don't like anyone who isn't fae." He smiled. "And they sure have taken a liking to your woman."

"She's not my woman," I growled and narrowed my eyes at the group.

He laughed. "So you say."

The group was made up of men with silver hair, jet-black hair, and golden-honey hair. They wore distinct clothing that likely designated their royal houses.

"There's a lot of fae congregated in one location," I stated nonchalantly.

The bartender nodded. "The Galactic Federation gathering is in two nights. This is the nearest outpost to there. You know the Federation doesn't serve spirits. We're making a killing in revenue this week with people taking their fill beforehand."

"Interesting." I sipped my drink, my eyes still trained on El.

"I've never seen folks this nervous before a Federation meeting, to be honest."

I paused and looked at him. "How so?"

"Can't say for certain . . . But you can sense the anxious energy. Always feels a bit like this before a war if you ask me."

War.

The chaotic destruction of Am-Re and Sethos was the first thing I could think of that would disrupt peace.

The bartender nodded toward the second floor of the tavern, where a balcony overlooked the first floor.

"We have a few interesting folks up there. Fae lords or something of the like. They've been meeting there for the last two hours. Their traveling parties"—he gestured back to the fae surrounding Elrie—"have been hanging here on the first floor while the bosses talk up there."

"Huh."

I thanked the bartender and got up after a few moments when he became occupied with other patrons.

Keeping my eye on Elrie, I made my way to the stairs running along the side of the tavern and slowly made my way up the second floor.

It was beneficial that my god aura was missing in times like these. I blended in with everyone else. No one batted an eye.

A second bar was on the landing, along with thirty or so tables with a few patrons. In the right back corner, a group of men and women sat arguing.

I headed to the bar and sat on a barstool.

"Need a refill?" a bartender asked, pointing to my almost empty goblet.

"In a minute." I nodded and stole a few looks at the group in the back.

A woman with long, beautiful, silver hair and pointed ears stood from the table and jabbed a finger at one of her companions. She was spewing insults at him.

I narrowed my eyes to see who she was yelling at.

A man with long black hair and red eyes smirked while leaning back on his chair, not bothering to look up at her. He wore a long cape that draped around him. A crown made of black iron and obsidian sat across his forehead.

I frowned. Why did he look familiar?

The bartender in front of me spoke. "What will you be having?" He nodded to my goblet.

"Do you have any ambrosia?"

The bartender chuckled. "Drink of the gods. Feeling fancy tonight, eh?" He nodded. "We stocked some just for this Federation gathering. You never know who might stop in."

I grunted. "Any gods stop by recently?"

The bartender frowned. "No." He shook his head. "Fae and elven royalty, yes, however. You would think they're gods with the way they carry themselves. Snobby assholes."

I laughed. People really didn't like the fae.

"Any royals in the group back there?" I asked.

"Who's asking?" a male asked from behind me.

I froze, and the bartender eyed me carefully. He slid me a glass of ambrosia and left to the other side of the bar, quickly busying himself with wiping down the bar.

I turned around.

The male who had been sitting at the table with the crown looked down at me.

He frowned and narrowed his red eyes, and a moment of silence passed between us.

"Khellios," he finally said, crossing his arms. "Mercenary god. We meet again."

I paused. It was my turn to frown. "My mercenary work has been over for a long time . . ." I sipped my drink. "You have an extensive memory."

"And you, as a god, do not." He chuckled.

"I have lived longer than you ever will. Faces blur over the years." I paused. "The woman yelling at you back there seems to have an excellent memory of who you are from the insults thrown your way." I gestured to the tables in the back and looked back up at the fae standing in front of me. "She sounded quite accusatory, listing past grievances from what I could hear."

His lips curved slightly. "Women insulting me is nothing new. When it comes from a fae queen of a neighboring kingdom, I have learned to hold my tongue. Fae wrath can be particularly nasty."

I looked to the group in the back, and they were still in a heated argument. A few members of the party looked our way.

"You still have no idea who I am, do you?" the male asked me.

I shook my head. "But I'm sure you'll tell me."

It was the truth. My brain blocked out many sad years in my past.

"I am Aeroth," the man said.

His name rumbled like electricity throughout the air. The lights in the tavern flickered, and a phantom breeze brushed my skin.

My eyes widened, and the blood in my body rushed through my veins in alert.

I knew who he was then.

Gods did not bow to others, but for *him*, all gods bowed their heads out of respect.

"Your Majesty." I stood immediately and bowed my head. "King of the Astral."

When the universe was created and the gods were assigned all that they were to oversee, Source gave dreams, the unseen, and the astral plane to the fae to rule. The astral plane was given to Aeroth's family. They were fae, elves to be exact, which were a type of fae, and the first elves to ever exist. As such, Aeroth hailed from the longest line of elven kings known.

Not only that, but Aeroth was also part Naaviri, from his mother.

Naaviri, or vampires, as humans had called them on Earth, were also a type of fae.

The combination of Aeroth's long elf lineage and the Naaviri side of him made Aeroth a deadly foe.

Every king of the astral ascended to power, and Source melded their essence with the fabric of the astral itself. In truth, it could be said that as king, he was the astral itself, forged into physical form. To gods, Aeroth was more god than fae, and if he was here at an outpost in the middle of space, in physical form, something was the matter.

"What has been of your life, God of the Moon and Stars?" Aeroth straightened, crossed his arms, and tilted his head. "You're a long way from your enclave."

"I would remark that you're far from home as well, but then, you are the Astral. As I recall, you can simply bend reality and travel to the astral plane with the snap of a finger."

Aeroth lifted his eyebrows and nodded once as if my remark made him uncomfortable. "All can travel to the astral plane during dreamtime or meditation. Most have no recollection of it by the time they regain consciousness."

His words made me pause.

I wondered if Aeroth could potentially help me in finding Renna.

"You look suddenly troubled, God." His burgundy eyes studied me carefully.

"I wonder if you would have the power to help me locate someone."

He leaned forward. "And who would that be?"

"My—" I paused before I described what Renna was to me.

She was not my wife.

Not my intended.

Not my lover.

I cleared my throat. "A woman very dear to me"—I frowned at how empty the description sounded—"is missing."

"Are you certain she is missing, or does she simply not want to be found?" he said, looking sharply at me. "I do not like to make it a habit to intervene in people's lives. Especially forcing women to be available for any man."

I clenched my jaw and straightened. "She was taken."

"I see." He put his hands behind his back and looked down at the ground. "The astral serves all seven universes. Many souls cross it at all times."

"You need to help me."

Aeroth observed me and dipped his chin down. "Her name?"

"Renna." I took a breath. "Renna Strongborn. A sea fae, parading as a god, known as Sethos attacked Taria to search for her. She vanished moments after his attack. I know he has her."

Aeroth narrowed his eyes. "Renna." Her name flowed off his lips, and an uneasy feeling overcame me.

"Do you know of her?" I said quickly. "Has she traveled the astral?"

Aeroth remained silent, his eyes assessing me. "I gave you something years ago."

I frowned.

"For your service to my kingdom."

My years traveling the galaxy flooded back to me. I had been lauded with a multitude of gifts in the centuries I was a mercenary. I slightly remembered being gifted swords . . .

And then suddenly it clicked.

My eyes widened. "The mirror."

The mirror that had morphed into a portal when Renna was taken.

The universe and Source were giving me a rare gift at that moment in meeting Aeroth.

"The mirror created a portal." I accused. "Renna had no knowledge of her magic—she could not have possibly created a portal on her own. That mirror must have aided her. She vanished through *that* mirror." I narrowed my eyes and stepped up to him, my fists clenched. "Why would you knowingly give me an enchanted mirror?"

He stared at me for a long time, expressionless.

"Tell me," I growled and stepped closer.

"Seven identical mirrors were created by an old queen in my family." He folded his hands behind his back. "You have one of the seven." He paused before continuing. "The mirror I gave you —I had no need for the mirror when it was gifted. I wanted to get rid of it."

I shook my head. "You could have warned me about the mirror's magical properties."

"The mirrors correspond to other each other like gateways. It aids in communication and transport. The magic in the mirror is only activated by another mirror. If she traveled through it, she must have been communicating with someone who had its counterpart."

Blood drained from my face.

Did Sethos have a mirror?

If he did, who would give him a mirror?

Nothing made sense.

"Can you track where the mirrors are?" I asked.

Aeroth shook his head. "The mirrors were given as gifts so the queen could communicate with her loved ones. I gave away the last one in my family's possession to you."

I rubbed my temples.

"Do you have the mirror through which Renna traveled?" he asked.

"No," I snapped and dropped my hands. "I was told the mirror disappeared through the portal as if sucked in through a vortex."

Aeroth crossed his arms and looked at me carefully.

"Have you seen Renna in the astral plane?" I asked him.

"What made her leave your side?" he asked.

My gut twisted. "A misunderstanding. She's in danger, Aeroth. I need to find her."

Aeroth continued to look at me for several moments. "Do you know why we're"—he looked back at his table—"*here*, Khellios?" Aeroth said, his eyes studying mine.

"Have you seen Renna or not?" I demanded.

Aeroth ignored my question. "We're here because the Galactic Federation demands we clean up after one of our own. He has caused significant chaos so far."

I frowned.

"You are familiar with him. You said his name a few moments ago."

"Sethos," I whispered.

Aeroth nodded and clenched his fist. "His stunt in Taria has garnered the attention of many. The Federation is holding a private meeting in addition to their gathering to discuss steps to bring him in line."

"I was under the impression the Federation did not want anything to do with Am-Re or Sethos. My enclave was told by the Federation to stay out of it. I am on my own searching for Sethos and Renna."

"You're right. The Federation *doesn't* want anything to do with him. *However,* Ukara, Goddess of War, directly petitioned the Federation to take a second look, given the risk. She called for backup to take down Sethos."

The news made my breath stop. Ukara's love for me and support of Renna's situation gave me strength.

"The Federation agreed with Ukara. They called in the twelve fae and elven kingdoms to bring him to heel." Aeroth looked to the table in the back, whose occupants were now all looking toward us. "The Federation has made Sethos our problem."

"If Renna traveled through a mirror to another, why would Sethos have a mirror created by a member of your family?"

Aeroth paused in that moment, and I could see his body tense. "I do not know."

"Do you know where Sethos is?" I asked. "I need to find her."

Aeroth shifted on his feet and crossed his arms. He looked back to his entourage and waved to them.

The people stood and began to walk over.

"I can only locate those accessing the astral as it is within my realm," Aeroth said. "I do not know where she is now. If she reaches my realm again, I can locate her, but understand that the soul does not go to the astral plane every time someone sleeps or meditates."

In that moment, Elrie came up the stairs.

I turned to face her.

"Khellios." She was breathless and gave me a brilliant smile. Her eyes moved to Aeroth and the rest of the monarchs who were approaching, and she slowed her gait.

"Who's your friend?" she asked, crossing her arms and narrowing her eyes at Aeroth. She put her hand on her sword hilt.

I looked to Aeroth as I spoke. "Elrie, this is Aeroth. He's going to help us find Renna."

38

SETHOS

y hands trembled as I searched the potion room inside the fortress for more vials again.

I had just come back from Etara's camp, seeking her help in controlling the darkness inside me, but Etara was gone. Her camp was vacant, and her star craft was missing.

This couldn't be happening.

My vision was blurry as the dark magic inside me moved like claws, chasing away my humanity. I could physically feel Am-Re's magic weave its way like needles up my body as it zeroed in on the path to my heart.

I needed more time.

More time for what? The familiar voice taunted me.

I gripped the sides of my head and squeezed my eyes shut. "Shut up!" I screamed.

Everything I wanted was so close.

I raged as I visualized everything slipping away—revenge against the gods, the respect of my people, and the opportunity to vanquish Am-Re.

I thought of Renna's face.

Her smile.

Everything was going so much better when you were just using her. The dark voice mocked me. *But you allowed your emotions to get in the way.*

I brought my forehead to the table, slamming it to get the voice out of my head.

You have lost sight of your goal. You are weak.

I rose and slammed my hands down on the table.

"Stop talking!" I yelled at the voice and bent down to the boxes of spell goods under the table Etara had left behind.

There had to be a vial somewhere, but I had ransacked the spell room.

I thought of the consequences of going without a tincture.

My body didn't feel different during the first two years of having Am-Re's powers. I felt like everything worked the same. The advantage was that I could easily call on the dark powers of the god as if they were my own. I knew the incantations; I knew how to use his commands because I had lived alongside him almost all my life. Wielding his powers felt natural.

In the third year, my body began experiencing tics and spasms after I used his magic. My body would become more tired, and my vision would blur for moments at a time.

When shadows began to visually mark my body and progressed upward, I knew Am-Re's magic was taking a toll on me—taking from me every time I used it. My body and soul in exchange for his magic.

Then the voices started, and Etara and I found a witch who created an antidote to slow the progression of the devastating effects of Am-Re's magic. The tinctures, which the witch made with my blood, helped stabilize me and drew out my genetic sea fae magic, encouraging it to establish dominance inside me to quell Am-Re's magic for moments at a time. Getting the doses was easy at first, but now . . .

Finish the task. The voice urged inside me.

Honor and greatness await you . . .

Don't you want to bring honor to the memory of your mother?

To the Fallen?

Traitor.

Lowlife.

Usurper.

Forget the girl.

I sank to the ground as the voice echoed inside me and curled up into a ball, the truth of its words battering my denials.

I was unworthy of the memory of my people and mother. Getting caught up in feelings for Renna was distracting me from my goal.

And now I was out of time.

You need her magic, the voice hissed.

You have trained her enough. She has vowed to stand beside you.

I nodded and squeezed my eyes shut as the magic began to nestle inside my body, claiming my bones, veins, joints, from the inside like deadly roots.

Renna promised to fight alongside me, but she didn't know who she had agreed to fight against.

Renna will betray you . . .

I shook my head and gripped my hair.

You don't deserve love.

Everyone leaves you.

Your mother let herself die.

It was much better than a lifetime by your side.

"Stop!" I screamed as my mind went back to digging for her in the rubble.

Renna will never stand by your side.

"She promised she would," I said, my voice breaking.

Then put her to the test. See where her loyalty lies.

There's only one way to find out.

39

RENNA

I held my breath as the arrow swooshed past my fingers and spun in flight toward its target.

A smile grew on my lips as it flew perfectly to its mark.

A shadow zipped past, and the arrow stopped midway.

I blinked, and Sethos stood with the arrow in his hand, a slow smirk spreading across his face as he casually observed the arrow in his fingers.

"Interesting design," he said, his voice somehow colder than I ever recalled. "An arrow with fletching and jagged thorn-like points on its base." He looked up at me. "You looking to kill someone with this Black Fire arrow?"

I frowned. "Injure. Maybe kill."

He narrowed his eyes. "Wrong answer."

I lifted my eyebrows.

He walked slowly toward me. "Always kill."

His voice had that darker quality that made me uncomfortable, and a chill spread through my back. I steeled my body so he wouldn't see me shiver.

"I'm still angry at you," I reminded him. "Your treatment of me the other day when you flew into Daya is still fresh in my mind."

So fresh that I had avoided him for two days, and my resentment only grew.

Sethos ignored my statement.

"If you're going to fight for me," he said, now in front of me. He handed me back the arrow. "You will need to kill."

"How very draconian. You're in another mood today. How was Vasarys?"

"You mean that place that keeps me from you?" He reached over and undid the braid that was over my shoulder.

I grabbed his hand and tossed it aside, stepping away from him. "Did you not hear that I'm still angry at you?" I tilted my chin up.

I had to stand firm.

Sethos dropped his hand and sighed.

"I hate what that place is doing to you," I said. "Right now, you don't even sound like yourself. We should just forget all this and leave."

He frowned. "*Leave?*" Sethos blinked and put his hands on his hips.

"Sethos," I began. "It's like you're two different people. I love when you and I are together, not thinking about Vasarys. It's like none of it—"

"You're asking me to run away like a coward?" He crossed his arms.

My heart began to race. "Can't you see Vasarys is costing you your peace?"

Sethos was silent as he stared down at me, and I squirmed under his gaze.

"I'm not calling you a coward," I said insistently.

Sethos suddenly wrapped his arms around my waist. "You

know why I like being by your side, Renna?" he asked, a slight edge to his voice.

I shook my head, my heart still racing.

"You are my peace when I leave Vasarys. I come here—*home* —to you, and I don't have to think about anything but you—*us.*"

He put a finger under my chin.

"Do you understand me?" There was a cruelty to his voice I didn't understand.

I tried to form a response. "Sethos . . ."

"Please, don't ruin what we have by getting involved in my duties."

My skin prickled with an uncomfortable heat that rose up my neck.

"I don't mean to dictate what you should do," I began. "I'm sorry if you think that's what I'm doing. I care about you—"

"Let's not talk about it anymore, mejtah." He ran a thumb over my lips, his eyes following his movement. "*Please.*"

I quickly stepped from his embrace to put space between us.

"Sethos, creating a division between us is the last thing I would ever want—"

"Good." He smiled. "Let's go take a walk." He grabbed my hand and led me outside.

The move startled me, but I had pacified his erratic moods in the past, and I would do the same now. My brain scrambled to change the topic.

"Where are we going?" I asked, forcing my voice to sound light.

"I've been so impressed with all the training you have been doing," he began.

"I have the best teacher." I forced a laugh.

I took a deep breath to recalibrate my mood.

"Is that so?" He looked sideways at me. "Or are you mocking me?"

An odd feeling spread through me, and it made me mentally pause.

Something was off.

I swallowed hard and forced a smile. "So where are we going?" I asked again.

"You'll see."

I should have pressed him more, but despite everything we had been through, I trusted him.

He was silent as we traversed deep into the woods, and I moved closer to him when it felt like the darkness of the woods seemed to creep closer to me, as if the shadows themselves wanted to meld into my skin, clinging to me like a second skin until I was swallowed into a pit of dread. A rotten smell like animal carcasses filled my nostrils, and I inched even closer to Sethos.

Sethos seemed oblivious to it all, his eyes almost dazed as he stared ahead.

After a while, he said, "I don't think I've been a good teacher, Renna."

I tilted my head. "Why do you say that?"

He shook his head. "I feel that I'm asking too much of you by wanting you by my side in a fight."

I scoffed and took my hand back. "Wait, what? You know I'm good." I stopped walking, and he spun to face me. "I'm better than good," I said, crossing my arms.

He smirked.

Was he trying to provoke a reaction from me? I had worked too hard to master my fear and my magic to be deemed unfit to fight.

I narrowed my eyes. "You don't think I'm good enough to stand by your side?"

"I think you may have what it takes," he said casually.

"*But?*" My voice rose.

"I'm just not sure of your follow-through."

Tension and fury coiled in my chest. "You're a fucking asshole, Sethos."

He shrugged. "Am I saying anything untrue? You've never seen war. What will you do in a real fight?"

"That's not my fault. I'm doing everything I can to stand with you. You know I've never seen combat. There's always a first time for everything."

A dark smile crossed his lips. "There is, isn't there?" He spun on his heels and continued through the forest.

My jaw dropped as he walked on without me.

"Sethos!" I called after him. "What the fuck is going on?"

He didn't respond and kept walking.

Anger thrashed inside me, and I cursed loudly, jogging after him.

When I caught up to him, I grabbed his arm and stepped in front of him.

"What gives?" I yelled. "What the fuck is up with you today?"

All humor was gone from his face.

"*You.*"

I shook my head. "I don't understand."

Sethos crossed his arms. "You know what I think about almost nightly now?"

When I remained silent, he continued.

"I think about how you have vowed to stand beside me, yet I'm sending you into conflict like a lamb ripe for killing."

"That's not my fault! I train every day—"

"You're right. It's not your fault. *It's mine.*"

"So what?" I demanded. "You're going to be cryptic as shit leading me through this fucking forest, not telling me where we're going?"

"I'm taking you beyond the shield."

My jaw dropped, and my eyes widened.

I blinked. "W-what?"

"Do you trust me?" he asked, lifting an eyebrow.

"Yes."

"In battle, you face the worst of people. That is what's beyond the shield. I need you to see it."

Daya was a safe haven for criminal fae. Wanting me to see the types of people I could face made sense.

"Why couldn't you tell me that?" I pushed against his chest. "I'm starting to have a huge problem with the way you've been treating me, Sethos."

"What?" he asked, lowering his chin. "You're angry that I'm trying to help you build character? To keep you alive?"

Anger rolled inside me.

"You're made of tough stuff." He crossed his arms. "Aren't you?"

I was comfortable using my magic and wouldn't be afraid to use it.

"I don't like you right now."

Sethos smiled. "Will you follow me into the dark, little serpent?" He put out his arm to me as if waiting for a response.

"Why should I go anywhere with you?" I challenged.

Sethos stepped up to me, the tips of his boots against mine.

"Because your place is next to me. Always," he breathed and ran his nose against mine. "Because I need you strong. For you and for me." He placed an arm around my waist and drew my body against his. "Because I want a future with you. I cannot promise you gentleness and flowers. Life has made me hard. This is my reality. And we need to make it out of this—together."

I placed my hands on his chest and looked up. "I told you," I whispered. "I'm on your side. Trust me."

"It gets darker the further we move forward." He looked to the forest beyond. "Are you sure?"

I knew his words held a double meaning.

But I wanted to be by his side.

Very, very much.

"I'll go anywhere with you, Sethos." I took his hands and squeezed. "Lead me into the dark."

A GLOWING WALL of angry purple electricity faced us.

Sethos's shield.

"Well, this looks painful," I mused. "No wonder nobody will cross this."

I looked side to side and saw how the shield curved around the forest as far as I could see.

Sethos laughed. "A good defense mechanism."

"Yeah. How the heck are we crossing this?"

Sethos waved a hand over the shield in the shape of an arch. He hovered his hand over it for a moment before moving toward it like he was going to push the wall.

The outline of the arch appeared in black, and like a door, it swung out.

My jaw dropped. "That's convenient," I chuckled.

Sethos shrugged. "It's my magic, Renna. I would hope I would know how to manipulate it."

I looked to Sethos. "How much is this magic affecting you?"

Sethos shifted on his feet. "What do you mean?"

"This shield is not insignificant." I unhooked my arm from his and crossed my arms. "From the fortress and clearing, when I look up, I only see a slight sheen of purple, which means it's very high up in the sky."

"I don't like to be bothered."

I shook my head. "This magic must be draining on your body, no?"

He ignored my question and gestured to the door. "Ladies first."

I clenched my teeth and pushed my body to move. I expected crossing through the barrier to have some sort of effect on me, perhaps react to my own magic's electric qualities or to feel heavy, but I felt nothing.

"Expecting it to hurt?" Sethos said, amused, as he walked behind me.

"You're a mind reader now?"

Sethos leaned into my ear and let his lips brush my skin there. "Reading your mind is my specialty, or has your body forgotten?"

My lips parted, and before I could respond, Sethos straightened, breaking the spell.

I forced myself to look away from him and at our surroundings.

The other side of Daya was much the same, with bioluminescent flora, but there were fewer trees. Instead, rolling hills met us, illuminated by two moons that bathed the landscape in a cool midnight blue.

"I take it the moons are also an illusion?" I asked, knowing the daylight was pure magic.

"Yes." Sethos nodded. "Otherwise, this would be all darkness."

"Convenient, though, for criminals looking to hide."

Sethos laughed. "War could be considered a crime, you know."

I frowned. "What are you saying?"

"Some would say you are becoming a criminal by choosing to back me."

"But—" I shook my head. "You're bringing justice to those who wronged you. This is different—"

"*Ah.*" Sethos smiled. "There it is."

I paused. "What?"

"Loyalty." He nodded. "You will need that, you know. Many will judge you for fighting alongside me."

I scoffed. "For standing up to injustice? I don't give a shit. I see how you have suffered. I will gladly stand by you. It's the least I can do."

Sethos pursed his lips. "Hmm," he said with a raised eyebrow. "Follow me."

Up ahead, I observed a small gold star craft, large enough to accommodate perhaps five people, in a clearing surrounded by trees.

A large bonfire was lit in the middle, signaling the presence of people. The soft crackling of the burning timber filled the air, and a smoky scent filled my nostrils, instantly warming me. I would have welcomed the calming sensation of a cozy fire, except my heart was racing, and I knew how dangerous the woods were.

Sethos looked to me and put his finger to his lips, gesturing for me to walk closer to the camp.

As we quieted and slowed our steps, advancing, soft music floated on the air.

"Do you know the people here?" I whispered.

Sethos didn't answer, and we kept walking.

We approached three hover motorcycles and a rectangular structure that had a symbol for toilet—an outhouse. Sethos nodded for us to stand behind the outhouse, and I followed.

"Why are we here?" I asked.

"Do you remember what I told you when you first began to train?"

I froze as I thought back. "That was like four months ago . . ." I complained. "Why don't you remind me?"

"I told you I would one day take you to the other side of the shield . . ."

I raised my eyebrows and put my palms up. "Yeah . . .?"

A slow, dark smile spread on Sethos's lips. "For real-life target practice."

40

RENNA

"**W**hat?" I hissed.

Sethos tilted his head. "You're a smart woman. I'm sure you know exactly what I mean."

I blinked several times.

Real-life target practice . . .

My heart dropped into my stomach as the realization hit me.

Sethos had told me he wasn't sure if I was ready to stand beside him.

That I hadn't seen battle.

That I was too green.

Inexperienced.

I came right up to his nose. "You brought me here to fight?" I demanded. "Are you serious right now?"

Sethos looked down at me, and suddenly I found myself with my back against the outhouse, hands pressed above my head.

Sethos pressed against me and brushed his nose along my neck, sending shivers down my body, which were heightened by the adrenaline shooting through my system.

"First lesson: When you stand next to me in a fight, Renna," he whispered against my skin, "you listen and do."

His tone was arrogant as if he were my master.

The fucking audacity.

I wanted to laugh in his face, but nearby voices had me shutting my mouth.

Sethos looked up and smiled at me. "Want to show me that you'll stand by me?"

My eyes widened as dread gripped me. "Say what you mean."

"There are three people in this camp. I want you to kill them."

My body tensed, and my vision tunneled as my throat dried up.

"E-excuse me?" I stammered, my body pulsing in time with my heart.

A dark look crossed over his eyes. "Did I stutter?"

His tone and words chilled me to the marrow.

My jaw dropped.

He was serious.

"*No!*" I said. "I'm not going to just kill people because you say so."

He frowned. "I thought you wanted to stand by me. This is what war is. This is what defending those you care about looks like. Or were you under the impression you would not have to kill?"

I gulped.

I knew I would potentially have to kill people. Heck, I was training to kill my father should he attack me. But my actions were always in the purpose of self-defense.

"They have not wronged me," I said quickly.

"Yet you have signed up to stand by me," Sethos argued and brought his face close to mine. "Will you falter like this in a fight?"

I shook my head. "N-no. I would be defending you and you, me."

"You think killing in self-defense absolves you morally?"

"And you?"

Sethos spit on the ground. "I never claimed to be moral, Renna. I do what needs to be done."

Doing what he had to do—like a true soldier in battle.

One who had overthrown my father to save his people.

To save me.

"You don't have to test my loyalty," I said quickly.

"Prove it," he growled, the ice in his eyes fading to a darker blue, almost black.

A nervous wave washed over me, and Sethos stepped away from me and walked toward the camp.

My eyes widened, and I took after him.

"*Sethos!*" I whispered furiously.

The voices in the camp quieted.

Firelight reflected off my face, sending a faint sensation of warmth to my skin.

Before us stood three fae males.

One had blue skin and bone, like spikes, on his arms and a green mane that was topped off with a bandanna. He wore a brown jumpsuit, the sleeves rolled up, and combat boots. A piece of twig was in between his teeth as he observed us.

To his right was a smaller-sized fae who had white, almost snake-like scales and yellow eyes. He was dressed in a green jumpsuit and combat boots. His arms were crossed as he looked down his nose at us.

The third was a tall fae who looked relatively human but was about eight feet tall. Tattoos covered his entire body, and the tips of his fingers were glowing red hot. He had a bored look on his face.

"Can we help you?" the snake fae creature snapped. "Are you new here?"

Sethos chuckled. "I'm hoping you can help us."

"Well?" the snake fae snapped. "We're busy. People in Daya

keep to themselves."

"What are you anyway?" Sethos asked him and folded his arms across his chest. "You're a weird fucking fae crossbreed."

The snake fae narrowed his eyes. "That's fucking rude. You think you can just come to our camp and talk to me like that?"

Sethos laughed. "I do actually."

The blue fae crossed his arms. "Looking for a fight?" he asked Sethos. His eyes slipped to me and then back to Sethos. "Or looking for a trade? She's pretty enough."

A slimy feeling spread over me.

Sethos stilled. "I'm not the sharing type, I'm afraid," Sethos replied.

"Then leave." The snake fae seethed. "Leave us now if you value your lives."

Sethos laughed.

I froze as I watched him double over to laugh.

And laugh.

And laugh.

The three fae across from us stilled, their expressions confused, and looked to me.

"Where the fuck did you get this loony?" the blue fae asked me. "Is he bothering you?"

Sethos straightened and wiped a laughing tear from the corner of his eyes and turned to me.

The humor drained from his face, and his features hardened. "Kill them."

My entire body froze as I processed his words, thinking I had misheard him. "*Sethos—*"

"I said," Sethos gritted out, his face furious, "kill them."

The fae males began to speak loudly over each other.

The blue fae spoke the loudest. "You think you two can just come here and act like you're tough shit?" he yelled. "You have no fucking clue who you're dealing with."

"Oh, I know." Sethos smiled at them. "But let me enlighten my friend here, who's a bit morally shy about killing. She's quite green, you see."

Sethos put his hands behind his back and began to pace, completely casual.

The fae men bristled as they watched him. They could see how unaffected Sethos was, and that could only logically mean one thing.

That Sethos was very comfortable in his power.

And that he had a lot of it.

"After some inquiries, I've learned the three idiots you see here," Sethos said to me, gesturing to the fae, "are hiding in Daya for a very specific reason."

The men shifted in place.

"There's a bounty out for three individuals who match their description for arson. They burned down a village with the sole purpose of looting. They killed children and women. Babies murdered in cold blood."

Anger rose within me, and my magic rushed to my fingertips.

The men jumped when my emerald and black magic crackled.

The snake fae lifted his palms. "What's your problem?" he asked Sethos. "You're here for a reason too, or why even come to Daya? Nobody who's here is innocent."

The tall fae growled, and his palms filled with what looked like molten lava and fire.

I narrowed my eyes and wondered if it was he who set the village on fire.

"Did you do it?" I gritted out to him.

The fae laughed at me. "And what if I did?" He tilted his head. "You going to do something about it?"

I took a step forward.

"No—" Sethos said suddenly. "Renna, use Darkness for these three."

I froze.

"Darkness will kill them instantly," I said.

"Whoa, whoa, whoa!" the snake fae said. "This is getting out of hand—"

"You have Darkness?" the blue fae asked, his eyes wide.

"She does," Sethos said proudly. "And she's magnificent."

His praise, which would have normally moved like sweet, light, fluttering butterflies inside me, felt revolting as he urged me to kill.

But these men were criminals.

I looked to the tall fae. "Did you do it?" I looked at his hands.

"Fuck you," he said and spit to the ground. "You fucking bitch. I'd kill you in the snap of a finger but not before I have a good round of fun with that pussy."

Rage boiled inside me at his disgusting words.

I knew he had started the fires at the village.

I hated men like him.

I called on my Darkness then, and it sped through my body, coiled in swirls in my chest, and rushed from me, surrounding me in a cloud of black shadows gathered at my feet.

The snake fae and blue fae began to panic and apologize. The tall fae merely looked down his nose at me, and the magic in his hands grew so that it dripped to the ground and began a fire.

They were nothing more than bullies who preyed on those weaker than them.

Men like my father.

Humans in my district in Andora had a word for men who behaved like they owned the world with no consequences while making everyone feel small: *machismo*.

I thought of the children and people killed in their attack, and I could feel the vessel of my magic suddenly overflow.

I screamed, and Darkness shot from me in both directions like a wall, just missing Sethos.

I groaned and molded and directed the Darkness to surround the camp in a circle. I made sure the trees were spared in my path as I enclosed the camp in a wall as tall as a three-story building.

"What the fuck!" the snake fae screamed and began to run around with his hands clenching his face. "What the actual fuck!"

The blue fae ran toward the star craft, but Sethos moved his hands, and the star craft levitated. In the next instant, it was thrown against the wall of Darkness. The impact of an object colliding with my barrier reverberated through my body, and I swayed.

We all stood with open mouths as the star craft disintegrated into dust.

"What the fuck, indeed," Sethos laughed and snapped his face to me, his eyes glittering with awe. "Look at you!" He gestured around. "This is all you! This is incredible."

I smiled slightly and continued to concentrate.

"Now." Sethos slowly clapped and looked to me. "Renna, darling," he said with a grin, "finish them."

"For what it's worth," the tall fae said. "I would do it again."

I frowned. "Why?" I asked. "You killed senselessly."

He shook his head. "The people we killed, they trafficked my wife. The camp had outlaws. Flesh is their trade. An eye for an eye."

A chill ran down my spine.

"Renna," Sethos barked. "Kill that morality inside you and end them."

The tall fae spoke. "You'd be doing me a favor. My wife was dead by the time I got there. I failed her and her family, who were waiting for me to return with her. I was too late."

I looked to the other two fae, but they remained silent, eyes trained on the ground.

"Is this true?" I demanded.

"Renna!" Sethos yelled. "*Enough!*"

"I don't deserve to live," the tall fae said. "Kill me. Take me to her."

I blinked, and memories of Khellios telling me how much he mourned my death in my first lifetime flashed in my mind. Haunting me.

My body began to shake.

"Do it!" the tall fae yelled. Angry tears tracked down his face. "Do it now!"

I knew then he was telling the truth.

Two wrongs don't make a right. My conscience reminded me.

Did I have a right to lash out in judgment like this?

Who was I to say who lived or died?

But they deserved to die for the killings they caused.

You are nobody to carry out punishment.

But if not me, who?

To take justice into your own hands would make you no better than your father.

This is not your responsibility.

Where would it stop?

My heart faltered as I locked eyes with the tall fae.

The magic in his palms ceased, and he fell to his knees. "Please," he said, arms extended and hands open.

"Renna!" Sethos screamed and stormed to my side. "Why do you hesitate? Take matters into your own hands! Kill them now!"

"I . . ." I whispered. "I can't."

"Can't *what*?" Sethos barked. "You can't kill murderers?"

I tried to form more words but couldn't.

"You had qualms about morality, and I delivered you the perfect first kill," Sethos gritted out. "They don't deserve to live! They killed children!"

A sob racked through my chest as my body was paralyzed by

conflict. "I don't support what they did," I said. "I never will."

"Then kill them!"

"I also don't support what they did to his wife."

"For fuck's sake, Renna!" Sethos screamed. "Do not be weak in this moment!"

My lips trembled. "I shouldn't have to do this. Don't ask me to do this."

"You were doing so good." Sethos urged me on. "Just let instinct take over, let your magic *do*."

"I can't—"

"Gods fucking damn this, Renna! What good is this magic if you don't use it!?"

I shook my head, feeling like a failure.

"Will you also fail me like this in my time of need?"

"*No,*" I sobbed, tears blurring my vision.

Sethos roared and spun to face the men, who only looked on silently at Sethos.

Sethos's voice was deadly. "We're done here."

When Sethos lifted his hands in the air, I gasped.

Tendrils of his magic extended to the men, and then they rose from the ground, suspended in the air. The snake fae and blue fae clawed at their necks as if they couldn't breathe. The only one who didn't fight it was the tall fae.

The tall man's eyes were locked on mine, and my words were locked inside my throat.

I wanted to scream.

I wanted all of this to end.

I turned away as I heard Sethos snap their necks and felt his magic ram against mine when he threw their bodies to my Darkness barrier.

It was too much.

I fell to the ground, and my magic snapped back into me.

Everything faded to black.

41

SETHOS

My body shook with anger when I arrived in Vasarys and was informed Cylas was there.

Viscous energy swirled within me, and I could feel the darkness rumble in my chest, moving with me as one unit.

Cylas had his eyes closed when I visited his cell.

I grabbed a bucket and threw the contents on him.

"Wake up!"

Cylas screamed and scrambled up to stand.

"What the fuck are you doing here?" I demanded, gripping the cell bars.

Cylas sputtered the bucket liquids from his mouth.

I sniffed.

Urine.

"You're a dead man, Sethos," Cylas growled, wiping his eyes.

I lifted my eyebrows. "You're the one on the other side of the cell, friend." I chuckled. "A mighty god. Subdued by a mere girl."

Cylas advanced to the bars and gripped them. "Where is she?"

I tilted my head to the side. I knew he meant Renna.

Iagon stood behind me as well as several guards. My overprotectiveness of Renna took over.

I moved my head to the side and looked back. "Everyone out."

The guards froze in place. Usually, they jumped at my command.

Did they doubt my authority?

"*Out!*" I screamed, startling them, and they quickly exited the dungeon.

Iagon remained and crossed his arms.

"Leave, Iagon," I said, looking back to Cylas.

Iagon stepped beside me. "You cannot be serious." He shook his head. "I'm your right hand—"

"And I am telling you to leave. *Now.*"

Iagon frowned. "Sethos, *he* is a prisoner here." He gestured to Cylas. "I have been in charge of the security of Vasarys while you have been gone—"

"I will not repeat myself again," I gritted out and felt the darkness slither into my hands, culminating in a black mist of swirling magic.

Cylas's eyes grew, and he stepped back.

Iagon shook his head. "Very well," he said in a muted tone and turned sharply to leave.

"Am-Re resorted to similar threats too," Cylas said in a disapproving tone.

"You will shut your mouth." I gripped the bars tighter and willed my magic to bring Cylas closer.

Cylas slammed against the bars, and he groaned.

"I told you to never return," I gritted out. "I let you leave last time because you had no role in the attack on Isyos. I considered myself merciful."

"Where do you have Renna, you miserable son of a bitch?"

Will you let him attack your mother like that? The dark voice inside my brain mocked me.

No. I saw red.

Attacks against my mother just wouldn't do.

The darker qualities of the magic within me suddenly exploded more rapidly than I anticipated, and Black Fire emerged from my arms and hands, grasping onto Cylas and burning him.

Cylas screamed as the smell of burning flesh filled the air.

"She will hate you!" he screamed as his skin burned a bright red.

I could see bone, and a smile curled my lips.

"Renna cares for me! She will hate you when she sees what you have done to me."

The mention of Renna's name made me pause.

I stumbled back and frowned, looking at my hands.

Something leaden moved inside my veins, and I shuddered.

Cylas doubled toward the ground, his wails filling the dungeon.

"You should have never come here," I yelled. "This is your fault."

"I came to save her from you," he whispered.

I walked to the cell and crouched next to his body against the bars.

"Renna is safe," I gritted out. "I left her sleeping in bed. She was clothed, don't worry, old man."

Cylas growled.

After Renna had collapsed in the forest of Daya, I portaled us back to the fortress and laid her down in her bedroom. I left a note next to her pillow telling her of my whereabouts and my return later in the night.

We had much to discuss.

"Of all despicable beings, I pity she is with you!"

I laughed. "She is safer with me than she would have ever been with *you*."

"You lie." Cylas struggled to sit up and screamed in pain.

I looked at his cuffs and urged my magic to clasp around them, pressing them against his skin.

Cylas's howls and curses echoed in the dungeon, and I could hear the rest of the prisoners we held stir at the noise.

After a while, Cylas was quiet, his eyes squeezed shut.

"Why not just let her be?" Cylas whispered, his voice hoarse.

"I need her."

"Of course you do," Cylas growled. "You want to siphon her energy, don't you? You're just like him."

"I am not her father," I spat. "*He* means to use her power. I only want to keep her safe from him."

Cylas looked at me then. "But you said you killed Am-Re." Cylas frowned. "We all heard you—"

"I killed him physically. But Am-Re's soul lives."

Cylas's eyes widened. "What did you do?" he whispered.

I stood. "I killed his physical body over seven years ago. I scattered his remains like you heard me say in Taria. Someone has gathered Am-Re's remains with, I'm assuming, the goal of bringing him back."

Cylas covered his face for a long moment and then looked up, his hands on his temples.

Cylas shook his head and spoke, his voice slurred. "You should have killed all of him . . ." He paused. "His wrath will be . . . like nothing we've ever seen." Cylas twitched on the ground in pain. "And you have condemned Renna to the worst possible reality."

I knew that.

I carried the guilt of not having killed Am-Re properly almost eight years ago.

I had never killed a god before, and my mistake was costing me.

"So explain to me *how* she is safer with you."

I laughed. "I don't have to tell you anything, Creator God."

"Have you hurt her?" he asked. "She deserves love. To be cared for. To be—"

"My goal is never to hurt her." I seethed.

"But you have!" he screamed. "You posed as Am-Re on her campus, terrorizing her."

"I did what I had to do. She is safe. Well looked after."

"Where is she now?"

I didn't hesitate. Cylas would die in this cell. The cuffs around his wrists would ensure it.

"Daya."

Cylas frowned. "You took her to a fae sanctuary for fucking criminals."

"As I said," I growled, "Renna is safe."

"Who looks after her?"

"I do."

Cylas shook his head. "Is she frightened?"

"No." I stepped closer to the bars. "I have been training her to use her magic."

Cylas blinked.

"You gods showed Renna how to wield physical weapons." I lowered my voice. "I have trained her to use the Black Fire. And she wields Darkness. And she is magnificent."

Cylas's mouth opened.

"If battle comes, she will know how to fight."

"She shouldn't have to fight. All she should know is peace!"

"Battle is coming, Cylas. Would you rather she remain docile and unable to defend herself?"

"Never." He tried to point at me, but his hand was shaking. "You are twisting my words."

"I will never let Renna be unprotected."

Cylas frowned. "You love her?"

I clenched my jaw and turned on my heels to leave.

"That is why you look after her." His voice was barely a whisper. "Even as you hurt her, you love her."

I didn't need a god dissecting my relationship with Renna. "I don't owe you anything."

"I may die here, Sethos."

I lifted my chin.

"Promise me, whatever happens, she'll be safe."

With conflict rapidly rising, I would do everything in my power to keep her far from pain and suffering. Whether it was Am-Re's magic threatening my life source, the battle with the gods, or Am-Re's return and the subsequent fight against Renna and me, one of these would be the end of me. I could feel death inch closer every day, its grip tightening with every passing moment. I would not be able to assure her safety if I were gone, and that thought rocked me.

"You are nobody to ask that of me."

"I may be nobody to ask you that," Cylas gritted out. "But still. Please ensure she is safe."

I didn't know how to respond to that without spiraling into panic.

"How does it feel?" I pulled back some of my magic and watched as Cylas screamed and bent over. "Knowing you will die here?"

"*Fuck you!*"

Cylas cried out again.

"I told you Renna was not yours. She is mine."

I pulled back more of my magic and bent down to level him with my stare.

"If I come out of this alive and battle comes . . ." Cylas said through clenched teeth, his spit hanging from his mouth.

I stood and turned my back to him.

"Do not expect me to be a friendly face," he finished.

I clenched my fists. "If battle comes, Creator God." I turned to face him. "Don't expect to be a part of it."

Cylas screamed as I pulled back the last of my power.

"Your penance will be to be left behind once more as slaughter ensues." I tilted my head. "Although this time, the dead will be your kin."

42

SETHOS

The day would not end.

I was in my war room with my commanders, going over the travel logistics of taking such a large army across the galaxies to Taria. It would be a long journey.

A man suddenly rushed into the room. "There's been a situation."

I looked up. "What kind of situation?" I snapped.

The man, a palace messenger, stood fidgeting with a scroll.

"There's—" The messenger began and blanched when he saw my face. "T-there's b-been an accident."

Conversation in the room stopped.

"*Well?*" I demanded.

The man flushed red and began to walk toward me, but I snapped a finger, and the scroll disappeared from his hands, appearing in mine.

I looked down and read the words, and it felt like my body began to tilt.

No.

"The mines," the messenger said. "They have collapsed."

I WALKED the length of the lava lake that emptied into the mining pit. The lava settled to the core of the pit and heated the walls, resulting in the precious mineral. The pit was as deep as the eye could see, with hundreds of ladders, pathways, and levels scaling the perimeter. While training to be a soldier, many of the endurance exercises had been held here.

Several of the council members stood at the foot of the pit with the mine overseers. They all looked on as workers formed an assembly line to bring the remains of the fallen to the top.

Hundreds of citizens gathered around.

The sounds of weeping and wailing filled the air.

Frantic women screamed in rage and had to be held back by others around them.

Grief gripped my soul as smaller bodies wrapped in white linen were carried up.

I had failed them.

I had failed my people.

"What happened?" I gritted out, my eyes concentrated on the bodies coming up.

Another small body was brought up.

I curled my fists as my body became hot with rage.

"Someone better speak!" I yelled.

The mining council members stepped up from the crowd, their perspiring faces pale.

"Ahtar." One of them bowed low. "Your Majesty."

He waited for me to tell him to rise, but I pressed my lips in a tight line.

"Sethos?" he glanced up in question.

"How many children?" I demanded, looking down at him and his councilmen.

Mothers in the crowd screamed for justice.

"We trusted you!" they screamed at me.

My heart sank.

My eyes darted as fingers pointed my way.

Men in the crowd spit toward me.

"That's a complex answer," the councilman said.

His response made me see red. I called upon the black magic ingrained in my body and raised my hand. The councilman rose with the magic in my palm, levitating off the ground.

Council members began to shift nervously, their attention on their fellow man, who now began to flail his legs.

I focused on his neck and clenched my fist. Clawing at invisible hands at his throat, he struggled to breathe. The action brought a familiar dark thrill through my body, and I felt trickles of my blood and cells begin to be set aflame. I knew there was a price to pay for this magic, but in that moment I did not care.

"I specifically said no children," I screamed. "How many children?" I asked, sparing a glance to where he was suspended.

He began to turn purple, foam coming from his lips. I looked around at the gathered councilmen. Nobody said anything. Nobody vouched for him. Everyone looked away.

"No one?" I yelled. "I will toss this scum into the fucking pit unless someone answers my question!"

His fellow councilman stepped forward and knelt. "One hundred and fifty-seven children." His voice was quiet. "Three hundred adults in total."

My eyes widened, and I dropped the councilman on the ground.

"Who made the order?" I screamed.

Silence met me.

I shot my dark magic at the councilman who was struggling for air and raised him up again.

"Who made the order for children to work?" I repeated.

The councilmen shifted uneasily.

"Cowards," I spat. "You only care about yourselves."

I felt the lifeforce dwindle in the man clutched in my grasp.

The man looked to me, his eyes bloodshot and skin beginning to turn purple. A guilty look passed in his eyes.

"Kill him!" mothers in the crowd wailed.

"Avenge us, Ahtar!"

My body began to vibrate with barely contained rage.

The man moved his lips and could barely form the words. "I . . . did . . ."

I clenched my jaw as years of anger rose to the surface. Images of the battered bodies of deceased children from the attack on Isyos haunted me, drowning me in a shrill ringing in my ears that began to fill me with fury until my eyes were blurry from the emotions coursing through my body.

The faces of the crowd began to blur, and my head began to throb.

I was no stranger to killing.

I had been one of Am-Re's assassins.

I had killed before.

Many times.

But today was the first day in seven years, since inheriting Am-Re's magic, that I had killed with my own hands.

And it felt good.

The disintegrating bodies of the men in the forest flashed in my mind, and a feeling of satisfaction burrowed itself deep into my soul.

But Am-Re's magic had a price.

And my time trickled closer to running out with every single use.

"Kill him!" the crowd shouted.

A woman stumbled forward, her hair silver like mine. Her

eyes were a different color, but her face reminded me of my mother's had been—haunted by grief.

"Ahtar," she sobbed at my feet, grabbing my cloak and pulling it to her. Two men from the crowd ran to her to pry her away. Her eyes bored into mine. "My child. They took my child. You are our only hope!"

I swallowed.

My magic demanded satisfaction to my people.

What shall we do? my magic cooed.

Kill.

Suffer.

Pay.

Glory.

I closed my eyes and welcomed the dark magic coursing through me kill once more. It quickly slithered within me to my entire body, as if violently pushing aside everything I was, slashing the sea fae soul inside me with sharp venomous claws.

I felt empowered.

And doesn't that feel good? the voice whispered.

Yes.

I was high off the feeling.

Opening my eyes, I locked gazes with the man suspended above. "May your soul be burdened with the choices you made here," I gritted out and released the magic within me.

Like the beast that resided inside, violent black swirls of magic erupted from me, encircling my arms like vicious serpents until the magic spread from my fingers and attacked his body, sending him higher and higher in the sky. As the dark magic inside overtook my actions, I suddenly felt like I was watching the events unfold before me out of my body.

And then came magic's payment.

I screamed as the magic intensified and began burning me

inside, but I could not stop. I had an urge to feel the man's body shatter and break.

I needed it.

My magic slammed him to the ground.

Silence spread over the crowd.

I stared at his limp body and trembled. My magic cast him into the middle of the mining pit, where his body would burn as the others had.

A just end.

My spine rolled with a dark shiver, and I cracked my back, something sinister settling within me.

I twisted my neck side to side, trying to shake the feeling off.

I looked to my council.

They all stood in silence.

They're eyes told me everything.

Respect.

Pride surged inside me, and a smile curled on my lips.

"Where is Velos?" I growled to the men present.

"Not here," a councilman said, his eyes glued to the ground.

"Interesting that the man who pushed for the mining changes chooses not to be here," I snapped.

"Velos has not been seen since this morning, Ahtar," another councilman shared solemnly.

I froze.

He must have known the accident would happen beforehand.

My body shook with rage.

"I want him found." I pointed to the group. "I want him hunted like a fucking animal. I want him dragged to me. *Now.*"

"He and his entire family are gone, Ahtar," another councilman said quietly.

"What do you mean *gone*?"

No one could leave Vasarys unless they used a portal. Only

supernaturals possessing magic could conjure portals. Am-Re had granted Velos immortality but he had no magic.

A councilman approached me. "He was not present at meetings today. My wife was to meet with Velos's wife today, but his wife could not be located. His daughters were not present for school lessons."

"So he just left?" I yelled at the group.

The men nodded uneasily, avoiding my eyes.

The man in front of me began to flush a deep burgundy red, and I looked to the group behind him.

There was one person who would help Velos.

"Bring Demira to me in the throne room. *Now.*"

The men quickly began to disperse.

I walked up to the workers who were still bringing up bodies. Their faces were charred from having to extricate the dead from the lava-damaged crevices in the mine shafts.

The workers looked up, their faces weary.

"Halt the mining work for a week. We will mourn the dead. Prepare the bodies for a burial. Iagon will make arrangements."

The workers nodded.

"And cut back to regular production," I added.

"Yes, Ahtar."

I forced my body to move from the pit to avoid seeing more bodies being brought up.

Without strong trade, there would be no money to pay the army.

With no army, I could not attack Taria.

And that would not do.

I curled my fists.

There had to be another way to sway the army to do what I wanted.

The dark magic that had settled within me began to move

freely through my body, like a slow serpent learning its new home.

There is always a way . . . the voice said.

Today you have ensured no one will ever question you again.

You have done good.

I cracked my neck side to side with newfound purpose and walked to my palace.

43

SETHOS

I was in the throne room, looking out toward the fiery lake that surrounded the cliffs where the palace was located. It cast the throne room in a red haze.

"You asked for me."

I turned from the windows.

Iagon stood in the middle of the room, hands on his hips, with the audacity to look disturbed.

"I did." I narrowed my eyes at him.

Iagon crossed his arms. "You killed one of our own. Do you seek to alienate the council? This is not the time to act irrationally. What overtook you?"

Anger swirled within me as he defended the life of the deceased councilman.

"Children died," I gritted out and took a deep breath to quell the magic inside me. "People *died*. That's what happened."

My head began to pound as the magic surged and thrashed inside me like a tempest.

"Sethos." Iagon shook his head. "I understand, but you can't retaliate in this manner—"

"And you expect me to do nothing? Simply so we don't *offend* the nobles?" I pressed my hands to my head to stop the dull pain.

Iagon continued in an admonishing tone. "You need the support of the nobles right now with the campaign. Killing one of them is—"

I pointed to him. "You're not here to think. You're here to do as I ask. And I did not ask for your fucking opinion."

He glared at me.

"Where were you?" I yelled.

Iagon turned red and stumbled over his words. "I was indisposed—"

"*You* are my second," I barked. "You were not there when I went down to the mines."

Iagon remained silent.

I rubbed my face in frustration. "I made inquiries as to where you were after I came back from the mines."

"I'm sorry—"

"You were told the mines collapsed. Apparently, you couldn't be bothered to leave the whore you were fucking to give a damn about the accident."

Iagon remained silent, his eyes on the ground.

If Iagon had been next to me when I surveyed the mines, he would have helped me not attack the councilman.

Right?

"I appointed you to be my second and stand at my side after fighting alongside you for years. I trust very few in this fucking place." I narrowed my eyes. "You failed me."

"I already apologized—"

"I come back to my lands, and it's chaos." Volatile magic rose within me.

"And you don't think being gone for long periods of time has something to do with it?" he yelled.

I glared at him. "We need to see what Demira has to say about all this."

He frowned. "What do you want with her?"

My hand twitched as dark magic swirled down my arm with the need to strike him. "Velos is missing."

Iagon's eyes widened, and his jaw hung slack.

Had he not known?

"How do you not know he is gone, Iagon?" I yelled.

He tried to form words, but I cut him off.

"I think Demira is behind the collapse of the mines."

Iagon shook his head. "That's not possible. We keep heavy surveillance on her. She has not been by the mines in a while. You know this."

"She doesn't need to go by the mines to be involved in them," I snapped. "If Velos is missing, perhaps he is—"

"I don't believe she is involved."

"They both have a vested interest in my failure. Velos and Demira are practically associates. I very much doubt he would do anything without her knowing. She wants to see me destroyed."

"I think you are gravely mistaken. She wants your crown but would not kill *children*—"

Rage boiled inside me. "You're thinking again!"

Iagon paused.

I pointed to him. "You tread on very thin ice, friend."

"Will you hurt her?" he gritted out.

"*Why?*" I demanded. "Are you enamored with her like the rest of the men at court? I told you she is not for you."

The dark magic rumbled and swirled off my body like a small tremor, and shadows began to fill the throne room.

Iagon began to back away. "Sethos . . ."

I snapped my eyes to him. "Do not speak."

Iagon looked around as the shadows reached him. He dragged his eyes back to me. "Friend, what has gotten into you?"

He held his palms up and took a step toward me. "A darkness has taken hold of you. These last few weeks, something has changed—"

"The guards are taking too long to bring her down. Go bring Demira to me."

Iagon frowned. "*No.* I will not have you hurt more people."

I lifted my eyebrows, and my shadows rolled around Iagon until they covered his body up to his neck. "*Excuse me?*"

Iagon lifted his chin. "Tell me you won't hurt her!"

"I don't owe you any explanation. Do as I say."

"You want a yes-man. That doesn't help a leader."

"You are a servant to the crown," I spat. "*To me.*"

I forced my shadows to bring him to me.

"I cannot support your actions any longer, friend." Iagon struggled to free himself.

Rage sent violent electricity shooting from my hands to Iagon, gripping his body and throwing him across the room until he slammed against a wall. My magic pinned him down, restricting his air.

Iagon's eyes looked at me with fear, and something within me rejoiced.

Iagon thrashed as he struggled for air.

I walked to him slowly. "The faces of the mothers down at the mines," I gritted out. "The suffering of my people. It haunts me. It burns inside me."

I could picture Etara speaking to me as if she were in the room, admonishing me. What would she say? "*This is not the way,*" she would cry. "*There is good in you still. Do not turn to violence as an easy solution.*"

I clenched my jaw. "Sometimes violence is the only way," I said.

When I got to Iagon, I crouched down beside him. "Oh, friend." My voice was low, and I put my hand on his head, brushing hair off his face as he struggled to breathe. "I don't like you questioning my actions."

Iagon tried nodding.

"You side with the enemy. The council."

"You—" Iagon struggled. "Are not above the law . . . Sethos."

I grimaced and leaned down to whisper. "That's where you're wrong, friend."

I tightened my magic around his throat, and satisfaction rose within me as his skin turned a dark red.

"You see"—I lifted my eyebrows—"I'm tired of waiting for my plans to come to fruition. I've tried to be patient. I've tried to stay within the lines. I don't want to wait any longer to take my revenge."

"What . . . will . . . y-you do?" he rasped. "Force . . . the c-council and . . . army?"

I smiled as the darkness overtook my body.

"All I wanted was for you to be my second. To be my friend and stand by my side."

Iagon blinked as tears streamed down his face.

"I was going to have you fetch Demira." I patted his face. "But I don't trust you. You would likely only help her escape."

I stood and called back my magic, bracing myself as it snapped back into my body.

"Guards," I called to the men standing outside the throne room without taking my eyes off Iagon.

Iagon rubbed his chest, and for a brief moment, guilt flashed through my body.

Twenty armed men stepped inside. "Yes?" one of them asked, coming to stand before me.

"Bring the palace Mage and the councilmen to me. I have an errand for them to run."

The guards bowed and marched out of the room.

Iagon scrambled to stand and immediately set space between us. "You are becoming like him." He wheezed. "Like Am-Re."

I shook my head. "Am-Re's hatred was due to vanity. His personality was simply an overinflated ego. I have a higher calling, Iagon."

Iagon rubbed his chest once more. "What are you planning to do to Demira?" he breathed.

"We're going to question her. Hopefully she'll know where Velos is."

"We?" Iagon asked. "You talk about yourself in plural . . ."

The magic inside me burst from my palms and drifted over to him, encircling him like a serpent.

Iagon shut his eyes, and tears fell on his cheeks. "Please don't kill her," he said, his voice barely a whisper.

"Enough with the dramatics, Iagon." I sighed and pulled my magic back, walking to my dais and climbing the steps. "I only kill those who are not useful to me." I didn't bother to look at him as I approached my throne. "You'd do well to remember that."

44

RENNA

My hands moved above cold fabric, and I immediately opened my eyes and jumped. Startled, I looked around.

I was in my bedroom, in my bed.

It was later in the evening, and muted light filtered in from the forest through my window.

I looked down to see myself covered in my sheets, my clothes still the same from what I had worn in the forest.

The forest.

I shot out of bed, almost stumbling from being tangled up in the bedsheets.

I gripped my pounding head and sat back down.

The events from the forest replayed on a loop, and my body tensed as the eyes of the tall fae bored into me in his final moments.

Sethos killed him.

He did ask to die . . .

And Sethos killed him.

In cold blood.

I shook my head slowly and groaned when the movement

made me dizzy. I knew intuitively that the amount of power I had used was the culprit of why I felt off.

I called my magic forth, and it began to swirl in my chest. I directed it toward my temples.

A rush of cool magic encased my head, and I sagged my shoulders and closed my eyes as the magic seeped into the areas where I ached.

As I focused my magic to heal me, my chest began to feel like it was caving in.

I placed a hand there and could feel the magic swirling under my skin as it sent healing magic to my head.

What was happening to me?

My body typically felt sore after I used Darkness, but this didn't physically hurt ...

It was like a dragging feeling, a cavity of black that made the muscles there tense. My breaths sawed in and out of me, and my heart beat loudly in my ears.

It wasn't physical pain.

It was the settling in of deep disappointment and rage.

Sethos had mistreated me and pushed me.

He forced me into a situation I had pleaded to have no part in.

He manipulated me to prove I was loyal.

A sob racked my body as the eyes of the tall fae flashed in my mind.

I covered my face with my hands.

I would never escape the memory of his eyes.

He was a terrible criminal and didn't deserve a happy ending.

But despite his abhorrent and disgusting actions, he, too, suffered his own loss.

I would never condone his behaviors, but to be forced to be his executioner?

After my father had forced me many times to perform dark magic as a child?

Sethos knew how much I struggled to overcome my trauma.

He was going to get a piece of my fucking mind.

Of all the people who would treat me like that, I would have never expected it to be *him*.

Asshole.

I squeezed my eyes and urged more magic toward my head to stop my headache, and a rush of super-cold magic stunned me with a terrible brain freeze.

I dropped my head to my lap and waited for the sensation to pass.

After a few moments of deep breathing, the headache abated, and I slowly straightened my back. The healing magic slowly left my head, and I stood.

I changed into fresh clothing, all the while cursing Sethos's name. He would come back sooner or later, and I would be waiting for him. Maybe I would try and summon my dretani to scare him shitless.

He would never ever treat me like that again.

I would make sure of it.

As I began to straighten my bed, I noticed a white paper on the pillow next to mine.

I frowned and leaned across the bed to grab it.

It was from Sethos.

I went to Vasarys. I hope to be back by tonight. If not, tomorrow.
-Sethos

Anger rattled inside me.

No apology.

No remorse.

Fuck him.

Oh, he was delusional if he thought I would let this pass for an entire night without talking to him.

I wouldn't wait for him to come to me.

I would go to him.

He said Vasarys was dangerous? That it was a risk to me?

That I couldn't go until I mastered my magic?

My magic was sufficient to protect me from anyone there. Tonight was a clear indication of that. If I had wanted to kill those fae, I would have.

Sethos also warned that it was inadvisable to portal to people but that it could be done if one imagined their essence.

I closed my eyes and moved my hands in a clockwise motion to create a portal, concentrating on my connection to Sethos and the magic we shared.

I couldn't wait to see the look on his face when he saw me in Vasarys.

Warning be dammed.

45

RENNA

My body slammed into stone, and I groaned as I rolled to my side to take in my surroundings.

I was in a dark corridor with low ceilings, lined with gray stone floors and walls. A lone window with black bars was in the middle of the corridor, casting a red tinge into the room. A dim, flickering green light farther down the hallway glowed as well.

I frowned.

Where was I?

I moved my hands along the stone floor and pushed myself to sit.

Sound suddenly came from next to me.

A groan.

More like a low moan.

I pushed my body against the wall nearest to me until my eyes adjusted.

The moan sounded again.

"*Water,*" a person croaked.

I covered my mouth as my eyes focused on a person before me—behind bars.

I quickly stood and, with my body pressed against the wall, began to move down the hallway.

Filled with bars.

So many bars.

It was a dungeon jail of sorts?

Where had I landed?

Was this Vasarys, or had my portal to Sethos failed?

I could portal back to Daya, but I needed to see where I was first. I couldn't give up that easily. Perhaps I had landed in the lower structure where Sethos was? Why had my portal led me here? Had he been here seconds ago?

I covered my mouth as I observed prisoner after prisoner in the cells.

Some were unconscious.

All of them were injured, some with open sores on their bodies.

Some were lumped over and sobbing softly.

Was this Sethos's true . . . essence?

Cruelty?

If this was Vasarys then Sethos had to know these prisoners were here.

Anger raged inside me, and it propelled me farther down the hallway.

My eyes focused now on the glowing green light.

It was coming from a lone cell.

My lungs paused as I felt a strange pull toward the light.

And then I saw him.

Cylas.

He was on the ground, eyes closed, with handcuffs of some sort around his wrists, blackening the skin as he openly bled gold. He was in a pool of gold blood.

Black and blue bruises marred his face, and one of his eyes

looked painfully bloated, as if blood could gush from it any moment.

My beautiful friend was broken.

My body was momentarily paralyzed as I stood outside his cell, and then all my emotions rushed in with no warning.

Tears filled my eyes, and I let out a silent scream.

I ran to the bars and knelt.

"Cylas!" I whispered loudly.

No response.

"No, no, no," I cried. "Stop this right now," I implored. "I'm begging you to answer me."

No response.

My hands trembled with sweat as I tried to reach for his body, but my arms were not long enough.

If I tried to break the bars, I would draw too much attention, and whoever put Cylas here would come looking for the source of the noise.

If Cylas, a *god*, had been incarcerated, I had to be smart and try to keep quiet.

I had to send healing magic to him, but would it work if I wasn't touching him?

You know you can trust yourself. My subconscious reminded me.

You got this.

I nodded and blew out a breath.

I had to try.

Closing my eyes, I called my magic forth and let the cool rushing energy move from my center, up my shoulders, down my arms, and to my fingertips. When I opened my eyes, the blue magic moved in tendrils toward Cylas. It reached him and settled on his body, covering him like a blanket.

I leaned my head against the cell bars as my magic worked, tears pouring over my cheeks.

I would never forgive the person who had done this to him. Never.

At the thought, my magic rushed out faster, and Cylas twitched, his back arching as the magic hit him.

Then his body slammed on the ground.

I opened my mouth in a silent scream.

Then silence.

I retracted my magic and sat on the ground with my hands over my mouth.

Had I killed him somehow?

"*Cylas!*" I whispered loudly and knelt again. "Wake up!"

"Fuck you," he whispered.

My body stilled as dread filled me. "Cylas?"

"Fuck you, Sethos, for this magic that sounds like her."

Blood drained from my face, and my jaw tensed.

"Fuck you to a million hells, Sethos," Cylas gritted out.

"*Cylas,*" I barked. "Open your eyes."

He cracked one eye open.

It felt like he stared at me for a million years before he spoke.

"Are you real?" he asked.

"Who the fuck did this to you?" I growled.

I already knew the answer.

Cylas opened both eyes, and his jaw dropped.

I just needed him to say it.

"Renna," Cylas breathed and sat up slowly.

I looked down to his wrists, where blood still poured from his body.

"Did Sethos do this?" I gritted out.

Cylas moved to lean against a wall.

"In part, yes."

Dark anger reared its ugly head inside me, and I rose.

"Renna," Cylas said, his eyes widening. "What are you doing in Vasarys?"

His confirmation of where I was made me release a breath I didn't know I was holding and also made my heart sink because my intuition screamed Sethos was likely at fault people were kept in these the prison conditions.

"I'm getting you out of here."

"You need to get away from here. It's not safe. He will return."

"Let him," I growled.

Cylas shook his head. "Renna, you don't know what you're up against—"

"Stand back."

"Renna."

"I said," I gritted out, "stand back."

I called on Darkness then, and the magic instantly rushed from me, shadows and tendrils pooling at my feet.

Cylas gasped, his face going even paler.

"No," he breathed, looking at my magic. "This isn't possible."

I smiled and lifted my hands to the bars, directing my magic to them with the intention of disintegrating them.

On contact, the bars turned into dust.

I lifted my chin, pride swelling in my chest.

I would never doubt my magic again for as long as I lived.

Cylas sprang up and staggered as he walked toward me.

I recalled the Darkness and caught him.

He flinched when I tried to support his arms.

"What are these?" I asked.

Cylas huffed. "Alaric Chains. Demonic handcuffs meant to bleed a person of their magic and lifeforce. Don't touch them."

"How can I get these off?" I asked.

"Can we try your shadow trick?" he said jokingly. "Just don't amputate my arms, please. Women love my fingers. Particularly my right hand." He winked.

I couldn't help but chuckle. Joking through pain was a very Cylas thing to do.

I called forth a smaller amount of Darkness, and a sole tendril of black magic extended out from my chest. I mentally directed it to one of the cuffs with the intention to dissolve it.

Cylas stayed very still as the magic encircled his wrist, and we watched as the cuff slowly dissolved into black dust.

Cylas flexed his hand, and I repeated the action with his other cuff.

When he was freed, I wrapped Cylas in a hug and began to sob against the crook of his shoulder.

As I held him he moved his arms around me and I could feel how weak he was.

"Don't cry," he whispered. "I'll get stronger. You saved me."

Cylas moved away from me and looked down at his wrists. The black charred skin was slowly regenerating. "See?" he said a gestured to his wrists. "I'm healing."

Watching his damaged body patch itself together was fascinating. The Chains had burned his skin down to almost the bone. I could see his veins, which were gold, throbbing as his body pumped blood to rebuild damaged muscle and ligaments.

"I will never forgive Sethos," I gritted. "*Never.*"

Cylas cupped my jaw. "Tell me what he has done to you." Cylas eyes looked me over as if checking for injuries.

"Nothing compared to what I will do to him."

"Not alone, you won't."

I shook my head. "It's my battle to fight, Cylas."

"Like hell it is." His eyes were furious. "You think you can take him on?"

I crossed my arms.

"Yes. *I can.*"

Cylas shook his head. "Renna, be reasonable. He'll kill you."

"No. He won't."

Sethos wouldn't kill me. He felt something for me. In a twisted way, he cared about me.

"Do you know what he's planning?" Cylas asked.

My breath caught in my throat, anticipating the worst. "No . . .?" I said, shaking my head.

Cylas sighed and crossed his arms. "He has assembled an army to attack Taria."

I blinked.

Cylas cursed.

"Why am I the one always assigned to share major reveals?"

Rage filled me.

"Why would he attack Taria . . .?" I asked slowly.

"Arios and some of the gods in the enclave attacked his home planet of Isyos when Sethos was a child. And when Am-Re wasn't successful at obtaining vengeance on the gods, Sethos killed him and took his throne. And now he's seeking his retribution."

My world tilted on its axis, and I forced myself to blink several times as a wave of nausea hit me.

He used me.

My lips trembled.

He fucking used me.

I took a deep breath and clenched my teeth as my chest expanded with rage.

He was training me to attack Taria and the Celestial gods.

I angrily wiped the tears from my face.

"Renna?" Cylas asked me carefully.

I remained silent as I took in the news.

"We need to get out of here. We need to inform Khellios and the rest of the enclave."

I nodded, unable to form words.

"I've recruited the Elemental Enclave to help us thwart his efforts," Cylas began. "I promised I would collect the God of Fire's half sister, Illona, from here in exchange for the enclave's support. We can't leave without her."

"My sister . . ." were the only words that escaped my mouth.

"Yes," Cylas said quietly. "I'm glad you at least know who she is."

I nodded slowly, my throat heavy with phantom words unable to escape.

"I'll go look for her and bring her back here. Together, we'll portal to a star craft that's waiting outside of Vasarys. I hope the star craft is there. I don't know how long I've been here."

Cylas gripped my arms and lowered so we were level.

"Do not move from here, Renna. Stay here." Cylas narrowed his eyes. "Please, stick to the plan."

I looked to his wrists and saw they were completely healed. Terror filled me that Sethos would hurt Cylas again.

My palms clammed up as my thoughts began to spiral, but I forced myself to nod. My throat was dry.

"I . . ." My body trembled as I croaked the words out. "I never thought . . ."

I never thought I would ever need to worry about Sethos targeting people I had grown close to. I knew the gods had lied to me at Khellios's direction, but Sethos knew I cared about them.

Cylas looked back and forth between my eyes. "I know you're in shock, but this nightmare will end soon."

"Yes," I breathed.

Leaning in, Cylas kissed my forehead and hugged me. "I'll be back for you," he whispered against my skin.

My eyes followed him as he portaled from the dungeon.

I could only stand there feeling numb.

Sethos betrayed me.

Knowing what Khellios had done and how I felt about being lied to.

Sethos lied to me over and over again.

I should have known to never let my guard down after Khellios, but Sethos had seeped into my pores and became a part of me.

He had been a part of my life for so long and made sure I knew it so that I trusted him instantly.

He guarded me.

Banished my demons.

Made me crave him, beyond thought.

But I couldn't in good conscience agree to be with someone who wanted to kill people I loved.

Don't you love Sethos? my inner voice asked.

I paused as I mulled this question.

Did I love him?

A shudder moved through me like a wave at the realization.

I did love Sethos.

I covered my face with my palms.

What was the correct way to feel?

Was I wrong to feel anger?

Should I only feel sadness?

I felt disgusted for loving him.

You could love someone but not accept their actions, right?

He had played with my mind in such a way that I was even now considering forgiving him for everything if he simply called off the attack.

I had seen the goodness in him.

Now, I only saw chaos.

And Sethos would never forgive me for raising the alarm against his attack.

But I would never forgive myself if I stayed complicit in the genocide he was planning.

Many would die under his hands.

Panic filled me, robbing me of the ability to take a full breath, and I placed a hand on my chest.

I had found love at last after being so afraid of allowing someone into my life, and for what?

Loving someone doesn't mean you're obligated to excuse evil acts. My brain reminded me.

How hypocritical of me when I was also ready to kill my father.

You killing your father would be an act of self-defense. Sethos is not acting in self-defense. The destruction of Isyos happened hundreds of years ago.

Self-defense is an immediate act in direct response to a threat. Self-defense would be just if it is of the same level as the pain inflicted.

I clawed at my head and pulled at my hair to stop my brain from trying to form logic.

I didn't want to think.

I silently apologized to Cylas for ignoring his plan and rushed from the dungeon into the light.

46

SETHOS

Screams rang out in the throne room, and I shifted on my throne to get a better look.

"Let me go!"

Demira.

The guards struggled with her as her purple magic shot out to fight the soldiers' hold on her arms, but the Mage who had gone with them zapped her magic every time to counteract it.

She screamed as the Mage fought to control her.

I made eye contact with the Mage and nodded to him to bring her over. As Demira struggled to be contained, the people present in the throne room, nobles and councilmen alike, stared with open jaws. Their faces were pale, eyes wide, as they watched their precious heir being dragged.

When they reached the foot of the throne dais, the soldiers threw her body down. Within milliseconds, Demira's purple magic created a barrier to brace her fall.

Iagon tensed next to me as he looked on at Demira. He clenched his fists as if he wanted to help her.

I narrowed my eyes at him before returning my focus to Am-Re's daughter.

"You tore me from my tower," she said, pushing off the floor to stand. "You had no right!"

When she wavered and a soldier tried to steady her, I glared at him, and he stopped in his tracks.

He forced his eyes to the ground.

"I was bothering no one." Demira straightened her black tunic and dusted off her leggings. "I was practicing my craft. Is witchcraft to be forbidden now, Ahtar?"

"Where is Velos?" I gritted out. "I know he is behind the mines collapsing."

She frowned and lifted her chin. "Are you certain?" she asked.

"He is the only council member not here. His family is suddenly gone. Curious, is it not?"

"I am not his keeper. Are you not ruler here?" she sneered. "Shouldn't you know?"

"Don't talk back to me, Demira."

She shrugged. "I don't know."

Rage churned inside me.

I wanted to hurt something.

Somebody.

Her.

I wanted her to hurt as much as I did.

Didn't hurt people hurt people?

"Come now," I said, lifting an eyebrow. "Don't you know where all men are in this realm?"

A collective gasp filled the room.

Demira's skin flushed, and she clenched her fists.

She took a breath and answered. "That is hardly true, Ahtar." She walked closer and stopped at the bottom of the dais. "I never know where you are."

I smiled. "We all know how you like entertaining men, Demira," I began. "Don't you hold private audience in your quarters? Several councilmen like to visit."

Demira tensed, and Iagon glared at me.

"This is not who you are," Iagon whispered fiercely.

I ignored him.

"I have long been patient with you, Demira." I continued and stood, then descended the dais.

Illona stepped forth from the crowd then and stood a few paces behind her sister. She eyed me in warning, anger flashing in her eyes.

Illona never bothered me. Despite her loyalty to her sister, I was neutral toward Illona. She lacked the cruelty of Demira.

I returned my focus to Demira. "I provide you shelter. Food. You think I don't notice how you gather my councilmen in secret to depose me." I shook my head.

Demira crossed her arms. "This is my home. I will not thank you for your charity for things owed to me." She narrowed her eyes. "Things that are rightfully *mine*."

The people in the crowd murmured and nodded in agreement.

I was losing control of the situation.

Without the respect of the people in Vasarys, I was a failure.

"Kneel," I growled.

Demira paled and froze. Illona rushed to stand next to her.

"Sethos," Illona said. "Please. You mean to humiliate us?"

My skin prickled with heat, and I looked around me. Most of the council members and dozens of soldiers had ushered inside the throne room, their eyes trained on me, waiting to see what I would do.

Demira was favored by many. She granted people boons of magic.

"Kneel!"

"Why?" Demira asked calmly.

"Because I am your king—your Ahtar—and I am commanding you to kneel."

"How dare you," she gritted out.

A dark feeling overcame me and chilled my entire body. A heavy energy filled my chest, spreading like a spider's web inside me.

"I said, *kneel.*"

Demira glared at me.

Her disrespect would lead to a coup, and she would overthrow me like I had Am-Re.

I called my magic, and it reached for her, gripping her forcefully and pulling her down to the ground so she knelt.

Demira cried out as her body shook from the force pulling her down.

She tried opening her palms, but my magic forced her hands shut.

"*Stop this!*" Illona pleaded and knelt next to Demira.

"Sethos, please," she cried. She kissed Demira's brow. "Don't do this. What do you need? I can help you, just don't hurt her."

"Where is Velos?" I asked again.

Illona stilled, and Demira shrugged her off.

"I don't know."

"Very few people can create portals in this realm," I snapped. "Who else would have the magic to help him but you?"

"You have limited my portal powers," Demira growled. "I cannot leave Vasarys. Illona and I are prisoners in this place, just like how my father kept us."

"I don't believe you." I looked to Iagon. "Pick her up and take her from here."

Iagon hesitated but nodded and walked down to her.

"Where are you taking her?" Illona asked and clung to Demira as Iagon approached.

Iagon reached them and seemed to be gently pleading with the women.

"I will not leave her side," Illona gritted out.

Iagon tried to pry Illona's fingers from Demira, but when he couldn't, I called my soldiers to assist.

I wanted everyone to watch as Demira was dragged from her.

When the soldiers approached her, Illona's pleas rang through the hall.

The soldiers paused, not wanting to put their hands on Illona.

"Hopefully, one day," I said to Illona, "you'll see there's nothing good about Demira. Your sister is a traitor to this throne."

Illona simply cried in response.

I crouched next to Demira and spoke, loud enough for the room to hear.

"Your father put up with you many times. That will never happen again," I said calmly at first before my voice turned deadly. "If you ever defy me again"—I leaned toward her—"or threaten any of my plans, I will rip you apart like I did him."

Demira whimpered.

"You will beg me for mercy as I end your pathetic life."

Demira refused to answer me.

"Do you understand?" I yelled.

Demira looked away from me and locked her eyes on the throne.

The heavy energy inside me demanded retribution.

"I'm going to give you one more chance." I warned her. "Tell me where Velos is, Demira."

"I. Don't. *Know!*"

I called my magic and pried Illona off Demira, sending Illona sliding across the floor. My magic held her there.

"Don't touch her!" Demira screamed. "You're a monster!"

I straightened and stood.

"Would you like to see how much of a monster I can be?" The words escaped my mouth so fast that I wasn't sure where they had come from.

"You should have died that night in Isyos," Demira gritted out and spit on the ground at my feet.

I froze.

"Pity you didn't die alongside your mother," she said.

Rage pummeled through my body, and I screamed. The anger within exploded from me, my magic lifting Demira off the ground, gripping her neck.

Demira coughed and tried to break free.

"You're working with Velos to undermine me."

She clawed at the magic.

"You meet with him and others in secret. My spies have seen it."

"Put me down!" she screamed.

"You and Velos had the mines collapse so I wouldn't have funds to pay for my army."

"You don't need funds for the army!" she screamed. "Your magic clearly has no boundaries! If you want them to do your bidding, then make it so!"

At her words, the darkness took notice.

What an excellent idea, the voice inside me hissed.

Iagon suddenly put himself between Demira and me.

"This cannot go on any longer," he said to me.

My temples pulsed, and my vision blurred. "Step aside, Iagon," I said.

"She told you she doesn't know where Velos is. Let her go! She can't portal out of Vasarys. She is already a prisoner here."

"Iagon," I gritted out, "step aside."

"Sethos. This is not you. This is extreme!"

In that moment, my magic surrounded Iagon with black shadows like a fast-moving vortex, and Iagon crumpled to the ground.

"I warned you not to interfere!" I barked.

"Who are you?" Iagon screamed. "This is not who you are at

your core! Even your voice is different. You're transforming into something vile and dark."

My magic gripped him harder, and Iagon struggled to stand.

"Can't you hear yourself? Even your eyes—they're changing to black."

The crowd began to step back, their eyes wary.

I was waiting for them to look at me with pride.

I was showing strength, trying to punish for the deaths at the mines.

They were afraid of me?

I couldn't win.

"You both are trying to undermine me!" I said to Demira and Iagon. "*Traitors!*"

"You are not fit to be king, Sethos!" Iagon yelled. "You are no better than Am-Re. And you will be killed in the same manner."

I'd had enough.

I called my magic in that moment and lifted Iagon high off the ground.

"Today is the last day you interfere, Iagon."

I closed my eyes and let my magic crush his windpipes, and moments later, my magic slammed him to the ground.

The crowd screamed, and chaos broke out.

My head swam, and I stumbled backward onto the dais.

A soldier helped me stand.

I blinked to where Iagon had been.

Had I killed him?

Horror seized me as I looked at a massive indentation on the throne room floor . . .

Demira's face was now purple. She gasped as she tried to speak. "If you think . . . my sister and I will live . . . one more day ruled by another monster, then you are mistaken." She coughed and gasped for air. "You have descended down a dark path."

"Mage," I called to the palace Mage standing off to the left.

He stepped forth. "Yes, Ahtar?"

"Demira is a traitor to the throne and Vasarys."

"No!" Illona screamed.

"Take Demira to the dungeons."

The Mage nodded. "Certainly."

"Please!" Illona cried.

"Also," I said to the Mage. "Bind her with Alaric Chains to contain her magic."

Demira paled.

"No!" Illona screamed, tears streaming down her face. "You are condemning her to a slow death!"

"Your sister should welcome the handcuffs," I told Illona. "She had no problem treating our recent guest to the same fate."

"Fight me," Illona begged. "Take your anger out on me, but don't hurt her!"

I shook my head. "You are the only good thing about this place, Illona. I could never hurt you. You are a flower amongst the blight."

My magic lowered Demira to the ground, and the Mage walked to Demira, the cuffs materializing in his hands.

"Please," Demira whispered to him. "Don't hurt me."

"I'm sorry," the Mage whispered and cuffed Demira.

Demira's screams of agony echoed in the room.

A dark thrill passed through me as her flesh burned, Illona's cries only fueling the darkness inside me, and it settled deep into my marrow, finding a home.

My chest heaved as a stretching and shifting sensation racked my body, as if accommodating and making room for the magic moving inside me.

When Demira lost consciousness and slumped in the Mage's arms, the voice in my head erupted in laughter.

You have done well, the voice in my head hissed. *She was worthless anyway.*

I tensed as the voice continued.

To have this power, you must show extraordinary strength, and you have done that today, the voice said.

Clear the room.

Now!

"Out!" I screamed at the people in the throne room. "Everyone out!"

Rulers are called to make hard decisions . . . the voice said. *And now you must make another hard decision. And it's headed to the throne room . . .*

As the people exited, I looked to the doorway.

47

RENNA

I had two options as to how to move about Vasarys.

Hiding in the shadows, crouching around corners, hoping people wouldn't see me and report me to Sethos.

Or be chaos itself.

Have people tell Sethos I was here.

Have him come find me.

Because, oh, how I wanted to talk to him.

I slammed the door of the dungeon open, and it sent a loud crack into the silence of the upper floor.

Opulent black obsidian walls and floors were drenched in gold accents, from chandeliers to sconces, chairs, and paintings. I knew the palace was done in the taste of my father. That over-compensating, showy, dripping-in-arrogance ostentatiousness he exuded.

He was a stark contrast to Sethos, who preferred a stone fortress that was being overtaken by nature.

If only Sethos completely opposed my father in personality as well.

Two men in identical black armor with long spears jumped

and faced me with their weapons drawn as if they had been standing guard at the entrance of the dungeon.

"*Halt!*" one of them screamed and jabbed his spear toward me.

I smiled and swerved the jab. "Now that isn't very nice," I said and shook my head.

I called on Darkness, and it emerged from my chest, palms, and feet.

The men's eyes widened, yet they kept their weapons firmly drawn.

"Where is Sethos?" I growled.

"Who are you?" the second soldier barked. "Identify yourself!"

I sighed and lifted my palms, waving them in front of me. Tendrils of Darkness moved like ribbons toward their spears, and my magic clung to their spears, instantly turning their weapons into dust.

The men jumped back but immediately drew their swords. I wasn't surprised, soldiers were quick thinking and resourceful.

"We can do this all day," I said calmly. "Where is Sethos?"

"I said," the second soldier gritted out, "identify yourself!"

I glanced up to large chandeliers lining the hallway.

"And I also asked you a question, asshole," I spat. "Which you have failed to answer. Or do you only respond to threats?" I cocked my head.

The men looked between themselves uneasily, and I took the opportunity to pause my Darkness. Calling my green and black electric magic to my palms, I directed the power to the men. I had seen Sethos lift the fae criminals in the forest by the neck, so I lifted the men before me just the same.

"Where is Sethos?" I screamed.

One of the men spit at my face and cursed.

A dark torrent of rage and Darkness erupted within me, and I clenched my jaw and hands to contain it. I would not let it out and hurt these men in the way I knew my power was capable of.

You are not Sethos.

Breathe in.

You are not your father.

Breathe out.

I pushed the Darkness aside and instead focused on the magic I was using.

"You should be grateful I chose self-control today," I screamed and tossed each man atop a chandelier.

The chandeliers swung violently as the men clung on for dear life.

I turned my back and called on my Darkness, and erupted around me in a cloud of smoke. I chose left and walked down the corridor.

48

___

RENNA

I followed the sound of screams.

Was Sethos hurting people?

I pushed harder as I ran, my heart thumping painfully in my chest.

Two large black doors stood at the end of the hallway, perhaps two stories high. The doors were open and unguarded.

As I got closer, I saw a lone figure seated on a black obsidian throne inside the room.

Sethos.

Rage filled me, and I barged inside.

As I crossed the threshold, Sethos looked up, and we locked eyes.

He stood immediately.

The throne room was almost cloaked in darkness, barely any lights on.

Sethos was alone.

"What the fuck is this?" he barked at me.

"This looks cozy," I snapped. "Seems like I just missed something. I heard screams. I'm guessing it was probably something you did."

Sethos stepped down from the throne dais. "Why are you here?" he yelled. "I thought I told you to never come here alone. You promised you wouldn't leave Daya!"

I smiled and crossed my arms.

Would he ever tell me the truth?

"And I thought"—I stepped forward—"that I asked you to never lie to me."

Sethos froze. "Do I mistreat you?"

"No."

He lifted his eyebrow as he kept advancing toward me. "Are you treated with anything other than respect?"

I stayed silent, backing away from him.

"You lied to me." I laughed bitterly. "Honesty is respect. I never meant anything to you."

"That's not true."

"You used me."

He looked down to the floor. "Sometimes we must do certain things for the good of all."

My jaw dropped. "You don't even have the decency to look me in the eye!" I yelled and called my Darkness.

Sethos looked up slowly, and each agonizing second felt like an invisible knife slashing my body.

"Say something!" I pleaded.

His ice-blue eyes glittered intensely.

A large lump formed in my throat as my vision began to tunnel. I felt like I was outside of my body, slowly disassociating as I spoke.

"You lied to me. After everything. You're no different from the other men in my life."

Sethos's jaw clenched, but he remained silent.

"It was you, wasn't it?" I gritted out. "Who created chaos at my university to lure the gods? You planned this from the beginning.

You used my father's magic to frighten me . . ." I shook my head as I felt my cold fingers wrap around my arms.

Sethos's eyes bored into mine, rage barely contained in them.

"You tricked me into going to Taria, but not for my safety." My blood now pounded heavily in my ears.

Sethos ran a hand through his hair.

"It was all a lie." I took a step toward him. "You don't care for me at all." I shook my head. "How could you care for me when you used me so cruelly?"

Sethos clenched his hands into fists.

"I let you touch me—I let you . . ." Anger began to rumble inside me, and he was in front of me in an instant.

"If you're quite finished, I would like to speak," he growled.

"You don't have to ask me for permission." I shook my head. "You have taken everything from me so easily—"

"I never meant to hurt you—"

"*Fuck you!*"

"I kept you safe for *seven years*," he gritted out. "I searched for you for *years* even before *that*!" he spat. "I never gave up—"

"With the goal to use me."

"No! And you have to know that. I searched for you because you are *mine*," he growled, and I jumped back, but he held me so I wouldn't move.

He gripped my arms, and I yelped.

"You're hurting me!" I said and pushed against him.

Sethos cursed and let me go.

"*I was* yours," I yelled, putting space between us.

He pointed a finger at me. "Do *not* say that!"

"You call me yours? You may not have hit me like my father. You may not have beat me." I looked him up. "But you instilled fear in me. You took my peace. And then you welcomed me with open arms." I spit at his feet. "You disgust me, Sethos."

Sethos glared at me, sending an ominous chill down my spine.

"You used me for personal gain—"

"There were lives taken!" he screamed. "Lives callously murdered by your *friends*! What did you expect me to do?"

"There is always another way—"

"Not in this. *Never in this.* I saw an opportunity, and I took it," he said fiercely and walked up to me.

I narrowed my eyes as we stood face to face, mere inches from each other.

His eyes suddenly softened, and he leaned down to my ear. "Even now," he whispered.

Suddenly, he grabbed my arms, and we descended into a portal.

49

RENNA

Sethos and I landed deep in the forest of Daya, and I rolled from him and set distance between us, calling a Black Fire sword.

I didn't want to use Darkness in the forest and risk setting the trees on fire. I would not and could not burn this forest because of Sethos. He had done damage enough. I refused to be an extension of the chaos he was creating.

Sethos told me to always think outside the box in a fight.

I could portal from here.

I waved my hand clockwise, imagining my room in Taria, and waited.

Nothing happened.

Sethos laughed and stood.

"You're under my shield, Renna." He dusted dirt off his jacket. "I call the shots here. The ability to portal is now blocked."

I blinked as I realized there was no remorse in his words or tone.

I would have to move toward the edge of the shielded area and leave so I could portal.

I began to move backward.

"Why did you kill my father?" I asked, hoping to keep his mind busy.

"Why? I saw the way he hurt you." His face twisted with disgust. "The way he would force your magic to hurt others."

My lips quivered, and my eyes became glassy. "Your manipulation also hurts, Sethos."

Sethos's eyes were filled with pain, rage, and hate. "Do not say that!" he pointed at me. "I did *everything for you!* I was only able to see you during your years in foster care when Am-Re would leave your home every evening. Then you would leave your apartment and walk through the district to clear your mind. I would walk beside you at night, using a glamour to hide myself from you."

I recalled those nights and the streets I would roam. I would let my mind go blank and aimlessly wander. It was riddled with crime, and sometimes I wished I would be killed to end my miserable existence.

"I kept you safe every fucking night. Did you never wonder why no one ever pulled you into a dark alley as you walked the streets alone? You lived in one of the worst fucking slums in Andora. You would have died without me."

My eyes began to water.

"When I found you, your mind was fractured." He shook his head. "I knew the way you hid the bruises on your arms. Or the way you would jump when you heard loud noises . . ." Sethos clenched his jaw. "The vacant look in your eyes those days. It broke me.

"The day of your eighteenth birthday, you went to the hill overlooking the district. I followed you. You sat there for hours in silence. I sat next to you, cloaked in invisibility. There was no life in your eyes, Renna."

He continued. "That night, you wished for two things out loud."

I hugged my arms around myself and held my breath for his

next words, knowing what he would say. It was the same two wishes I'd made since the age of six, when my father began to abuse me.

"The first wish was that you wanted him dead. And the second was that you wanted to experience normal life." His voice was raw, edged with anger and pain.

I covered my face and began to sob.

"And so—" Sethos's voice broke, and he cleared his throat. "I made sure Am-Re would never bother you again."

The realization of what he did for me and how he equally hurt me was overwhelming.

"For you, I would kill him every single time, in every lifetime."

"And what is the price?" I cried. "The magic has corrupted your soul into taking justice into your own hands."

"Justice that is needed. I have protected you, vanquished your enemies, given you shelter, and I have come to care for you deeply—all while using his magic. There can be goodness in it."

I shook my head.

"Renna." Sethos stepped closer. "I love you. Can't you see that?"

A cry ripped from me. "This is not love . . ."

"I have not lied to you in what we have shared intimately. I never expected to want you the way that I do. I never expected to —" Sethos stopped talking, and I dropped my hands to look up.

Sethos was staring at me with so much raw emotion that I wanted to cry from how much he was confusing me.

"I crave you," he breathed. "With every breath I take, I think of you. I can't get you out of my head, and heaven knows I tried to stay away from you emotionally in dreamtime. I never wanted to complicate our relationship, but I could not and I will not stay away from you."

I glared at him and extended my sword to point at him. "I'm supposed to forget all you have done to me—"

"I'm not asking you to forget, I'm asking you to understand me. *Join me.*" He held his hand out and began advancing toward me. "Together we can rule. With your power and mine, we would be *unstoppable*."

"Are you hearing yourself?" I continued to swerve branches, moving backward.

"I want us together."

I shook my head. "There is no *us*."

"You don't mean that!"

"Do you truly think my moral compass would condone you committing genocide? Or to join you and use my Darkness to terrorize civilians in Taria?"

"And about the civilians of Isyos?" he spat.

"As if that somehow makes it better."

Sethos glared at me. "It doesn't matter if you approve of my actions. You *know* the torment I live in. I shared my pain with you. The memories of my mother, my friends *dying*. Slaughtered."

"Your pain matters, Sethos. I will never diminish your sorrow." I shook my head. "But this is—"

"No different from you training to kill your father." His voice was cruel. "Or am I wrong?"

"I am not *seeking* to kill him." I stepped up to him. "But if he comes looking for me, I will be ready. I promised myself after I left my foster home that I would never be anyone's victim ever again." I clenched my fists, thinking of the power dynamic between Sethos and me. "And the problem is—" My eyes began to water as deep grief settled into the marrow of my bones. "I don't think you will ever see yourself as an abuser. You will never see me as your victim."

"Renna—"

"I'm *not* finished!"

Sethos clenched his jaw and looked away.

"I felt alone for so long." I wiped my nose on my sleeve. "I always wanted to belong somewhere. My university was a haven to me." My skin grew hot as my anger rolled inside me. "You *stole that* from me. You took me from an undisturbed life to"—I looked around—"*this!*"

Sethos narrowed his eyes. "Your life was only seemingly perfect because I protected you. I kept magic from you so you would not have to deal with it."

"I still battled every day to not be triggered and react."

"Which was made easier by the way I protected you! Never forget that I protected you first without an agenda."

I lowered my sword. "Tell me." I pushed against his chest armor with my hands. "Did you purposefully persuade me to study weaponry from Old Xhor? The city where I died?"

When Sethos remained mute, I knew the truth.

"What kind of a man are you!?" I roared and stepped back.

Sethos looked at me with a thunderous expression.

"*Speak!*" I walked back and extended my sword and tapped it against his chest, making contact with his armor. "You placed a lotus flower next to the post about Xhorian weapons when I was deciding on my PhD last year."

"I thought it would be one way to bring you to the proximity of the gods, *yes*."

Rage filled me, and magic rose within me. "How long have you been using me?"

Sethos remained silent.

"You and Khellios both lied, but *you*"—I pointed to him—"you are the biggest disappointment of all."

Sethos flinched as if I'd slapped him, and he clenched his fist.

"I don't mean to make an enemy of you, Renna."

I shook my head. "You stopped being anything to me moments ago," I snapped.

Sethos's eyes darkened, and a chill rolled through me.

I'd always felt safe with Sethos.

Now, as black overtook his eyes, pushing out the ice blue, I felt closer to danger than ever before.

"Call off the attack on Taria," I demanded. "Tell me you won't go. Don't do this. There's still time."

His silence was the confirmation I needed.

He refused to meet my stare, and I threw my sword down and hit his chest as sobs racked my body.

Sethos let me hit him until I slumped against his body, his arms gently encircling me.

I spoke into his chest. "Why are you ripping my heart apart?"

I looked up, and Sethos was looking down at me, his eyes glassy.

"I have a duty to my people, Renna." His words were a whisper, and he brought his lips to my forehead. "To my mother. They destroyed my life."

"Solve this a different way, I'm *begging you*."

Sethos's voice hardened. "A life for a life."

I gripped his arms. "You can't mean that."

He tightened his arms around me. "I've killed many people, Renna. For once in my life, these deaths will mean something."

"This is not the way—"

"This is the *only* way. Your father failed to give the people of Isyos and their descendants retribution. It now falls on my shoulders."

"It does not!"

He pulled back and gripped my biceps. "Why can't you see that I must do this?" He shook me. "I overthrew your father with the promise that I would bring honor and justice to my people—"

"There is no honor in killing for revenge," I yelled and pulled my arms free. "You are not responding to an immediate threat. I cannot let you do this!"

Sethos's eyes became harder. "And what of the survivors who still mourn their slain family? Their children?"

"Attacking Taria will not bring them back!"

"It will not," he yelled back, his face flushed red. "But I will earn their respect. I will earn control of my government. And my citizens will go to bed knowing the murderers of their loved ones have ceased to exist!"

"And become complicit in the same crime that robbed them! There is no rest of the mind—*of the heart*—for that!"

"You cried when I told you about Isyos," he yelled, coming within inches of my face. "You wanted to know if the attackers of Isyos were brought to justice. You vowed to stand beside me!"

He spit at my feet, and my heart sank.

"Justice sounded good to you before you realized they were people you knew, didn't it?" he screamed.

I shook my head. "Don't do this, Sethos." I cried.

"Why?" he barked. "You can't take away this pain. This endless torment I feel every time I see the faces of my people. The voices . . ."

"Sethos, I know so much darkness is adding to your pain, but there is goodness inside you. Remember how you protected me. You guarded me. You showed me it was okay to believe in myself."

Sethos wiped the tears from my eyes with a tenderness that confused me, and fresh tears streamed down my face. I knew this would be the last time he held me like this.

I ran my fingers along the sides of his face. "Sethos . . ."

"Renna," he said, resting his forehead against mine. "I need you. Love me in this. Support me. Stand by my side." He pleaded. "Love me *through* this."

"You cannot ask me to accept the slaughter of my friends—"

He pushed away from me slowly. "Yet you ask me to allow the murderers of my people to live."

I covered my face with my hands.

Sethos cupped my face gently, moving my hands aside.

"Were it possible for me to have found you sooner, Renna, perhaps you could have molded my heart into something else." He straightened and dropped his hands. "I will not change my course. This was always going to happen."

My rage returned, and I stepped away from him. "I hate you, Sethos. I will never forgive you for throwing our future away."

"No, you won't." His voice was soft. "You will go on loving me. For as long as you live."

"So you condemn me to a life of solitude without you!" I hit my chest. "I love you! And you are choosing to walk away."

"No." The tension in the air changed from desperation to something darker. "*You* are walking away from me."

I walked backward.

"Your voice . . . Do you hear yourself right now? You taught me to control Am-Re's magic, but it seems the lessons don't apply to you. It's poisoning you. You are somebody else."

"I *will* win this battle, Renna."

"If you win, that means the people I love have died. You expect me to rejoice at that?" I shook my head, disgust filling me.

Shadows began to rise around him as if the ground itself was encasing him in black fog.

I trembled and moved farther back. I called my Black Fire sword to appear back in my hand and extended it toward him to create distance.

"And what of me?" he screamed. "Does what I want not matter to you? Does my pain not matter?"

"I will never be able to look at you if you kill them."

"There is no future for me in a place where the murderers of my mother live."

I covered my mouth with my free hand.

"This may be the last time we speak. I will be enchanting the army to do my will."

I dropped my hand from my face and felt the blood drain from my face.

"It is the only way to ensure they have additional magical protection as they fight. I will not lose this battle."

I shook my head. The magic needed for such a feat was insurmountable. What would that do to his soul?

"Sethos, don't do this."

"If you are not with me, then you are against me."

His words chilled the blood in my veins.

"No." I shook my head and reached for him, but he was the one to step back.

"Will you stand by my side?" he spat. "Like you vowed?"

"I will never let you get away with this." I swore to him.

Sethos frowned, and the black overtook his eyes. He lifted his chin as his body radiated the sick, venomous energy that represented Am-Re. Black veins like the gnarly roots of a tree mutilated his pale face, making him look gruesome.

This was not my Sethos.

"*Sethos?*" I whispered and quickly considered what weapon I could use.

I needed to run and put distance between us.

But how?

"Renna," Sethos began, and I called a second Black Fire sword.

A chill ran down my spine as he smiled.

"Let's talk," he said, a wild look in his eyes.

"No!" I gritted out. "I don't trust you."

"I don't want to force you to listen to me." The voice coming out of Sethos's mouth was terrifying. "But I will if necessary."

Suddenly, Sethos lunged for me, and I jumped back, deflecting his move.

I conjured a dagger and willed my magic to launch it at him. When the dagger pierced his shoulder, he screamed.

I spun around, and a purple glow was visible up ahead.

The shield around the forest!

I vanished my sword and ran toward the shield.

"It doesn't matter where you run." Sethos's voice echoed around me. "Leave the shield," he gritted out. "You know I love a good chase."

I was so close to the shield that I could almost touch it. I reached out, but an arrow flew past me and grazed my cheek.

I screamed as the pain lanced through me like searing fire.

Then, another arrow.

This time, it barely missed the other side of my face.

When my fingers made contact with the shield, I was met with resistance, but I pushed through. And as I crossed the barrier, it felt like shards of glass scraping across my skin while being engulfed in flames, and I screamed.

Once through, I kept running and looked behind me to see Sethos now also on this side of the forest.

I wanted to call on my Darkness, but I couldn't bring myself to risk setting fire to the forest and the animals in it. But this was why Sethos had trained me thoroughly—so I wouldn't have to rely on one mode of defense.

I didn't need Darkness to fight him in that moment. I chose to bet on myself, and as I ran, I called on a Black Fire quiver, bow, and arrows.

I tried to erect my protective shield, but my mind struggled to control so many things at once. I couldn't waste time.

I turned slightly and shot an arrow toward Sethos.

He easily ducked my attack. "Put your weapons away, Renna."

"No!" I aimed another arrow his way.

I stumbled on a tree root and steadied myself as Sethos continued to advance.

"I will not let you get away with this," I screamed and shot again.

Sethos put away his bow and arrow and called a Black Fire sword and shield.

"You raised arms against me today," he gritted out and pointed his sword at me. "You remember that. I never wanted to fight you. But you leave me no choice."

A cry tore through me, and I released an arrow.

Sethos lifted his shield to catch it and cut the embedded arrow with his sword.

"And *you* stole my peace," I said and cocked another arrow. "You remember that."

I released the bow string, and the arrow lodged in his shoulder.

He looked down and then up at me.

"*Run*," he growled.

The sword and shield vanished, and Black Fire spheres rose on his palms.

I silently cursed.

Sethos raised a hand, shooting a sphere of Black Fire my way.

I quickly ducked to the side. Righting myself, I cocked my arrow with trembling hands.

Sethos had trained me for this.

I breathed.

I released my arrow, but his magic immediately thwarted my attempt.

I shot again.

Sethos blocked it again.

Sethos had taught me to keep my foe distracted.

I had to keep him talking.

"What would happen if you simply walked away from this chase?" I asked. "We could disappear into a different galaxy. Change our identities."

Sethos screamed in anger and shot a sphere of magic my way.

It brushed my leg, and fire consumed my veins. I screamed

and looked down to see my flesh burned and red. Tears spilled from my eyes. I stumbled back, clutching my leg. I couldn't shoot an arrow with one hand.

"Stop trying to change my course!"

I put a hand up to try and stop him and dragged my leg back. "Sethos, there is light in you. I know it."

"You have betrayed me," he screamed. "I knew when the time came, you wouldn't stand with me. My pain means so little to you."

He generated another sphere of magic, and I quickly called my Black Fire to change weapons.

A magnificent sword appeared in my hand, and I drew it just in time to deflect his magic.

"Don't give up, Sethos." I pleaded. "Please!"

Sethos screamed, and Black Fire erupted from his body like lightning and shot into the ground. It sped toward me.

"You said you would never hurt me!"

Sethos laughed, and I felt my father's presence then—as if he had completely taken over Sethos.

"Sethos, this isn't you. It's my father's magic controlling you. Don't give up. Let me help you."

"Sometimes, it's better to give up." His voice was my father's. "And give in."

Screaming, he launched at me then and hurled a sphere of Black Fire toward me. I brought my hands up, dropping my bow, and called up my protective shield.

Before the shield could envelop me, his magic brushed past my thigh, and excruciating pain radiated through me, blinding me for a second.

I screamed and almost collapsed, but I needed to keep fighting. I had a mission to stay alive. I needed to use healing magic.

Placing a hand on my wound, I clenched my teeth when the contact sent pain shooting up my leg. I allowed a small portion of my mind to imagine soothing energy pouring from my chest through my arm and down to my fingers.

A rush of magic coated my gaping wound, covering the flesh and pus in a cool layer. The pain lessened to a dull ache, and I watched as the skin began to slowly heal itself.

I looked back up to Sethos, who was closing the distance I'd put between us. His face looked monstrous, black veins a stark contrast to his pale complexion. He threw more magic my way, and my shield vibrated with the impact, but it held.

I called up a Black Fire sword and looked around. The forest was vast, and I didn't know where to go.

In my pain and lack of coordination, my back suddenly hit a tree trunk, and Sethos chuckled darkly.

"You should give up now," he said and threw another sphere of magic toward me.

"Do you want to kill me?" I demanded. "Is that what this is?" I shook my head. "We're both victims of Am-Re. Killing me solves nothing! Let me help you!"

"I merely want you to stop fighting me."

"I'm fighting for you. For us!" I cried. "You are supposed to be guiding my soul as my guardian. What you are asking me to do is not right!"

His lips curled with a slow, deadly smile that was not his, and he laughed, the mocking sound echoing in the forest.

My heart sank.

"I'm no guardian," he spat. "And I'm certainly not here to save your soul, little girl."

My heart felt like it would burst from my chest.

A Black Fire sword materialized in his hand.

"What?" I whispered.

"I made it all up, Renna. Soul guardians aren't real." Sethos stalked toward me. "You're nothing but a silly, spineless little woman, who has been so easy to manipulate—"

"No . . ." I ducked as he swung for me.

"A very pretty fool," he gritted out and launched himself at me. "You're either with me or my enemy."

"I hate you!" I screamed as he began to hack at my protective shield. "This is not you!"

I needed to try and summon my dretani now. I looked around the trees and saw a large body of water in the distance. It looked like a massive lake. If I reached the water, would I be able to call forth my beast to help me fight him off?

I had to try.

As I planned the logistics of calling my dretani once I reached the water, my protective shield faltered, and suddenly it was too late.

Another catapult of Sethos's magic hit me in the back of the knee.

I screamed as my skin burned and fell forward.

"Yield!" Sethos yelled.

"I will never yield to you!"

I pulled my body forward on my elbows, screaming with each movement. My thigh wound was now reopening with the scrape of the forest floor.

"You're making me hurt you. Stop this. *Now!*"

Sweat dripped from my brow into my eyes, but I continued dragging my body away from him. "You already hurt me. Repeatedly. I'm not making you do anything. You lying, manipulative asshole."

His magic erupted again, sending electrical currents of green and black and a bolt of Black Fire into the earth, racing toward me. The ground beneath me tremored. My eyes widened as the magic shot up around me violently, trapping me.

A fucking cell.

"What is this?" I panted as I scrambled in the small space. I had to move to be able to see him clearly through the bars his magic had constructed.

"You will stay here until you rethink your choice to oppose me. I don't want you as my enemy. You have magic to heal your wounds—do it. You will live."

"Are you listening to yourself?" I screamed. "Your voice—it's not you. Reject this power, Sethos!"

"This is exactly who I was meant to be. It took you long enough to realize. When will you stop fighting me?"

"I'm never going to stop fighting. I'm going to find a way to warn the gods and tell them of what you have planned."

He bent down so we were at eye level. His hands twitched sporadically, and he blinked several times. He whipped his neck back and forth, cracking it with unnatural speed.

A chill ran down my spine as a cruel smile spread on his face.

"You cannot say you love me and hurt me. You have and are actively hurting me," I cried.

"It's because I love you and want a life with you that I must do this. You will see this is right."

"You are blinded by ambition and hate, Sethos. There is no future for us. Not now."

"You knew how important it was to bring justice to my people. And you betrayed me." Sethos stood and dusted off his clothing. "I will send a palace Mage to collect you."

I spit at him.

Sethos turned from me and opened a portal. The red haze of Vasarys filtered into the black forest.

"But for now," Sethos said and turned to look at me, "think about what I offer you. You will never be as happy with anyone but me. We were made for each other."

I cried, and my body folded as the pain overtook me.

"You and I will be the greatest rulers of this universe, my sweet Renna. With my current god powers and the new ones I plan to acquire from the gods I kill, and you with your magic, we would be unstoppable."

I closed my eyes as tears streamed down my face, mixing with the dirt beneath me.

"No one would ever hurt us again. No one would dare. Can't you see that?" He laughed. "We will never be victims again!"

I shook my head against the ground.

"I love you, mejtah."

A sob escaped me at his endearment, and I opened my eyes just enough to watch him leave.

I was in a nightmare, and this time I was not dreaming.

50

SETHOS

Renna betraying me filled me with unimaginable rage.

I was so close to avenging the death of the Fallen, and I would allow nothing to stop me.

I looked at my army and how they assembled before me in formation.

The commanders and generals screaming orders.

The squadrons of mages I had recruited from all corners of this universe that had a connection to Isyos . . .

They all followed me on the promise of justice.

Justice they had been denied for years.

I could not throw this opportunity away.

I couldn't.

Not now.

I would redeem my people.

I had to.

The black magic within me moved like a turbulent ocean current.

Yes, the voice said. *Make the gods pay.*

I struggled to breathe.

Why couldn't Renna love me through this?

I loved her.

But my love wasn't enough.

Her love is not enough. She doesn't deserve you . . . the voice whispered.

If I couldn't have her love, if there was nothing waiting for me if I returned, then nothing but the battle before me mattered.

As the soldiers finalized their formation, the commanders and generals nodded my way, letting me know they were ready. They knew what was to come. My magic would pierce each soul, giving them supernatural protection. The magic would be given with the intention to make each of them stronger, faster, deadlier. The soldiers didn't know what was coming, but they would thank me once they battled. The gods were notorious for creating legions of soldiers to fight on their behalf to save their energy.

I paced on the hill where I stood, the magic within me restless.

Flashes of my mother's screams and outstretched hand flooded my mind. The way my hands were bloodied trying to dig her out and failing to free her. Her wails as she died entombed in concrete. I had gashed my head into the rubble after her screams ceased, willing to die myself. I should have died with her.

There was nothing left of my district that day. By the third day, Am-Re had patrolled my district, the day he'd found me, and the animals had begun pulling at the flesh of the Fallen. The growls of the beasts at night and the cries of the unfortunate who had lived and were too weak to fight back were embedded in my brain.

Then came the cries of violations perpetrated by the few criminals who had survived. I had walked the streets seeking help, only for my fourteen-year-old eyes to see criminals rutting on corpses and people who barely clung to life. I had returned to my home and lay in the ruins, seeking my mother's then-cold hand and holding onto it while I slept.

Never again.

Killing Arios's enclave would erase those memories.

I would start anew.

We all would.

It would be a new day.

If I survived the enchantment of the army, perhaps my body could take more magic still . . . I thought of the eventual deaths of the gods. I would be able to absorb their magic like I had Am-Re's, right?

That would ensure no evil was perpetrated by that enclave ever again.

Imagine what you could do with all that power, the darkness said. *You could become a god with so much accumulated power.*

Yes.

"Only if the magic I use today doesn't kill me," I murmured.

You won't know unless you try. The darkness reminded me.

"But what will become of me?" I asked.

Salvation. Hope.

And after?

You will have glory. All that your heart desires.

Renna's face suddenly flashed in my mind, and longing filled me. Part of me wanted to run back to her and let her talk me into the idyllic life she offered . . .

But I knew I would never be satisfied.

Suddenly, the army quieted, and I knew it was time.

I looked at all 100,000 troops.

The faces of the troops, all hardened by military training, looked up at me. Each one had signed up voluntarily to fight.

I walked down the hill and stopped midway. "Many of you stand here today," I yelled, looking at all the men, "having lived through the Night of a Thousand Tears or are direct descendants of the survivors. Each of us has had our lives affected by what was done. Like some of you, I have been cursed with long age and an even longer memory. I relive what happened in Isyos almost nightly. The faces of my brethren are ingrained in my brain. I was there when the fire rained from the sky like meteors. No mercy was shown to our people. Lives were cut short simply for existing under the rule of a tyrant."

The troops stood in silence.

"Many of you have been awaiting payment and compensation for your months of service . . ."

The soldiers began to shift uneasily.

"I can tell you today, payment of the greatest kind will be yours—glory. With your help, we will exterminate the gods who dared to attack Isyos on that fateful night. No mercy will be shown to you. And we will give none in return."

I began to call more power forth, and my body trembled as the magic lashed through me. I looked down, and the black shadows covered my entire arms. And then the fire burning inside began as more power moved through me, and it felt like flames were licking through my veins.

"The gods are a cowardly scourge. They send their dretanis and ghostly soldiers to fight on their behalf while they sit and watch battles. Their demonic creations will be deadly. But you"— I raised my arms and called for the power within me, a Black Fire ball emerging from my chest—"will have my protection. Today, each of you will be armored with supernatural strength, agility, and protection, unlike our Fallen who died in Isyos like slaughtered animals, and we will take our revenge. We fight for justice. We fight for honor. We fight to avenge the lives stolen too soon. We fight for our very survival."

The magic then shot up to the sky, and black clouds gathered and spread out above the soldiers. The soldiers ducked and looked above, pointing with alarmed faces.

"Do not fear," I yelled as the magic began to descend. "I do this as your Ahtar, your leader, sworn to protect you . . ."

The legions of mages to the right began to scream, erecting purple shields of protection.

There would be no escape.

We needed to win.

Soldiers began to desert their flanks, and chaos broke out.

"Cease!" I screamed. "Let go . . ."

The mages shot bolts of magic my way, and despite the protective shield around me, my body still felt the impact from so much magic.

I called on more magic and felt the shadows spread to the top of my chest and waist.

Once the magic reached my heart, there was no going back.

Soldiers began to run up the hill to attack me, and the last of my restraint broke. I screamed when, like a tidal wave, the magic left my body and exploded out. Screams broke out as the soldiers' bodies absorbed the magic, their chromosomes restructuring to accommodate the supernatural gifts I was bestowing on them.

My eyes widened when the mages' shields were destroyed, like the snuffing out of a candle. The black clouds filled with magic lingered above the army.

"What do I do now?" I asked the darkness inside me.

What good is an enchanted army if you cannot control them? They will turn against you. They will slay you in your sleep.

No.

That could not happen.

If you lose, you will never see Renna again.

"No."

How can you ensure you win this war? the voice asked.

"I must control the army."

You must.

I looked to the magic and moved my arms above me, directing the clouds to come down like black mist enveloping each soldier in shadows.

As the shadows spread, each soldier contorted until there was dead silence.

I screamed as the magic within me burned like fire toward my heart.

"Rise!" I bellowed.

One by one, each soldier wordlessly rose like a corpse, and the darkness shot through me like a jolt of adrenaline.

Arios's enclave would fall.

I would win this war.

Suddenly, my body began to burn, and I screamed. I looked down to see my skin boiling and vibrating. The boils became brown and orange with yellow liquid inside. I doubled over and began to vomit. My fingers dug into the soil beneath me, holding onto something as a blaze consumed my body from the inside out.

I clawed at my clothes.

I needed to get out of them.

I felt like I was dying.

Then I felt it.

I opened my mouth to scream out, but nothing came out.

I collapsed onto the earth beneath me and brought my hands to my chest.

My heart, it expanded painfully as if filling with a foreign liquid.

I couldn't breathe.

I was dying.

This is the price, the voice hissed like a serpent. *This is the price of ultimate magic.*

No.

Your body is dying, Sethos . . .

I squeezed my eyes shut.

And then my spine broke. It shattered into a million pieces, and only then did my screams break out as my body grew and morphed.

My gums exploded, giving way for sharp teeth. My hands dissolved as if acid had been poured on them.

My eyes changed, and suddenly the world was yellow.

And then the magic in my core, my own and that of Am-Re's, rose to the surface and exploded.

I was enveloped in white light before being plunged into darkness.

The world was still for a moment, and it felt like my body was drifting.

There was a quiet beauty about the darkness. It made me forget, for a moment, what was happening to me.

Rise! the voice said.

And I knew that nothing would be the same again. It had used the same command I used with my soldiers.

As the darkness dissipated, my body was stretched.

I was back on the field with my army.

The army was now quiet, looking up at me, like sleepwalking, lifeless husks waiting for my command.

I looked down at my body and realized I really had died.

My body had been transformed, gold scales covering where I used to have skin.

I was no longer Sethos, the man.

I was a beast.

Am-Re's dretani.

51

DEMIRA

I awoke in darkness.

Something was happening outside the cell I had been thrown in. The ground shook, and even though I was in a haze, pain rippling through my body as the Alaric Chains drained my energy, I noticed the change in the air.

It felt like a powerful force of energy, and I whimpered as the movements shook my battered body.

Another ground-shaking movement erupted underneath me, and I cried out.

I pushed up as much as I could to look around me. Sethos had demanded that I be placed in a windowless room in the dungeons as punishment, so there wasn't much to see.

Even though I was physically weak, my emotions still raged inside me. I wanted to scream, knowing Illona was unprotected.

She was my whole world.

I loved my sister.

Illona was the only good thing about this godsforsaken land we were forced to live in.

Our father had kept us in his kingdom out of some mercy I

never understood. I begged him to let us go and allow us to settle elsewhere. He never relented.

We were prisoners in a gilded cage, and I knew he enjoyed seeing us suffer.

We had nothing to offer Am-Re. We were failed experiments, abominations of birth, as he called us, but still, he refused to let us go.

And so, Illona and I became a unit, vowing and plotting to one day take revenge on the men who ruled our lives.

Sethos sought to marry us off, to be rid of us, but Illona and I refused.

We would not go quietly into the night.

I wanted my father's throne. Was it too much to ask for a woman to ascend to a higher rank than wife?

Suddenly, the room shook, and I couldn't scream as I tried to push my body into a corner.

Sethos?

Had he finally tired of me?

I closed my eyes and thought of the vision I had.

Metidons.

I had seen them in my mind over and over again, the vision so clear of me riding atop the wild beast from Konah into battle.

I would die in the cell. What was the use of that vision now?

The room shook again, and the wall of black bricks moved, green magic seeping through the mortar.

If it were Sethos, he would have opened the door.

He would not struggle.

Something or someone else was coming for me.

Fear thrummed in my veins, and despite the sluggish way my cells moved inside me from the restraints that were keeping me weak, I could feel my heart begin to accelerate as it fought to pump adrenaline into my body, urging me to move.

I whimpered, my eyes trained on the way the cell shook.

I was sure the magic outside my cell would smash the bricks in, and I would die from the impact.

I couldn't even erect my shield of protection to deflect debris because of the Alaric Chains.

Chains I now deeply regretted hurting Cylas with.

Illona had pleaded and thrown herself at my feet, demanding I free Cylas after we tossed him in the dungeon.

She was insistent that the ancestors had told her Cylas would help us escape, but I didn't want to escape like a coward.

I wanted to conquer my father's court.

Might is what they respected, and I had to show it if I needed to prove myself.

And now, as I lay weak and pathetic on the cell floor, grief and disappointment seeped into my bones.

I hadn't been good enough.

Perhaps my father had been right.

Suddenly, my cell exploded, and heavy bricks slammed into my body, pinning me down. I closed my eyes.

What a pathetic way to die.

Then I heard two voices.

"Demira!"

It was Illona.

My breath stammered out, but I was buried under debris and couldn't move, and my throat trapped any sounds or words I tried to make.

And then the second voice chilled me.

"I hope I don't regret this decision."

Green magic suddenly surrounded me, and the bricks levitated around me.

They were swiftly moved from me, and I blinked my eyes open.

My gaze landed on a pair of green eyes.

"Hello, little witch," Cylas drawled. "We meet again."

Illona raced to me and brought my body to her chest.

"Your sister just bought you a ticket out of here," Cylas growled. "There's a ship of Elemental Gods outside Vasarys. And if you so dare to attack me again, I will kill you."

52

KHELLIOS

I poured another cup of ambrosia and sighed.

"Someone should cut you off," a sharp voice said.

I frowned and looked to my right. The fae queen who had been yelling at Aeroth at the outpost stood next to me. She had her arms crossed while holding a goblet.

"You're drinking as well," I said, annoyed, gesturing to her drink.

"In moderation. You seem to be drinking to forget."

She sounded a lot like Ukara, and I rolled my eyes.

"With all the grace and honor due to you, Your Majesty," I said, sipping my drink, "do fuck off."

Unfazed by my reaction, she rolled her eyes. "My husband was an alcoholic, you know. I know the signs."

I grunted. "And you have concluded I am an alcoholic? Judging me like everyone else?"

"I have concluded you are a heavy social drinker."

"Meaning?"

"I've watched you. You find any excuse to drink when there are crowds around. But you don't join in the festivities. You drink alone."

"And? I have it under control."

"Do you? It's a fast track to self-destruction." She shook her head. "Have you spoken to someone about your drinking habits?"

I laughed. "You're funny."

"Gods are not immune to illnesses. Take Am-Re for example. From what we understand, he was ill before he was killed."

I shrugged.

I didn't have a drinking problem.

I wasn't violent.

I didn't hurt anyone.

I was angrier when I didn't drink.

People benefited from me being numb.

"If you grow ill, that young lady will need to nurse you to health. Do you want that for her?"

I paused and looked to where she gestured.

El was across the room, laughing with a fae king and elven queen and soldiers.

I stilled. "She doesn't need to look after me," I told the fae queen.

"Are you sure about that?" She frowned. "You don't notice the way she searches for you whenever she walks into a room. Her eyes light up whenever she sees you."

I rubbed my face with a hand.

She gestured to the elven and fae soldiers around Elrie with her goblet. "We fae collect beautiful things. The draw of something new and shiny always captivates us. The pretty commander is a beauty many already covet."

I growled. "She is not a shiny object to obtain."

"Territorial, are we?"

"I make no claims on her."

"So you don't want her."

I groaned. "I never said I don't want her—"

"Ah." The queen nodded knowingly, and my heart pounded fast.

My response caught me off guard, and I froze as El suddenly approached.

"Khel," Elrie smiled, stepping up to us. She eyed the elven queen and bowed her head in greeting.

The fae queen narrowed her eyes at us and walked away.

"That was odd," El whispered.

"I see you're enjoying the gathering tonight." I changed the topic and gestured to the room.

El chuckled. "By that tone, you're clearly not. I thought it would be good to toast our combined search for crew morale."

I rolled my eyes and drank.

A fae prince toasted to Elrie in the distance, and she blushed.

"The men around you clamor like chicks."

El turned to the room. "They're harmless, Khel."

I lifted my eyebrows. "*Allegedly.*"

"I don't know why you care anyway."

I turned to El. "What's that supposed to mean?"

El sighed. "I'm single, Khellios."

"Can I not care about men harassing my friend?"

El stared at me for a long moment, and I could see her jaw clench.

"They're not harassing me."

She turned her face back to the room.

"I don't need you to care," she said after a moment.

"You're my responsibility, Elrie."

"I am not. We've been over this."

"These men are looking at you like—" I shook my head, unable to finish the thought.

"Like what?" She put her hands on her hips.

"Like they want to eat you."

El's eyes dilated, and her lips parted. Her skin flushed a beautiful shade of pink.

"Well." She lifted her chin and looked at the room. "It feels good to be wanted."

A bitter laugh escaped me. "You want to be desired by *them*?"

"*So?*" She crossed her arms. "What's the problem?"

I shook my head.

"You're impossible." She pushed off the table and moved past me out of the room.

I turned to watch her walk away, and before I could think twice, I followed her.

"El," I called as she moved through the corridor past her crew.

"Leave me alone, Khellios."

"Let me talk to you."

"I don't want to talk to you."

She moved swiftly through the craft and headed for one of the command centers. Two crew members were there, and with a stern look from El, they left us alone.

El spun around and crossed her arms. "Speak now, Khellios. You already ruined my night, and now I'm tired."

"I'm sorry I spoke out of turn about the attention you were getting."

"Is that it?" she snapped.

"Yes." I shook my head and ran my hands through my hair. "It's not my place to interfere in what you do. I'm sorry. You're young. Have fun."

Elrie glared at me, and I put my palms up in defeat and spun to walk from the room.

"For once I thought maybe you'd care I was getting attention for another reason." She chuckled. "I'm so deluded."

I spun. "Don't say that—"

"But I am." She shrugged. "I thought perhaps . . ." She shook her head.

My palms clammed up.

Like a moth, I stepped closer. "You thought what?"

Her jaw tensed. "You don't get it, do you?" she frowned.

I wasn't an idiot. I knew what she meant.

She wanted me to desire her.

To not go a day without thinking about her.

To panic when I didn't see her in a room.

To not breathe easily until I saw her.

To not know what to do when my heart raced in her presence.

To crave her.

But there was Renna.

There was always Renna.

The gaping wound.

"Khel—" She sighed and closed her eyes. "I can't do this anymore."

"Tell me what you need."

Elrie's eyes fluttered open. "*You.*"

I froze. "Elrie . . ." I shook my head.

She began to walk toward me. "I want you, Khellios." She frowned. "Can't you see that?"

I took a step backward. "The timing of this . . . You're helping me locate Renna—"

"Only because you mean that much to me, Khel." She held her head in her hands. "I want to see you happy. Even if it's with her." She paused and covered her face that was now flushed red.

Moving back toward her, I wrapped my arms around her. I gently pried her hands off her face. "El, I'm not the man for you—"

She shrugged off my hold. "You don't get to decide that!"

"El—"

"I've wanted you since you arrived at my father's kingdom and stood at my bedside to cure me all those years ago. You gave me part of your divinity to save me. You were everything I thought of those first years you stayed with my father and me. You lived with us for three years."

"And you knew I was mourning Renna even then."

"And I hoped that one day you would be able to move past that. You helped train me in weapons. You never wanted me to be vulnerable like Renna had been, and so I aimed to please you. I trained hard. And then you left us." She wrapped her arms around herself.

"I never meant to make you believe—"

"You kissed me before you left."

I paused.

"The night before you left our kingdom, my father put on a festival in your honor . . . Other ladies and I wore masks for a dance performance we put on . . ."

My body began to prickle with awareness of that night.

"I waited for you and the others to get intoxicated," she said softly. "I'm not proud of it . . . but I adored you, Khel. I wanted to know what it was like to be kissed . . ."

I took a step away from her.

I remembered that kiss.

El continued. "And what it would be like to be touched by you."

The kiss with El had turned into the first sexual encounter I'd had since Renna's passing.

The guilt I felt after made sure I never forgot it.

"El, you should have told me it was you!" I shook my head and began to pace. "I took liberties that I should have never—"

"Liberties that were *freely* given. I wanted you to!"

I stopped pacing. "El, I almost slept with you."

Memories flashed of me pulling El into an empty room in her father's palace and pushing her against the wall.

"I never forgot . . ." El whispered.

I had pulled down El's top and hiked up her dress.

I knelt before her and put her leg over my shoulder . . .

"You remember . . ." she said softly. "Don't you?"

My body flushed with arousal as I recalled that night.

"Of course I remember!" I yelled. I shook my head. "El," I said softly. "You made me feel something for the first time in years. You should have told me it was you. Your father trusted me."

"You left that night!"

Rage filled me. "You knew I was leaving!"

El crossed her arms. "Does Renna love you?"

"I'm not discussing that with you."

"Does she or not?" she demanded. "It's a simple question, Khellios!"

"Why does that matter?"

"Because I've been waiting for you to move on. Because I am *here*, present, in flesh and blood, full of want for you."

"El—"

"I know grieving is not a linear process. I respect that. But at some point, you need to begin your life."

I shook my head. "You have no right."

"If you told me Renna loved you, I would step back. I would never interfere with your opportunity to be happy with her." She stepped closer.

"I've told you she doesn't remember our life. Nor do I wish to force her."

El's eyes glazed over.

I sighed. "I love her, El," I said gently. "I don't want to hurt her."

"But are you *in* love with her?" she whispered and wiped a tear from her cheek.

"She was ripped from me twice, El. This time, I have an opportunity to get her back."

"And if she rejects you when you find her?"

I closed my eyes and massaged my temples in frustration.

"What will you do then?"

"I don't know." I shook my head and looked up at her. I dropped my hands. "I don't know what not grieving and wanting her looks like. That's the truth."

El stepped up closer again and placed her hands on my shoulders. "Could you ever come to care for me?"

I groaned. "El, it's not so simple—"

"It's just a question."

"That requires a complicated answer."

"Do you find me attractive?"

I paused and thought about the moment we shared. Flashes of us came to the forefront of my mind . . . me on top of her, slowly riding up her dress as she spread her legs for me . . .

I swallowed.

El brought her face next to mine, her skin lightly touching mine. When she spoke, her voice was barely a whisper. "I tried to forget you, Khellios."

My pulse loudly thudded in my ears.

"I took a few lovers in the years I've been immortal."

I hadn't been intimate with anyone since Renna and I shared a fleeting moment on the beach in Taria. I wasn't prepared for El's closeness, and my body began to respond.

She was beautiful.

And she wants you.

"But none of them have been able to affect me the way you did. The way you do."

"El . . ." I groaned.

"Do you find me attractive?" she asked again, her breath next to my ear.

I looked away from her, but she grabbed my chin and pulled me back to her.

"I'm not that young woman anymore, Khel."

I groaned again.

"Tell me. Look at me and tell me if you find me attractive."

"Yes," I growled, my emotions ricocheting.

I felt like a traitor to my grief.

"I want you, Khel," she whispered. "I've always wanted you."

I shook my head. "El," I said gently. "You're not thinking clearly."

I stepped away from her. "I need closure for the chapter that is Renna in my life. It's not fair to you or me to give hope to something new."

She ran her hands through her hair.

I shook my head. "I never meant to cause these feelings you have for me."

"But I have them." She seethed. "And I can't get you out of my head. I—"

El looked beyond me, and her skin flushed red.

I followed her gaze.

Aeroth stood at the entrance to the command center. "Apologies," he said, looking to the ground. "I did not mean to interrupt."

"I was just leaving," El snapped and pushed past me. "This conversation is going nowhere."

53

KHELLIOS

I turned my back on Aeroth and moved to the wall of glass overlooking the passing galaxy.

My conversation with El had left me confused.

I couldn't offer what she sought . . .

Yet . . .

A part of me . . . *wanted to.*

Could I grow to be the man El believed I was?

When was the right moment to stop mourning for someone who was still alive?

Moving on from Renna's memory wasn't something that seemed possible. I mourned her for so long. It was normal for me to stay in the same stasis.

I was immortal. What was there to look forward to?

I only had my memories.

Elrie thought I could make new memories, but to be frank, change frightened me.

Change also felt like I was betraying my love for Renna. Love for the child she had carried. For the future we had planned.

I knew that if I talked with her, perhaps offered to give her more time—

I sat on a couch and dropped my head into my hands.

"I still remember feeling surprised when I learned you were a god. You had no divinity aura."

I'd forgotten Aeroth was still in the room.

I groaned and looked up.

He gestured to where I sat, asking to join me.

I nodded, and he took his seat.

"You gave up part of your divinity for El," Aeroth said. "And she's not even the woman you seek on this quest."

"Elrie will always be special to me."

"I apologize for walking into your argument with El."

I shifted in my seat and sat with my elbows on my knees. "It was not an argument. An argument leaves room for changing minds. She knows how I feel."

"When I met you years ago and you came to my father's kingdom, you mentioned you were mourning someone."

I rubbed my face out of frustration.

"Is Renna the same person you mourn?"

I dropped my hands and looked to Aeroth. "Yes. She has been reincarnated."

"You loved her in her past life."

"I loved her then and now."

"I see."

"Elrie can't understand that. She would rather I move on."

"Could you see a future with her?"

"It doesn't matter. I have a duty to Renna."

"And does Renna return your love?"

I clenched my jaw. "She doesn't remember what we lived."

"Ah."

Aeroth's intrusive questioning bothered me.

I didn't know what I would do if Renna rejected me again.

I knew the way I had revealed what she was to me was wrong.

We needed to have a conversation.

Closure.

If not for her, for me.

Only then would I allow myself to move on.

Was that too much to ask?

Aeroth lifted his eyebrows and shook his head. "I wonder what love like that feels like." He tilted his head. "My love for the fairer sex has not lingered on any single person more than a few years."

"You have elven and fae blood. The combination ensures you live for thousands of years. I would imagine a few years feels like passing dalliances."

He nodded. "They do. The rulers of the astral plane always had elven and fae blood. We have found that minimizing constant change of power when ruling the astral plane is best for the universe." Aeroth straightened. "You have loved Renna for a long time. What do you love about her specifically?"

I sat back and frowned. I hadn't been asked that question for some time.

I held my palms up. "I love her. I don't know what you want me to say."

Aeroth frowned slightly. "She must be very beautiful."

"She is."

"What else?"

"What do you mean, what else?"

"Surely, there are some qualities she possesses that signal her as the only woman for you. Are you *in love* with her?"

I thought of Renna when I first met her. She had been so frightened, and all I wanted was to protect her. She had been the first thing I truly felt was mine.

"She was so lost when I met her. She made me—"

"That was the past."

I paused.

"You're speaking of the Renna who died, correct?"

My eyebrows furrowed. "Well, yes."

"What do you love about her now?"

I stood. "I don't know what you're getting at."

Aeroth also stood, his palms up. "I don't mean to anger you. I merely admire your lasting love for her."

"She carried my child."

Aeroth stood silent for a moment and looked down. "I'm sorry for your loss. I would also search the ends of all universes for a woman I loved."

"The fae have mates. I take it you have not found yours?"

Aeroth locked eyes with me, his hard, and then looked away.

Rapid footsteps brought our attention to the door.

El stepped into the room, panting and her face flushed.

"Elrie," I said, stepping toward her. "Catch your breath."

She nodded and drew in a deep breath.

I looked her over and placed my hands on her arms. "What's the matter?"

El looked at me and Aeroth.

"A star craft from the Elemental Enclave has an injured Cylas. He was in Vasarys. Cylas has a message for you."

I cursed, and we all exited the room to run to El's command room.

"What was his message?" I barked.

"Renna is not in Vasarys. He believes Sethos took her to Daya. Guards reported they portaled from Vasarys."

"I can locate her," Aeroth said.

We stopped and looked to Aeroth.

"It won't be easy to find her," Aeroth said, "but if she accesses the astral realm, I can locate her."

I nodded and placed a hand on his shoulder. "Find her, Aeroth. I place her in your hands."

54

RENNA

I must have fallen asleep against the forest floor because when I opened my eyes, I imagined my body in deep space.

I knew in that moment I had to be in the astral plane.

Had I brought my body here to escape the pain, like when I had traveled through the mirror portal?

I looked down, and my body was free of scarring. Even the scars on my legs from when I had fallen as a child while practicing magic with Am-Re were gone.

I looked around me, floating in the nothingness of stars, planets, supernovas, and galaxies.

"Hello?" I said.

I'd spoken to the voice of the Astral before, but silence met me.

"Please help me," I pleaded. "I know you have heard me before."

I was completely alone.

Suddenly, in the stillness, *something* moved.

I paused and frowned.

This was my imagination. I had power over my dreams.

Right?

"Many will die. Please help me."

In front of me, space moved like a ripple of water.

I stopped breathing.

Since I was floating, I propelled my body forward to where I had seen the darkness move.

"Help me. If you can hear me."

I reached out to where the movement had been a moment ago, my fingers trembling.

Suddenly, my hand met something solid.

I gasped and pulled back, and the movement rippled again.

A body draped in a cloak of the universe moved as if awakened from slumber.

I was mute as a gigantic body outlined in the universe itself moved.

We meet again. The daughter of darkness and the astral night. How apt.

"I'm wounded," I said quickly. "I'm in Daya."

The darkness paused.

"I am in a cell, in the forests in Daya."

Who hurt you? Its voice was savage.

"I fought with Sethos, the ruler of Vasarys. He trapped me in a cell and means to attack Taria. I need to warn the gods in Arios's enclave."

The darkness moved around me, and I watched as space distorted and the astral figure hovered toward me.

I will be plain with you, Daughter of Darkness. Since our last encounter, I came across Khellios, the God of the Moon and Stars.

My body felt lighter as relief surged through me.

He and a mercenary contingency are looking for you. They have sought my help in locating you.

Khellios was searching for me.

I began to cry from the overwhelming emotion.

Imagine my surprise when I realized the woman who has been crossing into my realm is the same woman Khellios searches for. I will help you reunite with him. But only should you wish it.

"Yes! I need to see Khellios to warn him."

So it will be done.

"Sethos will be sending someone from Vasarys to collect me. He wants me in Vasarys. They may come soon."

That will not happen, the voice responded.

"There's no way for someone to find me here. It's nighttime where I am, and I can't see much outside of the cell he caged me in."

I will come and get you.

I paused. "*How?*"

I can locate anyone's physical body while their spirit is here.

"Even if you find Daya, only fae can access it."

I could almost feel the atmosphere electrify with a smile, as if it was coming from it and the body molded of space.

When I am not here, my physical body is fae. Entering Daya will pose no issue to me. I know of the realm.

I couldn't form the words to begin to express my shock.

I will guide your soul back to your body and emerge with you in Daya. Being the astral allows me to bend reality and pierce the veil between both places.

He extended an outline of a hand to me.

I lifted my fingers toward his and paused when a thought occurred to me.

"If you are the Astral, how are you fae?"

My lineage was given control over the astral. When a ruler ascends, our spirit and body become one with this plane.

I had been lied to three times before—by my father in childhood, Khellios, and now Sethos.

Enough was enough.

"How do I know you are who you say you are?"

You don't. But I have not hurt you. I have let you remain in my realm before, unharmed. And I am the best chance you have to return to safety.

He farther extended his hand toward me.

For as long as Source allows stars in the sky, my word will be true, Renna Strongborn.

I had no option but to allow him to help me.

Questions would come later.

I placed my hand in his, and suddenly my body was gently pulled backward.

He held my hand as stars sped past us as if we were moving at inconceivable speeds, but I felt like I was gently floating in a phantom breeze.

I wondered why I was traveling backward, and the Astral responded, as if it could read my mind. Perhaps it could.

You travel backward as you are drifting back to your body. You will drift off to sleep soon once more, and your body will feel like it's falling as you wake. This happens when the spirit returns to the body after leaving the astral plane.

I nodded.

Close your eyes. We are close to Daya now.

I closed my eyes, and everything went black.

55

RENNA

My body jerked awake.

I quickly opened my eyes and felt the cold forest floor underneath me.

Something moved outside the cell I was in, casting shadows on me as it walked.

I squinted at the shadows and noticed a red haze around the body as it moved.

"How do you feel?" the voice from the astral asked me.

I groaned as I took stock of my body. My wounds had healed significantly, but I was still sore.

"I'm not bleeding, but my body hurts."

"Good. What type of magic did Sethos use to erect these roots?"

"He used my father's magic."

"I see."

I groaned again as a fresh wave of pain pulsed through my body.

"Have you tried to break from the cell?"

"No," I gritted out as I pushed my muscles to sit up.

He approached the cell, the red glow around him a sharp contrast to the black caging me in.

"I need you to try." He sounded worried. "The magic is not allowing me to get closer."

I wasn't surprised. Sethos must have enchanted it to prevent this very thing from happening.

I nodded and tried to stand. The cell was at least twice as tall as I was, built in a dome-type shape.

"I'm not sure my magic will work either," I said quietly after standing. I tested reaching out to the roots, but strong magic repelled my touch. "It feels like a strong magnetic field fending off my hands. He must have anticipated me trying to escape."

"The antidote for any drug or spell is its exact opposite."

"What are you saying?"

"Your father's magic is made up of hate, Darkness, chaos. It destroys."

The opposite of his magic would be . . .

Love.

Hope.

Light.

Happiness.

Could it be that easy to counteract his magic?

Perhaps not in an attack but in a spell like this?

"I would need to channel magic while feeling things I don't feel right now," I said.

"I will help you. We can break through together. I'll direct my energy to the cell from the outside."

"And what are you suggesting I do? Close my eyes and imagine I'm in a field of flowers where I'm happy as I call forth my magic?"

He was silent for a few seconds.

"Imagine what it would look like to be blissfully happy. If it's that field, go there. Wherever your mind needs to go to imagine happiness. Peace."

I had thought I was happy just a few days ago.

"Go to that place and call your magic forth. Then summon your father's magic and cast it to the spot in front of you. I can see you through the roots. I'll also direct my magic to that spot."

It was hard to imagine happiness in that moment. I always felt like if I was too happy, something would happen to take my joy away. My anxiety was tied to my happiness like a noose—sometimes not too obvious, but the heaviness of the shadow of my anxiety was just a thought away.

But I had to try. I needed to help save my friends.

I closed my eyes and let my mind search.

Where had I been the happiest?

All my memories thus far were now marred by pain. Sadness. Betrayal.

I would have to look to the future, and I didn't know what that would look like.

I knew I wanted to find a place where I could feel safe, a place I would never be displaced from. I would never know fear there.

I felt safest among the stars.

I recalled Nera telling me once she preferred living among the stars in palaces made of stardust.

What would such a thing look like?

Then I recalled how peaceful it felt being in the astral.

Could I float in the nothingness forever?

My mind began to imagine a palace made of crystal among the stars.

The palace would allow me to overlook space all the time.

"Where is your mind?" he asked me in the stillness.

"I'm in space," I whispered.

"Where?"

"In a palace among the stars." In my imagination, I looked

around me. "I've never been here. The palace walls are made of crystal. I can see space anywhere I look."

"Why there, Renna Strongborn?" he asked. "What do you feel?"

"It's peaceful here. Quiet." I took a deep breath. "It feels like home."

"What else do you see?"

I turned and continued observing. "There's a tree. It's made of the same crystal material. There are red leaves on it, and they fall beautifully. We seldom have trees on Andora."

"Desert planets rarely do." His tone carried a hint of humor, and it made me smile. "What else?"

"There's a pool of water at the base of the tree. I would swim there all day."

"As one does with a pool."

"I can't swim." I almost laughed, but instead I felt a pang of sadness for the situation I was in. I was imagining something fictional. In reality, I was in the middle of a fae forest, wounded and incarcerated by a man who claimed to love me so I could learn a lesson.

"What else?" he asked.

I imagined my friends around me.

Khellios, Ukara, Nera, and Cylas.

Helena was there too. I could picture her smiling at me.

I saw another there too.

A shadow.

I frowned and focused on it.

It was the shape of the Astral in male form.

Faceless but with a red glow around it.

It made sense. He had provided me shelter twice when I most needed it.

He heard my voice in the darkness.

"What's wrong?" he asked.

"You're in my vision."

"I am honored."

I could never have my vision, but I could, in time, work to have a future like that. I would surround myself with those I loved. Nothing would ever hurt me again.

I vowed it.

I was tired of the pain.

"Now," he said. "Focus on where you are and the feelings it elicits. Call your magic, and when you feel it's time, bring forth Black Fire."

"Okay."

I commanded my magic to emerge, and my body ignited with what could only be described as electric waves of bliss. I kept my eyes closed but could feel my hands warm with my magic. I brought my palms close together and felt a ball of energy form between them.

I imagined my golden link to Source and asked for enough power to break through.

Suddenly, power surged toward me from my link to Source, followed by a great boom rocking the night.

I opened my eyes, and a great ball of white magic settled in my palms. It was blinding and lit up the forest around me. Without thinking, I directed it to the roots in front of me, and they immediately withered, creating a hole large enough for me to climb through.

I pushed my body through and exited into the night air.

Solid arms caught me and steadied me. The red glow remained, and my mind was brought back to that very first dream I had in Daya . . . running from my father in a labyrinth.

And of the red glow that enveloped me in a cocoon of safety and helped drive out the darkness . . .

"I have you now," he whispered. "You're safe."

I stood against him, my heart beating rapidly, and a familiar sense of calm washed over me.

"You broke free on your own," he said. "You didn't need me. This was all you. You would have figured it out on your own."

I straightened and slowly lifted my eyes to his.

Black hair draped down his shoulders.

Sharp jaw.

Elegantly pointed ears.

Red eyes.

A crown of iron and obsidian was on his forehead.

"Renna Strongborn." He smiled. "We meet in person at last."

He stuck a hand in front of him to greet me, and I was momentarily dumbstruck.

I was speechless as I beheld the personification of the Astral in front of me, and he smiled slightly as he saw my hesitation.

He put his hand down and turned to the side and opened a portal.

A darkened room with chrome accents was revealed on the other side of the portal. It looked like a star craft.

My eyes darted from the portal to his hands as red magic surged from his skin. "I have so many questions . . ."

"And I will answer all of them . . . but Sethos's people should be close by now. We need to go."

He held his hand out to me.

"What do I call you?" I whispered.

"I am Aeroth."

The sound of his name made the night move, as if the forest had been hit with a slow-moving phantom wind.

"Come, Daughter of Darkness."

I placed my hand in his, and the skin-on-skin contact super-charged the cells in my body, sending a rush of adrenaline through me that had my body shift forward, as if whatever energy was passing through me wanted to cling to him.

His eyes widened slightly as I watched his body tense and in sudden movement, move toward me.

His jaw opened and he blinked several times looking between us.

Had he felt it?

"Let's go," he said, his voice sharp.

"*Wait!*" I said, digging my heels in, feeling my skin vibrate in electric tingles against his. "What's happening?"

"Hopefully not what I think it is," he answered, his eyes skimming the forest and lowering to our joined hands. "We need to leave *now*."

He silently pulled me toward the portal, and I pulled him back.

"Aeroth," I began, panic ricocheting in my chest.

"I don't have time to explain," he said, his tight, almost on edge. "But it's not good. And you and I are now both in danger."

Vile rose in my throat, and I let him lead me to the portal.

"Don't let me go," I said before the portal absorbed us.

Aeroth turned to look at me, his eyes hard. "I will never let you go, Renna Strongborn."

In an instant, he wrapped my body against his as the darkness of the portal welcomed us.

56

RENNA

We portaled onto a star craft.

I had never been in one and had only seen them the interiors of them in exhibits on Andora. Only the rich and powerful had enough coin to travel on one in and out of Andora. My dream had always been to gather enough money and leave that planet. And here I was, a long distance from home on a star craft.

A gray interior with expensive-looking furniture surrounded me with enormous windows overlooking space.

Aeroth released his hold on me and stepped away from me. I watched as he closed the portal behind us.

He turned to me, and with the soft light of the craft, I could see his features more clearly.

His eyes were red but had lines of brown, making it a color I had never seen before.

"Thank you for helping me," I whispered.

He nodded once, his shoulders stiff, as if he was suddenly tense.

"Renna," he began and stepped up to me. "I need to speak

with you before Khellios arrives. He must already know we portaled in."

A foreboding feeling swirled inside me, and my stomach coiled with anxiety. Was he going to tell me what we experienced in the forest?

I clasped my hands as my skin still tingled the same way it had when I held his hands.

"Yes?" I asked, suddenly feeling uneasy. I shifted slightly away from him.

"Over the last few weeks, I have learned a lot about you from Khellios. I know about the university attacks. I know about Taria. I know how Khellios deceived you. And judging by how I found you, Sethos . . . betrayed you."

I bit my cheek as waves of emotion washed over me.

I would not cry.

I would *not* cry.

I clenched my jaw and fists to steel myself against spilling a single tear.

"What's your point?" I snapped, preferring anger to any other emotion.

"I need to tell you who I am," he began. "And what I suspect I am . . . *to you.*"

I chewed my lower lip as he ran a hand through his hair in frustration.

"What do you mean?" I fidgeted with my shirt hem.

"The Galactic Federation has entrusted me and a group of other fae monarchs to deal with Sethos. He is deemed too much of a problem. I intend to honor the Federation's request."

My heart stopped.

"*Deal?*" I asked carefully. "What do you mean deal? Sethos is trapped by my father's magic. It's not him— *He's not . . .*" I covered my face. "I just need to speak with him. I need to make him see reason before he attacks Taria—"

"I've been tasked with ending his life, Renna."

I brought my hands to my mouth and shook my head.

"No!" I said, grabbing Aeroth's black long cape that gathered at his chest. "You can't do that. He's good—deep down, I know he is. He has suffered and he needs to—"

"There is no goodness in him, Renna. Perhaps your proximity to him has blinded you—"

"No! We need to stop him. Not kill him." I gripped his cloak and stepped up to him. "I won't let you," I gritted out.

"I don't need you to let me do anything. I plan on honoring the Federation's request."

I pushed against his chest and stepped back. "And what else?" I yelled. "What else do you have to say to me?"

Aeroth stood motionless for a few moments as he regarded me.

"What am I to you?" I demanded. "*Speak!*"

"You are my mate."

Air rushed from my lungs, and I felt like I had been kicked in the stomach. But before I could respond, the doors to the room burst open, and Khellios and about twenty other people stepped inside.

Khellios rushed to me and enveloped me in a tight embrace.

A high-pitched noise filled my ears, blocking out all sound. I felt like I was suspended, apart from my body, as shock rolled through me.

A woman in silver armor came to our side and began to speak to me, but I was too shocked from Aeroth's revelations to understand her words.

And then Khellios began to drag me from the room with the group of people, and I turned to look back as I was jostled with the throng of people.

Aeroth stood in the same place, his red eyes locked with mine.

In that moment, despite what I had been through, nothing would ever be the same way again.

Aeroth had the eyes of a killer, and I knew without a shadow of a doubt he would kill Sethos.

And I was scared.

Like never before in my life.

ACKNOWLEDGMENTS

Thank you to The Creator, my family, and the female authors who have come before me (especially Mary Shelley and Jane Austen).

AFTERWORD
VILLAINS AND LOVE

For as long as I can remember I have always been a fan of villains. When I was a small child the telenovela *La Ursurpadora* was my first real exposure to a true villain character. The show followed Paola, a sophisticated and stylish villain who relished in being evil and the TV audiences loved her for it. I asked my mother to cut my hair like Paola's 90's bob hairstyle because I was obsessed with her sophisticated personality.

After that telenovela success, Latin TV audiences were graced by another villainous storyline in *Rubi*. Rubi, a vengeful law student, taught audiences about a good person turning evil. She turned evil to save her sister and bring her family out of poverty. Her storyline captured the hearts of many fans and the telenovela has had several versions throughout the years. *Rubi* cemented my love of villains and I knew if I ever became a writer I would have to write a villain.

In the *Daughters of Chaos Series*, Sethos's ultimate goal is avenging his mother and the Fallen. We learn Sethos's evil goals were not always present as he once planned to escape Vasarys with Renna before she died in her first lifetime. However, when

Renna dies Sethos loses all hope for a different life and thus begins his dark path.

It was very important to me throughout *An Heir of Darkness and Ruin* to ensure Sethos never deviated from his evil course. I wanted a true villain with a moral code so skewed none could sway him. I love current stories where the villain changes for the girl but that is not Sethos's story and I could not change his course simply for marketability. Sethos has an *unshakable* belief he is meant to bring honor to his mom and people and making him suddenly abandon those plans after so many years seemed... *wrong*. Hopefully you can understand that while the ending of book two was not a resounding happily ever after I did it to respect Sethos and his experiences. And besides, wouldn't you agree Renna deserves better? **She deserves true romance.**

I can tell you now that I truly love Sethos but like Renna I do not and will never agree with his actions. Writing the scenes where he was violent made me angry and there were days I had to step away from him. However, there would be no story without him. As I shared in the afterword of book one, he visited me in a dream like he did Renna and urged me to tell Renna's story. He needs to go through A LOT of inner work and healing to change. Hopefully this gives fans of Sethos a little sigh of relief that you have not seen the last of him . . . his story will continue in books three and four and perhaps (*whispers*) beyond the *Daughters of Chaos Series*.

Lastly, I want to address Renna and Sethos's dynamic. It's not healthy and its patterns we see all too often in our everyday lives. Renna has no one but Sethos to turn to while in Daya. She is isolated from her friends and old life and even though she has suffered DV in the past and can tell when Sethos is mistreating her, Sethos is all she has and does not want to be alone. We see her use some tactics DV survivors utilize such as pacifying her abuser by changing topics that are not too threatening, using sex as a form of communication in an attempt to find something to connect on, and other physical actions to not seem threatening. Don't get me wrong- I want Renna to succeed but like with Sethos's villain arc, I wanted to show the reader that sometimes victims of DV get trapped in subsequent abusive situations no matter how strong they are (or how much magic they wield). As a person who has lived through DV, I want Renna's growth to feel real.

We all want a happily ever after for Renna and I'm here to tell you it will happen (pinky promise).

With all my appreciation,
  Mina

GLOSSARY

THE GLOSSARY BELOW IS AVAILABLE FOR REFERENCE, BUT NOT REQUIRED.

Source: The Creator of the seven universes and all life.

Universes

Konah Universe: one of seven universes created by Source.

Galaxies

Milky Way: A galaxy that is mostly abandoned, inhabited by lawless beings. The galaxy includes the planet Earth.

Andromeda: A galaxy rich with life, inhabited by humans from Planet Earth and supernatural beings. The galaxy includes the planet Andora.

Sirius: A small galaxy inhabited by supernaturals.

Delphinus: A galaxy inhabited by supernaturals and the Elemental Enclave. The galaxy includes the planet Moringa.

Stars

Eusera: Closest star outside of Vasarys.

Planets

Earth: An abandoned planet in the Milky Way galaxy. Humans left this planet during the Great Migration.

Andora: A human inhabited planet in Andromeda galaxy. The planet is inhabited with descendants from the Great Migration. Includes supernatural beings who hide their magic and pose as humans.

Isyos: An abandoned planet destroyed by the Celestial Enclave.

Moringa: A small planet inhabited by the Elemental Enclave in Delphinus galaxy.

Tirose-B9: A planet inhabited by Arcadians.

Cities

New Xhor: An existing city on Andora.

Old Xhor: An old city on Andora currently in ruins. The ruins are an excavation site.

Dimensions

Taria: A dimension inside Andora where the Celestial Enclave resides. The dimension is not visible to humans. The dimension includes the ghost souls of old priests and priestesses of the Celestial gods and living people with magical powers escaping persecution from the Planetary Council.

Daya: A dimension suspended in outer space habited by criminal fae.

Vasarys: A dimension inside a black hole and Am-Re's kingdom.

Astral Plane: An alternative reality available to souls during dreamtime, meditation, and when the brain is in an altered state.

Civilizations

Arcadians: An advanced civilization inhabiting planet Tirose-B9.

Supernaturals

Naaviri: A type of fae that drink blood, also known as vampires on planet Earth.

Elves: A type of fae.

Mages: A being who is trained to practice witchcraft as a profession.

Kings and Rulers

Arios: The chief god of the Celestial Enclave

Istron: The chief god of the Elemental Enclave

Merida: The witch ruler of Taria's Witch District

King Miletak: A ruler from planet Tirose-B9.

King Oberon: A reclusive king of the Tatuiyah.

King Aeroth: The king of the Astral Plane.

God Enclaves

Celestial Enclave: The assembly of gods who oversee celestial bodies and related cosmic bodies and events.

Elemental Enclave: The assembly of gods who oversee the elements, fire, bodies of water, and weather events.

Spirit Enclave: The assembly of gods who guide the practice of witchcraft, oversee spirits, and supervise people's abilities in clairvoyance, clairaudience, clairsentience, claircognizance, and clairgustance.

Kingdoms

Tatuiyah: A fae kingdom led by reclusive king Oberon.

Kingdom of Nightmares: A fae kingdom of dreams and nightmares led by a king who mourns his dead wife.

Governments

Planetary Council: A human government formed during the Great Migration. The Council oversees the three human planets in the Andromeda galaxy, including Andora.

Galactic Federation: A multi-universe governmental body that creates and enforces laws for supernatural beings.

The Council of Vasarys: A governmental body that oversees Vasarys.

Events

Great Migration: Mass exodus of humans from Earth.

Night of a Thousand Tears: Term coined by Am-Re to describe the attack on Isyos by the Celestial Enclave.

ABOUT THE AUTHOR

Mina B. Castillo, formerly Mina Brower, is a Mexican-American and immigrant from Mexico who aims to inspire other immigrants to chase their dreams. Mina is a mother, wife, and fantasy author of the critically praised Daughters of Chaos Series.

Mina is an avid fan of science fiction and was obviously present during the Galactic Wars and likes to think she has a saved seat at Galactic Federation meetings. She attributes her love of the science fiction after her grandfather became a writer in the genre late in his life.

When she's not writing under her pen name, Mina is a partner at her law firm and mentors female pre-law and law students.

During her free time you can find Mina either hiking, at a museum, on a cruise ship, or beach side next to the buffet.